THE DARK WEB MURDERS
The Inspector Sheehan Mysteries Book 4

By

Brian O'Hare

Cover design by

Charlie Aspinall

Published by

Crimson Cloak Publishing

ISBN 13: 978-1-68160-664-4

ISBN 10: 1-68160-664-X

Edited by Denna Holm

Publisher's Publication in Data

O'Hare, Brian

The Dark Web Murders

1. Fiction 2. Mystery 3. Murder 4. Crime 5. Detective

Contents

ACKNOWLEDGEMENTS

I don't normally write acknowledgements, but this time I cannot miss the opportunity to mention the names of some people to whom I am deeply indebted, and one or two in particular who should have been acknowledged long ago.

Carly McCracken, owner of Crimson Cloak Publishing, and now, hopefully, my friend, has been publishing my books for a number of years and I have never thanked her for the faith she has shown in me. So, I thank you now, Carly. But surely you've always known how much I appreciate you even if I haven't stepped up and actually said it? Right?

And a big thank you to our indefatigable editor-in-chief, Veronica Castle. Veronica does sterling work in finalising my stuff … but she is much more than an editor. She is always there when my feathers are ruffled, when I need encouragement, or even when I need an ear just to sound off. She has to field numerous angst-ridden emails a month but remains always calm, sanguine and soothing. My heartfelt thanks, Veronica. Your constant reassurance is essential for me and always appreciated.

My thanks, too, to Denna Holm who was appointed to edit my last book, The Coven Murders. Unfortunately for her, she has been lumbered with this one as well. Thorough, painstaking, dedicated, I could not have asked for a better person to tidy up an error-strewn MS. Thank you for your brilliant work, Denna.

And a special word of gratitude to my long-suffering wife, Sadie, who is so often left alone for hours while I am buried in my study. You'll be pleased to know, dear, that after this I intend to take a break from writing for a while. But then, almost certainly, after a few weeks of me being under your feet everywhere you turn, you'll be begging me to go back into my study and write another book.

And then there's Jim Byrne, proprietor of Soapy Joe's famed Car Wash in my home town of Newry. Jim who?? Well, after The Coven Murders, I was searching around for a plot for my next book. I was chatting with Jim at his car wash one day and he jokingly suggested an idea I might use. "What about writing about a murderer who writes about his murders?" he said and went away, laughing. But I went home and thought about what Jim had said, and lo, The Dark Web Murders was conceived. Thank you, Jim. I hope you enjoy the book. (I might even stretch to a free copy!)

Brian O'Hare

INTRODUCTORY INFORMATION

The plot of this novel has demanded a greater number of characters than is usual in my books. I have had requests from reviewers of my earlier books to preface my stories with a list of the principal characters for handy reference, together with a glossary of Northern Ireland police terms and acronyms. If such lists were needed for my previous books, they are most definitely needed for this one. Both lists follow.

DRAMATIS PERSONNAE

Team of Detectives

Chief Inspector Jim Sheehan—Team Leader; charismatic, clever, independent, married.

Detective Sergeant Edwin McCullough—Long-time team member. Old school, stout, confirmed bachelor, lazy, but definitely showing signs of improvement.

Sergeant Bill Larkin—Forensics Liaison; bald, heavy glasses, married.

Sergeant Denise Stewart—Sheehan's detective partner; intelligent, resourceful, very pretty.

Sergeant Tom Allen—Newly promoted to sergeant; bright, well built, romantically involved with Stewart.

Detective Geoff McNeill—Allen's partner; fortyish, middle of the road, incurable stutter, married.

Detective Simon Miller—slim, always well dressed, extremely sharp, unmarried.

Detective Declan Connors—Miller's partner; heavily built, well over six feet, unhappily divorced; tends to be surly, but a good cop.

Detective Malachy McBride—McCullough's partner. New to the team; youngest member; excellent detective instincts; unmarried.

Members of the 'Fulfilment for the Enlightened Club' (A)

Judge Trevor Neeson—seventies, elegant, knows many secrets, questionable character, gay.

Judge Kenneth Adams—late sixties, slight, short, astute, enigmatic, cold, lacks empathy, hates Judge Neeson, gay.

Robert Bryant—wealthy surgeon, balding, fiftyish, flashy dresser, questionable sexual tastes.

Jaclyn Kennedy—millionaire property mogul, dangerously quiet but a planner and thinker, extreme sexual tastes.

Patrick F. Robinson—partner to Jaclyn Kennedy; millionaire; large, vicious, uncouth; questionable business ethics and methods.

Michael Stevens—barrister, squat, heavy set, bon viveur with decadent tastes.

Edith Gallagher—law professor, snobbish, worldly, mid-forties, superficially attractive, jaded sexual appetite.

Oliver Kane—senior civil servant, mid-fifties, bland personality, hidden depths, voracious sexual appetites, carries grudges to extreme lengths; hates Judges Neeson and Adams.

Members of 'The Club' (B)

[These are characters whose names are mentioned but who have little or no role in the story. The fact that they have sought membership of 'The Club' is an indication of their questionable sexual appetites.]

Thomas Downey—wealthy restaurateur; owns several restaurants in Belfast; likes to live dangerously.

Norville Keeley—inherited money, wasting it at a fast rate, not particularly bright.

William Martin—large shareholder in BBC television, elderly, millionaire.

Malcolm McAfee—makes a shady but very wealthy living hiring gambling machines to clubs, pubs, hotels and other places where people congregate; lacks moral integrity.

Martina Henderson—wealthy socialite, party girl, flighty, romantically linked with Norville Keeley.

Suspects

[Criminals who issued death threats against Judge Neeson.]

Gerald (The Toff) Delaney—immaculate dresser, burglar who parties at rich houses before robbing them.

Baako Kahangi—brutish African immigrant, guilty of rape and callous murder.

Thomas (The Hulk) McStravick—huge, villainous, guilty of aggravated assault and murder.

Terence Quinn/Eamon McKernan—members of the Real IRA. Quinn was arrested and imprisoned at eighteen years of age for shooting and killing a serving police officer. McKernan, a Real IRA sympathiser, was jailed for threatening Judge Neeson at Quinn's trial.

Ahdel Khan—Asian, but born and reared in Belfast. Vicious and violent bully, involved with sex trafficking gang operating in North Belfast.

Timothy Small—spousal abuser, killed his wife, arrested and imprisoned.

Other Characters

Kevin Lane—a young inmate at Magilligan Prison.

Dr Richard Campbell—pathologist, tetchy, very clever, good friend of CDI Sheehan.

Dr Andrew Jones—tall, well-built black man, with a deep, booming voice, pathologist, assistant to Dr Campbell.

Edgar Doran—Judicial Assistant to Judge Neeson.

George Rice—Scene of Crime Officer.

Margaret Sheehan—school-teacher, attractive, mid-forties, wife to Chief Inspector Sheehan.

Inspector Bob Williams—Friend of Sheehan's. Operates out of 'A' District.

Sam Gardener—retired cryptographer.

Superintendent Joseph Owens—Leader of the Task Force.

GLOSSARY

Police Service of Northern Ireland Acronyms.

Northern Ireland is part of the United Kingdom (Britain) and its police service has broadly similar ranks to its counterparts in England. The short glossary below, while not exhaustive, is offered to clarify for American readers the abbreviations used in this book.

RUC—The Royal Ulster Constabulary now redundant and replaced, in 2001, by:

PSNI—The Police Service of Northern Ireland which is peopled by:

CC—Chief Constable

DCC—Deputy Chief Constable

ACC—Assistant Chief Constable

CS—Chief Superintendent

Superintendent (tends not to be abbreviated)

DCI—Detective Chief Inspector

DI—Detective Inspector

DS—Detective Sergeant

DC—Detective Constable

SOCO—Scene of Crime Officer

NOTICE

The author is British. Spelling (and any common words) are U.K.

PROLOGUE
August 2012

It was a soft prison, he had been told. Medium security overall, with low security accommodation for selected prisoners. His friend had tried to sound cheerful but the concern in his eyes was inescapable. The unexpected display of feeling, however, had pleased the boy, despite his dire situation. They hugged, the boy tearful.

"I'll come and see you when I can," his friend had promised, and again trying to allay fears, he added, "Keep your head down, Kevin. Stay out of trouble and you'll serve only half your sentence. You'll be out in three years."

The words carried small comfort now. The young man stared apprehensively through the prison-bus window as Magilligan Prison came into view. He fought panic as his eyes traversed the bleak, lonely landscape, the seeming miles of fences surrounding low, concrete, H-shaped buildings. His breathing began to come in short gasps. *Deep breaths*, he urged himself. *Don't lose control. The hard men are in the Maze....*

To some extent the thought reflected truth. Prisoners convicted of scheduled terrorist offences had been transferred to the Maze prison, the notorious Maze where the most dangerous IRA and loyalist prisoners were held during 'the troubles', the prison where the IRA inmate Bobby Sands famously starved himself to death. This left Magilligan operating as a 'normal' prison, if normal was a word that might be deemed applicable. According to his friend, who had thoroughly researched the prison and its regime, the life here reflected its low security status. Sports, hobbies, library, education facilities, and excellent health care. "It'll be a breeze," his friend had assured him.

But as the bus passed through the huge security gates, topped by wire fences and frowned down upon by a dark, ominous watchtower, the young man's resolution wavered, and dread clutched his spirit once more. Trembling, he followed the other prisoners out of the bus as they were marched in single file towards the reception facility to be registered and processed.

An aggressive guard shoved him forward as he fell some steps behind. "Keep up," the guard snarled.

Hampered by the handcuffs holding his arms together, the young man stumbled but managed to regain his balance, almost bumping into the large, heavily tattooed prisoner in front of him. The man heard the scuffle and turned round to glare angrily at the slight, blond, blue-eyed prisoner who was struggling to remain upright. The anger dissipated almost immediately, replaced by a brutish leer. "Yeah, keep up, kid," he rasped. "Feel free to bang into me anytime." And guffawing coarsely, he turned back into the line.

"Shut it, McStravick," the guard barked at him. "Move on!"

Unnerved by the lout's crude interest, the effeminate young man was further disturbed by the fact that, given the guard's obvious familiarity with him, this was not McStravick's first time at Magilligan. *God! He knows his way around. What if he decides to come after me?*

The line of a dozen or so prisoners was efficiently dealt with by the receiving officers. Systems that had been in operation for some time were now smooth and effective. The staff knew how many committals were arriving and were prepared for them. Almost immediately the group was led into a stark, functional holding room where they were given a cold meal and some drinks. Most of them ate stolidly, heads down, not interested in conversation. McStravick kept staring at the effeminate newbie, trying to catch his eye. Each nervous glance in McStravick's direction earned the young man a view of misshapen teeth as the older offender's lips curled in a lewd and knowing grin.

After the meal, the young man was subjected to a total body search, as indeed were the other prisoners, and after the necessary documentation to record his arrival had been completed, he was led into another unprepossessing holding room where there was a television but little else to offer distraction.

McStravick tried to get a seat near the young man, but the guard tapped him on the shoulder with his truncheon. "Sit over there, McStravick."

The man glowered but did as he was told.

A Senior Duty Officer appeared at the door and called each prisoner in turn to a small outer office. When it came the young man's turn, he perched on the edge of a chair in front of the officer's desk, exuding extreme uneasiness. The officer looked up from the forms on his desk and stared at him with something almost approaching sympathy. "Name?"

"Kevin Lane."

"First time?"

"Yes, sir." It was a croak in which the words were barely discernible.

The Duty Officer studied the young man's file and his lips tightened. "Manslaughter?" His expression turned stern.

"It was an accident...."

The man glanced at him. "Of course it was." He studied the notes again. "You were sentenced to seven years?"

"Yes, sir."

"You don't list any next of kin here?"

"I am isolated from my family." The young man's voice remained tremulous. "I suppose you could say they disowned me. I don't really have any next of kin."

"Have you been living on the streets?" The officer's sympathy began to surface again.

"For a while, sir, but I've moved in with a very kind friend who's been helping me."

"Can you give me the friend's address?"

The young man hesitated. "It was only a very temporary arrangement. I don't think his address is relevant."

"If you say so." The officer regarded the young prisoner speculatively for a moment. "Okay. You'll be going through an induction process shortly, so I won't go into detail about what's going to happen, where you're going to be put, and so on. All I'll say is that if you behave yourself and strictly obey our rules, you can cut your seven years detention to a little over three. Got that?"

The shaking young man nodded and stuttered, "Yes, sir."

The officer kept staring at him, his head nodding constantly, as if trying to figure out how this effeminate young man's tenure at Magilligan might turn out. Eventually he breathed heavily through his nose and said, "Okay. You can go now. We'll chat again from time to time to see how you're progressing."

A couple of hours later saw Kevin Lane located in a cell in Foyleview where he had access to showers, toilet facilities, a television room, games room and a telephone. He was subject to another interview by an older, world-weary officer whose role was basically to make him aware of what to expect during his first twenty-four hours in the prison, wing routines, night sanitations arrangements, and details of the five-day induction course that all newcomers would have to attend.

"So, how are you feeling now?" the grizzled official asked him. His initial appearance, large, no-nonsense, tough, had almost given the young man apoplexy, but as the interview progressed, he had sensed a surprising aura of warmth in the man, and now here he was, asking him how he was feeling.

He opted for the truth. "I'm scared, sir."

"First time, son. To be expected. You'll settle down." He waved at a form on his desk. "I'm expected to note any immediate concerns you might have. You worried about anything? Is there something you feel you want to draw to our attention?"

McStravick's evil grin and bad teeth flashed into the young man's mind. He considered the pros and cons of mentioning his uneasiness about the man's odious intentions, but the thought of what might happen should McStravick ever hear of his complaint gave him pause. He simply said, "No concerns, sir. Everything's fine."

"Okay. The guard will take you back to your cell."

*   *   *

That Kevin Lane had been allocated a cell in Foyleview was pure happenstance. His location there had not been part of some sinister ploy. It did not spring from someone's evil intent. It was nobody's fault. It just fell that way. It was also an accident. New prisoners were generally allocated cells in the more rigidly guarded H blocks. Perhaps someone felt sorry for the timid new prisoner. Perhaps the person working on the allocations had been distracted in conversation with another guard and made a mistake. Whatever the reason, Lane was settled, on the first and only night of his time in Magilligan, in the comfortable surroundings of Foyleview.

One singular difference between the arrangements at Foyleview and the H blocks was that while prisoners in the H blocks had only restricted daytime access to showers, with guards accompanying them at all times, prisoners in Foyle had unrestricted twenty-four access to showers and toilets. These facilities were, of course, monitored, but only by a single guard whose supervision, at best, tended to be perfunctory.

Under normal circumstances, this would have mattered not a jot. Circumstances on the first night of Kevin Lane's incarceration, however, turned out not to be normal. Lane, as fastidious as he was slight, felt sweaty and unclean after a day's dusty travel to the prison in the August heat. Shortly after his evening meal, he made immediately for the showers where he proceeded to soap himself copiously in the warm, soothing water.

The fact that McStravick, with an equally huge and brutish companion, arrived at the facilities just as the young man was showering may well also have been a happenstance. Or it might have been a coincidence. Or it might have been the result of a vibration on the grapevine that somehow reached McStravick's ear and led to his decision to seek a shower at that particular time. Whatever the reason, it was never discussed in any of the prison records. Nor was there an indication in any subsequent report that either McStravick or his friend had been present in the facilities at that time. The only reference in later reports to the presence or absence of any other individual at the scene was a note that the supervising guard had '…unfortunately and regrettably…' chosen that moment to avail himself of the staff toilet facilities.

Eyes closed, soaping himself with an almost sensual appreciation of the hot water's cleansing properties, Lane was initially unaware that he was being observed by two hulking men, one of whom was the brute who had been seeking to catch his eye for most of the day. It was only when he leaned forward to shake some suds from his eyes that he became aware of the two men watching him. He became aware, too, with horrifying immediacy, that both men were naked and in a state of advanced arousal. Pressing himself back into a corner of the shower, he croaked, alarmed, "Wha ... what do you want?"

McStravick gave him yet another view of his misshapen teeth and said, "What do I want? You've been teasing me all day, you little prick. Now it's time to deliver."

Both men stepped forward and grabbed the trembling Lane, attempting to drag him away from the corner. McStravick pulled at the younger man's haunches, seeking to position himself behind his victim. Slender though he might have been, Lane possessed a wiry strength, and his struggles were making it very difficult for either of his attackers to overcome him. The two assailants moved further into the shower, clamping the young man with their thick, heavy arms, rendering his struggles futile. McStravick twisted the young man around and leaned over on top of him. Lane struggled violently again and, as the second attacker attempted to hold the young man still, he slipped in the soapy water on the shower floor and began to fall backwards. In order to protect himself, he clung to Lane but was unable to prevent himself from falling quite heavily. As he did so, he pulled both the young man and McStravick violently towards the shower wall. Momentum and McStravick's weight from behind caused the young man's head to smash against the wall tiles with a loud and sickening crunch. Blood began to stream down the white tiles and the two attackers stared at it, rattled. They stared, too, at the prone body of Kevin Lane, dumbfounded. Neither touched Lane nor attempted to discover if he was alive or dead.

"Fuck!" McStravick swore. "We need to get outa here ... now!"

Shortly afterwards, when the guard had completed his ablutions and was sauntering casually past the showers, he discovered the prostrate body of Kevin Lane. The shower was still running and washing away the blood that had by then become a trickle, oozing from the young prisoner's head. The shaken guard, casting frantic glances around to see if anyone else was there, immediately sounded the alarm before contacting the warden and the prison doctor, both of whom wasted little time in getting to the scene.

The warden glared at the guard. "How the hell did this happen?"

"I went to the toilet, sir," the guard said defensively. "But it was only for a minute. When I came out, I found the prisoner like this."

"Did you see anyone else skulking about the place?"

"There was no one. I'm sure of that, sir." The guard was determined to limit the damage to his status as much as possible.

"You had no right to desert your post, even for a second. You should have arranged cover."

"But we never—"

The warden waved an angry hand. "Move away from the scene. I'll deal with you later."

By this time the doctor was leaning over the body, having checked for a pulse but finding none. He was now studying the badly damaged skull.

"Well?" the warden said brusquely. "What's the situation?"

"This young man is dead, I'm afraid," the doctor said, moving the corpse's head into the light to examine the wound more closely. "We'll need a post mortem, obviously, but the prisoner has suffered severe traumatic brain injury. I suspect there has been bleeding in or around the brain, maybe in the brain tissue itself. I'm guessing, and the post mortem will correct me if I'm wrong, but I think we're possibly looking at an intracerebral haemorrhage."

"Any idea how it could have happened?" The warden's tone was brusque, almost angry. Clearly empathy was not a characteristic that overwhelmed him. Right now, all he could see was a future filled with endless reports, useless enquiries, government agents swarming all over the place, and pestering from nosy reporters who sought to decry the prison at every opportunity.

"Obviously his head hit the wall," the doctor replied, lips pursed, his words terse. A young man was dead, and the governor appeared to be utterly devoid of concern. "Why he hit the wall is a matter for the investigators."

"Could he have slipped and banged his head?" the warden persisted.

The doctor glanced around, saw the soap on the tiled shower floor, and said, "Soap and water on a surface like this? It would be possible to assume that, yes."

"All right," the warden said decisively. "The guard is certain that there was no one else around. Kid obviously slipped on the soap. We'll register it as accidental death, fatal head injury resulting from a fall in shower ... or however you medical types word it."

ONE

Sunday, 12th August, 2018. Evening

Judge Trevor Neeson studied his guests with a measure of satisfaction. The evening get-together was all he had hoped for. The powerful, the glitterati, the jaded, at his home. His lips curled in a sour grin. To outward appearances, the select group of guests mingling in the grand drawing room, in the adjacent hall, on the garden patio, were enjoying an evening out with old acquaintances and making new friends. As they drank contentedly, conducting their sotto voce conversations, all was calm, dignified, conventional. Benign smiles and familiar nods were cast back and forth across the lounge, the occasional glass was raised in friendly acknowledgement. A party like any other party.

Or so it seemed. But behind the façade of normality there lurked a deeper purpose. Dark information was changing hands, and appetites, long fatigued, were whetted in the anticipation of new experiences. Tonight, twelve new 'patrons' were to be initiated into *'The Club'*.

This the judge knew, and his guests knew he knew. His *outside-of-work* role was to act as a kind of broker for the seedier desires of the rich and famous, a role that he had fallen into almost by accident. His work in the courts had allowed him to identify and utilise many contacts, contacts multiplied by personal inclinations that had led him down many murky avenues and to many an unsavoury door. The occasional introduction of a close friend to deviant pleasures in secret rendezvous, the initiation of small, extremely select groups to arcane delights in the netherworld of the city, gained for the judge a reputation in certain circles as '*...the man to go to*'. Soon the demand for his services made him privy to significant knowledge about his 'clients', a level of knowledge owned only by the rare few.

Here was money. Here was power. Money, however, the judge no longer needed. But his appetite for power seemed to increase by what it fed on, and he found himself seduced ever more irresistibly by its lure. Hence his intimate association with 'The Club', an association which, in fact, concealed a level of proprietorship that his clients were unaware of. And after tonight these people would owe him ... and he would own them. The judge's eyes glittered momentarily before being darkened by the sudden frown that crossed his face. *If it wasn't for that bloody bastard phoning at eight o'clock, I could truly be relishing this.*

The judge, trim, an inch or so off six feet, elegant in his evening dress-suit, was just short of seventy. Few of the guests could have failed to recognise him, a key figure in the Appellate Court. His short, tidy hair was pure white, as was the distinctive miniscule moustache that clung precariously to the edge of his upper lip. This was a face many readers of Northern Ireland newspapers would often see staring out at them as they ate their breakfast cereal or drank their morning coffee.

The thin moustache was almost hidden now behind compressed lips as the judge glanced at his watch and began to move purposefully towards his study, shaking a hand here, stopping for a brief conversation there, but deviating not a jot from his intended destination. He spoke quietly to one of the hired caterers who was passing, carrying a tray of drinks. "Keep the drinks coming, Thomas. Don't let the party flag. I shouldn't be more than fifteen minutes."

"Won't be a problem, Judge. Take your time."

The judge nodded a curt thanks and left the lounge. As he entered his study, he pulled a smartphone from his pocket. Carefully closing the door behind him, he sat on the office chair behind his desk, eyeing the landline phone that sat there as if it was something repugnant. Prodding some numbers on his smartphone, he waited, drumming his fingers impatiently on his desk as he listened to the dialling tone's dispassionate repetitions.

Eventually a voice said, "Good evening, Judge."

"Weren't you expecting my call, Edgar?" the judge hissed.

"I was, Judge," his assistant answered coolly, offering nothing further by way of amplification.

"Well, this guy's going to phone in less than ten minutes. I need you to be ready," the judge said testily.

"Loads of time, Judge," came the same unflustered voice. "Keep your smartphone close to the phone when he rings. I'll start tracing the call immediately."

"All right. There was something else I wanted to ask you before he comes on."

"Go ahead, Judge."

The judge hesitated slightly and said, "The bastard always asks for five thousand. What if I offered him ten as a final payment, one that requires him to hand over all prints and negatives?"

There was a moment's silence on the line. Then came a somewhat disbelieving voice, "What century are you living in, Judge? Prints? Negatives?"

"Don't be impertinent, Edgar. What's so wrong with the idea?"

"Firstly, there is absolutely no guarantee that the prints he hands over will be all of them. Secondly, negatives went out with the dodo. He'll have the pictures on his smartphone. The only way to get rid of them would be to delete them. Can't see him doing that."

"What if I offer to buy the phone off him?"

"Pointless, Judge. He'll almost certainly have downloaded the pictures to a laptop or maybe an iPad."

"Well, what do you suggest?" the judge snapped. "If this bloody vampire thinks he can keep sucking money out of me indefinitely, he's got another think coming. I'm paying him nothing more."

Edgar was silent again, obviously mulling over the judge's dilemma. "Tell you what, Judge. Go with your original idea. Offer to buy the prints and the phone off him. Make sure you sound gullible. Make some sort of deal with him that he can't resist. Then get him to meet you … uh, what time's your party over?"

"Maybe around eleven, eleven thirty, but I have to take them somewhere first. I'll be about an hour."

"Oh? All right! Get him to meet you ... when? Maybe around one o'clock, on the top floor of the Victoria Square Q park ... alone."

"Are you serious? Why would I do that?"

"Something drastic is going to have to be done, Judge. This menace isn't going to listen to reason."

"You want me to meet this guy alone? What if he gets violent?"

"You won't be alone, Judge, but tell *him* it's essential that *he* comes alone. Tell him you don't want anyone to see you there. He'll believe that. Tell him if you see anyone there, you'll leave immediately with the money and he gets nothing. Don't worry. His greed won't let you do that."

"If I'm not alone, then who else is going to be there...?" The judge paused. "No! Don't tell me. But what if we are able to trace the call this time?"

"Doubt it, Judge. He always hangs up just before we can get him. He knows what he's doing. It'll be no different tonight. The other idea's a better one. And, now that I think about it, you won't actually have to be there."

The judge experienced a sudden guilty surge of relief. "I won't?"

"It's enough that he thinks you're going to be there. He'll be waiting for you. I'll take care of the rest."

The judge breathed deeply for a second, his brain whirring. Then he said, "All right, Edgar. I want the bastard gone, but I don't want to know any details."

"Understood, Judge." There was a click at the other end as Edgar hung up.

At that point the phone on the desk rang. The judge sucked in a deep breath, took a moment to ready himself, and reached out to answer it. "Judge Neeson," he said neutrally.

TWO

Monday, 13th August, 2018. Morning

The following morning saw Judge Neeson's luxurious lounge again full of people. But this time there were no revellers. This time, grim-faced men in white coveralls—scene-of-crime officers, forensic experts, police photographers—were engaged in a methodical examination of the room for trace evidence. Miniscule in nature, trace evidence might be less exciting than a shell casing or a footprint, but it was still of value to the forensic scientists who would later study it. That was why some of the SOCOs were on their knees with hand-held vacuums sucking up dust and debris that might contain evidence that could lead to the killer. Other officers, also on their knees, were searching for evidence that could be seen with the naked eye, using forceps to retrieve any loose fibres they might find, and even tiny fibres embedded in the crusted blood.

At times, however, trace evidence is too fine to be seen by the naked eye. Thus, one of the officers, wearing anti-glare viewing goggles, was checking the carpet with an oddly shaped, hand-held lamp attached to a cable. This was a Crime-lite 82S, a powerful and versatile 16-LED light source with available wave lengths from UV to IV. Red and infrared narrow bandwidth illumination is particularly useful for detecting blood, body fluids, drugs and fibres as well as for examining chemically treated fingerprints, while different light wave lengths can help illuminate fibres and other biological materials for easy observation and collection. These officers were carrying out their work efficiently and in silence, while others diligently searched the rest of the house.

A stricken man, slight build, early thirties, dark hair carefully coiffed, was seated awkwardly in an armchair. He seemed incapable of removing his gaze from the body of Judge Neeson, crumpled on the floor before a large onyx fireplace. If he heard the officer at the door say, "In here, sir," he showed no sign.

Detective Chief Inspector Sheehan thanked the officer and, accompanied by Sergeant Denise Stewart, he advanced into the room. Looking around, he said to Stewart, "No sign of Dick Campbell. Not often we beat him to a crime scene."

Stewart grinned. "Wouldn't worry, sir. Bet he's only a couple of minutes away."

Sheehan looked at the camel-hair overcoat that someone had carefully draped over the corpse, as if to protect its dignity even in death. It did not conceal the fact, however, that the judge's elegant evening trousers were bunched around his ankles. Sheehan frowned his disgust but spoke only about the overcoat. "Was that there when the body was found?"

The policeman, who had remained at the room door, looked blank. "Sorry, sir. Was what where?"

"That overcoat."

"Sorry, sir. Don't know."

"Who found the body?"

The office pointed to the slight man on the armchair. "That would be Mr Edgar Doran, the judge's judicial assistant, sir."

Sheehan moved forward and addressed the man. "Mr Doran?"

The man either didn't hear him or was too traumatised to respond.

Sheehan placed a hand on the man's shoulder and shook it slightly. "Mr Doran?"

This time the man looked up, his eyes expressing bewilderment. But he was able to say, "Yes?"

"Mr Doran, I'm Chief Inspector Sheehan and this is Sergeant Stewart. Are you up to answering a few questions?"

The man's eyes focused, seeming to recognise the blue-eyed, fortyish detective. "Oh, yes, Chief Inspector." He spoke with a slight lisp. "I have seen you a number of times in court." He gestured vaguely at the body. "But I don't really know much about … about…." He rose to his feet, nervous, uneasy, obviously not comfortable being seated while the chief inspector towered above him. Even standing, he was clearly below average height.

Sheehan noted the man's unease. *Won't have to push too hard to get this guy to spill what he knows.* "How did you come to find the body?"

Doran sucked in a deep breath, striving for the calmness he needed to relate his story. Then in the manner of one accustomed to summarising data, he stated, "I had a meeting with the judge scheduled for this morning at his office. He's very punctilious about such things and when he hadn't turned up after half an hour, I began to feel a little anxious. I phoned his home and his smartphone but got no answer from either. I waited for another half hour, thinking he might be on his way in to the office. When he didn't turn up, I tried phoning again, but there was still no answer." The man seemed to be reliving his anxiety as he spoke. "I have a key to his house, so I jumped into my car and drove straight here. When I came in, I shouted a few times but again, no answer. I was about to go up to his bedroom when I glanced into the lounge and saw … and saw…." He balked and his eyes slewed back towards the corpse again. He simply pointed but stopped speaking.

"Was that overcoat covering the body when you found it?"

"No, sir. I put that there."

Sheehan frowned. "You put it there? You're a judicial assistant, aren't you? You must have known that you were contaminating a crime scene. Clothes are full of static electricity. They can deposit miniscule fibres or magnetise them away. That was careless, Mr Doran."

The man backed away diffidently, cowed by the detective's tone. "I was shocked, sir. It didn't even occur to me to think about stuff like that." He gestured vaguely with both hands, distress overcoming him again. "The body was … it was … I couldn't leave it like that. I got the coat out of the closet and covered—"

"Okay. What was it exactly that you did for the judge?"

The man winced at the past tense, then said, "Are you sure you want me to answer that, Chief Inspector?"

"Why wouldn't I?"

"It would take several minutes to explain." He seemed to find a measure of backbone. "Minutes, I think, that might be better spent investigating the judge's murder."

The detective stared at him. "Just give me the highlights."

"Well, for a start, the judge has to be able to have an intimate relationship of complete trust with his assistant. I need to know everything the judge knows in order to be able to participate in every step of the appellate process alongside the judge. I screen cases, draft bench memoranda, summarise the different parties' briefs, draft court opinions, legal research and analysis, occasionally delve into the backgrounds of specific individuals at the judge's behest." He paused, looking uncertainly at Sheehan. "There's a lot more. Do you want me to go on?"

Sheehan shook his head. "No, that'll do. When was the last time you spoke to the judge?"

Doran's hesitation was disguised almost immediately, but Sheehan picked up on it. "Um … last night. He had a party here in the house and … he called me from here."

"In the middle of a party?"

Again that odd hesitation. "The judge is always working. His mind never quits. He wanted me to bring some papers to him after the party was over."

"What time was that?"

"What time did he phone or what time did he want me to come over?"

"Well, both."

"He phoned me around eight and asked me to come over sometime around one."

"You were here at one o'clock this morning?"

Yet again the man betrayed uncertainty. Sheehan wasn't having any more. "Look, Mr Doran, this is a murder case. If you know anything, you need to tell me. If you're hiding anything, you could be charged as an accessory. I can see that you are, at best, being economical with the truth. Now, what actually went on last night?"

"I wasn't here last night," the man admitted, eyeing the chief apprehensively.

"That's it?" Sheehan folded his arms and gave the man a hard stare.

Stewart glanced at her superior, surprise on her face. It was clear that she was thinking that her boss was being uncharacteristically harsh. Sheehan, however, was convinced that Doran was holding back information that could be useful.

"The judge had made an arrangement to meet someone at the Victoria Square Q Park and asked me to go in his place."

"Who were you to meet?"

"It was … em … one of the judge's confidential informants. He had papers the judge was looking for."

"A confidential informant was able to supply the judge with important legal papers?" Sheehan's tone was scornful.

The man's uneasiness was obvious even to Sergeant Stewart now. He shrugged his shoulders as if to say it had nothing to do with him. Sheehan allowed his annoyance to show. "I have warned you once, Mr Doran. I warn you again. There'll be no third warning. Who did you meet?"

Doran's head dropped and his face crumpled. When he spoke, his voice was low, defeated. "Judge Neeson was being blackmailed. He tried to do a final deal with the blackmailer and then asked me to meet the man to pay for, and collect, the evidence he was holding on the judge."

Sheehan strove to appear neutral, but this he had not expected. "Blackmailed?"

"Yes."

"And do you know what it was that the blackmailer was holding over the judge?"

"No." Doran's response was immediate and emphatic.

Sheehan's brows went up. "That was quick."

"I have no knowledge of what the blackmailer was holding over the judge," Doran said firmly.

"No knowledge, maybe, but suspicions perhaps?"

Doran shrugged and turned his gaze towards Stewart. He seemed anxious to escape those penetrating blue eyes. "I've heard some rumours but, in terms of my own knowledge, I can neither confirm nor deny them."

"Rumours?"

Doran hesitated briefly and said quietly, "I've heard a rumour that the judge has ... had ... a predilection for young boys, uh, teenagers. For myself, I have never seen nor come across any evidence of that."

"And you think the blackmailer might have?"

"I've no idea, sir. All I heard was a rumour. If the rumour has any basis in fact, then yes, maybe the blackmailer has photographs or a taped conversation or something. But I absolutely cannot confirm that. I simply offer it as a possibility."

"Okay! So, did you meet the blackmailer last night?"

"No. I waited half an hour, but the person didn't show up. I phoned the judge, that was around half one, and apprised him of the situation. He was surprised, obviously, but he told me to go on home and said we'd talk about it this morning."

Sheehan eyed the man, scepticism clearly visible in them. "How do you explain that? He knew there was a load of money coming and he just didn't bother to turn up?"

Doran shrugged, his expression mystified. "Yes, I found that odd. The only thing I can think of is that he was well-hidden when he saw me arriving. He'd have known I wasn't the judge, so he might have become scared, suspecting there was a trap or something."

"Do you think the blackmailer might have gone to the judge's house and killed him because he thought the judge tried to set him up?"

"Can't see why he would do that. The judge was paying him a small fortune. Why kill a goose that's still laying golden eggs?"

Sheehan nodded. That made sense. "So where did you get the money?"

Doran gave him a mystified look. "Money?"

"If the blackmailer had presented himself, I presume you were going to offer him money?"

Doran's eyes shifted away again, but his voice was steady again as he said, "Oh, yes. Of course. I got it from the judge's office safe before I went to the car park."

"The judge's safe?"

"Yes, he keeps a lot of money there. Significant amounts keep coming and going."

"That's strange. Why would he do that?"

"I often wondered about that myself, Chief Inspector. He knew I knew it was there and, while he normally kept me very much abreast of all his affairs, he never chose to explain this and, of course, it wasn't my place to ask."

"Do you have any idea of your own as to why there was so much money coming and going?"

"I can only speculate. I just assumed that the judge may have been engaged in some little sideline that was clearly lucrative, but I really couldn't begin to guess what it might be." He paused and, with a little shake of his head, added, "Uh, might have been."

"Okay. Apart from the blackmailer, did the judge have any other enemies that you know about?"

Doran seemed to stare inwards. "Not really, but when Judge Neeson operated in trial court, he could be very harsh in his sentencing."

Sheehan was not surprised by this. "Yes. I was a witness in his court a few times. I'm aware he had that reputation. Do you know of any defendants who might have felt victimised by a perception of unjust sentencing, or maybe family members?"

"He did receive a lot of threats, many of them anonymous, but, yes, some of the more hardened defendants would rant at him from the dock after sentencing, promising all sorts of dire repercussions."

"Would you have a record of the names of those individuals?"

"Well, I only started to work for the judge a couple of years ago when he had already been promoted to the appellate court, but I could ask around. Some of the trial clerks might have names."

"Thank you. I'd appreciate a list of any names you find, and maybe some of the more convincing threats. Oh, and when you're at it, could you also try to find out the names of the guests who were at the party."

"That won't be a problem, Chief Inspector. I was the one who sent out the invitations at the judge's behest. The list is in my office."

"Good. Send it to Sergeant Stewart here, would you, please?"

At that point a cheery voice sounded at Sheehan's right shoulder. "Ah, Jim. And the delectable Sergeant Stewart. How did you two get here so fast?"

"Good morning, Doctor Campbell." Stewart—blond, late twenties, very pretty, more than pretty, beautiful—smiled at the stout, balding pathologist. "We were in the vicinity."

"We just took our normal time, Dick," Sheehan cut in, his face expressionless. "You obviously dawdled the whole way here." He turned his eyes to Campbell's assistant, a tall, black man in his thirties. "Good morning, Doctor Jones."

"Good morning, Chief Inspector. Good morning, Sergeant." Jones' voice, a deep *basso profundo*, seemed to start somewhere near his boots, causing all sorts of reverberations in the floor before it got to his mouth.

Stewart smiled a greeting. "Good morning, Doctor Jones."

Sheehan gestured to the officer at the door. "Jack, would you take Mr Doran to another room and write down his statement." He turned to Doran who was still standing there. "Thank you for your help, Mr Doran. I will almost certainly want to talk to you again, but in the meantime, would you please give this officer a complete statement?"

Stewart, who was putting her notebook back in her pocket, added, "Please don't forget those lists, Mr Doran." She handed him her card. "My email address is there. Could you send the guest list right away, please?"

As he turned to leave with the officer, Doran took the card and said, "I'll do what I can."

Doctor Campbell laid his bag on the floor and struggled to his knees beside the corpse. This was not something his portly frame allowed him to do easily. "Judge Neeson," he muttered. "Called before him to give witness a few times. Seemed obtuse to me."

"How so?" Sheehan asked.

"Kept asking me to repeat stuff. Seemed to have difficulty understanding what I had to say."

Sheehan scoffed. "Dick, even I can't understand you ninety percent of the time. You can hardly blame the judge for seeking clarification when all you speak is gobbledegook."

The pathologist tossed his head. "Tosh, Jim! Nobody speaks with more clarity than I."

"So, are you going to look at the body or not?"

"All right! All right! Give me time to catch my breath." He reached for the overcoat, carefully pulling it down from the victim's head.

"Careful, Dick. There might be evidence there."

Campbell gave him a testy stare. "Now why didn't I think of that? And here was me going to roll it up in a ball and toss it in the fireplace." He handed the coat to Jones with exaggerated care. "Get that bagged and tagged, Andrew, and give it to one of the forensics guys. If, after having already done this so many times before, you're still unsure of the procedure, consult with Chief Inspector Sheehan and he'll write it all down for you."

He turned back to the body, which was lying on its side, back to the fireplace, and moved the head sideways. Stewart sucked in a horrified breath. Sheehan's lips just tightened. The judge's head had been brutally crushed. Bone splinters, blood, and globules of grey matter were oozing from a gaping wound.

Campbell sucked in a hissing breath. "My goodness! Somebody sure didn't like his lordship."

"Was it the blow that killed him?" Sheehan asked grimly.

Stewart kept her eyes resolutely fastened to her notebook, refusing to look any more at the shattered skull.

Campbell peered closely at the grisly lacerations before offering a response. Eventually he said, "Blunt force trauma. Judging from the abrasions and contusions, a single blow with a fairly heavy object. Our killer's strike was savage. I'd have to say it is almost certainly the cause of death, but obviously you'll have to wait for the autopsy results for confirmation."

"Big man, our killer, do you think?" Sheehan asked.

"Hard to say. A good swing with a weapon as heavy as this one appears to have been, could easily inflict these injuries. Even a woman could do it."

"Time of death?"

Campbell leaned forward and lifted the victim's wrist to check his watch.

Sheehan stared at him. "You're kiddin'."

Campbell replaced the man's wrist and shrugged. "You never know. A blow as aggressive as this may well have struck the watch if the judge had time to try to defend himself. No defensive wounds, however, and the watch is still functioning perfectly, so it'll be a rough estimate." He began to probe around the victim's neck and jaws, moving slowly down the large muscles of the shoulders and back. "Rigor mortis already settled in jaws and neck," he muttered, "and well on its way towards the hips, but the process isn't complete. I'd say death occurred between six and ten hours ago." He sat back on his heels and glanced up at Sheehan. "I can take a rectal temperature, if you like. Might be a bit more precise."

"Thanks, but no thanks," Sheehan grunted. "I've seen quite enough of that, thank you."

Campbell grinned and bent to continue his examination. As he was turning the body to explore further the back of the skull, Sheehan said, "Can you give me any idea of what the weapon might look like?"

The doctor, whose position on the floor was inhibiting Sheehan's view of the lower part of the body, jerked back a little. He waited a second or two before turning to stare at the detective. "I'm pretty sure it was an old-style police truncheon." He paused to raise a finger. "Not one of your modern expandable straight batons."

Sheehan offered him a startled look. "Aye, right! And how, pray tell, did you come to that conclusion?"

"Our killer has very kindly left us a significant clue."

Sheehan looked blank. Campbell moved slightly to allow the detective's gaze access to the nether regions of the body. "There it is." He pointed at the body's unprotected rear from which protruded a police truncheon. "A most painfully invasive penetration of the victim's rectum." He shuddered. "The things we see."

Sheehan, lips pressed angrily together, closed his eyes and slowly shook his head. Then he said, "Get that feckin' thing outa there, Dick. I don't want to look at it anymore."

Campbell removed the truncheon, but examined it closely before giving it to Jones for bagging. "I'm pretty sure this is the murder weapon," he said. "I think I see remnants of blood and residue from the head wound still adhering to it."

Stewart, who had injudiciously glanced up, turned her eyes quickly to her notebook again, obviously struggling to hold back the burst of bile that shot to her throat. Jones bagged the truncheon and left to give it to a forensics officer.

Sheehan turned to wander over to a couple of the scene-of-crime officers who were bagging small items for future forensic examination. "Thanks, Dick," he said as he left. "I'll call in to the mortuary in a day or two to see what else you can find." But Campbell was already engrossed in further examination of the corpse and gave no indication that he had heard.

Sheehan watched one of the SOCOs working the floor with forceps and goggles. The man finally noticed the Chief Inspector's feet and he stood up to greet him, removing the goggles as he did so. He was shorter than Sheehan and slimly built. His dark hair was thinning at the front, and his pale face was rendered somewhat effeminate by full lips. His expression was grave and his eyes guarded, but he held out a hand to Sheehan and said quietly, "Hello, Chief Inspector. George Rice."

Sheehan took the hand, surprised at how small it was, but simply said, "Pleased to meet you, George. You new here?"

"Yes, sir. I've just joined the team."

Sheehan pointed at Stewart. "This is my partner, Detective Denise Stewart."

Stewart reached out her hand with a smile and, as Rice took it, the sides of his lips flicked outwards before settling again.

That was a smile? Sheehan wondered. *Definitely of the blink and you'll miss it variety.* "So, George, having any luck with your search?"

The man shook his head. "Nothing, sir." Again that quiet demeanour, lacking animation. "Our perp was extremely careful. I'll carry on looking, of course, but from what I've seen, I wouldn't be optimistic."

Sheehan said, "Not surprised. The perps are seriously canny these days." His eye caught sight of one of his team, Bill 'Larko' Larkin, passing the lounge door. "Excuse me, George." He gave Larkin a wave, beckoned him in. George was back on his knees before Sheehan even spoke to Larkin. "Well, Bill? Anything?"

Larkin, balding, bespectacled, a rubicund face that was invariably wreathed in a cheerful smile, shrugged his shoulders and said, "We're only getting started, Chief. Just bagging odds and ends so far—laptop, office papers, the usual stuff." He paused briefly. "Oh, and the overcoat and truncheon that Doctor Jones gave us, which you already know about."

"Okay! I know that you and your boys are always thorough, Bill, but could you keep an extra eye out for hidden mobiles, smartphone, maybe a burner. There's going to be more than a whiff of scandal around this case.

I'd like to try to get us ahead of it, if we can. Check for hidden papers as well. I think there'll be some." Larkin's eyebrows asked a question, but Sheehan simply added, "We'll have a debriefing this afternoon around two. Set up the Incident Room in the Serious Crimes Suite as usual. Bring whatever you have found by then. The SOCOs can continue the rest of the search."

"Right, Chief. I'll alert the lads."

Sheehan turned to Stewart, still adhering to his side, as always. "Okay, Sergeant. I don't think there's much more to see here for the present. We'll head back."

As they left the crime scene, divesting themselves of their cumbersome coveralls, Stewart said, "I think I might look a bit more into Doran's background, Chief." Giving her boss a sideways glance, she added, "It's not unknown for the person who finds the body to be the one who put it there."

"Aye, right," Sheehan said, with a wry grin. "If only it were that easy." He gave it some thought for a minute. "He says he's only known the judge for a couple of years. Hardly enough time to build up the kind of animosity that would lead to murder."

"Maybe they've met before."

"Hmmm! Maybe. Still, wouldn't hurt, I suppose, to look into both their backgrounds and see if you can come across any connection between them in the past, however tenuous. It might tell us something." He shrugged. "Bit of a long shot, though."

"I'll see what I can find out, Chief."

"And we'll get the team to look into the background of the guests when we get that list. Don't give Doran time to hang around. Phone him in an hour or so and get if off him before the team debriefing."

They arrived at their car, an official vehicle from the station, and Stewart said. "You want to drive, sir?"

Sheehan headed for the front passenger door. "No, you drive, Sergeant. I need to think." Then he added as an afterthought, "Oh, and contact the team. Tell them about the two o'clock debrief. Everybody needs to get up to speed as soon as possible. My guess is there will be a lot of poky dead avenues in this one before we begin to find our way."

THREE
Monday, 13th August. Afternoon

"Maybe one of the guests hung back and hid somewhere until the rest had left." Detective Simon Miller, slight build, astute, smartly dressed in a grey suit, white shirt, green and maroon tie, tended to be the first to break any silences at the debriefings.

"Always possible," Chief Inspector Sheehan agreed, "but there were barely a dozen guests. Surely the judge would have noticed if one of them hadn't left with the others?"

"Yes," Miller said, "that's true, Chief. But maybe when he went back to check, yer man could have been waiting for him with the truncheon. It would have been easy to surprise him and do the deed."

Sheehan shrugged. "Plausible, but we've no evidence to support it. Plus, the guest would have had to hang around for a long time. Doran told me that the guests left not long after eleven and that he had been talking on the phone to the judge well after one."

Miller's eyebrows went down. "Oh!"

"Doesn't necessarily rule it out, though," Sheehan said, his tone placatory. "We'll keep it on the table for the time being."

"What about the Real IRA?" suggested Declan Connors, a strong, solidly built man, well over six feet, and also in his forties. He was popular with the team, but criminals tended to find him formidable and intimidating. "A judge, a police truncheon. They trying to make a statement, do you think?"

Sheehan looked dubious. "Nobody has claimed responsibility for the killing. You know how they like to trumpet from the rooftops their so-called retributions against the British State? We can wait a day or two, I suppose, but I don't think it's them this time."

It was customary for the Serious Crimes Unit to meet almost every day during serious cases. Sheehan believed passionately in sharing knowledge and ideas, convinced of the value of several heads gnawing at a problem as opposed to one. The Serious Crimes Room was large, with sufficient space to accommodate several desks equipped with phones and laptops, and banks of filing cabinets with box files and other papers stashed on top of them. On one wall near Sheehan's desk were two large whiteboards on which photos and other paper evidence were posted and, near that, a small table with a coffeepot, kettle, and some mugs. A couple of banks of fluorescent lights hung down on wires about three feet from the ceiling, giving the room a bright, airy feel.

Right now, the team members were seated at their desks. Sheehan had been debriefing them about the judge's murder. Bill Larkin, the forensics liaison and member of Sheehan's team, was at his usual place beside the white evidence boards, taking them through what little there was in the way of forensic detail.

"Did you find any documents in the judge's study after I left, Bill, or anywhere in the house?" Sheehan asked.

Larkin shook his head. "No, Chief. Bit funny that. Went over his desk with a fine-tooth comb for secret compartments or shelves. Gave it the full McCoy. But there was nothing there ... well, there were the sort of legal papers you would expect to find in the desk but none of his private stuff. Definitely odd. Everybody has private stuff."

"No safe?"

"Thought about that, obviously. We didn't find one, and we did a heck of a thorough search. That's not to say there isn't one. If you pay good money to have a concealed safe installed, then the chances are that concealed is what it's going to stay."

"Worth another search, d'you think?"

Larkin shrugged, grimacing. "I'll get the team back, if you like, Chief, but I wouldn't hold out much hope. We tried everything we could think of." He shook his head, lips still tight. "There might not even be a safe, or it might be in another premises altogether."

"Did you try his city office?"

Larkin looked miffed. "Of course we did, Chief. Same result ... or same no result. Well, actually there was a safe there, but the clerk ... uh, what's his name...?"

"Doran."

"Oh, yes. Him. He opened it for us. Nothing out of the way there at all. Well, actually, apart from the legal stuff, there was a big pile of money." He bent his head and looked at his boss over the top of his glasses. "It's still there, Chief."

Sheehan grinned and said, "Yes, I'm sure it is. Good work there, Bill. I'm sure you did everything that could be done. Didn't mean to make it sound like I doubted you. It's just I had a real feeling that if we could get our hands on his private papers, there'd be some serious info there, and it's a bit disappointing not to be able to find them." He turned back to the papers on his desk, shaking his head.

Larkin tried to maintain a straight face, but his open nature made it all too easy for the team to see he was clearly mollified by the boss's apology.

Sheehan glanced at Stewart. "On the issue of Doran, Sergeant, were you able to find out anything about him?"

Stewart pressed a couple of buttons on her keyboard and brought up a file. "Don't think he's our man, Chief. I couldn't find any connection between him and the judge anywhere."

"How'd he end up working for the judge?"

"By a circuitous route, I suppose you could say," Stewart answered. "He left school with good A-levels but didn't go to university. Went to work for some technology firm called All Solutions. He left them about six years ago to join Despard and McCullough's Law Office where he just worked as a research clerk. But he studied part-time in the evenings for paralegal qualifications and actually got a very decent law degree, 1st Class honours. It was shortly after this that he went to work as a judicial assistant for Judge Neeson." She looked back at her screen again and uttered a short chuckle.

"What is it, Stewart?"

"It looks like Neeson wasn't going to accept just anybody for this job. His criteria were pretty stringent."

"Like what, Sergeant?" This came from recently promoted Malachy McBride, the newest addition to the team and, in his early twenties, the youngest.

Stewart smiled at him. "You thinking of going into that line of work, Malachy?"

McBride was studying for a law degree a couple of evenings a week at Queen's University, but so far hadn't mentioned it to anyone. He chose not to mention it here either. "Just interested," he said.

Stewart's eyes went back to her screen. "He wanted somebody with a good degree, practical experience in legal research, high intellectual ability, incisiveness, an ability to work under pressure, significant levels of IT and written skills, and a preparedness to work long hours when needed." She looked up, grinning. "Some list that."

"And Doran got the job?" Sheehan said, his tone dubious.

She looked across to her boss, sensing his underlying query. "Yes, Chief, but my guess is that he got the job on merit. I didn't find anything that might suggest otherwise."

"From what he told us, he seemed pretty tight with the judge."

"Yes. Word from colleagues is that the judge trusted him with everything, although he's quiet and unassuming otherwise. He's polite with other staff, but generally keeps himself to himself."

"Okay. You get anything on his personal life?"

"Not much. Unmarried, lives alone in a two-bed apartment on the Lisburn Road, seems devoted to his work. Doesn't socialise that I could find, and spends long hours in the law library."

"That's all very interesting, Sergeant," Miller said, "but I'm beginning to think we're wasting time with this guy."

"I think you're right, Simon," Sheehan agreed. "Just clutching at straws. He seems clean enough. All right. We'll move on."

"Any real suspects, boss?" Tom Allen asked.

Sheehan glanced at the young, well-built, blond detective. In his late twenties, Allen was still filled with youthful exuberance but was dedicated and intuitive and had already earned his sergeant's stripes. "Not yet,"

Sheehan replied, "but Stewart is preparing a couple of lists for us. One consists of the names of the guests." He grinned at Miller. "That'll interest you, Simon. Stewart will distribute that now."

Stewart, seated at her usual place at the top of the room near Bill Larkin's boards, smiled at the group and waved a handful of photocopied A4 sheets.

As she left her desk to hand copies to the team, Sheehan went on, "And the other list still needs to be compiled by the judge's assistant. He's promised to let Stewart know the minute he has it ready."

"The other list, sir?" Allen had arrived at the meeting a few minutes late and had missed Sheehan's introductory comments.

"Yes, I mentioned it earlier. Doran, uh, you've probably gathered by now that he's the guy who found the body, hence Stewart's background check. Anyway, he's trying to work up a list of convicted criminals who might have had grievances against the judge or motive to want to harm him."

"He's working at it as we speak." Stewart paused to smile at Allen as she handed him one of the pages, a smile that was obviously affectionate.

It was an open secret in the group that these two were now living together in contravention of normal PSNI protocols. But mind-shattering events during a recent case involving a gang of Satanists had welded the team into such unity that Sheehan had no desire to break up any part of it. So, true to his tendency to ignore rules and regulations where they were of no consequence, he turned a blind eye to the relationship. He knew it would not interfere with the enthusiasm of either for their duties. If other problems were to arise, he would deal with them then.

"I spoke to him earlier," Stewart said. "He says he's working hard on the second list and hopes to have something for me tomorrow, or the following day at the very latest." As she went back to her desk, there was some rustling of sheets as the members of the team studied the list of names.

Geoff McNeill, mid-forties, medium build, ordinary features, victim to an incurable stammer, looked up and said, "What about the b-b-blackmailer, sir? Are we to treat him as a s-s-suspect?"

"We know absolutely nothing about him, Geoff, but that scenario on the roof of the car park might easily have set him off. He's definitely a suspect until we have information to the contrary."

"Can't see it being him," Connors interjected. "He was getting a small fortune every time he tapped the judge. He'd be mad in the head to chuck that away."

"Doran said the same thing," Sheehan said, "but it wouldn't be the first time somebody acted against their own interests in a sudden flare of rage or whatever."

"Anybody check the roof at the Q parking?" Connors asked.

"Yes. Stewart and I drove round there to have a look." Sheehan glanced up at expectant faces but shook his head. "Nothing. Just exactly what you'd expect. No sign of a damned thing out of the ordinary."

"Odd that," Miller interjected. "That assistant fella says he went at the time arranged for the meeting, but nobody was there. Doesn't make sense. You'd think the blackmailer would want his money ... unless he saw somebody that he knew wasn't the judge, suspected a trap, and scarpered?"

"Yes, it's a bit strange. We did go to the management and had a look at some CCTV footage for the hour or so between twelve thirty a.m. and one thirty a.m. Very quiet. Two owners came and drove their cars away. That was it. No one came to park."

"What about the blackmailer or Doran?" Allen asked.

"No sign of either of them. I'd expect Doran would have taken the lift to the top floor rather than drive. He'd have wanted to stay well hidden, so I'm not surprised we didn't spot him. No sign of any other car or person. Of course, we'll never know what the judge said on the phone or how he behaved, but it is possible that he might have said something to create suspicion in the blackmailer's mind of some sort of trap. He'd certainly stay away in that case and live to fight another day."

"Did the t-t-tape show the lift?" McNeill asked.

"Unfortunately, no. The manager's face was a bit red when we pointed that out. His focus was on car numbers. He'll make the changes, but that's no good to us now." He looked at the page in his hand. "We're going to have to do this the hard way, gather evidence bit by bit, until a scenario that makes sense emerges."

McBride held up the guest list. "Some heavy-duty names on here, sir. We're going to have to tread lightly around that lot."

It was on the tip of Sheehan's lips to tell the young detective that status should not inhibit their enquiries in the slightest, but with the thought came the realisation that what McBride was saying was more or less a fair comment. People with high social eminence could make things difficult for the police if they felt that their dignity and status were not being respected. Simple fact of life, and McBride knew it. With a wry inward grin, Sheehan acknowledged that he himself had never allowed status to temper his questioning of witnesses and suspects, regardless of their social rank or influence. Nonetheless, he said, "Which names have caught your eye, Detective?"

McBride was still unaccustomed to his new rank, and his sheepish, if pleased, grin as he heard it anew from the chief's lips was testimony to a persistent inner elation that the young man could scarcely conceal. "Well, sir," he said diffidently, "I don't know everyone on the list, but I see a couple of millionaire property magnates there, J.R. Kennedy and P.F. Robinson." He glanced up as he added, "Robinson's a bit of a rough diamond, hard man, dubious business tactics, questionable associations, but he got an OBE on the last honours list. Bit of a surprise that. And J.R., although it is not generally known, is a woman. She's the brains of the outfit but tends to stay in the background. The initials stand for Jaclyn Reanna." He shrugged, his expression sceptical. "Not sure if these rather grand-sounding names are her actual birth names."

"Friends of yours?" Sheehan said, innocent enquiry on his face.

McBride laughed outright. "I wish. No, there'd been one of those Real IRA bomb threats a while back, Chief. I was on the detail that was assigned to clear the area and protect the two developers. Scary, but it turned out to be another hoax."

"And you want to question them?" Sheehan asked casually, but with a twinkle in his eye.

McBride looked startled but shook his head. "No, sir. Indeed, I do not. I'd rather cut my teeth on somebody less eminent, if you wouldn't mind, sir."

"Uh huh! What other names do you see?"

McBride's eyes went down to the sheet again. "I recognise the name of Mr Robert Bryant, sir. He's a big shot surgeon with the Royal Victoria Hospital. My grandmother had—"

Sheehan held up a restraining hand. "That's all right, Detective. You can regale us with your grandmother's medical history another time. Anyone else?"

"Well, there's Thomas Downey. He owns a few restaurants in town." He glanced across to the detective at the desk next to him who was balanced, as he always was, on the back legs of his protesting chair. "Maybe Sergeant McCullough and me could have a crack at questioning him?"

McCullough, stout, balding, late fifties, and normally taciturn and indolent, was not given to volunteering for anything, but on this occasion he moved forward on to four legs again and tried to look interested.

Sheehan's face was expressionless, but he still found himself puzzled by the surprising relationship that had developed between the keen and bright McBride, and the…. He sought for adjectives to describe the uncouth sergeant. All the Ss: sullen, sexist, sectarian. His inner thoughts stumbled momentarily, tripping a bit over the final s-word that was slipping into his mind. *Stupid?* Well, maybe that wasn't quite fair. And talking about fair. McCullough had changed. There was no doubt about that. His experiences with the paranormal happenings in their recent encounter with LeBreton and his gang of Satanists had given McCullough a whole new perspective on the world. And, equally strange, he seemed to have developed a definite avuncular affection for his new young partner. Sheehan gave his head an imperceptible shake. *Who woulda thought?*

"Okay, McBride," he said. "The two of you can talk to Downey and see what he knows." He shifted his gaze to McCullough. "And, Sergeant, don't come down on him too heavily."

McCullough affected an expression of wounded surprise. "Me?"

Sheehan turned to the group in general. "Anyone else have anything to offer?"

Connors, who had drawn a short straw in his personal life and thus tended to be truculent, said, "Me and Simon will have no trouble chatting to the millionaires, Chief." Miller, almost dwarfed by his massive partner, gave him an acid look but said nothing.

"Does anyone recognise any of the other names?" Sheehan went on, glancing at different individuals for enlightenment.

"I've been Googling some of the names," Stewart volunteered. "There's a prominent barrister here, Michael Stevens. I think we all probably know him, or his name anyway. He's one of the top Queen's Counsels in the Northern Ireland Bar."

Heads were nodding in recognition of the name, and Sheehan said, "Yeah, I know him. Fierce prosecutor. Was cross-examined by him a couple of times. Not pleasant. Who else have you got there?"

"Kenneth Adams. I think he's the Honourable Kenneth Adams, another judge." She peered at her laptop screen. "Only a couple of other females apart from J.R. Kennedy. One is named Edith Gallagher. I have a Professor of Law at Queen's University who's called Edith Gallagher. Given the social level of the company, she would fit right in, so it's probably her. And it seems that the other woman named here, Martina Henderson, is a well-known socialite." She studied the screen in silence for a couple of seconds. "Funnily enough, she's been the subject of some gossip in the media lately. The social columns are engaged in a frenzy of speculation about a possible relationship she might be having with wealthy playboy, Norville Keeley." Another brief pause, and a couple of buttons clicked while she stared intently again at her laptop, "He seems to have loads of money, does Mr Keeley, but he doesn't seem to have any visible employment. And, as you can see, he too, is on our list."

"That name on the l-l-list there, Malcolm McAfee," McNeill interjected. "He's made hundreds of thousands p-p-putting one-armed bandits in golf clubs, h-h-hotel lobbies, lounge bars and betting shops. He practically has a m-m-monopoly on the infernal things." His face blackened. "What a d-d-disgusting way to make a living ... off the b-b-backs of poor people who think they might actually get a f-f-fair deal from them." It was probably one of the longest speeches McNeill had made at a debrief.

Sheehan gave him a sideways look. "You seem pretty het up there, Geoff?"

McNeill hesitated a minute before saying, "A friend of mine asked me to l-l-look into some poker gambling machines at their local. Her son was l-l-losing every penny he earned on them. When I spoke to the b-b-bartender, he just shrugged. No business of his, he t-t-told me. He said they just rented the space to a guy c-c-called Malcolm McAfee and told me to take it up with him."

"And did you?" Sheehan asked.

"I did, and much g-g-good it did me. Got a whole bunch of g-g-guff about how slot machines are perfectly legal, and how it was not his j-j-job to educate people about the s-s-sensible use of equipment that was only there for amusement." McNeill's lips compressed almost to whiteness. "He obviously didn't give a r-r-rat's ass about the poor people running themselves into debt and all sorts of d-d-depression. In the end, all I could do was s-s-speak to the young lad and advise him to get c-c-counselling for his addiction."

Sheehan gazed reflectively at McNeill for a moment before saying, "It might be interesting to see what McAfee was doing in that company at the judge's place. You and Tom take him, okay?"

"Damn right," McNeill growled.

Stewart, who had been tapping on her keyboard, looked up. "That's right, Geoff. It's the same guy. He's just come up on my screen."

"So who are those other two on the list?" Sheehan asked her.

Stewart briefly raised a hand, forefinger pointed upwards. "I'll have the answer in a minute, sir."

There were a couple of minutes of clacking while the rest of the team waited in silence.

"Here we are, sir. William Martin is a major shareholder in BBC TV, Northern Ireland, and the other is Oliver Kane, one of the north's most senior civil servants."

"Oh, yeah," Miller said. "Kane is a Permanent Secretary in the Department of Justice. I've heard his name mentioned a couple of times. Look like butter wouldn't melt in his mouth but behind the façade is a nasty piece of work. Friend of mine worked in his department. Hasn't a good word for him. Apparently, Kane can't stand anyone disagreeing with him and it's been said that if anyone does, they mysteriously lose their job within the next few months. Kane always denies any connection to that, of course. A man who takes the long view. Dangerous, I think."

"You fancy him for this killing?"

"God, no, Chief. I have absolutely no evidence for that. Just saying what I heard."

Sheehan nodded. "Interesting." He pursed his lips, staring at the notes in front of him. "So, we have a dead judge who has just been partying with another judge, a law professor, a couple of property millionaires, a prominent surgeon, a well-known barrister, a socialite and a playboy, a gambling machines tycoon, a media mogul, a top civil servant, and a restaurateur. What a motley crew! And what on earth can they all have in common?"

"Could well just be what it appeared to be," McBride offered. "Just a group of the judge's friends having a friendly get-together."

"Hmmph! I suppose. But when you're in this job long enough, Detective, you'll find it harder and harder to settle for the obvious and the innocent. And I have to say, there are some weird individuals in that group to be friends with a judge." He leaned back in his chair and sighed. "But that's not to say you're wrong. Maybe that's exactly what it was, just a party." He leaned forward again, brisk, business-like. "Okay! We'll talk to all of them. Maybe we'll have a clearer idea of what was going on after the interviews." He studied the sheet in front of him, ticking names with a biro pen. "A dozen names here. That's three for each team." He looked up. "McBride, you're still studying, aren't you?"

The young detective stared at him, clearly surprised. "Yes, sir," he said self-consciously, aware of the heads swivelling in his direction. "Studying law at Queen's a couple of evenings a week."

Miller said, grinning, "Well, now, aren't you the little dark horse?"

"All right," Sheehan said. "McBride and Sergeant McCullough will talk to Professor Gallagher as well as the restaurateur." He grinned. "Maybe you can exert enough authority to make her afraid to fail you when it comes to exam time."

McBride shook his head, grinning doubtfully and exhaling an apprehensive breath. "I think it'll be Sergeant McCullough who'll be doing most of the talking, sir."

McCullough patted his young partner on the shoulder. "We'll get it done between us, son."

Sheehan stared at the jowly cop, baffled. *Bloody hell! Is that McCullough or has somebody slipped us a clone?* He gave the sergeant a final glance. *Count your blessings, Jim. This is a good thing.* His eyes went to the list again. "Okay! And have a chat with that playboy fella as well." He looked at McCullough. "Mac, don't let your young charge get too close to that guy. Don't want anything rubbing off on him."

McCullough, whose affinity with humour was at best slight, nodded in mystification. "Right, Chief."

McBride had his head down, grinning.

"So, Connors and Miller are handling the two millionaires," Sheehan went on. "And Declan, don't be jumping all over them unless they give you a reason to."

Connors spread two innocent hands the size of baseball mitts. "Chief, you know me. Restraint is my middle name."

Sheehan ignored him, but could be heard to mutter, "Aye, right," as he flipped his page to study it. "Oh, and that wealthy socialite lady. You and Simon have a word with her as well." He glanced up at Connors, expression serious. "Try to resist her evil charms, if you can, Declan."

The others grinned widely, amused at the sight of Connors' mouth opening and closing. The man was obviously searching for a smart retort but, in the end, he just shook his head with exasperation.

Sheehan, still business-like, said to Allen, "Will you and Geoff also see what you can glean from that surgeon?"

"Right, boss," Allen said.

McNeill nodded but didn't speak.

Sheehan looked back at his notes, wrote a couple of names and drew a couple of lines and pointing arrows. After a moment studying the list, he turned to Allen again and added, "And talk to the BBC guy as well, will you, please?"

Both partners nodded.

"That leaves the barrister, the judge, and the civil servant, Kane. Stewart and I will take those on." He glanced over at Stewart. "You got all that, Sergeant?"

"Roughly, sir," Stewart replied, reading from a page. "I'll write up the names properly later. Allen and McNeill will interview the gambling machines guy, the surgeon and the media mogul. Connors and Miller will talk to the two property millionaires and the socialite. McBride and McCullough get the restaurateur, the playboy and the professor, and you and I will speak to the judge, the civil servant and the barrister."

Sheehan pushed the papers on his desk back into a manila folder and stood up. "Good. Match the names and addresses to the team members and text them out as soon as possible." He glanced around. "Well, unless anyone else has something to say, that's as much as we can do for the time being." He turned to Larkin. "Bill, keep pushing forensics and let me know immediately if anything interesting crops up, like the judge's personal papers, or a secret safe somewhere. I want to know about anything new right away."

FOUR
Monday, 13th August. Late evening

Lurking just below the surface of the clear web—that is, the normal Internet—is a vast network of vile and corrupt activity called the Dark Net, or the Dark Web, or even on occasions, the Deep Web. 'Deep' because of its enormous capacity. It is literally 'deep'. Searchers can only access 0.03% of the Internet via browsers like Google. The rest, and there is some statistical evidence to indicate that very few people are aware of this, is what makes up the Deep Web. Everything about it is anonymous. Browsers cannot even access it unless they themselves are anonymous. Identities and locations of Dark Net users stay anonymous. They cannot be tracked due to a layered encryption system which protects the users' identities. Those surfers who know what they are doing conceal their IP addresses by 'pinging' their activities around numerous international servers. Usually they rout the addresses via countries that are hard to police, like Russia or Serbia. They also use sophisticated encryption techniques, so trying to track them is virtually impossible.

To access this vast domain, users need considerable levels of technical expertise. Dark Net websites are accessible only through special networks, and even then, only by using special deep web browsers. The most famous of these is called Tor. Users are advised to exercise caution. The modern Dark Web's notorious reputation is well-earned, and the hidden Internet is undeniably dangerous. A careless slip, an identity falling into the wrong hands, and the consequences can be dire. Government agencies, among others, are becoming increasingly concerned that it is a haven for criminal activity. Concerned? They would experience emotions considerably more horrific if they were to fully inform themselves of what is available. Extreme pornography, so-called snuff movies, media exchange for paedophiles and all sorts of dangerous people, drug markets—these are all part and parcel of the normal services the Dark Web provides. It is possible to purchase firearms, or even hire a hit man. On a Dark Net site called The Human Experiment, sadists can view illegal human experimentation on homeless people, 'dross from the streets', expendable and worthless. Other sites show real-time streaming videos of young girls, maybe twelve or thirteen years of age, sitting or lying on beds in small rooms. Viewers with the correct code can bid to purchase or rent any of these children. Some of them, depending upon who is bidding at the time, will be sold to buyers for up to fifteen thousand pounds.

Every taste, no matter how corrupt, is catered for somewhere on the Dark Web. Even those who do not themselves engage in illegal activity, but who would have secret yearnings to do so, can enjoy vicarious experiences by following the blogs of those who like to boast in detail of their bizarre and unnatural exploits.

On the evening of Monday, the thirteenth of August, one such blog appeared for the first time. The blog design is professional, impressive, but singularly at odds with its location on the Dark Web. There is a predominance of gold and blue, with images of white marble busts of Plato and Aristotle set against a hazy background that seems to represent a thriving university. A Latin tag arcs over the scene like a banner: *Amicus Plato, sed magis amica veritas.* And below the scene, in smaller letters, sharp red letters, is another Latin tag: *Alterius non sit qui suus esse potest.*

There seems little here to attract the attention of Dark Web browsers. The immediate impression of classical culture, the implication of scholarship, the tone and theme of the blog—learned, philosophical—seem utterly out of place. But for those who take the time to read the piece, for those who have the intellectual capacity to delve into its argument, to penetrate its pseudo rationalisations, there is to be discovered a pernicious undercurrent. Here is meat for a certain type of jaded consumer who might seek vicarious access to the deviant and depraved, with the titillating promise of more to come.

NEMEIN'Σ ΒΛΟΓ

Συστιξε

Welcome to my blog, dear reader. Over the next few weeks I invite you to consider a series of arguments which I will set before you, arguments that will, I trust, encourage you to question the myth of social norms and examine the importance of impartiality in the role of Nemesis.

Today let us consider the concept of Justice. Philosophers from the time of Ancient Greece, such as Plato and Aristotle, have wrestled with this concept. There have been tomes on the subject from mediaeval scholars such as Aquinas and Augustine. Modern times have provided us with detailed analyses of the issue from Kant, Hobbs, and even more recently, Rawls. All of them see Justice as a moral concept, as doing the right thing, as giving everyone their due. It is defined as a fundamental moral virtue that ensures the establishing and maintaining of a stable political society.

Yet depending on the culture that defines it, Justice is different things to different thinkers. Plato held that Justice issues from God. Locke argued that Justice was inherent in the natural law. Social contract proponents claim that Justice is what is mutually agreeable to all concerned. Then there are those who claim that Justice is retributive and is about punishment for the wrongdoer.

But how are these ideas to be interpreted? Which, if any, offers a correct definition? Who exactly gives people their due? Who decides what is fair? Courts have been set up, as have been other institutions of government, to mete out Justice. But is what is meted out always truly Justice? Or occasionally truly Justice? Or rarely truly Justice?

Human interaction is multi-faceted. To what extent does society's view of Justice consider all of these facets? To what extent does the practical application of Justice spread its net to all those involved? Are there people who, caught up in the apparent meting out of Justice, actually suffer grave INjustice?

I have experienced the application of Justice. I have seen the dispassionate and uncaring face of so-called retributive Justice. I have seen the ramifications of Justice as its ripples spread beyond the ken of the principal actors. I have seen great harm result from the cold-hearted dictates of shallow judges who remain impervious to the evil they cause.

Philosophy is abstract, and philosophical Justice is abstract. But real Justice is in the here and now, in the acting out against the evil of the so-called defenders and protectors of society. Real Justice penetrates to all those who pervert, or cause to pervert, its action. Many thinkers may disagree about the precise nature, the fundamental essence, of Justice, but at its core there lies the clean, pure biblical eye for an eye, tooth for a tooth. And that is why I have appointed myself the agent of tangible Justice, the righter of wrongs, the one who sees beyond the immediate. Hand-washing after the deliverance of penalty does not alleviate blame for subsequent calamity. The prime mover must take a shared responsibility for events that occur as a result of his judgement.

And so I have identified and punished one who saw himself as the punisher. I live again the moment of his judgement. He is standing there in his room of opulence—arrogant, pompous, confirmed in his overweening superiority. He is initially unaware that Justice has finally found him. I experience a moment of satisfaction when, seeing me casually heft the Instrument of Retribution in my hand, his air of smug haughtiness wanes. His expression vacillates between annoyance and uncertainty, migrating to a burgeoning fear. Ah, Justice! He has no idea.

"What are you doing?" he stutters

"You'll learn in eternity," I say coldly.

Although Justice should be meted out dispassionately, and this is an issue that I will address at another time, I am aware of a sense of pride in my physical coordination, in the smoothness of the arc, the accuracy of the strike, as I swing the weapon. I draw back, with bent arm, behind and below my right shoulder and, turning my body with ineffable grace, my arm stretches and extends upwards as the club smashes, with a gratifying crunch of bone, against the side of the miscreant's head, precipitating an effusion of blood, grey matter and bone splinters. He crumples to the ground and I know that Justice has been done.

I draw down the pants of his black evening suit, and I savour the irony as I thrust the Instrument, a policeman's truncheon, so appropriately linked to the apparatus of the Justice system, deep into the malefactor's depraved rectum.

A prime mover cannot distance himself from the evil consequences in a chain of action which originated with him. He is responsible. He must accept blame. Justice has been served.

My next blog, dear reader, hopefully in a few days, will examine the morality of Vengeance.

Nemein.

FIVE
Tuesday, 14th August. Morning

"**P**ull over there, Stewart," Sheehan ordered.

"Double yellow line, Chief?"

Sheehan reached into the glove compartment and pulled out a rectangular plastic placard which bore the message, POLICE ON DUTY, and threw it on the windscreen shelf. "Let's go," he said, door already opening before Stewart had finished parking the car.

Striding across the footpath, Sheehan was soon on the walkway leading to the Royal Courts of Justice, Stewart almost running to catch up with him. Neither took time to admire the impressive building, with its imposing façade and giant Corinthian columns, as they hurried to the large entrance and went into the central hall. Stewart had been here a few times before but she never failed to experience a degree of awe as she traversed the long interior hall, thirty feet high, with its floor-to-ceiling panelling of Travertine marble.

Sheehan paused briefly. "Which floor?"

"Second, sir."

Sheehan strode off again, heading for the stairs. He couldn't be bothered waiting for a lift that would probably be too full to admit them anyway. He climbed the first flight of steps with ease before an abrupt reminder from the sciatic nerve in his right hip caused him to wince. *Dammit!* He strove to show no sign of the sudden pain, pausing casually as if deciding to wait for his sergeant who was several steps behind him. Keeping his voice as level as he could, he said, "Where exactly is the judge's office?"

"On the next floor, sir. If my laptop check was accurate, it should be the third door on the right."

"Okay, Stewart. You lead. Here's me rushing on and I haven't a clue where I'm going."

Stewart remained straight-faced as she went on ahead. Sheehan stared after her, still waiting for the spasm to pass, wondering if she knew about his sciatic hip. It was, to him, a weakness, and he hated that. He figured she had probably seen enough winces, heard enough soft gasps, to have alerted her to his problem. But if she did know, she gave him no sign. His mind flashed briefly to Allen, but he shook his head imperceptibly. *No, she stays. Loyalty like that? You keep it close.* He made it to the second floor with gritted teeth, but by the time he got to the office of Judge Kenneth Adams, the pain had subsided.

Judge Adams was a slight man, almost emaciated. The wrist that appeared from his jacket sleeve as he reached out to shake hands with the two detectives was almost skeletal. He had a full head of grey hair and heavy sideburns almost halfway down the side of his cheeks, but these did little to hide the narrowness of his face or the thin, aquiline nose. The eyes that peered out from beneath shaggy, grey eyebrows, however, were as sharp as a hunting hawk's.

His voice too, when he gestured to a couple of chairs in front of his desk and invited them to sit, was surprisingly crisp. When they were settled, he said, "And how can I be of help to you, Chief Inspector?"

"Thank you for seeing us, Judge," Sheehan said, "and please accept our condolences on the loss of your colleague, Judge Neeson."

Judge Adams nodded solemnly and said, "Thank you."

"In fact," Sheehan went on, while Stewart placed her notebook on her knee, with ballpoint pen in readiness, "I'm afraid it's your colleague's death that has brought us here today. I understand that you were at his house on the evening of his demise?"

The judge sat back on his chair and gave the detective a long and penetrating stare before replying, "Yes, I was there that evening, but both myself and several colleagues were long gone before anything ... ah ... untoward occurred."

"I understand, Judge," Sheehan said, his tone conciliatory, "but you will doubtless appreciate that we are obliged to interview everyone who was there and ask a few basic questions ... for the purpose of elimination from suspicion, if nothing else."

"Of course, Chief Inspector, of course." He waved a thin hand. "Ask your questions."

"You knew Judge Neeson quite well, I'm sure, sir. Did you happen to notice if he had been exhibiting signs of stress or any other signs of unease that night?"

Judge Adams seemed to look inward for a moment before saying, "Now that you mention it, he did seem a bit jumpy. His conversations with the small groups standing around were short and perfunctory. Oh, and yes, he kept looking at his watch. In fact, he disappeared into his study for fifteen or twenty minutes. Odd that, but, I'm sorry, I have no idea what was disturbing him."

"Do you know if he had any enemies that might have hated him enough to...?"

The judge quickly shook his head. "We make enemies on the bench more or less every time we deliver a sentence, but this was extreme. We get all sorts of threats and invective from uncouth morons in the dock, but their general level of intelligence would tend to militate against the possibility of them planning and executing a crime of this nature. The brutality of it, yes, but they'd be more likely to attack their victim on a side street or in an alley."

"Anything in his private life that might have earned him animosity?"

The judge showed no reaction to the question. He simply shook his head slowly and said, "No. Nothing that I know of."

Sheehan didn't miss the deliberate nature of the judge's composure and wondered about it. *It's almost as if he's trying to pretend that the question has had no impact on him. Odd!* Aloud he said, "Would you mind telling me, please, what was the purpose of the gathering at the judge's house?"

Adams spread his hands slightly and said casually, "Just a few friends meeting for a drink and a chat, basically. Nothing much more than that."

Sheehan sensed that Adams was holding something back. *Time to press.* "If you don't mind my saying so, Judge, the general social mix of the group is at odds with what one might normally expect at a high court judge's *soirée*."

Adams threw him a sharp glance, probably less than pleased with Sheehan's flippant French noun, but he simply shrugged. "All of them are people of some wealth and prominence. I suppose that gives them ... us ... some level of commonality."

Sheehan pursed his lips. "I'm sorry, Judge, but I don't find that explanation particularly convincing." Stewart's pen wavered, but she kept her head resolutely down. "I mean, judges, a socialite, a gambling machines vendor…" He paused a beat. "…a playboy? Money aside, sir, I struggle to even imagine what you might have in common."

Adams' eyes blazed. "You forget yourself, Chief Inspector," he snapped. "Are you impugning my word?"

"Not at all, sir," Sheehan said smoothly. "I just feel there's something you're not telling me. And to be honest, sir, when faced with that kind of obstruction, I tend to ferret out the withheld information eventually."

Judge Adams visibly bristled, and an angry retort hovered on his lips.

Sheehan held up an admonishing finger. "Sir, please. This is a murder enquiry. The normal niceties do not apply. If there is something else, I would appreciate it if you would tell us now."

Adams sat back again in his chair, folded his arms and studied the detective for some moments. Eventually he stated, his voice hard, "I have heard it said that you are no respecter of persons, Sheehan." He paused to stare at the detective again. "But I have also heard that you get results, so I will give you some latitude." He paused to gather his thoughts, and then said, "I suppose it's bound to come out at some point." He leaned forward again and said, "Brexit."

Sheehan blinked, surprised. "Brexit?"

"Yes. What the members of that group at the judge's house had in common was an implacable opposition to Brexit, particularly its inevitable and negative impact on Northern Ireland."

"Politics?" Sheehan was still thrown.

"The future of Northern Ireland, Chief Inspector. There are those of us who would seek a reversion of the decision to leave the EU, or at least pursue special status for our province."

Sheehan was baffled. This was not at all what he had expected, nor was he remotely interested in the details of the argument. "Okay. Can I ask where you went after you left the judge's house?"

Adams sat back. "I invited a few of the guests to my house for a late coffee and further discussion."

"Is there a housekeeper or someone who can confirm that?"

"No," the judge responded stiffly. "I live alone. I do have a housekeeper but she works normal daytime hours. You'll have to take my word for it, and, of course, the word of my guests."

"Can I have their names, sir, please?"

The judge's thin lips almost disappeared, but he held himself in check and said, with reluctant compliance, "Jaclyn Kennedy, Patrick Robinson, Oliver Kane, Robert Bryant, Michael Stevens, and Edith Gallagher. I don't know where the others went." Stewart was still writing busily when the judge added, "I think that is all the time I can afford, Chief Inspector, not, I am sure, that there's anything else I could add." He stood up and gestured to the office door. "I do hope you catch this miscreant, but I am quite busy and I must ask you to leave." He did not offer to shake hands.

Sheehan glanced at Stewart. "Got all of those names, Sergeant?"

Stewart nodded, her eyes on her boss, clearly not allowing herself to look at Judge Adams.

"Okay." Sheehan, too, stood up and said calmly," Thank you for seeing us, Judge. I appreciate you giving us your time." As he headed for the door, he glanced back. "If there's anything else, we'll get back to you. Thanks again."

*   *   *

As they walked down the stairs again, Stewart exhaled a shaken breath. "God, Chief, you don't give a crap, do you?"

Sheehan gave her a mildly inquisitive glance. "About what?"

"Status. Position. Authority. That guy's a high court judge, for heaven's sake, sir."

Sheehan stopped to look directly at her. "Actually, Stewart, I do believe in being respectful to those in authority, but the minute Adams started talking, I sensed a whiff of something off." He waved a hand. "Years of experience. But when that happens, I'm only interested in finding out the truth. And so I push." He gave her a reflective look. "But he's a clever one, that Judge Adams. Oh, aye! He fought not to tell me about Brexit. That threw me off. The fact is, that when he did admit it, it was only a bone to keep me occupied. Played me like a fish, he did. And now I'm mad as hell I didn't push harder. I know there's something else he was hiding, and it's nothing to do with Brexit." He resumed walking again. "I will find out eventually what it is, don't worry about that." He glanced at his watch. "Where to now, Sergeant?"

"Stormont, Chief. We're seeing Oliver Kane."

"Oh, yes. The civil servant. Remind me what he does exactly?"

"He's the Permanent Secretary at the Ministry of Justice."

Sheehan raised his eyebrows. "Oh, yes. Did you find out any more about him?"

They had reached their car and Stewart waited until they were settled in their seats before replying, "A bit, sir. He's in charge of one of the largest government departments with significant oversight of the Crown Courts and the prison system. You heard what Miller said at the debrief, sir. Kane tends to make enemies easily and holds grudges. He's clashed with both of our judges a couple of times, particularly about budgetary issues and excessive sentencing." She signalled and eased out into the traffic before continuing, "He runs the prison system as well and hates the costs associated with long sentences. A friend of mine told me about a finance meeting where Kane attempted to impose some restrictions on Court spending, and Judge Neeson called him '…a trumped-up little pipsqueak' and advised him to watch his manners when addressing members of Her Majesty's judiciary."

Sheehan made a face. "Humph! Subtle."

"Hates Neeson from all accounts. My source tells me that people have been waiting to see what misfortune might fall on Neeson. It seems that no one ever gets one over on Kane. Neeson's murder, however, was an unexpected intervention, and I'm told we'll never know now what nasty surprise Kane had planned for the judge."

"Unless it wasn't an intervention," Sheehan said dryly.

Stewart lifted her shoulders. "I suggested that to my source, but she couldn't see him going that far." She signalled to take a right turn and added, "She did say something else, however, that was oddly contradictory. According to her, Kane could do with a charisma transplant, but that despite his lack of personality there are some dark rumours that he is bi-sexual and has some voracious appetites. She couldn't give me chapter and verse on any of that. Just the rumour."

Sheehan remained silent for a while, staring vacantly through the windscreen. Eventually he said, almost muttering, "Holy heck! What is it with this group?"

*   *   *

The Stormont building, home of the Parliamentary Assembly for Northern Ireland, is located on the eastern outskirts of Belfast. In the somewhat incorrect usage in the province, the word Stormont, *('Stormount'* in common parlance), refers not only to the area where the building is situated but also to the Parliament, and to the Northern Ireland Government. *[The National Health Service is a laugh ... but d'ye think Stormount's goin' to do anything? Hah!]* The building is huge, sitting proudly at the top of a wide, impressive, mile-long avenue which meanders through acres of open green lawns and is surrounded by woods and parklands. The drive took the detectives past a huge twelve-foot stature of Edward, Lord Carson, standing on a large granite plinth, and on to an extensive space in front of the building. The impressive entrance, tented top, high columns, is built in classical Greek style, with long wings extending on either side. An ornate staircase, some distance from the entrance to the Great Hall, leads up to various rooms and offices. A quick query at a reception area furnished the detectives with the location of Kane's office.

In answer to their knock, Kane himself opened the door. He was a slightly built man, a little over five and a half feet in height, dressed in an undistinguished tweed jacket and charcoal grey trousers. His thinning dark hair was brushed straight back on his head and his voice, when he bade the detectives a good afternoon, was dull and uninflected. The office was much like the man, uninspired, sparse, containing little more than a largish table, laden with several files and documents, with some chairs around it, walls painted a faint nest-egg blue, bare but for three or four modernistic paintings, and a phalanx of filing cabinets along one wall.

"Please take a seat, Detectives," Kane said, gesturing to the table. The movement, like his general demeanour, was slight, lacking any animation. He sat across from them and enquired politely but demonstrating little interest, "What can I do for you?"

Stewart took a notebook from her pocket and laid it on the table as Sheehan said, "Just a few follow-up questions about the murder of Judge Neeson."

Kane showed no reaction. Instead he said blandly, "I believe I have already informed a couple of your uniformed officers that I know nothing about that."

"True, but there are some things that I need to get clear in my mind. For example, there are rumours that you were not on particularly friendly terms with Judge Neeson?"

Kane's expression didn't change. Neither did he shrug or move. His hands, which were loosely joined on the table in front of him, remained still. He simply said, using the same bland tone, "I have no control over rumours."

"Do you affirm or deny them?"

"I had little contact with Judge Neeson other than to be present with him at the occasional group meeting," Kane said in the same dry, monotonous tone. "My attitude towards him, or his attitude towards me, would have been of little significance in the broad scheme of things."

"He was murdered. People who were hostile to him would naturally demand the interest of the investigating team."

Kane looked calmly at the hands in front of him. "Hostile?" His tone suggested that he was considering a minor problem. "Hostility requires emotion. I have long ago discovered that emotion impacts adversely on decision making. I prefer to operate with a clear and uncluttered mind."

"How come then, given your ambiguous relationship with him, you attended a party at his house on the evening of his murder?"

Kane's fingers quietly meshed. Other than that, he remained still. "I would have to question the use of the word 'relationship', Chief Inspector. I had no kind of relationship with the judge."

"So what were you doing at his house?"

"I believe you already know the answer to that."

"I'd like to hear it from you."

Kane's eyes went down, again studying his hands before he spoke. His face remained expressionless as he said, "The people who met at the judge's house that evening are concerned about the impact of Brexit on the Northern Ireland economy. We met to discuss how we might best deflect future problems."

"What did you talk about exactly?"

Kane stared steadily at Sheehan. "It's quite complex."

Sheehan returned his gaze with equal composure. "Try us. We might be able to follow some of it."

Kane went through his moment-of-silent-deliberation routine, taking his time before answering. Sheehan watched him, thinking, *Still waters run deep.* When Kane spoke, it was a lack-lustre recitation of facts. "If the UK leaves the EU, it's more or less certain that they will also leave the customs union. There are those who fight that, but I think they will lose. However, if Northern Ireland, which is part of the UK, also leaves the customs union, then there will inevitably be a hard border between the north and the south of Ireland, with consequent impact on tariffs, trade deals, increased taxation on imports and exports, traffic and people border checks creating all sorts of delays for commercial vehicles on timetables. Need I go on?"

"No, thank you," Sheehan said. "That's quite enough. So what exactly is your group trying to do?"

"Our group is trying to come up with a plan that will persuade the British Government to keep Northern Ireland in the customs union, even after Brexit."

"Bit of a tall order," Sheehan said.

"I said it was complicated."

"You did indeed. Is that why you recruited such towering intellects as Norville Keeley, Martina Henderson and Patrick Robinson to help with your deliberations?"

Kane's eyes dived again to his hands, but not before Sheehan caught the flash of venom that appeared in them.

Ah! The real Kane emerges. Wonder if that's me in his sights now, as well?

Kane remained utterly still for some seconds before saying quietly, "I had no involvement in the selection of the group members. I simply went to the meeting in response to an invitation."

"From Judge Neeson?"

"From the judge's judicial assistant."

Changing tack, Sheehan said, "Do you know if the judge had any enemies who might have wanted to kill him?"

Again that insipid voice responded, "The judge was an arrogant man who seemed to thrive on insulting people. On top of that, he was vindictive on the bench, venting spleen on criminals and court personnel alike. I have no doubt he made many enemies. I'm afraid I can't help you with names, however." Unexpectedly, he sat back in his chair and folded his arms, psychologically cutting himself off from the two detectives. "I am due at a meeting shortly. Is there anything else I can help you with before I leave?"

Sheehan eyed him for a second, making no attempt to conceal his scepticism. Then he said, "I think that will do for now, Mr Kane. If we need anything more, we'll get back to you." He glanced at Stewart who closed her notebook and rose from the table.

Kane rose, too, and crossed the room, apparently already detached from the detectives and their reasons for being there. Holding the door open for them, he said neutrally as they passed by him, "Good afternoon, Detectives. Thank you for calling."

SIX
Tuesday, 14th August. Afternoon

A golden Labrador lay on a hearth rug, his head resting on his two front paws. He wasn't asleep, however. One eye kept cocking, constantly observing his master who was seated in a nearby armchair reading a newspaper. Eventually the man closed the newspaper, folded it, and threw it on to a nearby sofa. He stared through the window beside him for some seconds and then grinned at the dog. "What do you think, Fred?"

Fred's head came up and his body rolled to a sitting position. His tongue lolled out and he seemed to grin back.

The man, grey-haired, paunchy, looked out through the window again. "Bit of a breeze out there, Fred."

The dog got up, sidled over to the window and raised himself up so that his front paws were on the sill. He, too, looked out. He turned his head to his master, both eyebrows moving erratically.

The man chuckled. "I declare to God, Fred, you understand my every thought." Rising from his chair, he added, "So it's a walk, is it?"

At the mention of 'walk' the dog dropped back on to all fours, reversed a bit to face his master, and uttered a short, sharp bark.

The man reached out, patted the dog's head and said as he opened the lounge door, "A walk it is, Fred. Just let me get my coat and my stick." Fred bounded into the hall and stood facing the front door, tail wagging furiously, small excited wheezes and whines emitting from his mouth.

The man grinned again. "All right, Fred. All right. We're going. We're going." He buttoned his overcoat against the breeze he knew was out there and, taking a minute to attach a lead to the dog's collar, he opened the front door and headed out. Fred strained against the lead, dragging his master a few steps before the old man said calmly but firmly, "Heel, Fred."

As man and dog emerged from the stone-fronted, L-shaped bungalow, two cold eyes stared at them from an inconspicuous black car parked about fifty yards away. The watcher experienced no surprise, no emotion, no relief, when he saw them. He had made a point of observing the man's behaviours over the past couple of weeks and soon learned that he could almost set his watch by the man's comings and goings.

They had left the house precisely as anticipated. He continued to watch as they made their way to a small car parked on the drive. He watched the man open the back door of the car to let the dog jump in. He knew now their exact route and where it would take them, having already followed them on a number of occasions. They would drive to the Cave Hill Walk, leave the car in the parking area near Belfast Castle, and walk from there. He had studied their circuit in detail and had already selected the secluded spot where he would wait for them.

Giving the oblivious pair a couple of minutes to get en route, he started his car and, a few minutes later, drove calmly past them.

*   *   *

Man and dog loved this walk. It offered a challenging route over rough paths, crossing moorland, heath and meadows where the trills, shrieks and screeches of buzzards, kestrel, and peregrines could be heard overhead. And the weather today was cooperating. The rain and squalls of the previous evening had given way to a slightly cloudy but occasionally sunny afternoon, with just a hint of a breeze.

The early part of the walk took them through a woodland area containing many trees that had been planted at the latter end of the nineteenth century, the paths heading ever upwards towards a plateau.

Breaks in the trees offered magnificent views of Strangford Lough, Scrabo Tower, and the Mourne Mountains far to the south. Away to the north, easily visible, was Slemish Mountain, the first known home of the legendary Saint Patrick, and beyond that, the coast of Scotland across the Irish Sea.

The man never tired of these panoramic views and often stopped just to gaze and wonder. Fred, whose tastes were less aesthetic, would tend, when released from his lead, to bound along the paths and through the trees, following interesting smells. He seldom strayed too far, however, and invariably returned to check that his master was still behind him before scurrying off again.

Some twenty or thirty yards ahead of the man, Fred came to a high grassy bank at an isolated corner of a path that ran through the trees. A car was parked there with the bonnet raised and a man standing beside it. Seeing the dog, he reached out a hand and said cheerfully, "Hello, Fred. What are you doing all the way up here?"

Fred acted puzzled to hear his name from the mouth of a stranger whose smell was unfamiliar to him. He stopped, tail wagging uncertainly, cocked his ears forward and held his head slightly to one side, trying to make sense of what was happening.

The man smiled again. "Have I got a treat for you, Fred," he said and, opening his hand, he tossed some pieces of meat into the trees. Fred, catching the tempting aroma, was already salivating as he dived after the morsels. Two or three quick snaps of his head and the pieces were all gone. Fred licked his lips with a huge pink tongue and was coming back for more when he stopped, pawed his mouth, and reversed erratically, coughing, choking, whimpering at the sudden pain he was experiencing. Still reversing restlessly, his muscles started twitching, the twitching becoming more and more pronounced as convulsions began to manifest themselves.

The dog began to stumble. His twitching became more and more pronounced as he began to convulse. He fell to the ground, gasping. His legs and body began to stretch outwards while his neck curved down into his chest. His pupils were now dilated, filled with panic and fear, as spasms followed one another with increased severity.

The stranger watched impassively as the dog writhed and suffered, looking away only when he heard the footsteps of the dog's owner.

SEVEN
Tuesday, 14th August. Afternoon

"Awesome," Sergeant McCullough grunted, as he stared up at the three-storey building that constituted the new Law School at Queen's University. "Glass everywhere." He turned to his young colleague. "It does have walls, right? Have to say it looks very fragile from here."

McBride grinned. "I've been in it many times, Sarge. It's rock solid." He followed his partner's line-of sight and grinned again. "But I have to say, all that glass, makes you wonder." He moved forward. "We'll go in..." He paused. "...but remember, Sarge, you're doing the talking, right?"

McCullough nodded importantly, and said, "Sure, kid. No problem." But almost immediately, he added, "This is a law professor we're interviewing, you know. You're a law student. You understand this kinda stuff. If you feel that you'd like to chip in, don't let me stop you."

"Okay, Sarge. It's this way." He led his older colleague through the ground floor, past some informal student spaces and a café, and on to the upper floors where the School of Law staff had their offices and facilities. After a short walk along an upper corridor, McCullough was already showing signs of breathlessness. McBride pointed. "Those are her offices over there." He stood back with a slightly edgy expression. "You go first, Sarge."

"Will you quit, kid. It's only an interview. Way you're actin', you've got me nearly up the walls, as well. C'mon, let's go." He strode to the door and knocked firmly.

A female voice called, "Enter".

They found themselves in a substantial outer office where three secretaries at separate desks appeared to be working diligently. The one nearest the door, dark haired, thirtyish, wearing a black skirt and white blouse, smiled and said pleasantly, "Hello, can I help you?"

McCullough showed her his warrant card and said officiously, "Detective Sergeant McCullough and Detective McBride to see Professor Gallagher."

The girl rose from her chair. "Of course. Just a second." She went to a door in a side wall and knocked gently. She waited a beat and then stepped half-in, holding the door open. She emerged almost immediately and beckoned the two men to the room. "The professor will see you now," she said, and went back to her desk.

Unsurprisingly, given the huge glass panes that seemed to constitute the walls of the building, the room was airy and very bright, with magnificent views of the city from both sides.

The professor was a surprise to McCullough who had been expecting a stumpy, grey-haired, elderly lady. Edith Gallagher was, in fact, still in her late forties and, while her face might have been marred by some slightly crooked teeth and thin lips, it was an intelligent face, an appealing face, characterised by two soulful brown eyes that more than offset any seeming imperfections elsewhere. She had kept her figure trim, her short, chestnut hair elegantly styled and, when she stood up to greet the detectives, they could see that under her black professorial robe, she was wearing a lavender cashmere sweater with a purple skirt that barely reached her knees.

She came forward and offered her hand to both men, saying, in a pleasantly modulated voice, "How do you do, gentlemen? Please sit." She indicated three comfortable but armless chairs that were clustered around a glass-topped coffee table at one side of the room. Before she sat, she added, "Can I get you something to drink, tea, coffee, water?"

McCullough, who had sucked in his breath in an effort to reduce his girth, uttered a strangled, "No thanks," losing control of his paunch as he did so. He sat down quickly and waited for the professor to join them, trying not to allow his eyes to fasten on the two elegantly crossed legs that suddenly appeared beside him. "We'll try not to keep you too long, Professor," he said, struggling to regain some measure of control.

"Thank you," she said, wresting control from him immediately. "You are Detective Sergeant McCullough, right? And you..." She turned to McBride. "...are Detective McBride. I understand you are a part-time student here?"

McBride's face showed his surprise.

The professor smiled dryly. "I always like to know who's calling. And what are your electives?"

"I'm studying for the LLB single honours degree, Professor."

She nodded slowly. "Useful choice for a policeman, or are you thinking of practicing law after you graduate?"

"Not sure, Professor. I'm keeping my options open right now. Have to see how my career in law enforcement goes. Currently, I'm enjoying it very much."

"Good. So what have you come to see me about?"

McBride half-turned towards McCullough who had by now regained his composure.

"We were wondering, Professor," McCullough started, stopping again immediately to clear his throat, "if we could ask you a few questions about Judge Neeson."

Her face assumed an expression of sorrow. "Ah, yes. Poor Trevor. I was so sorry to hear what happened to him." She gave both men a direct encounter with her expressive brown eyes. "He taught me when I was a student here, you know. We were quite close, and that friendship spilled into our professional lives."

McCullough nodded. "We're sorry for your loss, Professor. Please accept our sympathies."

"Thank you, Sergeant. I appreciate that." Again that soulful look.

While McCullough may not have been the most perceptive of individuals, he did have behind him a number of years interviewing suspects. Distracted though he might have been by the professor's charm, he somehow found himself thinking, *Laying it on a bit thick, isn't she?* It was a fleeting thought, however, and he went on, "Did you know all the people at the judge's party on the evening he was ... uh, on the evening of the incident?"

"I am quite familiar with most of them. One or two would be very slight acquaintances."

"I see." McCullough hesitated. "Sorry to be so blunt, Professor, but would you be aware of any animosities that might have existed between the judge and any of his guests?"

"No, I'm sure that no such animosity existed. He was very friendly in his dealings with all of us."

McCullough nodded. "You say you knew him well. Would you know of anyone outside of the party who might have wanted to do him harm?"

Professor Gallagher shook her head. "I'm sorry, Sergeant, I don't. I'd love to help, obviously, but this kind of thing is—" She spread her hands. "—beyond my ken." She appeared to be giving the matter some thought for a few seconds. "Perhaps someone whom he sent to prison might...." She shrugged ingenuously.

"Obviously that would be one of our lines of enquiry," McCullough said. "Could I ask why the party?"

She leaned forward, puzzled. "What do you mean?"

"Well, lots of very different types there—legal types, property owners, playboys, gambling machines guy, others. Hard to figure out what you all might've had in common."

"Just some friends of the judge's meeting for a drink and a chat. No more than that." Her face was the picture of innocence.

McCullough had seen that expression many times before ... and didn't like it. What he had in the way of professionalism began to reassert itself and he said, rather more forcefully, "You do know, Professor, that we'll be talking to all of the people who were there that night. If there was anything else going on, we will definitely get to the bottom of it. It won't look good if we later find out that you were withholding something."

The professor lowered her head, seeming to contemplate McCullough's ultimatum. After a few seconds, she rose and went behind her desk where she stood looking out through the window. When she turned to them again, she seemed to come to a decision. Tight-lipped, she said, "Very well, Sergeant. This is something that I would much prefer didn't come to light, and I can conceive of no legal reason why it should, but the common theme, if you want to call it that, of our visit to Trevor's on that night was Brexit."

McCullough stared at her. "Brexit?"

McBride's hand, which was taking notes, also stopped, and he, too, looked up questioningly.

She nodded seriously. "Yes. Brexit." She sat behind her desk with her hands clasped in front of her. "I would ask you, please, to keep this confidential. We are not ready to tip our hand yet, but there are some small groups of us seeking to find ways to reverse the Brexit decision. Well, at least in so far as it applies to Northern Ireland."

McBride couldn't help himself. "Surely you can see that that is a hopeless endeavour, Professor."

She stared at him coldly. "Is it?" She turned to McCullough. "Did you come here to question my politics, which I should point out are absolutely of no concern to the police, or do you have other more pertinent questions?"

Both men were immediately cowed but McCullough persisted. "You're right, Professor. Sorry about that. Could you please tell us where you went after you left the judge's house?"

"A few of us went to Judge Adams' house for coffee and to have some further discussion about the Brexit issue." She stood up, fairly glowering now. "If that is all, gentlemen, I do have work to do."

McCullough stood up too, but as he did so, something of his normal personality began to assert itself. "Not quite all, Professor," he stated bullishly. "I'll need the names of those people who joined you at Judge Adams' house."

The professor sniffed, raised her nose, thought for a few seconds and quickly rhymed off some names, causing McBride's hand to fly back and forth across the page in his notebook. "Judge Adams, of course, and Michael Stevens. The others were Jaclyn Kennedy, Patrick Robinson, and Robert Bryant."

She left her desk, walked to the office door and held it open. "Now, I really must insist that I get on with my work."

McBride was first out, offering the professor a self-conscious nod and a mumbled, "Thank you," as he left.

McCullough, more assured, strolled out saying, "Thank you for your time, Professor, but please keep yourself available. We may need to speak to you again."

As they headed for the ground floor and the exit, McBride said, "Shit, I think that's my law degree out the window." McCullough didn't respond. He seemed puzzled about something. "Sarge, you listening to me?" McBride said, touching his boss's arm. This earned him a quizzical glance, and he grinned, "Hey, it worries me, Sarge, when you start looking thoughtful like that. Are you okay?"

McCullough stopped and said, "Good lookin' woman, that, and she was really nice to us at the start. But then she went all *prima donna* at the end. What was all that about? I mean, I don't think we said anything that could have set her off." He stared at his young colleague. "You were watching her, kid. You think all that bluster might have been about trying to hide something?"

"Wow! That's very perceptive, Sarge. Tell the truth, that hadn't occurred to me. But now that you mention it...."

McCullough grunted. "Stick with me, kid. You'll soon find out that I'm not as stupid as I look."

The young detective clapped his superior's back as they walked forward again. "You're not, Sarge. You're definitely not." Then he grinned and added quickly, "Oh, I'm not trying to say that you look stupid, Sarge."

McCullough just grunted. But his thoughts were puzzled. *A year ago, I'd have bawled him out for talking to me like that. Must be gettin' old.* He stopped again to look back at the high building. "I wish I'd asked her what they all had to eat, or what the curtains were like in Judge Adams' house, or what room they were in for their meeting, or where they all sat in relation to each other," he muttered. "Definitely stupid. Good mind to go back."

McBride looked blank. "What are you talking about, Sarge? How are these things relevant?"

McCullough shook his head. "I'm not much good with this sort of stuff, kid. Wish the chief was here. He'd know what to do."

McBride was half mystified, half amused. "Don't get it, Sarge. What am I missing? What the heck does it matter what they had to eat?"

"It doesn't matter at all, son. It's just the way she got miffed so suddenly. I think she was covering something up with her anger. You get that a lot and learn to see it over the years. To tell the truth, I'm starting to wonder if there even was a meeting at Adams' house. She'd know the answer to silly little questions like that if there was. If there wasn't a meeting, these questions would trip her up. And in that case, you'd have to wonder where they really went after they left Judge Neeson's." He walked on. "We'll definitely go back again if we have to, but in the meantime, we can try the questions out on the next guy."

McBride looked at his companion with something close to respect in his eyes. "Sarge, I'm impressed."

McCullough tossed a dismissive head. "Humph! You'll be the only one, kid. Who do we see now?"

"That restaurateur, Thomas Downey."

"Right. Let's see if he knows the colour of the curtains wherever he went."

EIGHT

Tuesday, 14th August. Late afternoon

A number of laptops and computers in houses and apartments all over Northern Ireland and, indeed, over much of mainland Britain and further afield, pinged around five o'clock that Tuesday afternoon. Many hard-core users, forever glued to their electronic devices, stopped what they were doing when they saw the name on the message that had appeared at the lower corner of their screens and immediately clicked on it.

NEMEIN'Σ   ΒΛΟΓ

Γενγεανξε

Nemein calling.

Hello again, and welcome to my blog. I am pleased to see from the number of 'hits' and 'likes' accorded to my last modest post that I am beginning to acquire a sizeable following. I do hope that you find today's post of equal interest. As usual, I feel initially obliged to clarify some philosophical issues that, properly understood, will explain and vindicate the course of action upon which I subsequently embarked.

Vengeance is mine, saith the Lord. Yet the Good Book says, 'An eye for an eye.' Food for thought. Imagine if someone causes irreparable harm to someone you love. Would you seek revenge? Would you rely on the justice system? Think before you answer. If we had a perfect justice system that meted out consistent punishments, there might be a case for patience. But, is not that a huge IF? Would you leave the aggressor's fate to the Lord, or would you exact an eye for an eye here on earth? Or would you simply follow the New Testament and turn the other cheek? We are called on to forgive, not seek revenge, are we not? Hah!!!

Let us look at that. South Africa's Truth and Reconciliation Commission was set up on the understanding that Restorative Justice can help victims to forgive, perpetrators to find remorse, and both parties to find lasting peace. But I ask, how genuine is offender rehabilitation? How realistic is the concept of restorative justice in which BOTH the offender and the offended are genuinely willing to—in the one case seek, and in the other offer—forgiveness?

Forgive me if I bristle with scepticism. I see people. I observe people. I know people. I work with the best and the worst of people. And this concept makes me sneer. Liberal idealists cannot force forgiveness on others. What do they know? Life experience, as Dewy would claim, has so much more to teach us about the truth and reality of things than empty ideologies and liberal posturing. And the reality is that people do not forgive. It is not in their nature.

So, which path does one take? Do we seek vengeance? Or do we attempt to walk the path of forgiveness?

Simone de Beauvoir, French writer and existentialist, writing after the Second World War, talks about the rage and the hate experienced by the ordinary French citizen during the occupation of their country by the Germans. She wrote that one does not hate plague, or hailstones, because they do not consciously cause evil. One only hates man, because only man has the will to do evil. The French swore that the Germans would 'pay' for their atrocities. De Beauvoir argues cogently, and to my mind with sound justification, that the word 'pay' reflects the human desire of victims to visit upon their tormentors a pain and brutality equal to the pain and brutality inflicted upon them.

In other words, they seek the Law of Retaliation, the biblical eye for an eye. De Beauvoir sees so clearly that where there has been a great injustice, a terrible dehumanisation. There follows also a primal desire to seek vengeance upon the wrongdoer.

Thus a balance must be restored by making the perpetrator experience, or, to use De Beauvoir's psychology, to make him 'viscerally understand' what he has done, by forcing him to undergo an equal and brutal victimhood. He viscerally understands the pain he has caused by undergoing it.

But then, incomprehensibly, De Beauvoir drifts into a banal and spiritless questioning of the morality of the desire for revenge. She suggests that vengeance has a 'disquieting character', and thus the idea of vengeance becomes suspect. How could she have drifted so erroneously from the inevitable conclusions of her earlier argument? Oh, it is wonderful to sit in an ivory tower and philosophise intellectually without experiencing the compulsion of emotional involvement. But how one's view can change, how fragile becomes one's intellectually held beliefs, in the face of the actual and dehumanising experience of injustice and pain. Who can say, if they have not experienced the pain of abuse, of degradation, of loss, whether vengeance is retribution or tyranny?

De Beauvoir attempts to argue that if acts of retribution are undertaken, if one acts in response to a passionate hate, then the avenger is no better than the original aggressor. What tosh! If the legal system fails, if vile indifference leads to the destruction of a noble soul, and no one attempts to balance the scales with justice, then what course of action is left to us? Do we simply weep and cease to act? Philosophy is objective. Suffering is subjective. Philosophy simply examines ideas. Suffering is real. And when the right to vengeance is denied, there comes great outrage and a deep-seated infuriation that cries to heaven for action.

And I have answered that cry for action. It took time. It took patience. It took a manipulation of work schedules to allow monitoring of the target. It took extreme caution and no little skill to ensure that I remained invisible during my surveillance.

I soon discovered that my quarry was a man of rigid routine. His comings and goings were so precise, I could have set my watch by them. He left his house at the same time every morning, went into town and visited the same shops in the same order, and arrived home always at the same time. In the afternoon he walked his dog. Again, the timing was meticulous in the extreme, his habits punctilious. At precisely three in the afternoon he would emerge from the front door of his bungalow, call the dog to heel, direct the dog into the back seat of his car, drive to the Cave Hill Walk, park always in precisely the same spot near Belfast Castle, exit the car with the dog, and begin his walk. His route never varied. That allowed me subsequently to walk the route alone and identify the ideal place to exact vengeance.

There was always the problem with the dog, of course. It was a large dog, it clearly loved its master, and at any sign of threat it could doubtless have turned vicious. How could I have achieved my goal with a huge dog and its slavering jaws snarling and tearing at me? But as I considered possible solutions to the problem, I came to realise that the dog was not at all a problem, but a boon. If I could somehow incapacitate the dog near the ambush area, the man would rush to its aid, bend over to examine it, and leave the back of his head an exposed and unrestricted target.

I know little about poisons, but research soon taught me that I had a number of options. My plan required that the dog not die immediately but remain alive, twitching and gasping and struggling to move. These effects would best guarantee that the man would cast himself on his knees at the dog's side. I isolated a number of possible poisons and finally reduced that list to three: cyanide, arsenic, and strychnine. I had to research each further, in order to decide which of the three would be most appropriate to my needs.

Thus, when I learned that cyanide, which interferes with the red cells' ability to extract oxygen, causes the victim to suffocate almost immediately, I had to reject it. The dog's sudden death would not have suited my purpose. If the man happened on the scene, finding the dog dead and me standing nearby, his first response would almost certainly be suspicion and blame. Arsenic, too, causes severe gastric distress, pain, vomiting, and diarrhoea with blood. No, too much, too soon. Such symptoms, immediately after the healthy animal had bounded vigorously around a nearby corner, would again almost assuredly arouse suspicion.

My decision became clear when I discovered the effects of strychnine. It is not as fast acting as cyanide or arsenic, and early symptoms are confined to the head and neck which simply become stiff. Shortly, however, the front and back paws begin to spasm, and the body later begins to stiffen and arch. Ideal for me. These symptoms, and their slow development, are sufficiently innocuous to make it appear that the dog could have hurt itself against a rock or a tree. It would then have been perfectly normal for me, the innocent bystander, to point at the writhing animal and say, "Is that your dog, sir? It seems to be having some kind of seizure."

Unfamiliar as I am with poisoning (you will understand that it is not something I do every day), I was at a loss as to how I might acquire strychnine. There was a time when strychnine could easily have been purchased over the counter in any local chemist's shop, particularly for pest control. However, the effects of strychnine poisoning are unacceptable to modern attitudes to animal suffering. During the whole process the animal is horribly and painfully aware of what is going on, as the nerves of the brain are also stimulated to give heightened perception. It is an agonising way to die. And so, in 2006, strychnine was banned, even as a pesticide, because it causes unnecessary suffering to animals. It is now illegal to purchase strychnine in the UK.

This was an unexpected setback. But further research informed me that where strychnine is needed for agricultural use, a special license can be acquired. I am fortunate in that I have some access to the dark underbelly of society, and thus privy to skeletons lurking in many cupboards. It was the work of one afternoon to peruse records to which I have convenient access and uncover a member of the agricultural community who not only had quantities of strychnine, but who also had secrets in his life that he was desperate to conceal. A single phone call, with what I rather fondly imagine was just the appropriate hint of menace, ensured that I was able to acquire the small amount of strychnine that I needed.

Thus, and oh the irony of it, the precision by which my target had lived, was the same precision that guided him to his dispatch. Events transpired exactly as I had envisaged. His predictable pattern led him to the Cave Hill Walk, led him with almost serene inevitability to the site where Retribution would claim its due.

I heard them approach. I waited beside my car, bonnet up to offer the illusion of a motorist in difficulty. The dog, as always, lurching some yards in front of its master as it romped excitedly from one new scent to the next, was first to appear. Some juicy pieces of meat, laced with the strychnine so generously supplied by my agricultural acquaintance, ensured the dog's unwitting complicity in the drama that followed. First came the tortured writhing of the dog, followed by the anguished fall to his knees by its master, and then ... then came the moment, the moment when the undefended head presented itself for the coup de grâce!

It was but the work of a second to seize the Instrument of Vengeance from its concealment on top of the car's radiator, tread softly across the forest path, swing with grace and fluency, and crush the back of the target's head with a gratifying disintegration of bone. Although haste was imperative, it was impossible not to pause and relish the visceral elation engendered by the sudden spurt of blood, mingled with grey matter from the cerebellum. Oh, the joy of it! But, sadly, there was little time for jubilation.

I tore my eyes from the shattered skull and, in the briefest of moments, wrested the fallen one's pants to his ankles. Turning him face down, I thrust the weapon (as before, a large police truncheon) deep into the corpse's rectum with all the force I could muster.

Although I had scarcely moved during my wait, I spent a few vital seconds using a leafy branch to scrape the earthen path where I had trod. You will appreciate that it was imperative to ensure concealment of any footprints or even partial footprints that I might have made.

I returned to my car, replaced the bonnet, and allowed myself one final moment to savour the triumph of vengeance. Something of balance has been restored. Another malefactor has been brought to understand the suffering in which he has been complicit. One final look and I drove quietly from the scene.

I hope you found today's blog interesting, dear reader, perhaps even informative. Very soon I will return with an examination of the Philosophy of Hate. Until then, I urge you to ponder the real truth of what it means to be human.

> *Nemein*

The blog was followed by two comments. The first read: *From SmartCat. Hi Nemein. Seriously cool stuff, dude. Do you hire out?*

The second was Nemein's reply: *Hi SmartCat. I appreciate your approbation. Regrettably, since my energies must remain inflexibly focussed on my current project, I cannot be available for other undertakings. However, although it is not given to us here below to peer into the future, who knows what circumstances might arise? I trust you will continue to follow my blog.*

> *Nemein*

NINE

Tuesday, 14th August. Late afternoon

At Sheehan's behest, Stewart drove the car as close to the crime scene as she could. Neither paid any attention to the beautiful views, to the wild and rugged landscape, or to the screeching birds above. Another murder had been committed. Both were grim-faced as they quickly exited the car and ducked under the yellow police tape that was already cordoning off the area to deter curious walkers from entering and contaminating the crime scene.

Sheehan stopped to talk to a scene-of-crime officer who was hunkering down as he poured some liquid plaster-of-Paris on to some tyre tracks. He recognised the slight figure of George Rice. "Hi, George. Think you'll get a good impression?" he asked.

The man stood and nodded seriously to Sheehan. He wore the same dispassionate expression that he had worn at the judge's house. "Yes, sir. But I don't believe that will benefit us much."

Sheehan gave him an enquiring look but said nothing, waiting for the man to continue.

The officer pointed to some continuation tracks just beyond the slowly setting mixture. "Good threads, no wear, so no obvious irregularities. We'll get a first-class impression, sir, but the thread here is what you call symmetrical." He pointed again. "See. Same pattern across the whole tyre.

Very, very common. Just about everybody, unless they're driving high performance cars, uses this kind of thread." The officer brushed his hands against each other and shrugged. "We'll make the cast as usual, sir, but it'll be a match for about seventy percent of the cars on the road."

Sheehan nodded glumly. He cast his eyes backwards and forwards across the path. "Footprints?"

The officer's lips tightened as he turned his head sideways towards the area where the car had been parked.

Oh, oh. Something's actually stirred him up a bit, thought Sheehan.

"I think there might have been some, sir, but the perp took the time to erase them with a stick or a branch or something. I couldn't even find a partial."

Sheehan scowled. "So he's a smart fella, huh? Okay. Thanks, George." He turned and headed to where Doctor Campbell was just rising from his knees beside two shapes concealed under crime-scene throw blankets. Campbell, too, was brushing his hands together when the two detectives approached him.

"Hi, Dick," Sheehan said.

"Good afternoon, Chief Inspector," the pathologist said, smiling. "And good afternoon to you, too, Sergeant Stewart. I trust you are well today?"

"I'm fine, thank you, Doctor," Stewart answered, returning the doctor's smile. Doctor Campbell never seemed to take things too seriously. "Just a pity we had to discover this lovely area because someone has been murdered."

The doctor nodded, serious now. "Indeed, someone, and—" He pointed to the smaller heap. "—a beautiful dog, as well."

"A dog, and ... a human being," Sheehan said, a little tersely.

"And I am fully aware of that and all its implications, Jim," Campbell retorted, "but that does not mean one cannot also have sympathy for a poor, blameless animal that must have suffered a most painful death." He noted Sheehan's questioning look and said, "If my suspicions are correct, the unfortunate creature was poisoned with strychnine. Not only does it produce some of the most dramatic and painful symptoms of any known toxic reaction, but the victim's awareness of what is happening is heightened to extremes." He shuddered. "This lovely Labrador died a most horrible death. How could one not have sympathy for it?"

Stewart was almost in tears. "The killer did that to the poor wee dog just to keep it out of the way? That's .... that's sick." She turned to her superior and said fiercely, "Sir, we're going to get this creep and make him pay."

"We will, Sergeant," Sheehan said, "and we'll make him pay for killing the poor wee human being as well." He turned his gaze to the pathologist. "What can you tell us, Dick?"

"White male, late-sixties, maybe seventy. Blunt force trauma to the head. Pretty much a carbon copy of the Judge Neeson murder, right down to the truncheon in the rectum."

Sheehan glanced at him sharply. "Is it now?"

"Well, the blow is slightly higher on the back of the head. I'd guess the victim was kneeling at the side of his dog trying to comfort it, or maybe trying to figure out what was wrong with it. The killer struck from behind and above. One blow. And it was more than enough." He pulled back the cover from the corpse's head. "Very precise. No angry hammering."

Sheehan studied the victim and frowned. "Odd. I'd swear that I've seen this face before, but I know I've never spoken to him nor have I ever had any dealings with him." He stared a while longer, searching his memory but came up with nothing. Shaking his head in puzzlement, he said, "Nah! Nothing. Must've just come across him on the street or in a supermarket or something." His lips tightened as he stared around the scene, his eyes searching.

Campbell pointed to a SOCO walking up the path, studying something in his hands. "That officer over there might just have the information you're looking for."

Sheehan stared at the officer, then back to the doctor. "What? You clairvoyant now?"

Campbell grinned. "Maybe."

"Dick!"

"Oh, God. I hate to explain. I'd rather leave you guessing." Campbell's grin remained wide. "Actually, that officer was standing exactly where you are a while ago. He said he was going down to the car park to find the victim's car. Maybe he found some useful information in it ... the guy's name, maybe, or something that might ring a bell for you."

Sheehan turned and stalked off, leaving the grinning medic standing there.

Stewart almost ran to catch up. "Boss..." she said, "you know I didn't mean—"

"It's okay, Stewart. I know what you meant. And don't worry. We'll nail the bastard and make him pay for all his crimes."

As they walked down the path to meet the approaching officer, Sheehan recognised him. They had met on crime scenes before. Sheehan offered his hand. "Hi, Frank." He nodded towards Stewart. "You know my colleague, Sergeant Stewart."

Frank gave her a friendly nod.

"Find anything in the car?" Sheehan asked.

Frank gave him a sharp look.

Sheehan shrugged modestly and said straight-faced, "I'm a chief inspector. It's my job to keep tabs on everything."

Frank didn't look very convinced, but said, "Yes, Chief. His wallet was in the glove compartment, along with his driving licence and insurance papers."

"Who is he?"

"Don't have the full story yet, but I've sent a couple of officers to question his neighbours. According to the insurance papers, he's Mr Seamus Redmond, and he has an address in Strathye Park on the Malone Road, sir."

Sheehan absorbed this. "Redmond?" He shook his head and muttered. "No, doesn't ring a bell." His eyebrows lifted. "Strathye Park? Classy neighbourhood."

The SOCO nodded agreement. "Yes, sir." He looked again at his notes. "Date of birth on the insurance policy is the nineteenth of April, nineteen forty-nine."

Sheehan did a brief mental calculation. "Dick wasn't far out."

"Sir?"

"Nothing. Just thinking out loud. Anything in the wallet?"

"Some cash, couple of credit cards, organ donor card. Oh?" He stared at the card, seeming reluctant to continue.

Sheehan pursed his lips. "Yep. Somebody's life is going to take a massive turn for the better this evening." He seemed to focus on the distant hills but his eyes weren't seeing them. "Life's vicissitudes. Somebody dies. Somebody lives. Weird," he said eventually. "Okay, Frank. Send those couple of men to my office as soon as they've finished canvassing the neighbours. I want to know right away what they find out." He nodded to the officer, and said across his shoulder, "Let's go, Stewart."

TEN
Tuesday, 14th August. Early evening

"Smug b-b-bastard." McNeill was clearly annoyed as, close to evening, they headed towards their car in the Royal Victoria Hospital car park. They'd had to wait over an hour before Robert Bryant would interrupt his late afternoon clinic to speak to them. "Bloody B-B-Brexit! No matter where you go."

"Did you not find that a bit odd?" Allen asked. "I mean, businessmen, yes, but you don't often find surgeons beating themselves up about Brexit."

"Dunno. National Health's in a s-s-state."

"Uh huh, but the NHS was in a state long before Brexit." He shook his head, "Just something funny about it."

"Or maybe it was just him. Smarmy sort of individual. All p-p-politeness and manners. Like an act, you know. He d-d-didn't seem to be feeling anything."

"Yeah." Allen nodded absently as he unlocked the car and climbed in. "Now that you mention it, his answers had a bit of a rehearsed feel. He was obviously expecting us."

McNeill gave him a wry grin as he fastened his seatbelt. "Aye, well, can't b-b-blame him for that. He was with the judge an hour or so b-b-before he was killed." He waited as Allen reversed out of the bay and headed towards the exit.

Allen still looked bothered. "But why act so guilty about trying to derail Brexit? Half the country's shouting about it from the rooftops. I can't see why they're making it such a big deal."

McNeill didn't reply as they stopped at a large busy roundabout before heading back in to the city. Their exit safely negotiated, he said, "Maybe they actually have something p-p-planned and are getting ready to do s-s-something about it."

Allen nodded. "Maybe. We'll push McAfee a bit harder on that and see what he has to say. What's that address again?"

*   *   *

McAfee's office was on the fifth floor of a tall building in Chichester Street. It was plush, spacious, had plenty of armchairs, a large ornate desk and a substantial drinks bar in one corner. As the businessman invited the two policemen into his office, he pointed at the bar before sitting down and said, "Can I get you two gentlemen something to drink?"

"No, we're fine, sir," Allen said politely. "We don't drink on duty."

The man pointed to a group of armchairs near a large picture window that overlooked the city. "Please, sit." Once they were settled, he said, "So, how can I help you, Officers?" He stopped, slightly puzzled as he stared at McNeill, "Have we met?"

"I had to s-s-speak to you a while ago about the effect your m-m-machines were having on young lives," McNeill said stiffly but with some heat.

McAfee sat back in his chair, unfazed. "Ah, yes. I remember now." He said nothing further, clearly wrong-footing McNeill who looked uncertain before taking out his notebook and subsiding into silence. McAfee waited a beat before adding, "Is this what you're here to see me about?"

"No," Allen said. "We'd like to have a word with you about Judge Neeson."

McAfee settled back into his chair and said, "Ah, yes. Sad business that."

"I understand that you were at his house a while before he died?"

McAfee was immediately on the defensive. "You think I had something to do with it? I remind you that I was also well away from the house before the judge was ... was so tragically deprived of his life."

Allen stared at him briefly. *So tragically deprived? How long did he spend working on that one?* Aloud he said, "How did you come to know the judge?"

"I occasionally met him at the odd bash here and there."

"Here? As in here in your office?"

McAfee looked annoyed. "As in here and there, different places."

"What places?"

"Friends' houses, the odd evening at a hotel, usual social gatherings."

"Uh huh. And the bash at the judge's house was just a social gathering?"

"Of course. Just a few friends meeting for a drink and a chat. That's all it was."

Allen's expression didn't change but his brain was racing. *Just a few friends meeting for a drink and a chat. Exactly what Bryant said and exactly the way he said it.* "To the outsider's eye, the ... uh, social mix was extremely diverse. Hard to imagine what such a group might have in common ... and in a judge's residence."

McAfee glared at him. "Was that a question?"

Allen raised a couple of laconic eyebrows. "Just an observation, really, but okay, let's make it a question."

McAfee shrugged. "Money. The higher you climb the social ladder, the more likely you are to meet with other high climbers."

Allen looked thoughtful. "I see. So you, something of a hustler with limited educational experience, suddenly find common ground with a cultured judge, just because you've made a few pounds?"

McAfee leapt angrily to his feet. "If you've come here to insult me—"

McNeill had risen equally quickly. He laid a strong hand on McAfee's shoulder. "I suggest you sit down, Mr McAfee." Something very angry simmering inside of him completely eliminated his stutter. It also eliminated McAfee's resistance.

Allen remained calm during this exchange. When McAfee was seated again, he said, "It is you who's insulting us, Mr McAfee, if you think for one moment we would believe your absurd explanation for the meeting." He sat forward in his chair, eyes narrowed. "Now, sir, let me make it plain. The judge has been murdered. You're sitting here lying through your teeth. What you're really making us believe, sir, is that you are somehow involved in the judge's murder."

"That's ridiculous. What motive would I have?"

"That's why we carry out investigations," Allen said grimly. "To find these things out. Okay! I'll ask again. What was the purpose of the gathering at the judge's house?"

Neither policeman missed the crafty gleam that appeared momentarily in the witness's eyes. Neither did they indicate that they had seen it.

"If you must know the truth," McAfee said, striving to appear earnest, "and I would have to ask you to please keep this private, if at all possible, the common denominator of the group is a desire to deflect Brexit ... from Northern Ireland at least. We were simply meeting to consider options."

"Do you hire your m-m-machines to places down south?" McNeill asked.

McAfee looked slightly thrown, but he said, "No. I just operate in Northern Ireland."

"What about Europe? D-d-do you have business there?"

"No. I told you. Just Northern Ireland."

McNeill sat back, a derisive expression on his face. "So why are you b-b-breaking your neck about Brexit?"

McAfee said loftily, "I happen to have wider political interests than those affecting my own narrow concerns."

"That's very noble," Allen interjected. "And what political problems in particular are you concerned with."

"Well, we definitely don't want a hard border."

"What was the border like b-b-before Britain joined the EU?" McNeill asked. "There was plenty of f-f-free movement then, was there not?"

Whoever had urged McAfee to offer Brexit as the purpose of the meeting had neglected to brief him on the essential arguments about the issue. He spluttered for a minute or two, and then, affecting anger once more, he said, "I understand I have to talk to you about my movements on that evening, but I'll be damned if I'll sit here and allow you to examine me on the arguments for and against Brexit."

"Just making c-c-conversation, sir," McNeill said calmly.

"On that point, Mr McAfee," Allen added, "would you care to tell us where you went after you left the judge's house that evening?"

"One of the guests, Mr Downey, invited a few of us around to his house for coffee and a chance to continue the conversation on Brexit."

"Invited who?"

McAfee stared sideways at the carpet, apparently searching his memory. "Well, there was me, obviously, and Thomas Downey, Norville Keeley, Martina Henderson and, let me think, oh yes, the media guy, William Martin."

"Downey's wife can confirm your presence there that night, can she?"

"Sorry, no. She's away for a few days. That's why Downey invited us there ... for the privacy."

"Nice house?"

"Yes, lovely."

"What room were you in?"

"It was a large sitting room, plenty of seats."

"Curtains?"

McAfee looked nonplussed. "I presume so. That's not something I would ever pay any attention to."

"You'd hardly remember the general colour of the carpet, then, or of the furniture?"

McAfee shook his head, trying to appear impassive. "Sorry. Wouldn't have a clue. I'm just not interested in that sort of thing."

"And you talked about overthrowing the government."

"We did not," McAfee snapped. "We were trying to find ways to make Downing Street consider a special Brexit deal for Northern Ireland."

"What sort of special deal?"

McAfee blew air through his lips as he searched for a response. Eventually he said, "We haven't arrived at any hard and fast options yet."

"Okay! Any idea if the judge had any enemies who might wish him harm?"

McAfee shrugged. "None that I know of." He paused to think. "Job like his, you might be looking for some hardened criminal who held a grudge or something."

Allen glanced at McNeill who nodded and put his notebook back in his pocket. Both detectives then stood up. "All right, Mr McAfee," Allen said. "That'll do for now. But we'll almost certainly wish to speak with you again, so please keep yourself available."

ELEVEN
Tuesday, 14th August. Evening

The venue was a large country mansion just south of the city. It was set in its own substantial grounds at the end of a long tree-lined drive. Exclusive, ultra-private, it purveyed very specific services to an exponentially growing number of wealthy members. Access to the mansion's menu of experiences, broadly categorised under the common heading, *Fulfilment for the Enlightened,* was available only through recommendation, and even that was dependent on the result of an intensive vetting process. The names and professions of those who were granted membership remained secret, but The Club's mysterious founder, whose identity was carefully protected, had full details of all members locked carefully away in a hidden safe. That safe was hidden in the house of Judge Trevor Neeson. To the members, the judge was an intermediary who introduced them to the arcane diversions of The Club. The truth, however, was that the judge was the owner, architect and creative force behind this flourishing venture.

The wealthy members seldom socialised, although occasionally a few would meet for drinks and the exchange of experiences. But reputations tended to be held sacred, and most of the members preferred to fulfil their extreme desires in the privacy of one of the many upstairs rooms in the mansion, or even in the 'dungeon' cellar. When 'group entertainment' was organised, participants wore specially designed masks to ensure that identities were protected. Wealthy doctors and surgeons, members of the legal professions, businessmen and women, scions of multi-nationals, were among the elite of this secret society whose fantasy experiences had become increasingly hardcore to satiate palates already too jaded to find diversion in the offerings of normal sex clubs. Masked fetish balls, dominatrix training, sado-masochism—there was no proclivity that could not be gratified. Patrons, as the members were called, would pay several thousand to star in their own adult movies, or to have 'fun' sex parties with young children, or to be kidnapped and abused by their captors, or even to be a 'mediaeval gaoler', equipped with whips and chains, to physically abuse 'recalcitrant prisoners' until the floor of the cellar ran with blood. For those to whom money was no object, opportunity for experiences involving extreme sadism could be arranged with precision and discretion.

Although The Club was of relatively recent vintage, a few members, owners of private jets or luxury yachts, were from England, Europe, and one from as far away as South Africa. The menu was as varied as it was imaginative, with numerous options to suit all tastes. Few questioned how the 'fun children', the young porn actresses, the 'prisoners', or the many other essential 'supporting actors', were sourced for the delectation of The Club's affluent clientele, nor did any express curiosity as to how or where those 'dream extras' lived their lives when not engaged in The Club's business.

The Club's house provided the patrons with a number of bars, one of which was an L-shaped drawing room, comfortably furnished, with a fully-stocked bar at the shorter end. While drinks were free, there was no bartender to serve the drinks. The members served themselves. Privacy was paramount.

The evening of the fourteenth of August, a Tuesday, was typical for Northern Ireland. Despite the fact it was late summer, it was cold, wet, with windy squalls forcing the rain to beat heavily, if spasmodically, against the windows of the big house. A small group of patrons was comfortably ensconced before a large natural fire near the free bar, oblivious to the night's tantrums, sipping drinks and talking quietly. Masks had been discarded to allow an unimpeded flow to what was clearly a tense conversation. The deviant delights on The Club's menu were clearly far from their minds.

Professor Edith Gallagher, perched awkwardly on the edge of a deep armchair, the quivering of an illicit cigarette in her fingers betraying her nerves, said, "Christ! We've only just joined The Club and already I've had the police around."

"I've had them, too," Judge Adams said calmly, more comfortably ensconced in his own chair, nursing a large brandy glass. "They're only fishing. They know we were at Neeson's house that night. That's all they know. So keep your heads and this will blow over."

Gallagher wasn't convinced. "I know The Club's management, whoever they are, has our names, but would the judge have kept a record as well, do you think?" Her expression belied any hope there might have been in her words.

Judge Adams gave her a patronising look and almost sneered, "For god's sake, Edith. Does Bill Clinton smoke cigars, do you think?"

"This kind of knowledge is power, Edith," said Michael Stevens, offering a more conciliatory response to the professor's comment. The barrister was a squat, ungainly figure whose unprepossessing face was characterised by a bulbous, veined nose that hinted at an excessive acquaintance with the finer pleasures of life. He was possessed, however, of a rich baritone voice that helped minimise his physical defects and had made him a fortune defending wealthy clients in court. "Whatever about The Club's owner or owners, the judge will have compiled his own list for sure, and our names will be on it. He's probably got it tucked away in some secret place. I know I would have if I were in his shoes."

"Humph!" This came from Jaclyn Kennedy, a thin, angular woman in her late forties who was sitting rigidly upright on the small sofa she was sharing with her business partner, Patrick Robinson. "Maybe whoever killed the judge has done us a favour." She stared speculatively around the group. "It wasn't one of you, was it?"

Immediately the expressions of all the room became inscrutable, unreadable. Oliver Kane was the only one whose expression did not change at all. But that was the nature of the man. His expression was invariably inscrutable. Most, maybe all, might have been innocent of the judge's murder, but none wanted to show any facial expression that could be misread or misinterpreted.

But there was no misinterpreting Judge Adams' expression. He was clearly angry. "Don't be silly, Jaclyn," he snapped. "Stick to the issue at hand."

Kane, sitting primly upright in his armchair, knees and feet rigidly together, tended not to speak much at meetings. His dark eyes, however, followed the conversation, studying every speaker, observing, analysing. There was a moment of surprise, therefore, when his spiritless voice made itself heard. "Somebody needs to meet and remind our absent colleagues to not move an inch on the Brexit story. I am not altogether sure that they can be trusted to hold fast." He was referring to the other members of the group who had partied at Neeson's house but who, for various personal reasons, had been unable to attend this meeting.

"Don't think we need to worry too much about McAfee or Downey," Judge Adams said, "but I would have less faith in Bill Martin. He's weak. And Henderson and Keeley seem to take nothing seriously."

Patrick Robinson clenched his huge fists and growled darkly, "I'll have a word with them."

"Have either of you two legal eagles heard anything about what the police are doing?" Robert Bryant asked. "I, too, had a couple of detectives questioning me this morning. They give me some peculiar looks when I offered them the Brexit story." The surgeon, fiftyish, balding, immaculately dressed, sounded calm but his constant fidgeting betrayed that he, too, was disturbed.

"Let them look all they want," Adams replied. "Just keep repeating the Brexit excuse like a mantra. They can't prove otherwise." He sipped his brandy, savouring its flavour. Holding his glass up to the light, admiring its colour, he added, with a slight curl of his lips, "I phoned Neeson's assistant this morning to extend my sympathies. He didn't have time to talk because SOCOs were tearing the judge's office apart looking for private papers or a hidden safe. Apparently they found neither."

His listeners visibly relaxed, but Jaclyn Kennedy said, "If there is a safe, we're going to have to find it before the police do."

"And how, pray tell, do you propose we do that?" Bryant said. "We can't just waltz into his house and start searching."

Kennedy gave the surgeon an angry look. "We'll see how many of your private patients suddenly start cancelling operations if your name appears all over the media as a member of the *Fulfilment for the Enlightened Club*." She held his gaze until he looked away and then said, "I was hoping that we might have a contact who can at least tell us where the safe is. We can figure out after that how we might make it disappear before the police get their hands on it."

"Looks like we might be back to the judge's assistant again," Stevens said.

"Might be hard to convince," Adams replied. "These chaps are fiercely loyal and tend to guard all secrets zealously."

"Bribe?" suggested Kennedy, studying her long red nails.

Adams shrugged. "I don't know the chap particularly well, but if he's going to be approached, it will have to be done with extreme delicacy. One doesn't know exactly how he might respond." He raised a skinny finger for emphasis. "What we do not want is to have him looking into the 'person' offering him the bribe and finding his way to The Club."

Several heads nodded agreement. It was clear that they looked to the diminutive judge for leadership.

"Damn Club," snarled Robinson, heavy-set, unrefined, intellectually outstripped in this company. "Nothing but stress. And for all that we've got out of it, couple of bloody days."

The others glanced briefly at him but made no response.

"Maybe the killer's got the papers?" Kennedy suggested.

A sudden silence reigned. "Christ, we better hope not, "Robinson said. "Names on that list, he'd make a fortune blackmailing them ... us."

"Let's cross that bridge if we come to it," Adams said.

"That's easy to say," Professor Gallagher snapped. "We're sitting ducks right now because someone decided to murder the judge." She threw a speculative glance in several directions as she eyed the different members of the group. There was nothing in her attitude to confirm whether her glances were genuine enquiry or calculated to deflect suspicion from herself. She frowned and added, "Wonder if the motive was connected with The Club?"

Stevens glanced at her. "Got to be loads of possibilities. You know how vicious his sentencing was in court. He was a sadist. We all knew that. Plenty of people hated him."

"Jaclyn could be right," Bryant said. "That blackmailing opportunity is as good a motive as you could ask for. Somebody might've killed him for the list."

"Or there are The Club's more ... refined activities," Adams said laconically. "He's obviously high in the pecking order. Maybe he acquired too much information on some wealthy client. Maybe something in the cellars went too far and the judge had to sort it out. That's too much knowledge right there." He let the possibilities hang in the air.

"What about his taste in young boys," Bryant offered. "Maybe some father discovered what the judge was doing to his son?"

"Like I said," Stevens responded, "loads of possibilities."

"Back to the immediate issue," Adams said. "That list remains a serious complication. I don't think we can assume the killer has it." His listeners watched as he calmly took a sip from his brandy glass. "I know Trevor. He was obnoxious, but he was streetwise to the nth degree. If there is a secret safe, it won't be anywhere obvious. Could be buried in a floor, or deep in a wall. Unless the killer knew him intimately, he wouldn't have found the safe. So, if we are to get our hands on that list, we'll need access to the secret hiding compartment, wherever that is, and then the combination of the safe itself."

"Well, the police haven't found it," Gallagher said. "That's something, at least."

"But for how long?" Judge Adams asked. The others were giving him their undivided attention. He looked back quizzically at them as if to say, who made me your leader? He smiled thinly. "I did suggest extreme delicacy in our dealings with Neeson's assistant. It occurs to me now that if this problem becomes pressing, we might have to consider extreme measures. We do have a lot to lose."

Several pairs of eyes guiltily skittered away from the judge, focussing on aspects of the room's decor, but there was no indication of disapproval. Robinson, clearly unburdened with squeamishness, grunted, "Now there's a suggestion that makes some sense. If we don't do anything, the police are going to find the damn safe at some point. I say we grab the wee shite, take him somewhere quiet, and kick the living daylights out of him until he tells us where the safe is." He sat back, folding his arms with some smugness, before leaning forward again and adding truculently, "And while we're at it, we can beat the combination out of him as well."

There were some expressions of distaste at the large man's crassness, but again, no obvious disapproval of what he was suggesting.

"When you say 'we'…" Judge Adams said, waving a thin hand at the people around him. "…to which of us exactly are you referring?"

Robinson, whose reputation for dubious tactics in his business dealings was well known to the people in the room, gave the judge an arrogant smirk and said, "Shoulda known. You intellectual types can look down your noses, but you don't have it when it comes down to brass tacks." He leered again at the others. "I can get a couple of guys, reliable. We can throw on balaclavas and pretend to be loyalist gangsters. That'll scare the crap out of him. We mightn't even have to touch him." He paused and grinned sourly. "Well, maybe he'll need a whack or two to soften him up a bit." He sat back again, obviously satisfied that he was the real go-getter in the room.

There was silence for some minutes while the group digested this. Their manners might have been fastidious, but the veneer was thin. Self-preservation quickly quelled any sensibilities.

"These two fellows," Bryant said, "I presume they wouldn't know why they are looking for the judge's safe?"

Robinson gave the surgeon a scathing look and grunted. "Money. Maybe jewellery and other valuables. It wouldn't occur to these guys that people would keep anything else in a safe. I'll see that the job'll be worth their while."

Stevens cleared his throat. "Perhaps it would be best if the judge and I remained ignorant of the details." He stalled in the face of the contemptuous glare Robinson threw at him.

"Jesus! You barristers. Don't worry. You won't need to get your lilywhite hands dirty. I didn't make my money without knowing how to get things done, and done quietly." He didn't see the frosty look his partner-in-business gave him. He rose from his chair and sneered, "I'll leave you all to your blether. I'm going now to sort this mess out."

After he stalked out of the room, the remaining members were silenced, staring at the floor, or at their shoes, or at anything that wasn't one of the other people in the room.

Gallagher finally broke the silence. "What about the others who were initiated with us? Do we tell them what we're doing?" she asked, preparing to light another cigarette.

"I really would prefer that you didn't do that," the judge told her, and waited while she fiddled the cigarette back into its packet. He ignored her angry scowl and said, "About the others. I don't think it would be advisable to bring them in on this. The more people who know about it, the greater becomes the possibility of information leaking out." He thought for a moment. "If any of the others bring it up and want to discuss it, just say it's being taken care of. No more than that."

TWELVE

Tuesday, 14th August. Late evening

E dgar Doran was seated at his desk, his back to the living room door. The clicking of his keyboard was muted but it was enough to prevent him hearing the faint click of the handle as the door behind him eased slowly open. A figure in a dark anorak and a black balaclava mask peered through the slit and saw the unsuspecting back of the judicial assistant at the far side of the room. A quick nod backwards was a signal for two other figures, similarly dressed, to burst into the room alongside him, seize the suddenly terrified man, tie his hands behind him, and cover his protesting mouth with duct tape. Doran's eyes flashed wildly from one assailant to another, filled with panic, while his mouth uttered incomprehensible questions from behind the duct tape.

One of the figures dragged him towards the room door. "You're coming with us. Give us a hard time and we'll cut you to pieces."

Doran tried to protest. "Mmph! Mmph! Mmph!"

The man flung the back of his hand against Doran's defenceless face, almost knocking him off his feet. "I told you to shut up," he snarled, his voice low and gruff.

Doran was wearing only trousers, a pullover and carpet slippers, but the intruders allowed him no time to grab a coat. His muffled protests continued as the trio hustled him down the quiet stairs from his apartment to the entrance door, and out to the street. The biggest of the three glanced right and left to ensure they were unobserved and, seizing the hapless victim by an arm, threw him aggressively into the back seat of a waiting car.

One of the other men climbed into the back seat with Doran and tied a black cloth across his eyes and around his head while the car drove away quietly and without fuss. A screeching getaway would have attracted the kind of curiosity they didn't need.

The car drove through the city for about twenty minutes, taking right turns, left turns, turning back on itself, driving a couple of miles without any turns. If the prisoner was trying to keep a mental track of the various turns in the hope of later following the route, he was doomed to disappointment. No one in a blindfold could have retraced that maze of turns. Not that Doran looked like he was alert and functioning. He had squeezed himself into the corner of the rear seat, arms clasped tightly across his chest, his knees drawn up in a defensive huddle, and his breath issuing in small, fearful gasps.

No one spoke during the twenty-minute journey until the car stopped on a side street outside a dilapidated roll-up garage door. The man in the back seat got out, went around to the other side of the car, opened the rear door and pulled Doran roughly out on to the road. Grabbing him by an arm, he dragged the stumbling man after him, growling, "Keep moving." The biggest man had already slipped a key into the garage door and was rolling it up as Doran was flung past him into the darkness. The helpless man staggered blindly for a moment, lost his balance, and fell to the oily concrete floor, landing heavily on his right shoulder and side. He grunted in pain behind the duct tape, but one of the thugs kicked his side and snarled, "Shut up until we tell you to speak." The thug then seized him by the armpits and held him erect, standing behind him, a hand clasped around each arm.

The large man switched on a light, a single bare bulb hanging from the ceiling, and stepped forward. He pulled the black cloth from Doran's eyes and ripped the duct tape from his face. He stood back for a few seconds while his captive's terrified eyes darted wildly around the room and from one balaclava covered head to the other.

"Wha ... what do you want with me?" Doran croaked. "I don't have any political affiliations. You've made some kind of mistake."

The large man swung an angry hand at the prisoner's face. Were it not for the thug behind holding him up, he would have fallen again.

"Shut it," the man snarled. "Now, tell me where it is."

Doran could scarcely speak. Blood was trickling from the side of his mouth and he was quivering with fear. "Wh ... where what is?" he stammered.

"Dammit, I knew you'd start with these shitty denials." His fist shot forward and buried itself in Doran's solar plexus.

Doran gasped with pain and shock, trying to suck in air. He struggled to bend over to ease the pain but the thug holding him wouldn't allow him to move.

"Please, I ... I don't know what you want."

Another heavy punch to the left side of his face knocked the stricken man's head sideways. "So you want to do it the hard way?"

Doran cringed. "I don't. I don't. Please, please. Tell me what you're talking about."

"Where is the safe?" The man's voice was low, menacing.

Doran's eyes closed and he moaned, "Oh, dear God. What safe? What safe?"

Another brutal fist slammed into his left side. "The judge's safe, you bastard."

For a moment Doran seemed confused and incapable of coherent thought. "The judge's safe?" he repeated, as if he didn't know what the words meant.

His head was battered to one side by yet another vicious blow. "Yes, the judge's safe, you stupid shite."

Doran was crying now, tears mingling with the blood on his face. "It's in his office," he moaned. "It's in his office."

The large man was becoming increasingly frenzied. He buried his fist again in the groaning man's abdomen and rasped, "Not that one. The other one."

Doran, wheezing and gasping for air, tried to wrest himself from the grasp of the thug behind him, but he was too slight and too dazed to succeed. Almost whimpering, he cried, "There is no other one. That's the only one I know about."

The large man struck him on the side of the head with such fury that Doran was knocked violently sideways, falling to the ground and bringing the thug who was holding him to the ground as well. Doran lay still, unconscious.

The third man, who had been silent during the interrogation, said diffidently, "Boss, I don't think this guy's tough enough to take a beating like this without spilling what he knows. I don't think—"

"You're not getting paid to think," the large man snarled. "Go get some water and wake this prick up."

The third man looked around the garage. Apart from a couple of shelves with bottles of car wax, a plastic bottle of engine oil, sponges, dusters, a toolbox and some cardboard boxes, the garage was bare.

"Uh ... where?"

The large man held his hands out, fingers clawed, looking as if he was about to strangle his companion. "Just get it," he hissed.

The third man left the garage and returned in a few seconds with a bottle of drinking water, obviously from the car.

"Throw it over him," the larger man ordered.

The third man held the bottle close to Doran's face and kept pouring the water on him until the unconscious man choked and tried to rise. He fell back, groaning anew when the large man kicked him in the side.

"Last chance," the man shouted. "Tell me where the bloody safe is or you're dead."

Doran fell back and mumbled in a resigned whisper. "If you're going to kill me, do it now. I don't know about any other safes."

The large man glared down at him and kicked him again. "Fuck you, you useless bastard." He turned to his companions. "Throw him back in the car."

THIRTEEN
Wednesday, 15th August. Morning

S heehan had just left Margaret home from Mass and was sitting at his office desk. *Working on a Holy Day, Jim?* He shook off the thought. *Murderers don't care what kind of day it is, and they have to be stopped.*

He picked up a couple of pages of handwritten notes from a file on his desk. It was his habit to jot down random thoughts and observations as each case progressed. He never shared these with the team because of their speculative nature. Often, however, as the case moved forward, patterns and ideas would emerge from his notes, spurring his brain to formulation of loose hypotheses, some fruitful, others no better than blind alleys. With little real information available to this point, he was mired more in the zone of bafflement than in the postulation of theories. Why did the blackmailer not turn up at the car park for his money? Or did he turn up and see something that sent him scarpering? Did whatever he saw send him to the judge enraged? But then, the judge's death, with his questionable personal life, was producing a myriad of other suspects. And what was the connection between the venal judge and the apparently respectable teacher? There seemed no logic to that, yet given the identical MOs for the killings, there had to be something.

Hearing the outer room filling up, he sighed and left his office. He sat at his usual place at the head of the room as the team prepared to deliver the summaries of their interrogations carried out the day before.

About a half an hour or so later, McNeill was the last member of the team to report on the interviews. "Looking at my n-n-notes, I discovered s-s-something a bit odd," he began. "When we asked McAfee what he had been d-d-doing at the judge's house that night, he said, and I wrote it d-d-down exactly, 'Just a few friends m-m-meeting for a drink and a chat'."

Miller frowned. "That sounds familiar."

"It does. My notes show that B-B-Bryant gave us exactly the same answer. And, although I d-d-didn't note it at the time, I'm sure William Martin used p-p-pretty much the same words."

"That's it," Miller clicked his fingers. "Should've noticed that. Our lot used those words, or ones very like them, as well."

Sheehan nodded, "So did Judge Adams." He looked at Stewart. "I'm sure the other two did, too."

Stewart checked her notes. "Michael Stevens and the civil servant guy, Oliver Kane." She spread her hands apologetically. "I didn't write down what they said verbatim, but I did note that they had been at the judge's for drinks and a chat."

"Pretty close," Sheehan said.

Others were nodding, and McBride said, "I noticed that, too. Slight variations, but the same idea each time, definitely."

"This has more than a whiff of collusion about it," Miller said. "Wonder why they felt it was necessary?"

"Same with that Brexit thing," McBride said. "Our lot tried to pretend it was a huge secret and that we were forcing it out of them."

"Yes," Stewart said. "Adams made a particular point of asking us not to make it public, if that was at all possible."

"Yeah, we got that all over the place, too," Connors said. "They made it sound like some serious anti-government plot."

"Yet the ones we sp-sp-spoke to didn't seem to have m-m-much of an idea about Brexit," Mc Neill said.

"That's right," Allen agreed. "McAfee was making a big deal out if it, but for all his bombast, when it came to even the basics of Brexit, he didn't seem to have a clue."

"Exactly like that playboy idiot, Norville Keely," McCullough said. "I mightn't know much about Brexit, but I sure know a helluva sight more than he does." He raised a fat finger. "On top of that, he hadn't a clue what the inside of the house they were in looked like. Tried to stave us off with some bogey answers but you could see he was chancin' his arm."

"Oh, aye! Him. You didn't say where he gets his money, Sergeant," Connors said. "Has he businesses in the EU or anything like that?"

"No way," McBride almost scoffed. "He had three wealthy aunts and he was their only relative. All dead now. He got left a fortune ... uh, three fortunes." He shook his head. "But from the way he's going through them, I can't see them lasting much longer."

"So, they're all each other's alibis?" Allen said. "Which probably means we don't really have an alibi for any of them."

"True," Sheehan said. "We didn't get much in the way of real information but we definitely have some oddities to consider." He held up a finger. "First, we have everyone initially trying to pretend that they were friends of the judge's, meeting for drinks and conversation. But if they weren't friends, what were they doing there?" Another finger went up. "Second, they made it look that we were forcing the real reason out of them with their 'Please don't tell anybody, but we were discussing Brexit' thing. But this story is too well rehearsed. What were they really talking about?" He brought up a third finger. "And third, it's clear they had a meeting about what to say to the cops, and all agreed on the same story, even down to the reluctant Brexit admission. What was going on that they felt such a subterfuge was necessary?"

"Something seriously iffy about it, Chief," Allen said.

Sheehan gave him a wry grin. "Aye, right." He looked at his hand and, deciding against holding up any more fingers, put it back on the desk. "So, we have a couple of possibilities here. They're up to something nefarious and the murder has come as a shock, throwing them off their stride, or the nefarious activity is somehow linked to the murder."

"Or," Miller offered, "the murder is down to the judge's cruelty in court."

Sheehan looked at him. "So you're saying that whatever is going with the group is irrelevant to our investigation?"

Miller shook his head. "No, I'm not saying that, sir. Just ensuring that we don't neglect other possibilities. For example, there was all that money in the judge's safe. Where the hell did that come from?"

Sheehan nodded. "Uh huh. Doran said that the judge wouldn't tell him about it even though he knew that Doran knew it was there."

"Huh! Do you believe that?" Connors said.

"Hard to say. He sounded convincing, but obviously we need to keep an open mind."

"Maybe the judge wasn't above a wee bit of blackmail himself," McCullough suggested. "Wouldn't be long filling your safe with money if you knew a few secrets." He let his chair fall forward on to four legs as he warmed to his theme. "And it wouldn't take up a lot of his time. Any other sideline that raked in that kinda dough would take a fair chunk out of his week if it was legit. Should be easy to find out what the sideline was, if there was one."

"Good point, Sarge," Miller said. "Like I say, Chief, other possibilities."

"On that," Connors interjected, looking at Stewart, "did that assistant guy give you the list of hotheads who threatened the judge in court?"

"As a matter of fact, Declan," Stewart replied, "I was on the phone to him just before the debrief. He's been working on it, but he now thinks the list he has is too long and contains names that would be a waste of our time. He's going to go back over it this evening and trim it down. We should have it by tomorrow."

"More work," McCullough grumbled.

The room ignored him.

"And where does that teacher, Kennedy, fit into this whole scenario?" Allen asked. "What connection does he have to the judge, or to that group?"

"Yes, indeed," Sheehan agreed. "I was coming to him." He pulled some file pages towards him. "Got a report here from the officers that checked him out. His name is Seamus Redmond, retired principal of the local high school, lives alone, classy area, Strathye Park on the Malone Road, never been married, a man of precise routine that tends to keep himself very much to himself. The Labrador was Fred, six years old."

"Vile, horrible thing to do to that poor dog," Connors growled.

"What he did to Redmond was pretty vile, too," Sheehan said, eyebrows raised.

"We're only too aware of that, Chief," Miller said. "But Serious Crimes sees a lot of that sort of thing. What happened to that poor, innocent animal is new to us, vicious, nasty, unforgiveable." He paused, staring stone-faced at the top of his desk, before adding, "And distressing."

"It was," Sheehan agreed, looking back at his notes. "Redmond had a brother in England, but he died last year. Some nephews and nieces in England, but apparently they've never visited him here."

"Serious loner, then," Connors said.

"Yes, but according to the neighbours he was a gentleman, very polite and mannerly any time they bumped into him at the supermarket or in town." Sheehan put the pages back on the desk and turned to Larkin. "Forensics discover anything?"

Larkin shook his head. "Nothing yet. Nice tidy wee house, all the papers were the usual stuff—house and car insurance, bank statements, some bills, deeds to the house, a small portfolio of ISAs, some diplomas—nothing to excite any attention."

"Did you see a will?" Miller asked.

"No. Must be with his solicitor."

"Did he have a computer?" Sheehan queried.

"Yes, sir, a laptop, but it was clean, too. Writes a bit of poetry. I think he was getting a collection together for a book. Reads a lot, has a huge store of ebooks on his kindle reader. Does some research into gardening, animal training, astronomy, quite a bit of that stuff on there, but nothing weird. No porn, no strange pursuits. Clean as a whistle."

"There has to be something," Allen said. "He couldn't have ended up with a truncheon stuck up ... him, just like the judge, unless there was some sort of connection."

Larkin shrugged. "Well, we still have to go through the hard drive yet, but I wouldn't hold out much hope."

"We'll need to find something," McCullough said, "or we're nowhere."

"Don't focus too much on the judge connection," Sheehan said. "We still have to carry out a normal investigation, check out his work colleagues, any friends out of town, clubs or societies he's a member of. Will you and McBride look into that and see what you can find, Sergeant?"

McCullough gave him an affirmative nod, but he wasn't finished. "He wasn't married. Maybe he was homosexual."

"So?" Connors asked.

"Well, he might have been up to something kinky with the judge's group," McCullough said. "There's your connection right there. Maybe he just happened to miss the party that night for some reason or other."

"Sergeant!" Stewart exclaimed, exasperated. "If the police heard you talking like that, you could be fined or arrested." Her eye caught Allen's grin and she had to fight to conceal her own.

McCullough shrugged. "Just sayin'."

"Didn't you get the memo on unconscious bias?" Sheehan said dryly.

McCullough looked puzzled. "Musta missed that one, Chief."

"Well, first of all," Stewart explained, "we have no evidence to suggest that he was homosexual, so you're just jumping to conclusions. He might just have been a confirmed bachelor. And secondly, even if he was gay, that doesn't necessarily point to involvement in anything kinky, or even involvement with the judge's group."

"Doesn't mean he wasn't," McCullough persisted. "There's obviously some connection between the two murders, so there has to be some connection either with the group or the judge. Me and Malachy'll try to get more info on the guy."

"I'm pretty sure the officers that checked him out were thorough," Sheehan said, "but maybe when you are looking into his background, you could take your young colleague for a drink in a neighbourhood pub or something and see if there's any gossip to be found. Maybe a name will crop up."

McBride nodded, and McCullough said, "Okay, Chief," adding as an afterthought, "Are we drinking on expenses?"

Sheehan studied him. *Did McCullough just say something humorous, or is he actually serious?* Straight-faced, he replied, "If the drink is personally consumed, Sergeant, it becomes a personal expense."

"The group went to a fair bit of trouble, boss," Miller said, too involved in his thoughts to listen to this by-play. "They have to be hiding something a lot more serious than a bit of anti-Brexit plotting."

"Aye," Sheehan agreed. "But what?"

"Might give us a motive for the murders if we could discover what," McBride said. "If we could only find the judge's papers, we might get a lead."

"It wasn't for want of trying," Larkin said, slightly peeved.

Sheehan nodded. "I get that, Bill, but it doesn't mean that there aren't any. I'll bet my life there's a secret safe somewhere. We need to find it."

"Yeah, we talked about that," Miller said. "And where does this blackmailer fit in? Is he one of the group at the party, do you think?"

"The answer'll be in the papers," Sheehan said." He turned to Larkin. "Bill, no reflection on you and your team, but you're going to have to go hunting again."

Larkin nodded agreement. "I was thinking that, Chief. I know we searched more thoroughly than normal because you did hint at the importance of any private papers, but this time we'll take the house and office apart. Count on it."

"Thanks, Bill." Even as he spoke his mobile phone rang. He pulled it from his pocket and said, "Yes?"

"Chief Inspector Sheehan?"

"Speaking."

"Officer Johnston here, sir. Grosvenor Road Station."

The man sounded serious, so Sheehan said, "Hold on one second, please." He rose from his desk, pointed at the phone to indicate he had to take the call, and went into his office. Back at his own desk, he said, "Yes, Officer. What can I do for you?"

"Not sure, sir. We were dealing with an assault last night and the victim said we should report it to you. He was pretty out of it, sir, in the hospital, sedatives, painkillers, you know, but I'm sure it was you he spoke about."

"Who is he?"

"Victim's name is Edgar Doran, sir. Worked as a judicial assistant for Judge Neeson."

Sheehan paused, puzzled. "And he told you to contact me?"

"Yes, sir."

"Okay. Tell me what happened."

"I don't have the full story yet, sir. Someone found him about one o'clock in the morning on the road near his apartment, bleeding and badly beaten. He rang 999 and the victim was collected by ambulance and brought to the Royal Infirmary. We were called, but I was given only a few minutes to speak to him, sir. Apparently three masked men broke into his apartment, dragged him out to their car, drove off with him somewhere, and beat him to a pulp. According to the doctor he has severe bruising all over, black eyes, a couple of broken ribs, injuries to the abdomen, but nothing life threatening."

"Is he still at the Royal?"

"I don't think so, sir. The doctor said that he would likely be discharging him this morning to recuperate at home. Serious need for the hospital bed, sir."

"Where's home?"

The policeman gave the DCI Doran's address, an apartment on the Lisburn Road.

"Okay, Officer Johnston, thank you for contacting me. I'll take it from here."

Sheehan remained staring at the desk in front of him for some minutes. *Why me?* He sat back in his chair, aimlessly stroking his chin. *Must have some connection to the judge's case.* With that thought, he rose briskly from his chair, stopping just as suddenly with a grunt of annoyance as his sciatic hip protested sharply. "Damned thing," he muttered, reaching behind him to rub the offending spot with the knuckles of his right hand.

Finally making it to his office door, he called over to Stewart who was working at her desk. "Get a car, Stewart. We're going to the Lisburn Road. Pick me up at the gate." In response to the puzzled glances from the rest of the team, he added, "Edgar Doran has been attacked. He's in hospital. Stewart and I are going there to see what's what."

FOURTEEN
Wednesday, 15th August. Mid-morning

E dgar Doran's face was a mass of purple bruises when he opened his door for Sheehan and Stewart. One arm was in a sling, and he was limping as he stood aside to usher the detectives into his apartment. The two-bedroom apartment was on the second floor of a large terraced house. The sitting room was reasonably spacious but quietly furnished— cream painted walls, plain beige carpet, a small maroon leather sofa and matching armchairs facing a forty-inch flat-screen television that stood in a corner just left of a small marble fireplace. A couple of doors leading out of the room were closed but would obviously open to the kitchen, bedroom and bathroom. One wall was shelved from top to bottom, each shelf loaded with books. They were large and heavy legal tomes for the most part, although one shelf was lined with leather-bound fiction classics. Obviously the room of a serious student.

At the wall opposite the entrance door was a functional kneehole desk with three drawers down each side. On the middle of the desk's surface rested a laptop, with a printer on the right. On the left was a three-tier stack of trays holding some papers and files. And on both sides of the laptop were small ornamental jugs filled with biros and pencils and a paper opener. Efficient, space saving, a desk that had clearly seen a lot of use.

"Pleash sit down, Detectivesh," Doran said, having trouble pronouncing the words. His swollen jaw was clearly still painful.

Sheehan sat in one of the armchairs while Stewart sat on the sofa. Doran lowered himself painfully into the other chair.

Sheehan waved a sympathetic hand. "Sorry to see you like this, Mr Doran. You'll forgive me if I say you don't look great."

Doran's swollen lips allowed him only a semblance of a grin. "I look a lot better than I feel." The words were slurred but reasonably clear.

"I can imagine."

"Doctor says it'll pash quickly. Jush bruises. Be right ash rain tomorrow."

Sheehan cocked an eyebrow. "Aye, right!" Then he said, "Officer Johnston says you told him to contact me?"

Doran nodded vigorously. "Yesh. My attackers almost beat me to death, wanting to know where the judge's other safe is."

"Other safe?" Sheehan parried. He refrained from mentioning that the team already had suspicions that one existed.

"Yesh. The biggest guy kept hitting me and kicking me, shouting at me over and over, 'Where is it? Where is it?'"

Stewart winced as she wrote in her notebook.

Sheehan said, "Oh dear, that must've been painful. Did you tell them where it was?"

Doran turned a strained face to him. "How could I? I didn't even know of its existence."

"Is there one?"

Doran shook his head. "I don't know. Those thugs seemed to think there is. Thash why I contacted you. Maybe theresh another safe somewhere." He was still struggling with his pronunciation and, aware of it now, he made a determined effort to speak more clearly. "It occurred to me that the judge might've been holding something on someone and was murdered for it, and that the killer is now trying to recover any damaging information the judge might have left in this other safe."

Sheehan nodded. "Feasible. Thanks for letting us know. Did your attackers say anything that might've given you a hint as to who they were?"

"No. Apart from the constant questioning about the safe's whereabouts, they said nothing."

"Can you tell us anything about them? Heights? Accents? Anything?"

Doran pondered this. "Well, they all wore balaclavas. I thought sure they were loyalists who were going to shoot me, although I had no idea why. It was terrifying. So I wasn't paying a great deal of attention to details." He thought back to the incident. "I was in a bare kind of garage. Empty. Just a few shelves with car polish and stuff. One guy, he was average size, maybe five-nine, held me by the arms while the leader hammered me. He was a good deal bigger than the other two and was obviously the boss." He paused again. Then he went on, "Uh, accent? He wasn't ordinary working class, of that I'm sure, but he was definitely from Northern Ireland. The other two spoke very little but their accents were very raw Belfast." Doran gave them another lopsided grin. "Hardly narrows it down."

Sheehan chuckled. "I guess. We'll initiate some enquiries, see if any neighbours saw the car, check out if it shows on any nearby CCTV cameras." He shrugged. "But I wouldn't hold out a lot of hope. Criminals are very savvy these days. They seem to have a better knowledge of where CCTV cameras are than the police."

Doran nodded. "I understand. I suppose letting you know about the safe was my primary purpose for contacting you. If you find the safe, its contents might give you a lead on the thugs who assaulted me."

"You think they were specifically focussed on the safe?"

"Seriously so. The big guy was getting more and more frantic when I couldn't tell him where it was. At the end, when it began to sink in that I didn't know anything, I think he was just battering me because he was frustrated."

"I don't suppose you have any sense of where they might've taken you?"

"No. I was very scared when they threw me into their car, although I did try to count turns. But they were driving too fast. And I have a feeling they drove back on themselves a couple of times to stop me trying to memorise the route. I got lost and confused almost right away."

Sheehan stood up. "Well, sorry again you had to go through that. But you were right to contact me. This gives us a whole new line of enquiry." He extended his hand. "Thanks again for the information. It's been very useful. If you think of anything else…."

"I'll be sure to call you right away," Doran interjected, taking the chief's hand. He extended his hand to Stewart as well. "Thank you for coming to see me. I hope you catch the culprits."

"Thank you again, Mr Doran," Stewart said. "And sorry you had to experience this suffering," she added, shaking the man's hand before following her superior out into the corridor. Struck by a thought, she turned back, "Oh, Mr Doran, were you able to get any further with that list of suspects?"

Doran slapped his forehead with his free hand. "Of course. Stupid of me. I have it here." He went to the desk and lifted an A4 page. "I'll put it in an envelope."

"No. No need," Stewart said. "It's fine as it is."

Doran handed her the sheet. "I was intending to send it to you today but…" He lifted his injured arm, his swollen lips attempting to smile. "…I got distracted."

Stewart smiled and said, "Thanks again, Mr Doran," adding as she left, "and get well soon."

FIFTEEN
Thursday, 16th August. Late morning

Another frustrating day or so had been spent by the team, not only interviewing the principal suspects in the case, but speaking to peripherals—neighbours, acquaintances, possible witnesses—the usual slow, relentless search for even the tiniest morsel of information or evidence that might move the investigation forward. When they got a text from Stewart to go to the Serious Crimes Room for another debrief, they were happy to drop what they were doing and come in.

The debrief had already started when Bill Larkin, carrying a manila file, slipped into the Serious Crimes Room and tiptoed over to his desk. In answer to Sheehan's quizzical glance, he winked and held up a triumphant thumb.

Wonder what that's about? Sheehan thought, puzzled. He gave Larkin another glance, but the forensics officer already had his head down, sorting papers from the file he'd been carrying. Sheehan shrugged mentally. *We'll know soon enough, I suppose.* Aloud he said, "Carry on, Sergeant."

McCullough, notebook in one hand and fiddling with a ball-point pen in the other, said, "We couldn't have been more thorough, Chief." He glanced at McBride. "Right, Malachy?"

McBride nodded confirmation.

"He's seriously clean, but…" He paused to ensure that he had the room's intention. "…I wasn't as far out as some of you seemed to think at the last debrief."

"Okay, Sarge," Miller said, grinning. "We're all ears."

"Well, the scene-of-crime officers who checked Redmond out did a first-class job. The teacher was highly respected and there seemed to be no breath of scandal. But, like the chief suggested, I took my young trainee here—" He grinned at McBride's mock scowl. "—for a wee drink at The Bridge Bar near where Redmond lived. The place was almost deserted, but there were two old guys there, so we joined them and bought them a couple of drinks. That got them going. We chatted about football, snooker, this bloody stalemate up at Stormont, until one of them asked if we'd heard about the murder."

"We pretended we hadn't," McBride said, "and asked the normal questions anyone would ask. They didn't know a lot about the actual killing, but one of them said he'd known Redmond for over thirty years."

"That was our cue to order another round of drinks," McCullough interjected, adding with a grin, "although my young colleague took rather longer than he should have to figure that out. Anyway, while he was getting the drinks, I asked the old guy if he thought there was anything iffy in Redmond's past that might have got him killed."

"The old guy thought about it," McBride chipped in, "and I was back with the drinks before he'd even gotten around to saying he didn't think so. But there was something about the way he said it made me think he knew more than he was saying."

"You shoulda seen the way my man here worked him," McCullough said, beaming at his young partner. "If he quits the police, he has a great career as an actor waiting."

McBride looked embarrassed. "Will you quit, Sarge," he said.

"I'm telling you," McCullough said, "he easily got him to tell us that there had been a small incident in Redmond's past, although the aul' fella tried to stall, saying that it was a long time ago and he didn't see what it might have to do with anything."

"Thanks to my senior colleague finally discovering where his pocket was," McBride said, "and putting another couple of pints in front of them, it was easy enough to push the old guy. Turns out that Redmond had been caught thirty years ago soliciting for homosexual favours in a public toilet in Portadown. He should have been arrested, but the patrol cop was from Belfast and knew the family well. It was hushed up. Rumours flew around for a while, but mostly in Portadown. Redmond was teaching in Belfast at the time, and somehow the rumours didn't seem to get that far. He was lucky to keep his job."

"So, I was right," McCullough said. "He was gay."

"That's it?" Sheehan asked.

McBride nodded. "The old guy said the episode must have scared the living daylights out of Redmond. There was no further scandal attached to him since that."

"So what are your thoughts, then?"

McBride shrugged. "The sergeant and I have not found common ground about this yet."

"All that talk about the disagreements at Stormont," Miller said, laughing. "It's infected you."

"To be honest, I think the guy is pretty much as clean as he appears—" McBride started.

"And I think if the tendencies were there thirty years ago, they didn't go away," McCullough interrupted. "I think Redmond just learned to be careful."

"So?" Sheehan said.

"So, we didn't know anything about the judge either. They were all careful. And yet, now we know something's going on. And that truncheon business. Both of them? That's no coincidence. There has to be some connection between Redmond and Judge Neeson."

Sheehan, watching their expressions and listening to their banter, was baffled anew. He'd never seen McCullough so engaged. "Conjecture, though, isn't it?" he said. "You've no real evidence?"

McCullough shook his head. "No, but we're not finished, Chief. We can still come at it through questioning those other people who were at the judge's house."

"Yes, we'll work out a rota in a couple of minutes," Sheehan agreed. He looked at the others. "Anybody got any further leads on what might have been happening at the judge's house?"

There were some shamefaced shakings of heads. Only Allen spoke, "We've been back to a couple of them, Chief. Same stonewalling. Can't break their stories." He looked expectantly at Sheehan. "What about you? Got any ideas which one we should be looking at?"

Sheehan grinned. "I never get ideas until all the evidence is in. You start focussing on ideas before you have the evidence and soon you're twisting whatever evidence comes in to fit the ideas. Road to nowhere."

"But what about your instincts?"

Sheehan grinned. "Instincts? I don't have instincts. I keep anything like that in check. Always."

There were a few scoffing grunts, but Sheehan just shrugged and smiled.

"Well, I fancy Judge Adams," Stewart said, immediately grimacing in anticipation of the hoots and jibes she knew would follow her injudicious choice of wording.

"Way too old for you, Sergeant," Miller shouted.

"Go for it, Denise. He's got loads of money," Connors advised.

"Okay! Okay!" Stewart said, grinning. "He's a good candidate, icy, no empathy. He's dry, controlled, and his eyes look merciless to me. He's clearly the intellect in the group and if one of them is the killer, he's the one I would pick."

"I can see why he might be considered a suspect in the killing of Judge Neeson," Sheehan said, "and he's certainly canny enough to have left a clean crime scene, but why would he kill Redmond? Where's the connection there?"

"Well, as Sergeant McCullough says, there has to be one," Stewart replied. "We just don't know yet what it is."

"That big builder guy, Robinson, might be a runner," Miller said. "He was aggressive and ignorant when we spoke to him. And he has a brutal track record. Wouldn't put it past him." He studied a list he had in his hand. "Not sure about the others."

"Big, aggressive, brutal…." Sheehan seemed to look inward, mentally leaving the group. He was muttering the words so quietly that he could scarcely be heard. It was clear from the teams' expressions that all were wondering what the chief was thinking.

"What is it, Chief?" Connor's asked.

"Just filing away a random thought. Nothing important."

Connors shook his head. Trying to access the boss's thoughts was like trying to grab smoke.

"What about any of the others?" Stewart asked

"I don't rate the socialite," Allen said. "Too airy fairy. But the professor ... hard to say. Strong personality, all eyes and soulful looks. Don't know what's lurking behind that façade."

"You're sure it's a façade?" Sheehan asked.

Allen nodded. "That would be my guess."

McCullough voiced agreement. "She's hard all right, Chief. Say the wrong thing and you'll soon know all about it. Intimidating woman."

"Yeah, like that property millionaire lady, Jaclyn Kennedy," Miller added, "she's too studied in what she does. She's a planner and schemer, that one. Deep."

"I'm not sure if it c-c-could be any of the women," McNeill offered. "The k-k-killings are a bit too brutal."

"And that idiot playboy would have been too stupid to carry out the deed without leaving forensic evidence all over the place," McBride said. "Might be worth having another chat with him, though. I think if anyone is likely to crack about what's going on, it could be him."

"Good point," Sheehan said. "The two of you visit him again. See what you shake out of him."

"McAfee's a runner," Allen said. "He has no empathy, and if somebody threatened his thriving existence, I think he has a murder or two in him."

"Too r-r-right," McNeill said. "A far better suspect than that B-B-Bryant. He might be a b-b-bombastic so-and-so, but he doesn't h-h-have the iciness McAfee has."

"He's a surgeon, though," McBride pointed out. "He'd have been around death a lot. I don't think killing would trouble him. I'd keep him on the list."

"I dunno," McNeill argued. "I think he would have more f-f-finesse than our killer. With his skills, I think b-b-bashing somebody over the h-h-head would never be an MO of choice for him."

"People have hidden depths," Stewart said. "Kane, the civil servant, is as bland as they come, practically invisible. When we talked to him, he was dull and monotonous. Bit puny, too. But there was something about his eyes, the way they seemed to miss nothing. Kinda sinister. He's dark, for sure. He's a genuine suspect in my eyes."

"You could be right," Connors agreed. "Just because he's puny doesn't mean he couldn't have delivered a blow. Doctor Campbell says a woman could've done it."

"You're right about the eyes," Sheehan added. "I noticed that, too. Very intense. And I tell you what, he takes offence easily. I saw that a couple of times." He uttered a half chuckle. "I think I might be on his list now. He can really experience sudden anger. He tries not to show it. His eyes go down, maybe to hide it, and he holds the anger in. But it's there, bottled in. People who hold stuff in like that can be dangerous."

"Okay," Miller said, "so we're looking at Judge Adams, Malcolm McAfee, Patrick Robinson and Oliver Kane." He checked his list again. "Are we ruling out the women or not? Given what Doc Campbell says, I'm not so sure about that. But we can always come back to them. I think we can definitely forget about Norville Keeley and Robert Bryant as well. What about the BBC guy, William Martin?"

Allen was shaking his head. "Can't see it. Clever. Made a lot of money. Fair age, getting on a bit. He was crappin' himself during questioning. Not cool under pressure. Our perp clearly is." Allen shook his head. "Not Martin, for sure. Wouldn't have the nerve."

"What about the barrister, Stevens?" Miller asked. "What did you think of him, Chief?"

"Same stonewalling as the others. He had no trouble keeping the pretence together ... if it is a pretence." He paused for a second, weighing possibilities. "You and Declan go back and have another chat with him. Push a bit harder this time and see if anything happens."

"Right, Chief," Miller agreed.

"Okay!" Sheehan said. "I think that's enough guesswork. It's all highly speculative and normally I'd have dismissed it as a waste of time except for one useful offshoot."

All eyes were upon him again.

"Your discussion has identified some members of the suspect pool who might cave under intensive questioning. I think that's something to work on, so let's get back out there and start pushing. But first, dig more deeply into the backgrounds of Judge Adams, McAfee, Robinson and Kane."

"Let's just keep Bryant and Stevens on that list, too," Miller interjected. "I'm not sure that we can sideline them just yet."

"Okay," Sheehan agreed. "So, two lines of enquiry. We go back and push the weaker members and hope somebody cracks, and we try to find dirt on the serious suspects. If necessary, we can dig into the others later. We can only do so much."

That earned him a few heartfelt grunts.

"Miller and Connors, will you also see what you can find out about Judge Adams' private life, his past relationship with Neeson, any—?" He caught the look Miller gave him and held up a conciliatory hand. "Okay! Okay! You don't need me to tell you how to do your jobs. Anyway, when you've got something, go and see him. He'll get ratty as hell but don't back off."

The two detectives nodded.

Sheehan checked his notes. "Allen and McNeill can take over on Robinson." He looked up. "Fresh eyes. You never know." He checked his list again. "And Bryant can be seen instead by McCullough and McBride." He put the page back on the desk and leaned back on his chair. "This is all still in the very messy stage. Loads of speculation and nowhere nearly enough information. But ask around, talk to friends and acquaintances ... the usual. We might find something that helps with the push." He paused briefly before holding up an admonishing finger. "But no trampling all over their human rights. Keep it inside legal."

He ignored the eyes raised to the ceiling and went back to his list. "So this is what we now have. Miller and Connors are going to investigate Judge Adams and the barrister, Michael Stevens. McCullough and McBride are talking again to the playboy chap, Keeley, and digging into the surgeon, Bryant. Allen and McNeill have switched to the construction bigwig, Robinson, and will also go back and have another word with Martin, the BBC mogul." He glanced at Allen. "If he was nervy the first time, he might crack when he sees you again."

"We'll all do whatever digging we can, Chief," McBride said, "but we really need something to hit them with, something to knock them out of their complacency. If we could only find that other safe."

Sheehan made to answer but turned away when Bill Larkin loudly cleared his throat. "Bill? You've been acting funny since you came in, and not a word from you. What's going on?"

Larkin did, indeed, seem to be in a state of suppressed excitement. "Was waiting for the right moment, Chief. Good news and bad news."

"Humph! We could do with a bit of good news. That first, please."

Larkin didn't share McCullough's penchant for theatricals. He simply said, "We found the safe."

That created a stir.

"Wow! Brilliant, Larko!" Allen almost whooped.

Sheehan curbed the sudden elation he felt. There was bad news coming. "And?" he said.

Again Larkin was short and to the point. "We can't get it opened."

There were groans and deflation where seconds earlier there had been tense excitement.

"All right, Bill," Sheehan almost snapped. "Enough with the macho silent stuff. Start talking."

"You know how we went back to the judge's house three or four times, searching everywhere for that safe. I was convinced there wasn't one." Larkin started making gestures with his hands and arms to amplify his story. "The judge has this big, fancy bath in the bathroom. It's up high, maybe three or four steps up to it. It's all surrounded by these dark green Italian tiles. There's a shower unit at one end and a big three-foot shelf between the back of the bath and the wall at the other end, all covered with these tiles. They're all down the whole side of the bath as well. Uh, everything's all green tiles and the bath is just sunk down into them. Loads of toiletries are sitting on the big ledge at the back. And the tiles are expertly fitted. Very posh looking. But from the point of view of a safe, we never gave the bathroom a second thought."

He went to the whiteboard and started sketching on it with a black felt marker. "But here's the strange bit. When I went in earlier this morning, I noticed a slight discrepancy in one line of grouting. Look, here's a sketch of the bath." He pointed to the back end of the sketch. "Just here, a section of the tiling, the whole way down the side, had come out about a tenth of an inch from the rest. I fiddled with it, you know, pressing on it and so on, and suddenly a whole piece of the tiling moved inward and slid sideways to the left, behind the rest of the tiles, leaving a three-foot opening."

"The safe was in there?" Sheehan asked, eyebrows raised.

"Yes. Weird, huh?"

Sheehan frowned. "How did you miss that before?"

"Gimme a break, Chief. It wasn't there before."

"So, what are you saying?"

"Two possibilities. One. Someone came back there to access the safe and didn't close the opening properly when they left. But I don't rate that as an option. I worked the mechanism a few times and the tiled cover slides into place as neat as anything. The only way it stays open like the way I found it, is if you stick something thin in there, like a knife or nail file maybe, to stop it closing. When the tiled cover hits the knife, it judders a wee bit and stops. It doesn't close when you take the knife out. It just sticks where it is."

"You think someone left it open on purpose?" Sheehan sounded dubious.

All eyes in the room went back and forth from Sheehan to Larkin, like spectators at a tennis match, listening intently to every word.

"That's my second possibility," Bill said, "but to my mind, it's really the only one."

"Can you explain why anyone would do that?"

"No, other than to say that whoever did it must have wanted the safe found."

"You reckon? Whatever's in that safe is probably worth a mint to a blackmailer. Any idea why he led you to it?"

"Not a clue. Maybe he had no way of getting it open, so he just gave it up."

Sheehan looked far from convinced. He stared at Larkin, his mind racing. Then he shook his head. "This has a more studied feel to it, Bill. I think whoever it was wants the police to know what's in it." He shook his head, frustrated. "Whatever. We'll figure that out later. You say you can't get into it?"

Larkin nodded. He reached for an A4 sheet on his desk and pinned it to the whiteboard. It was a black and white photograph of a safe. The team could see it was square, heavy-looking, had a solid door-handle, two keys, and four very thick, metal locking bolts down along the inside edge of the door. It was an impressive sight.

Larkin turned his back to the board and said, "I need to explain something to you. You can get very reasonable electronic or digital home safes for sixty or seventy pounds. And with a good combination code, they will do an excellent job. But if you really want to push the boat out, you can get up-market ones with digital locking that will defeat just about any burglar for four or five hundred pounds. You would rarely see anything more expensive than that."

"One minute we can't get two words out of you, the next you're bletherin'," Connors growled. "Get to the point, Sarge, will you."

Larkin turned to the board and pointed at the photograph there. "This is the safe we found in the judge's bathroom. It's a Burton Eurovault Mark IV." He paused for a second, simplicity and directness gone. This time he was looking for effect. His tone was slow, measured and emphatic when he turned to face them again. "And it costs almost three ... thousand ... pounds. That's in the stratosphere for safes." He nodded with slow deliberation, looking at his colleagues over the top of his spectacles.

"Holy shit!" Allen exclaimed.

"Yep! Top of the range. Loads of specs, but I'll just mention a couple," Larkin went on. "Solid steel door, special steel armouring devices, double three-way locking bolts, special drill protection of the lock and bolt work, multiple re-locking devices to secure the door in case of attack, high security key lock as standard ... I could go on, but I think you get the picture."

"Whew!" Miller exclaimed. "No getting in there without the combination code, right?"

Larkin nodded. "We have electronic devices that can run hundreds of combinations in a very short time, but the expert I spoke with this morning reckons we wouldn't crack the code of a safe this sophisticated even in a week."

"I saw a m-m-movie a while back," McNeill offered, "where the burglar d-d-drilled a tiny hole near the lock so he could p-p-push in this wire camera probe thing to scope out the l-l-lock. Once he could see inside it, he had the thing open in m-minutes."

Larkin grinned. "Aye, Hollywood can sure make it look easy. Drilling is nowhere as easy as it sounds. Apart from the time spent just cutting, you're up against new, advanced interior technology. So, if whoever's doing the drilling isn't familiar with the lock he's working on, things could get very ugly and even more complicated."

"Like what?" Connors asked.

"Well, apart from the actual hardness of the door, all sorts of relocking devices that you can't even see start closing the door down worse than ever." He spread his hands. "The fact is that top safe engineers will go to massive lengths not to drill a safe. It takes forever on a decent one, never mind a Burton Eurovault, and those re-lockers that I mentioned can lead to, like, a four or five day wrestling match, wearing out a few hundred carbide-tipped drills on the way. Imagine what it would be like trying to drill into this thing?" He pointed at the photograph and shook his bald head. "Out of the question."

"What about drilling in through the back, Sarge?" McBride suggested.

"Good point, son," Larkin said. "Looks like that might be the way we have to go, but it'll be messy, noisy, time consuming, and damaging to the safe, although, in this case, that's not something we'd care about. The real problem is the material the safe is made out of, and this one has a double-walled, steel body filled with ultra-high-performance concrete. Several sets of saw blades will have to be utilized trying to cut into this stuff. My man reckons a week minimum."

"A week?" Sheehan exploded. "No way. Get your man to employ a couple or three teams on it ... non-stop, day and night. I'll have a word with the new Assistant Chief Constable about covering the overtime."

"I'll talk to the guy, Chief, but it'll still take days. They'll only be able to drill into that stuff a millimetre at a time, and they'll have to pause for overheating, watering, and stuff like that. It'll be slow going."

"Dammit! That's frustrating. We need to know what's in that safe. Do they need to take the whole back off? If it's papers we're after, would a hole big enough to get a fist and an arm into it not do us?"

Larkin nodded. "Never thought of that. I'll see what he says." He paused, thinking. "But it might be files, Chief, you know, with stiff covers. No pulling them out of a fist-sized hole."

Sheehan made shooing actions with his hands. "Well, go. Go now. Get this thing started."

Larkin gathered up his file and papers and hurried out, offering Sheehan a quick nod as he left.

"Bloody hell!" Miller said, exhaling a deep breath. "You're right, Chief. This sure as hell is frustrating. Questioning the suspects isn't going to take us that long. We gonna be sittin' around on our butts until they get the safe open?"

"No, Simon, we aren't," Stewart said, holding up a sheaf of A4 pages. "Mr Doran has finally sent us a list of possible suspects from some of the judge's court cases. He sends his apologies for the delay. Says he suffered some minor distractions that caused the list to slip his mind."

There were some grins. Sheehan had earlier briefed the team on Doran's kidnapping and assault.

"We still working that angle?" Miller said.

"We work every angle," Sheehan said, "until we get some kind of handle on what's going on with this case."

Stewart left her desk and handed copies of the list to the team. There were six names on the list, each name followed by a paragraph explaining why the suspect had appeared before Judge Neeson and offering verbatim the threats they had issued to the judge when sentenced. Stewart then went to the whiteboard and pinned six photos there. "Doran also sent these," she said.

The team stared at the photographs. "Unprepossessing bunch," Miller said.

As Stewart was returning to her desk, Sheehan said, "I think we should all take a few minutes to read this stuff before we make any comments."

The detectives were already engrossed in the pages, scarcely aware that Sheehan had spoken.

MEMORANDUM

To: Serious Crimes Unit

From: Edgar Doran, [Judicial Assistant, Crown Court]

Date: 15th August 2018

Subject: Criminals Who Issued Death Threats To Judge Neeson In Court.

Preamble

As you know, magistrates in Northern Ireland can hear less serious criminal cases, i.e., summary trials, and they can also conduct preliminary hearings for indictable offences. Generally, these serious offenses, however, are committed for trial in the Crown Court, where the widest range of sentencing powers is available to a judge. You are also probably aware that Judge Neeson was invariably prone to lean towards the maximum tariff when passing sentence.

All the criminals on this list, partly because of their attitudes and criminal records, had their cases moved up to Crown Court for indictable trials. They are vicious criminals. In each trial, Judge Neeson was the presiding judge, and in each case, he passed the maximum sentence. My research has disclosed nine offenders whose final comments to the judge at the end of their trials were extremely threatening. Of the nine, three remain in prison. Four of the six below have now completed half their sentences and are currently released on supervised licence. I do not have their present addresses, but I am able to append the names of their probation officers. Access to these officers can be arranged through The Probation Board for Northern Ireland (PBNI). One offender served his full term and therefore is not on probation. I was able to ascertain the general area where he lives. The sixth possible suspect is still in prison but, for reasons that are explained, his friend's name is offered as a substitute, together with the name of the friend's probation officer.

The comments to the judge attributed to the offenders at the time of sentencing are taken from their trial transcripts.

1. Gerard 'The Toff' Delaney—Aggravated Burglary/Attempted Murder

Always immaculately dressed, and seen often at soirées in wealthy houses, Gerald 'The Toff' Delaney was a well-known and recognisable figure. He had never been officially invited to any of these gatherings, but such were his social skills that guests generally assumed others had invited him, and his presence was never questioned. His purpose for attending these functions was to survey and scrutinise the residences which he would later rob of cash, jewellery, and other items of value. He was finally caught in the act by one owner. Delaney shot him in the stomach while escaping. However, the owner survived to identify him, and Delaney was charged with aggravated burglary. During interrogation, he revealed where he had hidden the proceeds of several robberies in exchange for a lighter sentence. The Public Prosecutor Service agreed to the deal, but Judge Neeson sneered at it in court, refused to accept it, and sentenced Delaney to the maximum sixteen years. Delaney stood in the dock and, although he appeared to speak calmly, witnesses claimed that he was 'menacingly cold'. The court records indicate that his words were, "I am an intelligent and resourceful man, Judge Neeson. Be assured that one day you will pay for this."

He was imprisoned in 2009 and released on supervised licence three months ago. His probation officer is Geoffrey Wilson.

2. Baako Kahangi—Rape and Murder

Baako Kahangi, an African immigrant who had been living in this country for five years at the time of his offence, was charged with the rape and murder of a defenceless housewife in Dundonald. After raping her, he strangled her and stabbed her multiple times. Following the murder, he took time to ransack the house and left with two bags of items that he intended to sell.

At the sentencing in the Crown Court, Judge Neeson professed himself astounded at the utter lack of remorse shown by the defendant and imposed the maximum sentence of 22 years, to be served in full without the possibility of parole. Kahangi began yelling and cursing the judge when this sentence was announced, demanding deportation back to Africa. As he was being dragged away, the court record shows that he shouted, "You not get away, f***ing b***ard. No matter how long, I get you, motherf***er. You dead, you f**k. You dead."

Not having been granted parole and having served the full term of his sentence, he is not obliged to report to a probation officer. He was aged twenty-three at the time of sentencing and, since he is still relatively young at forty-five, he is, by all accounts, strong and fit, having made full use of the prison's gymnasium during his incarceration. No address is available, but he was last reported to have been sharing a flat with an African friend in the Poleglass area.

3. Thomas McStravick—Assault Occasioning Actual Bodily Harm (with intent)

Thomas 'The Hulk' McStravick (the nickname is occasioned by his heavy build and extremely strong arms) was a senior member of the Lannon gang from the Short Strand. The Lannon-Morgan feud had become extremely vicious about ten or so years ago and, although there was no hard evidence, some twelve murders inside of two years were attributed to this feud.

In 2013, one of the Morgan members was attacked by three of the Lannon gang, kicked, hammered with an iron bar, and had his head violently stamped upon several times. The victim survived the brutal assault but continues to suffer severe mental health problems. He identified McStravick as one of his attackers, and forensics were able to match the marks on the victim's face to threads on a pair of boots seized from McStravick's flat. Bloodstains on the boots also matched that of the victim's.

In court, McStravick was belligerent and aggressive, and despite repeated warnings continued constantly to shout at the prosecution, accusing them of lying, and swearing that he had been framed. He had to be removed from the court on three occasions, during which periods the trial continued without him. Judge Neeson imposed a sentence of ten years, the maximum permitted to him, but added another two for contempt of court, both sentences to run consecutively. McStravick began screaming and swearing at the judge, in what the court recorder described as a "...mostly incomprehensible diatribe of menace, obscenities, and threats." The words the recorder was able to distinguish were "...the Lannons have long memories. One week after I get out, you will die, you b***ard and no one will know who did it. But you'll know, and I'll know, you f***ing w**ker. You're going to die, Neeson."

McStravick was released on licence a month ago. His probation officer is Gerald Gribbon.

4. Eamon McKernan/Terence Quinn—Terrorism Offences (murder, possessing arms)

As a result of the Good Friday Agreement in 1998, the larger terrorist organisations have laid down their arms and are seeking political avenues to promote their causes. But, as you are aware, there are still on the Republican side a number of diehards who oppose the Agreement and have formed new independent military groups, calling themselves Dissident Republicans, The Continuity Irish Republican Army and the Real Irish Republican Army. These groups, though short of numbers, still pose a serious threat, and a number of bombings, murders and attempted murders over the past several years have been attributed to them.

One sniper killing was carried out by an eighteen-year-old member of the Real IRA, Terence Quinn. He was in possession of a rifle and shot dead a serving police officer who was leaving his house one morning in June 2013. The sniper was recognised as he sought to escape and was later arrested and charged with terrorist offences.

At his trial in 2014, Judge Neeson, citing Section 36 of the Criminal Justice Act 1988—*terrorist murder of police officer earns life imprisonment for adult offender*—imposed a tariff of 25 years. The defence argued that the defendant should have been sentenced as a youth offender (a 14-year tariff) but Judge Neeson stated that at eighteen years the offender was now deemed adult and fully deserved the maximum sentence for a violent offence of this nature.

There was uproar in the gallery and one voice was heard to shout, "You will be followed, watched, and stalked until we know your every move, Judge Neeson. Then we will strike." The shouter was seized, arrested, and identified as a Real IRA sympathiser called Eamon McKernan. He was sentenced to two years for threatening an officer of the court and for contempt of court.

Terence Quinn is still serving his sentence. McKernan was recently released on licence. His probation office is Horace Fisher.

5. Ahdel Khan—Rape, Sex Trafficking, Prostitution, Assault, manslaughter

Ahdel Khan, a vicious and violent bully, is Asian but was born and reared in Belfast. He was a member of a sex trafficking gang operating in North Belfast. He was finally caught, arrested and charged with numerous offences including violent rape of minors, assault, sex trafficking and prostitution, unlawful imprisonment of minors, and causing death by drugs.

The gang had seduced several young girls, imprisoned them, raped them, and forced them into prostitution with hundreds of men. Khan, in particular, beat them constantly, force-fed them drugs until they became addicts, and threatened to kill their families if they tried to escape.

One of the girls, whose badly beaten body was found dumped in some waste ground, had died of a massive heroin overdose. Fingerprints and DNA evidence linked Khan to the girl's death. Judge Neeson imposed a 22-year sentence on Khan who then shouted at the court, "How is this sentence f***ing justified? These f***ing slags were worthless whores, bloody rubbish, not worth a s**t. Twenty-two years for one of those good-for-nothing sluts? How does that make sense? It's the colour of my f***ing skin, isn' it, you racist b****rd? You'll pay with your f***ing life for this, you hear me? Your f***ing miserable life, you bigoted f***er. Count on it."

Kahn is now released on supervisory licence. His probation officer is Anthony Pearce.

6. Timothy Small—Domestic Abuse resulting in Death

Timothy Small's record shows a history of spousal abuse. Despite being arrested for a number of vicious attacks on his wife, the charges had to be withdrawn because of his wife's refusal to testify against him. The attack for which Small was finally arrested and charged was the worst case of spousal abuse the arresting officers had ever seen. Small's merciless tendency to attack the face and head first was already a matter of record, but on this occasion Mrs Small's eyes and face were horrifically bruised. Her nose was smashed and there was massive dislocation of her jaw. Her skull, too, was fractured. This fatal assault also resulted in several broken ribs, a ruptured spleen and other serious injuries. The attending physician was reported to have said that had she survived the attack, she would have required facial reconstruction and would have suffered irreparable scarring and nerve damage.

At the end of the trial, the defence entered a plea for clemency because of provocation, but Judge Neeson rejected the plea, saying, "When psychological, sexual or physical violence, especially when the assault results in death, are carried out by a partner or spouse, the intimate relationship raises the charge to aggravated status, and there can be no mitigating factors that would permit any plea for leniency. The defendant is sentenced to life without parole, no minimum tariff recommended."

Small, still in the dock, completely lost control, roaring profanities and obscenities at the judge. The most printable part of his recorded invective is what he screamed when officers pulled him from the dock to transport him to prison. "You're worse than the f***ing hanging judges in the Wild West. You know nothing about justice. I have good friends who will make sure that you get what's coming to you, Neeson. You hear me, you b****rd? You have only weeks to live. F***ing weeks."

That was two months ago. Small is still in prison but his best friend is Frank Hosford. He is now out on supervised licence, having served time for Battery and Grievous Bodily Harm. Hosford's probation officer is Maurice Parker.

I hope this information is of some help to the Serious Crime Team.

Edgar Doran [Judicial Assistant]

Date: 15th August, 2018

After several moments of silence, Allen exclaimed, "Geez! There are some rare specimens of humanity on this list. How could the judge have lived with those kinds of threats being hurled at him all the time?"

"Well, not all the time," Sheehan said. "Doran has selected these six for us because they are extreme examples." He turned to Stewart. "He put a fair bit of work into that. Send him a thank-you note on our behalf."

Stewart said, "Will do, Chief."

"Looks like any one of them could have killed the judge," McCullough said. "Those threats sound very real. Could that mean that members of the other group are in the clear?"

"And did whoever it was kill the teacher, too?" Sheehan asked. "You said yourself, the two cases have to be connected."

McCullough's face screwed into an expression of puzzlement as he wrestled with this, but he offered no answer.

"Good point, Chief," Miller said. "The two killings are almost a hundred percent linked. Could it be that one of these guys is somehow linked to the other group we're looking at?"

"You changing your mind about the blackmailer, then?"

Miller stared speculatively at Sheehan, rubbing his chin with thumb and forefinger. "Just looking at scenarios."

"Well, no point in speculation until we have spoken to them to see if any of them have alibis," Sheehan said, adding firmly, "And if they do have alibis, check them within an inch of their lives. That should at least cut down the list a bit."

McBride, chin resting on his hands, mused thoughtfully, "So, six good suspects from Doran's list, a blackmailer who is a total ghost about whom we know nothing, at least four, maybe more, members of the judge's group who have the will, the temperament, and maybe the motivation, whatever that is." He looked around, bemused, counting on his fingers. "What's that? About eleven serious possibles all in the frame for these killings?"

Miller grinned. "Piece of cake. The chief will have it figured out by tomorrow."

There were a couple of feeble chuckles and Sheehan raised his eyes to the ceiling, but McBride's candid summary left the team in no doubt about the complexity of the task that faced them.

"Okay, Miller and Connors, check out Khan and McStravick. McCullough and McBride, find Timothy Small's friend, Frank Hosford and see if you can learn anything from him." He studied the list. "Allen and McNeill, you take on that Real IRA guy, McKernan, and keep your wits about you and your eyes open when you are with him. Don't let him have any information about you." He glanced over at Stewart. "We'll see what we can find out from the Toff chap, Delaney, and the African guy, Kahangi."

Stewart nodded grimly but didn't speak.

Sheehan added, "You got a note of who's seeing who?" *Or should that be whom?* he wondered absently.

"Yes, Chief."

Sheehan gathered up his notes. "Right, it's been a long meeting. Take an hour or so to get some lunch and gather your wits before you go hunting. We'll meet again on Monday morning to compare notes."

SIXTEEN
Thursday, 16th August. Evening

Sheehan entered the house and hung his overcoat in the hall closet. Margaret poked her head out from the kitchen door. "Dinner's nearly ready. Want a wee aperitif?"

"No, I'm fine."

"Okay. Wash your hands, and I'll put out the soup."

Sheehan shook his head, grinning as he went to the bathroom. *Wash your hands. Never would have thought of that.*

The soup was already waiting for him when he sat down. "So, how was your day?" he asked.

Margaret raised her eyes to heaven. "Don't ask."

"Don't ask? Somebody acting up?"

Margaret sat down, unfolding a napkin. "I wish. One of the first-years arrived in with her mother ... his mother ... crap! Its mother...."

Sheehan turned to her a bemused smile. "What are you going on about?"

"This kid in first-year has decided that she ... he ... is a boy. Arrived in with her mother this morning in boys' clothes, short haircut. Of course, it had to be one of my pupils."

"Grief! What did you do?"

"I asked them to wait in the reception area, got somebody from the staffroom to look after my class, and went in to have a chat with the principal."

"Well?"

"She went up to high doh. We haven't had a transgender pupil before and she almost panicked. She's afraid of getting her approach wrong and ending up a target for the zealots in the media."

"So what did she say?"

"Well, we've had memos from the Department of Education about introducing gender neutral protocols, but she hadn't given them a great deal of attention. 'Where do we even start, Margaret?' she asked me. She was almost wringing her hands."

Sheehan made a face. "I can see why."

"I said all we could do was help the parent seek a referral to a gender identity clinic. I mean, if the kid's a boy and we're a girls' grammar school, he can't stay here."

"How did she react to that?"

Margaret laughed. "She almost kissed me. She told me that she had started to panic when I brought the problem to her office. Her mind was racing ahead, spending a fortune that would decimate the school's budget. She saw herself having to use money we couldn't afford to set up Transgender Monitoring Policies, build gender neutral toilets, set up staff training programmes, and God knows what else."

"And you said that if the kid was a boy, he was out of her hair, and out of her school?" Sheehan said, grinning. "And suddenly the problem was solved?"

"Exactly. She was so relieved. We went straight out to the parent and child. Oh! She was good. Seriously good. Very sympathetic and understanding. 'But we're a girls' school, etcetera.' She should be on stage."

"Washed her hands, eh?"

"Sort of. Well, actually, not quite." Margaret seemed a little surprised. "She did spend time with the parent and got the secretary to find a clinic the family could be referred to for advice and support. Actually, she handled the whole thing very well once she realised that her budget wasn't in any danger. Spent a good hour with the parent and child and sent them away reasonably happy." Margaret went to the hob to check a saucepan. "But she must have been worrying about it all day. She called all the staff to a meeting immediately after school to discuss what we might do if the shoe was on the other foot." She sat beside him again.

"Other foot?"

"Well, she had begun to wonder what might happen if one of the boys from the Christian Brothers School decides to change gender and come to us. We're not ready for that. The pupils are not ready for that. So, she arranged for an adviser from the Education Board to speak to the staff on Monday after school. We'll see where we go from there."

Sheehan finished his soup and wiped his mouth with a napkin. "Strange times. There was none of that about when I was a kid."

Margaret got up and picked up the two soup dishes. "Well, it's something we're going to have to deal with now. And from what I read in the papers, it's becoming increasingly prevalent." She put the dishes in the sink. "Dinner'll be about fifteen minutes. So, how was your day?"

"We've got no joy from our questioning of our existing suspects, still no clue about the mystery blackmailer, and today we got six new suspects, all violent criminals."

Margaret grimaced. "That good, eh? So, anything striking that famed intuition of yours?"

"Not really."

"I know that look. Not really what?"

"Well, something Miller said about one of the early suspects we are talking to, a property dealer called Robinson. He described him as being big, ignorant, aggressive, and with a brutal track record. He could have been describing the gang leader that kidnapped and beat the daylights out of that judicial assistant I was telling you about. There might be a connection there, but I don't have any evidence yet."

"Oh, yes. Uh, Mr Doran, wasn't it? How's he doing?"

"Improving, I understand. Strapped up a bit but no lasting damage."

"You think that Miller's suspect did this to Doran?"

"Don't know, but the kidnapper was really anxious to get his hands on the judge's other safe. Our suspects would definitely want access to it as

135

well, given the very iffy connection they seem to have with the judge. Robinson, whose reputation leaves something to be desired, might have thought the judge's assistant would know where it was and decided to beat the information out of him. Who knows? But, yes, there might be a connection there, or it might be a coincidence. But you know me and coincidences."

"The other safe? You mean, the one you said you couldn't find?"

"Aye! Well, actually, Sergeant Larkin found it today."

"Oh, good." She noticed his expression. "Not good?"

"So far we can't open it. Larkin says it'll take a week. Frustrating. We need the info that might be in there."

She sighed. "Well, fretting about it isn't going to change anything tonight. Forget about everything for a while. Go into the lounge and relax. But don't just sit there thinking. Clear your brain. Read the paper."

"Clear my brain? Aye, right," Sheehan said. "One of the victims is a retired schoolteacher. I'm ready to swear that I've never spoken to him in my life nor have I had any dealings with him, but his face keeps flashing in my brain, and I feel that I should know him. Can't think why that should be, but it keeps happening."

"Just stop thinking about it and maybe it'll suddenly hit you."

"Aye, maybe."

Margaret stopped as she headed for the door. "Oh, I almost forgot. Niall phoned."

"The bishop?"

"Yes. He's taking us out to dinner on Saturday evening to catch up. So, keep your diary empty. We need a night out, and you need it more than I do."

Sheehan agreed. The idea pleased him. "Actually, I'd like that. We haven't had a real chat with him since that terrible night at LeBreton's crypt."

She shivered. "Jim," she said sharply. "You're not to talk about that. I never want to hear LeBreton's name again, or Baphomet, or any mention of covens. We'll just eat, drink, and be merry, right?"

"And hope we don't die tomorrow," he said, grinning. He headed for the lounge. "I think I will have that drink."

SEVENTEEN
Friday, 17th August. Morning

S heehan stopped by Stewart's desk, pulling on his overcoat. "Ready?"

"Yes, Chief," Stewart replied, shutting down her laptop. She grabbed her anorak from a peg on the wall behind her desk and scurried after Sheehan who was already striding through the door.

"You get the address?" he asked, when she caught up with him.

"No problem, although Mr Wilson, Delaney's probation officer, said he needed to know why we wanted the address before he would give it to us."

"Hummph. What did you tell him?"

"More or less the truth. I said we needed to talk to Delaney in connection with a violent crime we were investigating."

"Did he push any further?"

"No. Funny enough, he just laughed."

"Laughed?"

"Yeah. I asked him what was so amusing. He just said, 'the violent bit', and added that I would find out when I talked to the suspect. Then he said he had a client and hung up."

"Not overly impressed by your dulcet tones, then?" Sheehan said, grinning.

Stewart chuckled. "Either that or he was genuinely busy. It'll be interesting to see what he meant."

They had to run to the car through a sudden rain squall, one of many the blustery August day had already inflicted upon the city. Wipers barely keeping the route visible, Stewart finally turned into a narrow street.

"You have arrived at your destination." The sat. nav's tones were also dulcet.

Delaney's house was one in a row of small terraced houses in Short Strand, one of the less affluent areas of Belfast. A couple of low sparse hedges, no more than ten feet apart, separated his property from the houses on either side. Sheehan opened a small iron gate and walked up a narrow concrete path to the front door. On the right of the path was a very scraggy patch of ground that by no stretch of the imagination could be called a lawn.

Just as Sheehan raised his hand to ring the bell, the front door opened and a harassed, stout, grey-haired lady, probably late fifties, exited the door at some speed, almost bumping into Sheehan who, by dint of nifty footwork, prevented what might have been an awkward collision.

"Oh, I'm so sorry," she said breathlessly. "I'm way behind schedule and it's all rush, rush, rush."

Sheehan grinned and said, "We were looking for a Mr Gerard Delaney?"

"Yes, yes," she said hurriedly, pointing with her thumb over her shoulder. "I'm his carer, but I have to rush on to my next charge. You'll find him in the sitting room." And literally running, she headed for a small Fiesta parked at the kerb.

Neither Sheehan nor Stewart had consciously formed an image of Delaney in their minds but hearing this, both glanced at each other bemused. Sheehan gave the open front door a staccato rap and the two detectives let themselves into the house. Perhaps, in view of Doran's description, they were expecting to meet a dapper, personable, well-dressed individual. Instead they found an emaciated man who sat on an armchair in front of a meagre fire with a rug around his knees—pale, gaunt, straggly grey hair, plastic oxygen tubes attached to his nose.

Delaney looked up, clearly surprised to find two visitors standing in his minimally furnished sitting room. Sheehan said apologetically, "Your carer told us to come on in. She had to rush away."

Delaney made to speak but was suddenly convulsed with a bout of coughing. Eventually he managed to ask, in a weak, rasping voice, "Who are you?"

"I'm Chief Inspector Sheehan. My colleague here is Detective Sergeant Stewart."

"Police?" He made another sound that could easily have been an abbreviated cough or a weak chuckle. "Heh! Heh! Okay, I'll come quietly." This was followed by another wheezing cough before he was able to look up at them through tired, watery eyes. "So what is it I'm supposed to have done?"

"Not a thing," Sheehan said, experiencing some empathy for the man's condition, despite his criminal past. "It's just that your name came up in an investigation we are conducting. It's a tedious part of the job, but names that come up have to be checked out."

The man's rheumy eyes studied Sheehan again. "If you're looking for an alibi, it'll be the same no matter what the time of whatever crime you're investigating. I was here." He looked away from the detective into the smoking coals, adding almost inaudibly, "I'm always here."

Sheehan, noticing the man's blue-tinged lips, suspected that he had a lung infection. "What happened to you?" he asked.

The man shrugged and sighed heavily. "Emphysema. Didn't even know I had it until it snuck up on me after a couple of years into my sentence. It was always there, I suppose, but cold prison cells, little exercise, and smoking far too much, brought it on. I've been like this for about five years."

"That's unfortunate. National Health able to do anything for you?"

"I'm waiting for a lung transplant." He hacked into a dirty handkerchief that he had in his hand and, after an extended period of wheezing during which he seemed to be trying to clear his lungs to breathe, he added with a mirthless grin, "Not sure how useful that'll be. Doctors tell me there's a significant increase of pressure on the arteries. So I have heart problems to look forward to as well." He pulled the rug more tightly around his knees, and Sheehan couldn't help noticing how thin and veiny the man's wrists and hands were. He stared again at Sheehan. "You gonna tell me what I've got mixed up in?"

Sheehan pursed his lips. Normally he would have dodged the question, but he thought, *What the hell! He's going to do nothing with any info I give him.* "Your trial records show that you threatened Judge Neeson after he sentenced you."

Delaney spat angrily into the fire, his eyes staring unseeing into the feeble flames as he revisited the past. "Him? His Honour? No honour, none. Totally reneged on a deal I did with the prosecution. Doubled the sentence I was promised. Of course I threatened him. I was beyond furious." He turned back from the fire, a speculative look on his face. "I saw on the News that he was killed recently. You fancy me for that?" An attempt at a laugh turned into another hacking cough.

Sheehan said, straight-faced, "Witnesses said that you were very scary when you issued the threat. I might have to keep you on our books until a more viable suspect emerges."

Delaney was able to grin for once without wheezing. "Well, whaddyaknow! A cop with a sense of humour."

Sheehan looked round the bleak room, the faded linoleum on the floor, the lack of any real comforts, and felt sorry for the man. "You haven't really got out of prison, have you?"

Delaney just stared at him.

"We'll leave now," Sheehan said. "Anything we can do for you before we go?"

The man shook his head, tight-lipped. "No. I'm fine."

Stewart noticed the almost empty coal scuttle beside Delaney. "You want me to refill that for you? Where do you keep your coal?"

The man looked down at the bucket and shrugged resignedly. "That's it, right there."

"My God!" Stewart said. "It's forecast to be cold and wet tonight." Any hostility she might have harboured towards the suspect couldn't survive the pity she suddenly felt.

Sheehan pulled out his mobile phone. "Where do you normally get your coal?"

"Hanna's," Delaney said, his expression puzzled.

"Do you remember their contact number?" Sheehan dialled as the man called out the numbers and ordered four bags of coal to be delivered immediately to Delaney's address. He gave the vendor his credit card number and, as he ended the call, he said to Delaney, "How are you for food?"

Delaney, looking increasingly puzzled, said wearily, "Half a loaf, no milk, a few tea bags."

Sheehan shook his head. "Bloody hell!" He pulled out his mobile again and dialled another number. After a few seconds, he said, "Hi, Kiaran, it's Jim. Look, I have a man here needs a visit. Uh, you'll probably assess that he needs regular visits. Can you come and see him?" He listened for a second and called out Delaney's name and address. Then he added, "Come as soon as you can, and bring a decent food hamper with you."

Delaney looked up, protesting, "But you don't have to—"

"I know," Sheehan interrupted him, "but I do have to sleep tonight. The man who's coming to see you is a friend of mine from the St. Vincent de Paul Society, Kiaran Carr. He'll make a point of seeing what you need and will arrange regular visits from now on to make sure you're all right." He stared at Delaney and added, "I'll talk to the team. I might be able to convince them to scratch your name from the suspect list."

Delaney didn't look up or respond to Sheehan's wry humour. He sat still, hands holding the rug, staring into the fire, obviously struggling to remain expressionless.

Stewart put her hand on his shoulder as they were leaving and said, "Keep yourself warm. It's going to be cold tonight."

As they drove away from the house, Sheehan said sternly, "Not a word about this to anybody, right?"

Hands on the wheel, eyes firmly on the road, Stewart said, face impassive, "Wouldn't dream of it, Chief."

*   *   *

They stopped at a nearby café for a coffee and a sandwich before visiting Kahangi.

"Sat. nav's hardly going to help us this time," Sheehan said, finishing the last of his coffee.

"No, sir," Stewart replied, taking her smartphone from her pocket and fingering the screen. "Here we are, Chief, Poleglass." She studied the screen for a few moments and said, puzzled, "Oh, I didn't know that."

"Know what, Sergeant?" Sheehan said, a trifle impatiently.

"Says here that Poleglass was one of a number of housing schemes established in the early 1980s to alleviate the overcrowding in the Catholic areas of West Belfast. It's been around quite a while."

Sheehan gave her a sardonic nod. "We've been made very aware of that during the past thirty or so years, especially during 'the troubles'."

Stewart studied her phone's screen again. "Lisburn? Asking for trouble building a Catholic estate near a largely loyalist town, was it not?"

Sheehan shrugged. "Ours not to reason why, but the area certainly has gained a reputation for itself—joyriding, vandalism, gangs of hoodies, fights with neighbouring loyalist youths, stones and bottles constantly thrown at ambulances and police vehicles, and the never-ending joy-riding—any God's amount of anti-social behaviour, that's for sure."

Stewart made a faint whistling noise through her lips. "Pretty lawless. Is it well policed?"

Sheehan grinned mirthlessly. "We did try, but you're too young to know what it was like back in the day. In the 1990s, some of the local residents did try to keep the hoods under control with a Neighbourhood Watch scheme. They set up night-time patrols, blocked small streets to prevent access to joy riders, imposed curfews for large groups of youth. They did have a certain amount of success, but the scheme was criticised by some as vigilantism, especially when some of the nationalist paramilitaries began to butt in on it. That's when there were claims made by the families of some youths that their sons were forced out of the estate and made to leave the country. Members of the Neighbourhood Watch rejected these allegations, of course, but not many believed them. Too much evidence to the contrary."

Stewart gave him a dubious look. "Two cops going in there to look for a hardened criminal ... on our own? Are we wise in the head?"

Sheehan grinned. "Ach, it's not so bad now, although we won't be knocking on doors, that's for sure."

Stewart consulted her screen again. "There's loads of small estates there now, Chief," she said, and began reading some of the names, "Glenbank, Glenbawn, Merrion Park, Woodside, Glenwood, Glenkeen, Laurelbank...."

"Yes, I know," Sheehan said, "and a lot more besides. The place has gotten a lot bigger since the expansion in 2000 after the demolition of the Divis high-rise flats."

Stewart looked baffled. "So where do we start? Kahangi doesn't even have his own address. He's just hanging out with somebody."

Sheehan shook his head. "We're going to have to think of something." And he glanced at her from under lowered eyebrows.

Stewart knew that look and grinned. "You're playing with me, Chief. You have a plan?"

"Any mention of a church on that screen of yours?"

Stewart checked. "The Church of the Nativity."

"That's the one. When we get back in the car, set your sat. nav for that. It's a fairly new building, very modern looking. I've seen photos of it, so we won't miss it."

"And that's going to help us how, sir?" Stewart asked.

"I know the dean there. He's been in the district for over twenty years and has his nose to the ground, always trying to find trouble before it starts. If anybody knows where Kahangi is, it'll be him."

*   *   *

Half an hour later they were driving away from the church towards an address in Ardcaoin, one of the smaller Poleglass estates.

"That was a nice priest," Stewart said.

Sheehan nodded. "One of the good 'uns. Working his butt off to get the youth in the area involved in all sorts of positive activities." He shrugged. "Long way to go but...." He glanced at his sergeant who clearly was not fully engaged in the conversation. "Something up, Sergeant?"

Stewart didn't answer immediately. Eventually she said, "Do you not think we're taking a risk, sir, heading into Poleglass without a couple of armoured Land Rovers for protection?"

"Two armoured Land Rovers and a police car driving through Poleglass in broad daylight?" He shook his head. "Word would spread like wildfire. Then what?"

Stewart had read enough reports and seen enough television coverage to get the chief's point. In no time they'd be surrounded by dozens of masked youths with bricks, bottles, stones. There could even be a riot. Not something they would want to stir up right now. Somebody else's problem for another time. "So we just drive in?"

"Unmarked vehicle drives to somebody's house. Happens all the time. Who's gonna pass any remarks? We'll be fine."

Despite its reputation, the first impression of the area was reasonably positive. Many residents had tidy little gardens in front of their houses; others had fresh paint on their doors and window frames. As the detectives drove into the smaller estates, however, signs of poverty and deprivation became more evident—crumbling walls, graffiti, litter. Stewart's lips tightened, but she continued towards their destination at a steady pace. After some moments, as she pulled up in front of a somewhat dilapidated red-bricked, terraced house, she said, "We're here, Chief."

Sheehan wasted no time. He climbed out of the car before Stewart had even switched off the engine. "Let's go," he said, crossing the pavement to the small rusting gate that was part of a rickety wooden fence about two strides from the front door. Sheehan had already knocked on the door by the time Stewart caught up with him.

After some moments the door was answered by a huge black man, heavily built and massively muscular, wearing a stained white singlet and torn jeans. *Steroids for sure*, was Sheehan's immediate thought as he studied the man. The large face, thick lips, yellowed irises, and a cascade of flowing black ringlets tied back with a small coloured bandana, gave the man's head a distinctly leonine appearance.

"No hawkers," the man growled, already closing the door.

Sheehan stopped the door with his left hand and held up his warrant card in the other. "Police," he said neutrally. "Are you Mr Baako Kahangi?"

"Why you want know?" the man snarled belligerently.

If he's on steroids, he could easily go nuts. Keep it calm. "Nothing to get concerned about, sir," Sheehan said easily. "Just a routine enquiry."

The man drew himself up to his full height, something in the region of six and a half feet, folded his immense arms across his chest and growled, "I not do nuthin'."

Sheehan was uncomfortable on the doorstep. Prying eyes could quickly discern what was happening here. "If we could just step inside for a minute, sir, we could clear this up very quickly."

It was obvious that the suspect was struggling to retain his macho 'not-give-an-inch' attitude, but eventually, responding to some glimmer of prudence in the face of the policeman's calm and unthreatening demeanour, he stood to one side and wordlessly nodded the two detectives into a tiny hall. That was as far as he permitted them to go. "What you want?"

"Our records indicate," Sheehan said smoothly, while Stewart hovered nervously just behind him, "that you threatened Judge Neeson when he sentenced you at the end of your trial."

"That bastard," Kahangi exploded, anger suffusing his face. "He lucky I blocked by guards in courtroom or I rip him apart."

"Where were you between nine o'clock on the evening of Sunday, the twelfth of August and nine o'clock on the morning of Monday, the thirteenth of August?" Sheehan said smoothly, attempting to deflect the man's intemperate rage.

Kahangi continued to glower at him, breathing heavily, until suddenly he turned, half opened a door behind him, and shouted, "Fahim. Where I Sunday night, twelve August?"

"Here, with me," came the immediate response from the other side of the door.

Kahangi closed the door again and turned to Sheehan with a smirk. "I here. You satisfied?"

Sheehan raised his eyebrows. "Your friend didn't take long to figure that out."

Kahangi smirked again. "Fahim brain like computer." Then his expression changed, scowling again. "Why you ask these questions?"

Sheehan pondered his response. Usually he would have thanked the suspect and left, but he wanted to watch Kahangi's response to what he had to say. "Judge Neeson was murdered on that evening. Your name is on the list of suspects."

Conflicting emotions crossed Kahangi's face. Sheehan saw immediate anger flash there as the man's fists tightened in response to the word 'suspect', but, more revealingly, he saw the anger almost dissipate, replaced by surprise and a gloating satisfaction.

"Murdered?" Kahangi queried. "That good. He deserve. How happen?"

"You deny any involvement?"

Kahangi spread hands the size of garden spades and almost smiled. "I here. Not involve." Then he offered the detectives another vicious scowl and added fiercely, "But I glad."

Sheehan said simply, "Thank you, Mr Kahangi. I think that's all we'll need for now." He nodded to Stewart who opened the door with some alacrity, and they departed quickly, leaving their mountainous suspect staring after them.

In the car, Stewart said, "What do you think, Chief?"

"He's not our man?"

"How can you be sure?"

"You mean, apart from the fact that he was genuinely surprised to hear that Judge Neeson was murdered? Obviously doesn't read the papers."

"Maybe he can't read the papers."

Sheehan grinned. "There's that. And subtlety is hardly his middle name, wouldn't you agree?"

"A heartfelt yes, sir."

"So, whatever profile we come up with about the murderer, subtlety will be part of it. Kahangi doesn't fit, Stewart. Forget about him."

EIGHTEEN
Friday, 17th August. Early afternoon

Miller replaced the phone in its slot on his desk and said to Connors, "Arrogant wee shit."

"What did he say?"

"He can give us fifteen minutes in his chambers at one forty-five. He's due in court at two o'clock." He leaned back on his chair, folding his arms, his face expressing distaste. "You wanna hear him, dry, dusty oul' voice. Treating me like dirt under his shoe. Never met the guy, but I hate him already."

Connors chuckled. "I just love your professional neutrality, Simon. That's what makes you such a great detective."

Miller tossed his head. "Shut up. So what did your *professional* enquiries uncover?"

"Conner took a notebook from the side pocket of his jacket. "Have to admit I wasn't doing well initially until someone gave me a hint to enquire at the Youth Justice Services. That's all I got. But then I got lucky. I bumped into a woman I used to know as she was coming out of the area office in Duncairn Gardens. We had a wee chat at the door, and I invited her for a cup of coffee."

Miller reached across and slapped his giant partner on the shoulder. "Good for you, Dec. Are you putting your toe back in the water?"

Connors scowled at him. "You gotta be joking. Be a long time before I go that route again." His face assumed a pained expression. "I mean, the house and garden, the four by four, the kids, on top of the bloody alimony. And she was the one who had the affair. I just can't get my head around that. It was all her fault, but she gets everything, and I have to slum it in a poky wee apartment. Where's the justice in that, huh?"

Simon nodded. He'd heard all this many times before. *This is a wound that isn't going to heal any time soon.* "I know, Dec, but you're going to have to stop brooding on this. You need to find somebody new and start again." He cocked his head sideways as if studying his partner. "You know, if you weren't such a big ugly brute, you could be quite attractive."

Connors scowled at him. "Bugger off."

Miller grinned back at him. "What's she like, this woman?"

"Dawn, if you can believe that, is her name. Actually, she's very nice, but I never knew her the way you're talking about. We were just friends in school. I just happened to ask her what she was doing there, and it turns out that's where she works. Definitely my cue to invite her for a coffee."

"Is she married?"

"Give over, will ye! She's divorced, like me. We had a bit of chat about old times and things, but I wanted to get on to what she knew about Adams. That's what we mostly talked about."

"Are you seeing her again?" Miller asked. Then, wagging his eyebrows up and down, he added, "Is this a new Dawn-ing?"

Connors groaned. "Oh, God. What's with this feckin' Dear Abby stuff? It was just a casual meeting."

Miller grinned knowingly. "You are, aren't you? Go on, admit it."

Connors couldn't hide his grin. "She gave me her number and I said I might call. That was it. Now can we get down to business?"

"You're going to call, right?"

"Gimme a break. What about you? You're thirty now. About time you stopped playing the field, don't you think? Leave it any longer and you won't have kids." He laughed. "You won't be able to."

"Between relationships at the minute. Just can't seem to find the right one." He gave Connors a regretful look. "I find somebody nice and we get on for a while, but then somebody else nice comes along and that's it. Can't stay in a relationship. Vicious circle I can't find my way out of."

"Well, if you want to be a daddy, and that is the one good thing that came out of my time with that ... that.... Anyway! Somebody'll come along." He gave Miller something of the same scrutiny that he himself had been subjected to a minute earlier. "Actually, if you weren't such an ugly wee wart, you could be quite attractive, too."

"Feck off! So what did your friend, Dawn, tell you?" He gave his partner a quizzical look. "Are you sure her name's Dawn?"

"Better than bloody Simon. Yes, it's Dawn, and once she got started, she was a mine of information. It turns out that not all judges are fair, reasonable and dispassionate, and it seems that Adams, and Neeson as well, were unreliable on the bench and universally disliked."

"Universally?"

"Well, by the barristers, clerks, solicitors, secretaries, anybody who had dealings with them in court. Dawn herself hated the pair of them."

"How does she know them?"

"She's one of the team leaders in the Youth Justice Department."

"Okay. Plenty to say, then?"

"Apparently both judges suffered from what the legal people secretly call 'Black Robe Syndrome'. These kinds of judges see themselves as big-shots. They forget the pressures legal teams are under, forget their manners, just become totally arrogant. It appears these two in particular were rarely influenced by legal arguments. They had no compassion or patience, and if they took a dislike to counsel on one side, the other side would almost certainly win their case. Adams is notorious for that. Both, it seems, were downright nasty in court and had everybody cowering."

"What did she say about Adams' background?"

"Came from a wealthy family. Thinks he's above everybody. Was clever enough when he studied law and had a good record as a barrister. A nasty little terrier in court, apparently. Got a name for himself and finally made it to the bench. Thing is, once he became a judge, his arrogance got in the way and his judgements were frequently questionable. According to Dawn, Adams has gotten lazy in court and tends to take the easy way out, or goes by his likes and dislikes instead of focusing on the niceties of legal argument. In a recent case in family court, logic was crying out that the father should be awarded custody of the children, but Adams gave them to the mother, an unfit bloody alcoholic."

"Ouch! Poor kids."

"Aye! You get anything?"

"Not half. I know one of the court judicial assistants quite well. It cost me a couple of pints and a boring night in a pub but, yes, I got some dirt."

"Do tell."

"Well, for a start, both judges are homosexual with a liking for teenage boys. My contact was able to tell me some gruesome stories. And, get this, both took a fancy to some unfortunate young fellow a few years back. Fought over him likes cats and dogs, but in the end the youth wanted nothing to do with either of them. But that's what started them off and they've been sworn enemies ever since, each blaming the other for the lad walking away with somebody else. At that time Adams was still a barrister, and the couple of times after that when he appeared before Neeson on the bench, he lost both cases."

"Holy shit! So what was Adams doing at Neeson's party?"

"Seems odd, alright." Miller gave the question a few seconds thought. "Maybe their antagonism to Brexit overcame their antagonism to each other."

"Aye, if Brexit had anything to do with why they were there, which I very much doubt. We'll ask him that when we're talking to him. Might rattle him a bit." His expression changed as an idea hit him. "Do you think Adams might be the blackmailer the chief was talking about?"

"Never thought of that," Miller said slowly, speculatively. "Don't know. It's possible, I suppose. They probably had loads of dirt on each other."

"Any word of anything else that might provide a motive for murder?" Connors sounded excited.

"No, they were both generally quite circumspect," Miller said. "But hate's not a bad motive, I suppose."

"Yeah, but what would have been his beef with the teacher? We're thinking same killer, right?"

Miller shrugged. "Don't know. But we do know now that they're all gay. Bit tenuous, I admit, but it's a connection."

Connors closed his notebook and put it back in his pocket. "Well, you know what the chief says. No point in trying to form conclusions when we don't have all the facts. Maybe something else about them will emerge during the course of the investigation."

Miller looked at his watch. "Quarter past one. We'd need to head off. We have to get through the lunch-time traffic."

*   *   *

Judges' chambers tend to be functional and relatively characterless, a place for the judge to be alone, to hold the occasional short meeting with barristers and solicitors, to rest between court sessions, or read up on complex aspects of law that occur during the course of a trial. Judge Adams' chambers, however, were rather more flamboyant than the norm—polished mahogany desk and matching book shelves covered with impressive tomes, all meticulously tidy. A couple of dark brown leather armchairs. A thick pile patterned carpet. And one wall covered with squares of faux-leather panelling.

Sumptuous surroundings to feed a small man's big ego, was Miller's first thought when he and Connors were led into the chambers by a court official. The judge was sitting behind his desk, already gowned and wigged. *Trying to intimidate us*, was Miller's second thought.

The judge did not invite the detectives to sit but addressed them from his seat as they stood there. "Why am I being bothered again about issues already dealt with?" he snapped in his reedy voice.

Connors' scowl was already beginning to manifest itself, but Miller gave him a cautionary shake of the head and said to the judge, "Just a follow-up visit, Judge. We're not sure that everything was covered in the first round of interviews."

"Humph. Very inefficient."

Miller again glanced at his volatile partner. Too soon yet for dramatics. "Well, you know how it is, sir," he said, with a disarming grin. "They don't call us PC Plods for nothing."

The judge gave him a suspicious look and glanced at his watch. "You have ten minutes," he said, making little effort to hide his disdain. "What do you want to know?"

Connors' usual struggle with patience ended with patience in defeat. Struggling now with belligerence, he said, trying to sound neutral, "We have discovered during our investigation that you and Judge Neeson had an antagonistic relationship."

Adams looked up, annoyed. "And how is that any business of yours?"

"You do know that Judge Neeson has been murdered?" Connors countered, bordering on disrespect.

The judge stared at him. "I'll thank you not to be impertinent, Detective."

"You are also aware that you are obliged to answer questions legitimately posed by detectives in the pursuit of their duty?" Connors persisted.

"Depends how you define 'legitimately posed'," the judge snapped.

"I'll define it for you, Judge," Connors said, moving his forbidding bulk closer to the desk.

"If you are attempting to intimidate me with your size," the judge said angrily, "you'll earn only censure and the loss of your job. Now step back from my desk immediately."

Connors opened his mouth to make an angry retort, but Miller caught him by the arm and pulled him gently backwards. "Just a second, Detective. We're drifting off course here." He turned to Adams. "Your relationship with Judge Neeson at this point in the investigation must of necessity be an issue. Can you confirm that you were not friends?"

"We were not friends," Adams answered brusquely.

"Is it not odd then that you attended a party at the judge's house on the evening he was murdered?"

"That was fully explained to your superior," Adams said with an arrogant lift of the head. "We're people who are anxious to combat the impact of Brexit on Northern Ireland and were meeting to discuss options."

"It was important?"

"Too urgent to allow petty animosities to interfere with it."

"So how did the recent meeting go?" Miller asked innocently.

"What recent meeting?"

"You said the issue was urgent?

"Of course."

"Then you must have had a meeting, maybe two since that night. That was a while ago. How did the meetings go?"

Adams struggled to maintain his composure, but both detectives could see that he was not prepared for this question. "Given the circumstances and the death of a colleague, it would hardly have been appropriate—" Adams began.

Connors cut in before the judge could finish. "A dead guy you didn't like, an urgent issue that couldn't wait, and yet you let it slide for twelve days? So just how important is this issue of yours?" He stared grimly at the judge for a couple of seconds and suddenly said, "What were you really doing at the judge's house that night?"

The judge snapped back in his chair. "How dare you?" he blustered. "Are you impugning my integrity?" He rose angrily from his chair and pointed at the door. "This meeting is over." He turned to Connors. "And you. Your superiors will hear about this, of that you can rest assured."

The detectives turned to leave, but at the door Connors looked back. "And you can rest assured, Judge Adams, that we will be back with further questions."

On their way out of the building, Miller said, "So what do you think?"

Connors grinned. "Might have overplayed my hand a little bit, but did you see the little runt jump? I couldn't have gotten a much better reaction with a cattle prod."

"He's definitely hiding something," Miller agreed. "But what? And obviously it's not just him. There were nearly a dozen others involved. Whatever it is might well have nothing to do with the murders."

"He hated the judge," Connors argued, "so he might have been operating independently. Maybe there's a couple of things going on, stuff maybe the others aren't in on."

"Here we go," Miller said with a sigh. "Speculating without facts. If the chief could hear us now."

"Aye, right!" Connors said with a grin. "Okay. Let's get on. Who's next?"

Miller looked at his watch. "Let's get a bite of lunch first and then we'll go and see this Khan guy."

NINETEEN
Friday, 17th August. Evening

Michael Stevens cocked his eyebrows, grinning an obvious suggestion. The answering smile from his companion was clearly affirmative, so he pulled his mobile phone from his pocket, saying, "I'll order us a taxi." He dialled and, while waiting for a response, he said, "One for the road?"

His companion smiled acquiescence, rose and headed for the elegant cocktail bar. "Make your call. I'll get them."

Two hours earlier, Stevens had been thinking of an early night. He'd had a long and difficult day in court and had spent much of the afternoon and late evening preparing for a nine o'clock start the next morning. Thus, he was much too exhausted to even contemplate the rigors of an evening at The Club. Still tense and high-strung after the efforts of the day, however, he had decided to have a bite to eat and a quick drink in the Green Room of a small intimate bar he favoured on Union Street. Prior to its opening in 2003, the Union Street Bar had been a shoe factory and evidence of this was still visible in its wrought iron pillars and various odd plaques on the walls. Its publicity brochure claims that, *"It's that touch of antiquity that fuses with modern loft styling to create a venue that is comfortable for a quiet drink..."* A sentiment with which the barrister fully agreed. The Green Room was a particular preference of his, a unique upper level above Union

Street, restricted to a certain clientele. It was comfortably furnished, with cosy lighting, and offered privacy to those who desired it.

He had earlier been drinking on his own in a quiet corner alcove and had caught the eye of someone he recognised at the cocktail bar, slim, a little below average height, attractive in a stern, withdrawn fashion. They had been in shared company before on a number of occasions but had never conversed. A couple of shyly exchanged glances and a tentative smile resulted in the two of them spending an hour and a half in each other's company in the alcove. Surprisingly, he found his new escort to be a person of significant intellectual depth, an absorbing conversationalist, and apparently willing to spend the rest of the evening pursuing even more intimate dalliance. He grinned to himself as his companion returned with the drinks. He had some surprises up his sleeve that he would refrain from mentioning. Time enough to show his hand when things got interesting. There was always the chance, of course, that his proclivities could bring their intimacy to a fractious and brutish end, possibly ending also any chance of future meetings. *But what the hell! Live for the hour, right?*

The taxi took them to Stevens' well-appointed apartment in a matter of fifteen minutes, during which time Stevens maintained an urbane and attentive conversation with his new acquaintance. When they were entering the apartment, however, Stevens staggered slightly and had to hold on to a doorpost for support. He shook his head for a second before saying with a grin, "Wow! My head's spinning a bit. Did we drink that much?"

His companion was solicitous and led him to one of the armchairs in the huge, opulent sitting room. Smiling, the visitor began to explore and, pointing at a large door with an ornate surrounding frame, said coyly, "That wouldn't be the master bedroom, would it?"

Still feeling somewhat dizzy but excited by his visitor's obvious implication, Stevens rose and said grandly, "Indeed it is."

"And are there handcuffs in any of the drawers?"

Stevens stood still, his expression suddenly lecherous. "Wow! You don't waste time, do you? But of course. What self-respecting hedonist would be without them? And whips ... and leather bindings ... tape..." He was staggering again and beginning to slur his words. "Gosh! Mush be havin'... attack of ver ... vertigo."

The visitor reached out and took his hand. "Come. We'll get you on the bed."

Despite his increasing wooziness, Stevens was enjoying this uninhibited directness, and lurched towards the bed, saying with a lewd leer, "You'll get no ar-argument from me."

The bed was a massive king-sized affair, an antique replica, with intricately designed metal head and foot frames cast in a gleaming expensive bronze. Stevens fell rather than climbed on to the bed and turned to settle with his head on the pillow, smirking, but with sagging eyelids.

"No. No. Not like that. The other way. Come on." The visitor helped the increasingly drowsy barrister to turn so that his back was resting against the foot frame, his head lolling back, exposed. Stevens lay still, trying to regain his equilibrium as he watched the visitor search a bedroom chest-of-drawers. He waggled a pair of sluggish eyebrows and mumbled, "Naughty! Naughty!"

The visitor's search reaped a pair of handcuffs covered with a kind of pink fur, and two leather thongs.

"Are you going to arresht me, Officher?" Stevens slurred, with an inane cackle.

The visitor didn't answer but quickly divested the increasingly helpless barrister of his clothes, and was able, with little difficulty, to persuade him to lie on his stomach with his back exposed, handcuffing his hands to the bottom frame, and tying his feet and knees tightly together with the leather thongs.

Stevens, still unaware that he was struggling to stay conscious but aware of his nakedness, gaped at his visitor. His words were becoming increasingly garbled, but the stupidly expectant grin was still on his face as he said, "Are you going to ... to ... play a new game?"

"No."

He tried to bring his head forward, suddenly aware that something was amiss. "No? What are you gon ... gonna ... do?"

"I'm going to kill you," his guest said calmly.

TWENTY
Friday, 17th August. Late evening

A shadowy figure sat hunched in front of a laptop screen. It was the only light in a darkened room. The face that was bathed in the pale light was impassive, expressionless. There was no hint of stress, of strain, of emotion, just blank concentration. Blank like the blank screen. For several moments the cold eyes stared at the pale light. Nothing moved. Not the hands, not the head, not the lips, not even the eyes, as if the figure was in some kind of trance. Then suddenly the hands moved forward and the fingers began to type.

NEMEIN'Σ BΛOΓ
Συστιφιξατιον

Today, my many faithful followers, I wrestle with the concept of JUSTIFICATION. While the elements of Justice and Vengeance can be defined objectively, separated from thought and deed, Justification strikes me as an inner belief that extends beyond the objective. Justification cannot reside in broad generalities other than as literary examples that are inherently empty. Real justification, the essence of a specific deed, can be found only in the belief and in the psyche of the doer. In other words, justification is immediate and real. It has no place in empty philosophy.

It is, however, based on intellect, too. When claims are made, such as those made in my earlier blogs, justification is used to support and affirm those claims. Justification can emerge from various sources, some empirical, some based on authoritative testimony, but obviously, in the cases I have presented, justification derives from intellectual consciousness and logical deduction.

This, I know, is a complex argument. I won't bore you with a too philosophical analysis, but it is important that you understand that justification focuses on beliefs, and that justification is the reason why people hold and maintain a belief. It is the inner belief that gives justification its focus, its essence, its power, what Socrates in his Dialogue 'Theaetetus', identifies as 'a justified true belief'. In other words, a justified belief is one that we are within our rights in holding, a belief that is neither political nor moral, but simply intellectual.

Our beliefs, of course, do not come from the air. We form our beliefs based on empirical and logical evidence and thus, when those beliefs fall within the confines of normal human conduct, when we act within the ambit of those beliefs and are true to them, then our actions are justified.

There are many different theories of justification, among the most popular of which are:

Externalism, where a person seeks to justify a belief by having recourse to outside sources of knowledge, or:

Internalism, where a person must be able to justify beliefs or actions through internal knowledge already deemed true.

There are other theories that move to more extreme versions of justification but, since they are not relevant to my argument, I will ignore them. Suffice to say, any theory of justification must correspond to reality as the doer sees it, BUT, intrinsically, must correspond also to the reality of the external world. In other words, his beliefs and attitudes must reflect the beliefs and attitudes of normal life; they cannot be a compendium of the delusions of the insane.

I have given much thought to the justification of my own cause, my own pursuit of justice. Two major elements apply, elements that match the key components of justification as defined above. ONE, my belief that a major miscarriage of justice has been done is informed not only by my own inner belief but also in terms of the normative behaviour of the world around me. TWO, everything I believe about my quest coheres strongly with the entirety of the rest of the beliefs in my values system.

Therefore, I continue my crusade with renewed confidence and a renewed sense of the rightness of what I do. And so, I happily relate the story of the pursuance and dispatch of the next perpetrator of the injustice that has all but destroyed my life.

I saw him come into the bar. I experienced a small frisson of anticipation. I could not have been certain, I could only have hoped, that on this night he might eschew the frenetic delights of his more extreme haunts for the emptiness of a lonely drink. It was a slim hope, but there he was. That fortuitous confluence of timing truly made me wonder if Justification and Karma are somehow aligned.

He seemed distracted and went to a corner alcove where, having given his order to a waiter, he remained deliberately isolated. I was seated at the cocktail bar, carefully positioned so that if he should glance my way, our eyes would meet. And inevitably they did. We had seen each other at occasional functions before, even in small groups, but had never had any form of intimate conversation. He recognised me and offered me a ridiculously raised eyebrow, accompanied by an arrogant leer which, I presume, he fondly imagined was attractive flirtation. Despite my repugnance, I smiled back, and was soon invited to join him in the alcove.

Determined to act out the role I had planned for myself, I engaged him in a series of short, sharp debates, ranging in topic from politics to law, to philosophy, and, ironically, to justice. For a while the conversation flowed. He may have been a brute and a predator, but he did not achieve the eminent position he held in society without enjoying significant levels of intellectual acumen. And I could see that he was both surprised and impressed by the depth and variety of my own conversational gambits.

Despite his veneer of culture, however, he was lacking in finesse or refinement. His hands brushed mine rather too often and too obviously, his knees searched constantly for mine despite the distance between us. True to my determination to maintain my adopted character, I allowed him no sense of the revulsion stirred in me by his crude advances. Instead, I offered him enough hesitation to inflame his already hyperactive libido.

Predictably, the offer to join him for a drink at his apartment was made and, since I was playing the coquette, the offer was coyly accepted. He suggested a final 'drink for the road', and I offered to purchase them at the cocktail bar while he phoned for a taxi. It was but the work of a second to slip a slow-acting soporific into his glass before returning to the alcove. I calculated that the effects of the drug would not fully incapacitate him until we were well and truly settled in his apartment.

Almost from the moment of arrival, the man's brute nature began to manifest itself. Had I not ensured his impairment, I dare suggest that his superior strength would have allowed him to overcome me with little difficulty. As it was, I was able to take charge, and by dint of some overtly sexualised remarks and gestures, I quickly had him acceding to my every whim. He was almost crawling like an over-excited pup when I helped him on to his antique, king-sized bed. He made to put his head on the pillow, but I turned him so that his head was lolling over the back rail. Under the impression that what was happening was a prelude to some unusual wanton activity, he meekly accepted my instructions.

There was no doubt in my mind that a depraved pervert of this person's ilk would be possessed of a cache of sadomasochistic paraphernalia. And so it proved. Within seconds, a search allowed me to choose from many loathsome items a set of handcuffs and some leather thongs. The man, who was demonstrating a contrasting mix of lustful excitement and drooping eyelids, was by now physically helpless.

I easily persuaded him to lie on his stomach although I dare surmise that his own perverted tastes were probably more persuasive in this instance than my own blandishments. It was but the work of a few moments to handcuff his wrists to the back frame of the bed, undress him, and tie his knees and ankles together with the leather thongs. And still he remained oblivious. With a stupidly expectant smirk on his face, he turned his head to ask if we were going to play a new game.

At this point, no longer burdened with the need for role play, I said simply, but with cold contempt, "No."

I could see something akin to fear flash behind those increasingly sluggish eyes. Some awareness of the fact that he was now bound and utterly helpless must have crossed his mind because his next question was suddenly devoid of all lechery.

"No? What are you gon ... gonna ... do?"

Despite an almost overwhelming excitation that suddenly permeated my entire being, I fought to remain dispassionate as I looked into his eyes and said calmly, "I'm going to kill you."

It is at moments such as this that detachment is tested. My brain and my very body were aflame with a dark turbulence that I could scarce control. I knew, however, that the purity of my purpose depended on quelling my emotions. Exercising a prodigious level of restraint (of which, looking back, I am now manifestly proud), I placed a gentle hand on the man's shoulder. Inevitably he was threshing about and shouting obscenities, his eyes bulging from his head. Hampered by the sedative, his efforts became increasingly feeble. I positioned his head so that his chin was extended over the rear frame and said, "But not yet. I must leave you now to retrieve my Instrument of Justice." He had still sufficient presence of mind to resist my positioning of his head, tossing it this way and that. I stroked the flailing head and smiled sweetly. "I won't be long. I trust you can endure a few moments of loneliness until I return?"

Macabre humour, I know. But one employs whatever psychological techniques one can in order to retain emotional equilibrium.

You will have intuited by now that the events of that evening had been carefully planned. Part of that planning included driving to the location earlier in the evening and parking my car in a nearby entry. A few minutes brought me there to retrieve a truncheon and a Du Pont Tyvek Coverall suit, easily acquired on the Internet. The suit was particularly useful in ensuring that no droplets of blood or other foreign matter attach themselves to my person, and equally, in ensuring that in the flurry of activity that was to ensue, no tiny speck of skin, hair or clothing would fall from me, later to be discovered by some painstakingly conscientious forensic officer.

When I returned to the bedroom, he was still there waiting for me. (Ha! Ha! He did not have a great deal of choice in the matter.) Fear must have generated a measure of adrenaline because he was still awake and fighting the sedative. When he saw me, he began to shout, to remonstrate, to curse, struggling violently but fruitlessly against his bonds. I went back to his toys and found a roll of duct tape from which I cut a strip and, moving to the back of the bed and bending down, I pressed it over his spitting mouth. It was not that I feared someone might hear. Given the history of activities that room must have witnessed, it would have been imperative for him to ensure it was fully sound-proofed. No, his sound and fury were both irritating and distracting. I needed to focus intently on what I had to do, to savour its every second, to absorb to the full each iota of his terror and suffering, with, of course, a carefully maintained disinterest. Purity of intent had to remain paramount. For that I needed uncluttered silence.

But, ah, the delicious anticipation! I had to force his head forward a couple of times before he would allow it to hang over the rail. Indeed, I had to threaten to pummel his face with the truncheon in order to ensure his cooperation. And so came the moment of truth. His head, shivering and shaking, presented itself to me at exactly the optimum angle as I stepped forward to deliver the coup de grâce.

My friends, I do declare that I seemed to have stepped out of myself to watch the grace, the elegance, the rhythm of that wide, inexorable arc as the truncheon flew with ever increasing speed from behind my right shoulder to crash against and to shatter the back of the evil-doer's head. And, oh, the crunch, the blood, the bone splinters, the spurting grey matter! All of my senses—hearing, sight, smell, touch, even, to a degree, taste— were fully engaged in that sublime moment of retribution. One blow, one devastating blow, and the matter was all but ended. There remained only the one final, symbolic act.

I released the lifeless wrists from the handcuffs and tried to pull the knees forward so that the buttocks would be raised in a symbolic posture. His ponderous weight, however, and his utter lifelessness, rendered this manoeuvre too difficult for my limited strength. As I struggled with the flaccid body, I did note that some blood, grey matter and bone splinters spilled out from the shattered skull on to the bottom of the bed and on to the floor. That, for me, was simply an observation. It had no impact on my sensibilities. Once I had the body fixed in position, it was but the work of seconds to thrust the truncheon forcefully, handle first, into the malefactor's rectum.

I fell to my knees, filled ... filled with an elation so transcendent, a satisfaction so sweet, a triumph so overpowering, that I was transfixed, mesmerised, motionless. For how long I remained in that mystical state, I do not know. I was teased out of thought. I had lost awareness. I had lost emotion. I had lost feeling. But at some point consciousness returned, and with it a draining ... a draining of passion, a draining of energy. I was now experiencing only lethargy.

I climbed to my feet, devoid of impulse, and robotically I went to the vestibule, removed a large towel from the bag I had brought with me and spread it on the floor. Standing on it, I divested myself of the protective suit and rubber gloves that I was wearing and, wrapping all in the towel, pushed everything once more into the carrier bag. I allowed myself one final, indifferent glance at the lifeless barrister, and left.

Again I thank you, my faithful readers, and hope that you now have some additional understanding of the importance of justification in the execution of justice. No vestige of passion, no emotional energy, must be allowed to contaminate the lucidity and the clarity of unalloyed nemesis.

Until the next time, dear readers, and do not doubt there will be a next time, I remain, your friend and mentor,

Nemein

TWENTY-ONE
Monday, 20th August. Morning

Sheehan was in his office, poring through the case files and notes, searching for some clue, some inspiration, that would help him find some order, or shape, or even some kind of pointer to what had transpired so far. But it was a frustrating search. So many suspects, so many disconnections, so many possible motives without any clue as to the real one. There was nothing that led to any form of continuity, nothing that could enable him to formulate any kind of pattern. True there were the truncheons, but what did they mean? And why their brutal placement in the victim's rectums?

There was a brief frantic knock on his door and Stewart rushed in without waiting for his usual invitation. "Sir." She was almost gasping. Her left arm was raised and pointing erratically back towards her station. "You really need to see this."

He raised a calm hand. "Slow down, Stewart. Explain."

Stewart inhaled a deep breath and standing on the opposite side of his desk, she calmed herself enough to say, "You've heard of the Dark Web, sir?"

Sheehan nodded. "Just enough to know that it's not a place for ordinary people to be poking around in."

"You're right about that, sir. It's very dangerous for people who are not computer savvy. I would normally never go near it myself, but that remark my friend passed about Kane's dark and voracious appetites made me wonder."

"You've found something about Kane on the Dark Web?" Sheehan was suddenly very interested.

"No, sir. Nothing about Kane." She hesitated, frustrated, searching for words. "Sir, it's all a bit complicated. You're right. The Dark Web is one scary place. I had to disguise my IP address and my identity just to even browse there, but eventually I felt safe enough to initiate a search." She waved her hands in front of her making vague diagrams in the air. "You know how when you're searching for something on the net, you throw in a few connected words or phrases and all sorts of stuff comes up? You might get a sentence on a page from a book with a couple of the words you have been searching for highlighted in it, or an advert, or a page from a blog. It could be anything."

She backed towards the office door, urging Sheehan to follow. "Come on, sir. You need to see this." Sheehan was now on his feet, interest piqued, as he followed her to her desk. "I was getting nowhere for a while," Stewart went on, rushing in front of him to pull her chair out from her desk, "but I put 'judge', 'murder', and 'truncheon' together in the search box, and what came up has taken my breath away."

She ushered Sheehan into her chair and leaned forward to touch the keyboard of her laptop, scrolling back to the beginning of the post she had been reading. "It's a blog, sir. Read it." She stood back, watching the chief as he read, her hands moving endlessly together in a washing motion.

As Sheehan read, his expression became bleak. Consumed by what he was reading, his eyes never left the screen, nor did he utter a sound. Stewart eventually sat on a chair at one of the nearby desks, waiting for her superior to finish. Sheehan's ability to focus on an issue to the exclusion of everything around him rendered him unaware of the signs of strained impatience exhibited by his sergeant until he was finished studying the strange blogs.

After a prolonged period of scrutiny, Sheehan finally said, still studying the screen, "Good grief! This guy's deranged." He looked at Stewart, almost stunned. "You've found our killer, Stewart."

"Not on the Dark Net, sir," she said. "Just his blog. There's no way I could trace his IP address from here."

Sheehan was blowing heavily from both cheeks, clearly distracted. "This is huge, Stewart. Copy it out to the team's smartphones immediately. They all need to see this stuff. Message them to get up to speed with it during lunch and to get in here for a debrief at two o'clock Get me a print of the blogs as well. I need to study them." He stared back at the screen and shook his head. "The guy is clearly a mental case but, jeez, he's seriously well-read and intelligent. My God! There is so much stuff here. I've never seen anything like it."

"Me, neither, sir. It's strange, terrible. I don't know what to make of it. To tell the truth, I have trouble understanding the half of it." She pointed to the screen. "But you can see there's been a third murder, Chief. I take nothing has been reported in?"

"No," he said, staring at nothing across the room as his brain worked at speed.

"Saturday evening according to the date," Stewart said. "Monday morning and some poor individual is lying dead in his bedroom. If he lives alone, and the indications are that he does, it could be ages before we find the body." She stared at her superior, daunted. "Where can we even start, Chief? How many drinking establishments in the city have snugs and cocktail bars?"

Sheehan shook his head. "Somebody is not going to turn up for work this morning and he won't have phoned in. Hopefully one of his colleagues will be concerned enough to try to contact him. That might lead to the body's discovery."

"That could take a while, sir."

Even as she was speaking, the phone in Sheehan's office rang. He almost ran to answer it, casting a questioning glance at his sergeant. Grabbing the phone, he said sharply, "Sheehan."

"Boss." It was Miller, and he sounded excited. "We weren't able to get hold of Michael Stevens on Friday afternoon, so we tried again this morning. The caretaker of the apartment block he lives in said that he hadn't seen him all weekend, and that he found that unusual and worrying. So we got him to open the door to the apartment. You'll never guess what we found there, Chief."

Sheehan paused a beat before saying neutrally, "You didn't happen to find a naked man in a room full of sexual paraphernalia lying in bed on his stomach, head bashed in, and a police truncheon rammed up his backside?"

There was a blank silence at the other end of the phone. Then a whispered, "What the f—?" followed by an astounded, "How in the name of— How did you know, sir?"

"Miller, I'm the chief," Sheehan explained patiently. "It's my job to know these things." He grinned over at Stewart who was standing in the office doorway, listening. "Is Doctor Campbell there?"

There was some background noise on the phone, then Miller came back on. "He's just arrived, Chief."

"Okay, hang about a wee while and see what you can glean from him. If you get a chat with him, suggest that the time of death might have occurred between ten p.m. and one a.m. on Saturday night. Don't tell him how you know." He winked over at Stewart as he added, "That'll keep him up all night."

"Just that, sir?"

"Just that. And try to look intelligent when you tell him. More importantly, the two of you will be receiving an email from Stewart in a few minutes. It's a shocker. Read the stuff during lunch. Chat with Connors about it and get in here for a debrief at two o'clock."

He replaced the phone and turned to Stewart. "No need for us to go traipsing over there. We already have a full and detailed description of the killing. But we'll pay Dick a visit at the mortuary after the debrief. Okay. Get those emails out and bring me that print-out."

"What about lunch, sir?"

"Oh, crap! I don't have time." He rooted around in his hip pocket and pulled out his wallet. "After you send out that stuff, is there any chance you could get us a couple of sandwiches and some coffee from the canteen?" he asked her, with a disarming grimace. "I'll pay," he added, handing her a ten-pound note.

Stewart smiled, not in the least offended. "Done, Chief. Always up for a free lunch."

TWENTY-TWO
Monday, 20th August. Afternoon

McCullough was looking even more baffled than usual. Even before the team had settled down for the debrief, he said directly to Stewart, "What was that stuff you sent on my phone. I couldn't make head or tail of it."

"Did you read it all?" Stewart asked.

"I know they're blogs, but I couldn't get past the first dozen or so lines of any of them."

"The good stuff comes at the end of each of them, Sarge," Miller said. "Stewart found them on the Dark Web."

"The Dark what?"

"I'm with the Sarge on this one," Connors said. "I know we had to read this stuff for the debrief but it was away over my head too. And what are you talking about, Dark Web?"

"One dangerous place," McBride interjected. "You're better well away from it."

"Well away from what?" Connors growled, his patience already wearing thin.

McBride glanced at Sheehan for permission to speak. Sheehan shrugged.

"Okay," McBride said. "You know about Google on the Internet?"

"Of course," Connors said. "Everybody searches for stuff on there."

"Huge source of information, right?"

"Absolutely." Connors was on firmer ground now.

"Well, Google's network is only a fraction the size of a much darker, much deeper, much more sinister network that not only supplies all sorts of off-the-wall information, but provides all sorts of criminal services, support, access to just about anything a depraved appetite can seek. It's a terrible place."

"How come I never h-h-heard of it either?" McNeill asked.

"It's not somewhere ordinary people would go," McBride said. "For a start, you need to know how to protect your anonymity, and you need to know how to access special search engines such as the TOR Hidden Service Protocol."

"Now what are you going on about?" Connors growled. "You've lost me again."

"The Dark Web is becoming better known now," Stewart joined in. "Many people have heard of it, but its users are generally shady or criminal types. Some people who are very familiar with computers can try to browse there, but unless you are very sure about what you're doing and know how to stay anonymous on it, you just don't go near it." She glanced over at McBride. "You seem to know a bit about it, Malachy. How come?"

McBride blew air from puffed cheeks. "One experience, Sergeant. That was all I needed to have me running for the hills."

"Do tell, boyo," Miller said.

"Well, a guy on my course was telling me about it. I couldn't believe what he was saying. I said I was going to have a look, but he told me I could only do so by using a deep web browser like Tor. I made him show me how to use it so that I could browse anonymously. He did warn me to be careful, but he didn't warn me about hitting random buttons. There I was at home one evening, trying to sneak on to the hidden wifi via Tor, doing random searches to see what might come up. What happened next scared the ever-loving shit out of me." He glanced apologetically at Sheehan. "Uh, excuse me, sir. I was waiting for this webpage to load, it was taking a long time, much longer that the normal net. Anyway, when it finally loaded, giant black capital letters leapt up on my screen. They said, 'YOU BETTER START RUNNING.' Needless to say, I almost shit my pants. I couldn't get the machine switched off quickly enough, and I have to say I was in a panic most of the night. I didn't dare go back since."

"Sensible," Sheehan said laconically. "Okay, enough about the Dark Web. It's a place where paedophiles can get access to children, addicts to drugs, people looking for hitmen, swingers looking for depraved sex. It's all the bad stuff you can think of."

"Yes," Stewart agreed, "and I think it'll become more and more the haunt of those awful trolls who post hate messages on social media, abuse videos, extreme pornography. The ordinary people have now started to react angrily to that sort of stuff and, with the authorities stepping in, the trolls are not getting away with it the way they used to. The Dark Web is probably their next step."

"It's also a place where murderers can boast about their killings," Sheehan added, "and that's what we're here to talk about. If you want to know more about the Dark Net, Stewart can fill you in later." He waved a hand at Miller. "But there's a couple of other things we need to get out of the way. This Dark Web stuff is not today's only bombshell. Detective, the floor's yours."

Miller nodded and said succinctly, "Connors and I have been trying for a couple of days to interrogate Stevens but couldn't get him in. After we had been back and forth a few times, even the concierge got worried and he let us into the apartment this morning. And there was our man, naked, face down on this huge bed, sex toys all over the place, back of the skull bashed in, and a police truncheon rammed up his wazoo."

There were some sharp intakes of breath, followed by a moment of shocked silence, before Allen said, "Holy crap! This guy isn't going to stop, is he?"

"That's who the third b-b-blog was about, wasn't it?" McNeill guessed.

"Oh, aye! On that, Chief...." Miller said, with an arch look at Sheehan.

Sheehan gave him a grin and a dismissive wave.

"There you go," McCullough said. "Another direct link to the group." He pointed at the pages on his desk. "If this is the connection between the victims, the teacher has to fit in somewhere. We're going to have to look into him again."

"This is messing with motive again," Miller said. "This whole stuff about the judge being blackmailed seems less and less relevant."

"Unless the other victims had some involvement in whatever the blackmailer had on the judge," Sheehan said.

"We're still not hearing much about the blackmailer," Connors said. "He seems to have disappeared off the map."

"Blackmailers are cowards. They work in the shadows," Sheehan said. "When the judge was murdered, he probably cowered down somewhere, scared out of his skull in case we find out who he is and accuse him of the murder."

"Or maybe the other victims knew about whatever the judge was involved in and the blackmailer bumped them off, too, to make sure that nothing gets pointed towards him," McCullough offered.

"Bit of a stretch," Miller said. "That doesn't account for the obsessive nature of the killer's MO. I mean, the truncheons? The skull bashing? The nakedness? All of that's gotta be significant in some way."

"Three k-k-killings, same MO," McNeill said. "M-m-makes you wonder about those criminals D-D-Doran gave us. Might have been reasonable suspects for the judge's m-m-murder if that had been the only one, but things are moving f-f-further away now."

"I think you're right, Geoff," Sheehan said. "These murders are well planned. The suspects Stewart and I talked to couldn't have done them. Delaney is very ill and housebound, and Kahangi is just a thick, muscle-bound idiot. I'm ruling out both of them."

"Yes, Khan's the same," Miller agreed. "Nasty, vicious bully, but clearly knew nothing about the judge's murder." He eyed the room. "But I tell you what. He was acting guilty as hell. I'll bet anything he's back at his human trafficking again. As soon as we left his house, I phoned Superintendent Murray of the Specialist Investigation Unit. Gave him a heads up. Hopefully Khan'll be off the street in a couple of days and a few more innocent wee girls will be saved. But as a far as the judge's murder is concerned, no way he's a genuine suspect."

Allen was nodding. "We also spoke to McKernan. Apart from the fact that he has pretty much forgotten all about the kid that was jailed, and that his threats to the judge were just empty bombast, he was partying at his girlfriend's house at the time of the judge's murder. There were several others there. It was the girl's birthday. We checked it out, Chief. His alibi's solid. Loads of people saw him there. And, just like Miller with Khan, I can see no possible connection between McKernan and the other two victims. He's out too, sir."

Sheehan looked at his notes and raised his eyes at McCullough. "Mac?"

McCullough spread his hands. "Malachy and I were just talking about this earlier today, as a matter of fact, Chief. Small, as you know, is still in jail, but we went to see this friend, Hosford, who was supposed to carry out the threat. He never could've done it. He's a cowardly weasel. Blustered at us but scared of us at the same time. Nasty piece of work, but he was drinking in a late-night pub that Sunday evening. No way he's involved in the judge's killing."

"His alibi's sound?"

"Yes, we checked," McBride said. "Several witnesses saw him there. Actually, he's not even visited his mate in jail. I'd say he never had any intention of supporting Small's empty threats."

"All right." Sheehan looked at his notes again. "Oh, there's one more. McStravick."

Miller raised a forefinger. "That's us again, Chief," he said. "He's not long released from prison and hasn't yet got himself somewhere to live. His probation officer, uh, Gerald Gribben, said he was staying with his brother and gave us the address. But when we spoke to the brother, he told us he couldn't put up with that gorilla at his place any longer. Apparently, McStravick started acting like the house and everything in it was his, so the brother threw him out. Says he doesn't know where he went after that and doesn't care. We got back to Gribben, but he doesn't know where McStravick is either. He was mad as hell. McStravick was supposed to notify him if he changed his address. Gribben says if the bastard doesn't turn up for his next meeting, he's going to have his ass tossed back into prison. He's promised to notify us when he sees him. Supposed to be the day after tomorrow." At this point, Miller shrugged and spread his hands. "But judging from what's being said here now, it seems hardly worthwhile pursuing the so-and-so."

"I've no doubt you're right," Sheehan agreed. "But just to be thorough, have a wee chat with him anyway." He reached out and pulled the prints of the Nemein blogs towards him. "Okay. You've read these blogs. What does anybody think?"

Allen was first to speak. He held his smartphone up and said to Stewart, "So, where did you get this stuff?" His voice and his expression contained more than a hint of accusation.

"Just an idea I got when the word 'dark' was used to describe Permanent Secretary Kane. We had heard about his secret vices and I wondered if I could find something about him there."

"You were taking a hellava of a risk," Allen said, trying to keep his voice normal, but there was anger there.

"I knew exactly what I was doing," Stewart responded, trying to sound calm, but the rosy spots on her cheeks indicated she was not pleased with Allen's over-protectiveness. "I hid my IP address using a VPN connection with a proxy server and made sure I was browsing via TOR."

"Stewart's excellent work has gotten us a massive step forward," Sheehan said, interrupting this by-play. "We need to examine this stuff and see what we can learn from it."

"I've had a couple of reads through it, Chief," Miller said. "My immediate reaction is that the guy might be brilliant but he's a feckin' nutcase."

"Is it a guy?" McBride asked.

"What do you mean?" Miller said.

"Well, I thought it was a guy, too, when I was reading the first two blogs, but all through the third, I thought it was a woman. So I went back through the first two and couldn't find a male gender pronoun relating to the blogger anywhere."

Connors was studying his sheets, brow furrowed. "We ruled out the females," he said. "Maybe that was a mistake."

"We ruled them out because we didn't think they would be capable of murder," Stewart said.

"Maybe that was a mistake, too," McBride said diffidently. "I read a book a while back about woman serial killers. Some of them were worse that the worst men."

"Like who?" Connors asked

"Well, some I remember were Aileen Wournos, Nannie Doss, Amelia Dyer. Tillie Klimek."

"Never heard of any of them," Connors said dismissively.

"Check them out on the net. You've heard of Lizzie Borden?

"The one with the axe? Is that not just a nursery rhyme?"

"Oh no. She was real, very real." He glanced apologetically at Stewart. "Women can be as vicious and as merciless as any man."

"On that point," Sheehan said, "there was something in the first blog that caught my attention?"

The others turned to hear what he had to say.

"If you look at how he described the blow, he says, or she says, *'I draw back, with bent arm, behind and below my right shoulder and, turning my body with ineffable grace, my arm stretches and extends upwards as The Club smashes, with a gratifying crunch of bone, against the side of the miscreant's head'.*" He looked up. "There's a couple of things there. First, the judge is not quite six feet in height, yet the killer had to strike upwards. I think our killer is below average height. Who fits that profile?"

"The two women, certainly," McBride said.

"Judge Adams is small," Stewart offered. "And so is Permanent Secretary Kane. If he's five six, that's about the height of it." She finished with a slight giggle, suddenly aware of her unintended pun. "And this last blog, it could be an account of a girl/boy thing as Malachy suggests, but it could also be an account of a gay meeting, and we know Adams is gay and Kane swings both ways."

"So now we have four suspects from the group," Allen said. "What else can we deduce from these blogs?"

Sheehan said, "We've hardly had time to look at them, of course, but another little throwaway line in the third blog has me puzzled." Fingers enlarged phone screens as the detectives searched for the blog referred to. "Almost immediately after all that bullshit about justification," Sheehan went on, "he starts to talk about his victim whom we now know was Stevens. It's the bit where he says, *'I could not have been certain, I could only have hoped, that on this night he would have eschewed the frenetic delights of his more extreme haunts for the emptiness of a lonely drink. But here he was'.* Two things. One, the perp obviously knew a fair bit about Stevens' comings and goings but wasn't sure if he'd come to his usual drinking hole because he sometimes went to the more '...frenetic haunts'. The question is, what exactly does that imply, and is there any way we could find out where or what these haunts are?"

There was silence in the room with some despondent shaking of heads.

"This is why we need to know what's in that bloody safe," McBride said, his frustration evident. "I bet it has loads of info about all of these people."

McNeill poked at his phone. "Strange way of expressing h-h-himself," he said. "Bit like the b-b-books I studied for O-levels. Can we d-d-deduce anything from that?"

"Bloody nutcase," Connors snarled.

Stewart chuckled. "Yes, it's almost a bit Gothic in style, I think. Certainly it's closer to nineteenth century writing than twenty-first century. The guy must have been big into Jane Austen, R.L. Stevenson, the Brontës, H.G. Wells, and loads of others. My guess is he's trying to reproduce that style, for whatever reason, and that's why he sounds generally weird to modern ears."

Miller laughed. "Will you listen to her. Where's all this coming from?"

"I loved Advanced Level Literature at school," Stewart replied, smiling. "I probably read a whole lot of the books our killer has read."

"Well, he sure likes to use loads of five-dollar words where five-cent words would do just as well," Miller said.

"And bloody fifty-dollar ideas. I can't follow them at all," Connors growled.

"The writing definitely has a strangely weird obsession with self," Sheehan said, "but it's quite clever. Not just anybody could express themselves the way this blogger does, even if he does go over the top. He's clever and well educated. And you're right, it does have a somewhat classical feel, a bit like those old novels by the likes of Edgar Allan Poe, Anthony Trollope, maybe even Bram Stoker. Definitely not modern in style."

Connors raised his eyes to the ceiling. "Now he's at it."

"Our four suspects are well educated and, doubtless well-read," McBride said. "I know the professor could easily write at this level."

"And Jaclyn Kennedy has at least two degrees," Miller said. "We discovered that when we went to interrogate her. So this quality of writing wouldn't be beyond her."

"It would be no problem for Adams or Kane either," Stewart added.

"You said there were a couple of things, Chief?" Miller prodded. "What was the other one?"

"Yes, the word *'miscreant'.*"

They all looked at it.

"What about it, sir?" McBride asked.

"Well, it seems to imply that the judge has done something very wrong, at least in this blogger's eyes. That's where all that justification stuff is coming from. Each of the murders was a punishment." He shrugged. "But a punishment for what?"

"You're right. Chief," Stewart said. "I've been through all the blogs a couple of times. The whole tenor of them is about revenge and justice. Obviously all three victims have done something to set him, or her, off."

"I can see why Dark Web browsers would love all the juicy details of the killings," McBride said, "but what is all this philosophical justification and introspection at the start of each blog?"

"He's a killer, isn't he?" Miller said, a slight grin at the edge of his lips. "Probably thinks he needs a killer blog."

Stewart glanced over at him and said, her voice sounding as if she had just eaten something sour, "Simon, that's terrible."

Miller, grinning widely now, shrugged. "Just a wee smidgin of gallows humour."

"He obviously doesn't see himself as a killer," Sheehan said, ignoring both of them. "He or she ... aw, feck it, I'm just going to say 'he' from now on. He's under the impression he's some sort of avenging angel who's carrying out some sort of retribution. Even his cognomen, Nemein, is a Greek word that means 'to give what is due'." He caught their bemused stares. "What? You think I can't do a Google search?" he said, adding, "Matter of fact, I was able to figure out the Latin stuff and the other weird headings, as well."

"Yes, what about those?" Allen said. "I can see Latin there but what are those bold headings? They look like Swahili or something."

"It took me a while to figure it out, but I was fiddling about with letters in a Google search and discovered that the bold blog titles are simply English words written in Greek letters. I suppose he or she is trying to beef up the impression of scholarship. All that the fancy titles really say, however, is *Nemein's Blog.* The word underneath the title in the first blog, is *Justice*. In the second blog, the word under the title is *Vengeance*, and the third sub-heading is *Justification*."

"I told you he was a nut," Connors growled. "Why does he need to write all that rubbish?"

"Well, it's obvious he loves the whole intellectual classical thing. He's revelling in it. Probably never had a chance to express himself like this before and he's indulging himself to the full. Looks like he is seeking admiration, as well, seems to need it, in fact." He moved his right hand slightly to add emphasis to his next point. "But there is a more pressing motive for the philosophy, I believe. I think he feels instinctively that murder as an act is wrong, and he's turning himself inside out to justify what he says he has to do. He seems to think that if he can do the deed and keep his emotions detached from what he's doing, then he's simply an instrument of justice and not a murderer."

"Sounds more like f-f-female thinking than m-m-male thinking," McNeill mused.

Stewart glanced up at him but didn't speak.

Miller said, "Well, whatever kind of thinking it is, and whoever it is, he has a definite motive for killing these people. It's obvious that something happened somewhere, and the guy is bumping off these people because they were somehow involved in it."

"Whatever it is," Connors said, "to me he still sounds like a bloody lunatic."

"Miller's right," Sheehan said. "He's not just picking random victims. There's method in his madness. We really need to find out what the connection is between the victims."

"So what exactly are those Latin quotes at the top of the blogs?" Allen asked.

"Just part of the image he wants to create," Sheehan said. "The more scholarly he can seem to be, the more likely his many followers, as he calls them, are to accept his arguments. The first one, *Alterius non sit qui suus esse potest,* means 'Let no man be another's who can be his own'."

"Bloody hell," McCullough said. "That makes no more sense than the Latin does."

"He's probably saying that a person should not be a slave to anyone else's thinking. That's part of his self- justification."

"What about the other one?" Allen pressed.

"Amicus Plato, sed magis amica veritas," Sheehan quoted. It means *'Plato is my friend, but truth is a better friend.'* I think he's saying that Plato is a great philosopher and people would benefit from reading him, but that truth is more important. It's probably a cry to his readers to believe the 'truth' that he is trying to convey in these philosophical blogs."

"Do you think anybody actually reads them?" McBride asked.

Sheehan shrugged. "They have their own morbid fascination, especially the descriptions of the murders."

"He certainly has some f-f-following," McNeill said, "and they s-s-sound as insane as he is. Look at those ones after the third b-b-blog— *'Bring me with you n-n-next time, Nemein. I've got a seriously m-m-mean right arm'.*"

"Yeah, and this one," Allen added. *"'Crush their skulls? Call on me, Nemein, and I'll knock the heads right off their shoulders for you'.* Who are these people?"

"What do you make of all of this, Chief?" Stewart asked.

Sheehan shook his head. "It would take a psychologist to explain it." He looked at his watch. "In fact, I've emailed copies of the blogs to Professor Nigel Greenwald. You remember him. He's a professor of Psychology at Queen's University and he's helped us out a couple of times before. I told him to phone as soon as he's had a look at them."

"Well, it's obvious that there are all sorts of psychological issues here," Miller said. "The killer is clearly letting it be known that he's highly intelligent, that he's educated to at least third level, and that he enjoys philosophical analysis. I suppose it's what you said, Chief. He probably thinks that the whole professorial image thing will make people accept that his arguments make sense."

"But they don't," McBride sad. "I need to study them some more, but I can see where parts of them are full of spurious logic and sophistry. He wants to explain that he has no choice but to carry out these killings, that justice demands he act in the way he does. He argues that so long as he remains detached from what he's doing, he's not guilty of any crime." He indicated the screen of his phone with his right hand. "But in the second half of each blog he is no more detached from the killings than ... than Lizzie Borden was detached from her hatchet."

"That's true," Sheehan agreed. "He is right in there, living and reliving every violent and murderous second, with an almost orgiastic pleasure. And he can't see that. To quote our resident expert, Detective Connors, 'he's a bloody nutcase' ... or she."

Connors leaned back in his chair and put his hands over his face, chuckling.

"Keep reading these things," Sheehan said. "All that self-analysis, there might be other clues to the person's identity, or at least enough to come up with a comprehensive profile."

"Leaving the actual c-c-content aside for a m-m-minute," McNeill said, "could we not track the p-p-person who is writing this by trying to f-f-find his IP address, or whatever you call it?"

"No, it's impossible," Stewart replied. "Identities and locations of Dark Web users stay anonymous and can't be tracked due to what's called 'the layered encryption system'. The Dark Web encryption technology routes users' data through a large number of intermediate servers. That protects the browser's identity and guarantees anonymity. And because the encryption is at a very high level, websites are not able to track the location and IP addresses of their users, and, on the other side of the coin, the users are not able to get any information about the host."

"That makes a kind of sense," Miller said, "or would for people with something to hide, or who have seriously kinky interests."

"Yes," Stewart replied, "the whole point of all these encryption layers is to ensure that Dark Web users who want to talk or blog or share files can always be sure that what they share is kept confidential. And so our perp happily talks about his murders and his inner thoughts about them. He knows he's safe. Nothing anyone does in the Deep Web can be monitored, and for that reason it's becoming a very attractive option for certain types of Internet users, or for those know about it, at least." She shrugged and spread her hands. "So, whatever way we might manage to track our perp down, it won't be through finding his, or her, IP address on the Dark Web."

"Thanks for that, S-S-Sergeant," McNeill said, with a baffled grin. "I think."

At that point the phone on Sheehan's desk rang. He answered it immediately and after listening for a second, said, "Ah, Nigel. Good of you to get back to us so soon."

There were some faint mutterings in reply as the team craned forward, trying to hear.

"Oh, hold on a minute," Sheehan said, and reaching forward pressed a button on the phone. "You're on speaker now, Professor, and the team is listening with all ears. Saves me the bother of having to go over all of this stuff with them at a later date."

The Professor's voice boomed out loud and clear from the speaker. "Assuming you would be able to repeat it, Jim." The team could easily detect the smile in the Professor's voice.

"Aye, right," Sheehan chuckled. "Go on ahead, Nigel."

"Well, you have to remember that I had barely an hour to consider this material."

"I know. I know. Just a brief analysis."

"The subject is complex. I really should take more time to study it."

"I understand, Nigel, but we need this right away."

The professor sighed. "Everybody wants the condensed version these days. Whatever happened to analytical enquiry?"

"We're trying to stop a madman from killing again, Nigel, and we're seriously pushed for time," Sheehan said. "Anything you can give us now will be really helpful."

"All right! All right!" Another deep sigh. "You've heard of a narcissistic personality disorder, I presume."

Sheehan caught the look of bafflement that crossed McCullough's face. "One or two members of the team would like a little clarification on that."

"Okay. Narcissists are characterized by a pervasive pattern of grandiosity either in fantasy or in behaviour—"

"Gee, God, Nigel! Hold on a second. Can you tone that down a bit?"

"Okay. Okay. Goodness! Anyway, it's an antisocial personality disorder and the narcissist is characterised by a huge sense of self-importance, an excessive need for admiration, the sense that he or she is special and unique. On top of that, he has a complete lack of empathy, and tends to demonstrate arrogant or haughty attitudes."

"What about violent tendencies?" Sheehan asked.

"Well, the thing with identifying disorders is that while they have recognised general tendencies, these can be found in individuals to varying degrees. That said, narcissists do not necessarily exhibit violent tendencies."

"But our guy does, in spades," Sheehan argued. "So why are we talking about narcissists?"

"And that's the interesting point about this case," Greenwald replied. "Your killer is also a psychopath or sociopath." The Professor hesitated. "There's been some to-ing and fro-ing about the use of the terms sociopath and psychopath since the1930s ... ah, we'll not go into that. We'll stick with psychopath. The point is that while psychopaths can usually fit the profile of a narcissist, narcissists are not necessarily psychopaths."

Miller stepped up to Sheehan's desk and spoke into the speaker. "Detective Miller here, Professor. Our guy is definitely violent and some of us think he's a dangerous nut-case, uh, excuse the less than scientific language. Would you agree that he is a dangerous psychopath?"

"Of course," Greenwald responded. "Just to clarify. Psychopaths manifest extreme antisocial attitudes. They are aggressive, perverted, and they can exhibit amoral behaviour without remorse. Not all are criminal, but many are. They possess a complete disregard for the feelings and needs of other people, absolutely no empathy, and a total lack of conscience."

"Sounds like our man," Sheehan said.

"Yes. They're also often highly intelligent and skilled at manipulating others. They think they're above the law. Rules simply don't apply to them. As a result, their behaviour can be reckless. They don't think they're like normal people. They feel invincible, or even immortal. So they think they can get away with doing anything they chose to do."

"You're pretty much describing the guy who's writing those blogs," Sheehan said.

"Maybe so," Greenwald replied, "but so far, all I've been giving you are textbook traits. Individuals will demonstrate these to varying degrees and levels, but not all will be exactly the same. To be definitive, I would need time with this person."

"Not gonna happen, Nigel. You know that. We don't even know who he is. Can you just go with your gut for once and forget about scientific accuracy?"

The heavy sigh again emerged from the speaker. "Okay! Don't hold me to this, and don't quote me in a courtroom. Your killer comes across to me as a narcissistic psychopath. His blogs reveal a hugely inflated self-image, and he's clearly on the borderline of uncontrolled psychosis. The self-glorying blogs are calculated to paint a picture of himself as a unique and a superior being dealing with complex issues with the controlled dispassion and inevitability of Nemesis."

Sheehan caught Connors' frustrated glance at McNeill. "You're going back into the stratosphere again, Nigel," he said. "You're losing some of my team."

"Sorry," Greenwald said, sounding anything but. "Have to say that I am surprised he has retained control over his MO across the three killings. Three single blows? I'm sure his natural instinct would have been to engage in a great deal more violence. The story he's acting out in these scenarios seems to help his control, but I don't know how much longer he can rein his violence in."

"Hello, Professor. Sergeant Stewart here," Stewart called across to the speaker. "He sounds very controlled in his blogs. I can't see any indication that he might lose it."

"Good afternoon, Sergeant," Greenwald purred. "Nice to hear your voice. Yes, your killer likes to portray himself as the voice of reason but, remember, he's utterly lacking in empathy. In his own distorted mind, he's a heroic crusader, an avenging angel who has to tolerate doing bad things to achieve a good outcome. I would guess, since he says he's seeking vengeance for some evil visited upon someone who meant something to him, that he's replicating in some way the manner of death of the victim he's avenging. But he's living a delusion and it wouldn't take much to set him off on an orgy of violence. Believe me, this so-called control is fragile. Like all psychopaths, he's a deeply disturbed personality. That said, he's very clever and I would guess that he's living a respectable life somewhere. The really smart ones can shut down their fantasies and delusions, and not allow them to cross over into their normal existence."

"You're saying our killer in his normal life just comes across as an ordinary Joe?" Miller sounded annoyed.

"Yep! My guess is that he can compartmentalise the different versions of his life, living each one independently of the other. He will have established an identity of sorts, wherever he works. He might generally be seen as arrogant, maybe self-important and disdainful, or maybe at the other end of the spectrum, introverted, or cold and inscrutable. Whatever it is, he'll keep it consistent. But he'll be compulsively orderly, a good worker, and unlikely to be overly friendly with colleagues. Nonetheless, he's someone who has an excessive regard for his own feelings. He's also very, very dangerous if he thinks he's been crossed or if he perceives some kind of slight, real or imagined. He won't forget and won't rest until he has achieved payback."

"You keep referring to our killer as 'he', Professor," McBride called. "Oh, Detective McBride speaking."

"Hello, Detective. And your question?"

"Some of us are not fully convinced that the killer is male. There are some indications that it might be a woman. Is that likely?"

"The third blog? Yes, interesting question. I'm sorry if I've misled you. I was using the single male pronoun for handiness. Yes, everything I've said could apply equally to a female killer."

"We don't hear so much about female psychopaths, Professor," Stewart said. "Why is that?"

"That's true," Greenwald replied. "Research indicates there are likely to be fewer female psychopaths than male, but I'm not so sure about that. Women are so much better than men at hiding their true nature. I believe that current statistics are probably an underestimation of the percentage of female psychopaths in our society."

"And would they be as violent?" Stewart asked.

"Well, as I said, Sergeant, not all psychopaths are violent. But some are, and violent female psychopaths can be just as dangerous as their male counterparts."

"I'm a bit puzzled by our killer, Nigel," Sheehan said. "You say he lacks empathy and normal human feelings, yet our blogger seems to have had strong feelings for whoever it is he is avenging. Could psychopaths ever really fall in love?"

"Excellent point, Jim. And you are right. Psychopaths lack normal human emotions. But I was reading some new research recently that discusses that very point. Yes, emotional detachment and lack of empathy are two key indicators of psychopathic personality disorder, but some do form relationships. Such a relationship, however, may not be based on psychological intimacy in the traditional sense of the word. Instead, a couple may enter into a relationship based on a shared sort of view of the world in which both try to get as much out of other people as possible. Or, and research would seem to bear this out, sometimes the healthier of the two partners, who may not even be a psychopath, will strive to make a relationship work and can influence the other. Over time, they might form an intimate bond that allows both to become more trusting, sharing, and able to see things from the partner's point of view. Not love as we know it, for sure, but a definite attachment."

"Following the Chief's point," Stewart said, "about psychopaths being incapable of normal feelings. I might be wrong, but from the tone of these blogs it appears to me that our psychopath is wrestling with some form of guilt. He is constantly seeking to excuse his actions. Is there not some kind of a contradiction there?"

Greenwald chuckled. "I always said you were sharp, Sergeant. Your blogger definitely wants to give the impression that he is wrestling with guilt. But be assured, he isn't. Yes, I agree that this business of justification that seems to permeate all the blogs would seem to imply a streak of empathy which, of course, would be inconsistent with a diagnosis of psychopathy. The only explanation I can give for that is that your killer, judging from the style of his writing and the vocabulary he uses, has been a reader all his life, particularly of the classics where morality invariably prevails. He has somehow ingested this literary sense of morality as an abstract kind of awareness, but in him it's ... ah ... just data being uploaded on to a computer."

"Okay, so why bother to pretend?"

"Psychopaths are very manipulative, and he believes that by analysing, questioning, and finding justification for his behaviours, he is providing his readers with what he considers the image of him as a hero. He works very hard at this but there is still something of the charade in it. On one level he strives to give meaning to what he is saying, but on another he knows that most of his readers are perverts and voyeurs. He aims to impress them with this faux-moral stance on the one hand, and the gruesome details of his killings on the other. It's a weird mix. It would never work in ordinary society. But he has won a huge following as you can see from the myriad comments after each blog, and that is vital for him. Approval is huge for narcissistic psychopaths."

"So all this serious philosophising is all bluff."

"Not quite bluff. It's a scenario he is acting out in his head, and to a degree his delusions buy into it. But it also serves to show how clever he is, of course, and there is adulation to be acquired from that. So that would make all the complex analyses he offers his readers worthwhile for him. But regarding feelings of guilt, he cares not one jot about why he is doing what he's doing. He does it because he wants to."

"We might well have him, or her, on our radar," Sheehan said. "What should we be looking for in our interrogations of suspects?"

"Not sure, Jim. As I said earlier, psychopaths can seem to appear normal. You would probably never guess there was anything wrong with them. So, if you've already interrogated your killer, you probably would not have recognised him, or her, for what he or she is, unless…." He paused, seemingly unsure about whether to proceed.

"Unless what, Professor?" Sheehan urged.

"Well, this might not be the right advice to give unless you're very sure of what you're doing, but sometimes you can sense the difference between normal human warmth and cold lack of feeling. I mean, your killer will be able to act as if he cares about normal aspects of life and living, but to the trained eye, he'll be a little bit off. The problem is that most psychopaths are, as I said, extremely clever, and they have superb skills in knowing what signals they're supposed to give off when being interrogated. They're great actors. They can appear disgusted, perturbed, upset, etcetera, but it's all just an act. If you hit a nerve, you just might get a wee reaction, but you'll need to be quick to spot it. You'll just have to follow your instincts on that one, Jim."

An image of a flash of venom in two hostile eyes surged briefly through Sheehan's brain as he looked around the room to see if anyone else had a question. There were no takers. "All right, Nigel. Thanks for that. You've given us a lot to think about. Obviously, you'll get back to me if anything else occurs to you?"

"Of course, Jim. Glad to help. 'Bye!"

TWENTY-THREE
Monday, 20th August. Late afternoon

Sheehan and Stewart stared at the half-covered corpse of Michael Stevens, feeling faintly repulsed, as always, as they watched Doctor Campbell examine the cadaver's facial features from a distance of two inches, watched him smell the open cavity that was the cadaver's mouth, watched him examine the arms, the hands, the fingernails, all the while muttering incomprehensibly. Sheehan was waiting for a judicious moment to interrupt, when suddenly the doctor stopped still and said, "Well, this is a surprise."

Immediately alert, Sheehan said, "What's that, Dick?"

The doctor turned with a start. "Ah, Jim? You're here? And your delectable sergeant. Didn't hear you come in. Good afternoon to you both. And may I say, Denise, you're looking lovely as ever."

"Thank you, kind sir," Stewart said with a smile. "Your door was slightly open when we arrived, but you seemed intent on your examination, so we didn't want to interrupt."

"What did you see, Dick?" Sheehan repeated, unconcerned with niceties.

Campbell eyes crinkled as he turned again to Stewart. "I think perhaps you can convert your plural personal pronoun from 'we' to 'I', Sergeant."

He waved a hand at Sheehan. "This one undoubtedly does not share your qualms about interrupting my work."

Sheehan sighed and gave the pathologist his bleakest look.

Campbell raised his hands in defence. "All right! All right! Don't get excited. The actual find is not the cause of my surprise. In fact, I really don't know what to make of it. My surprise is occasioned by the fact that there is actually something there to find. Our perpetrator has to date been meticulously careful. I have not found a single item that might be called a clue since these murders began and, as I understand from Bill Larkin, neither have the SOCOs. So, this is definitely a surprise."

Sheehan's hands were held almost rigidly in front of him, ostensibly to express pleading, but it almost seemed as if he was threatening to strangle the pathologist. "For the third time, Dick, what have you found?"

At that point the door opened, and Doctor Jones came in wearing a white lab coat and carrying a manila file and some sheets of paper. "Good afternoon, Doctor Jones," Stewart said.

Jones, not one for casual talk, gave her a nod in return and said solemnly, "Good afternoon, Sergeant. Good afternoon, Chief Inspector." He continued walking across the mortuary, left his papers on a nearby desk, donned a white rubber apron, and was quickly absorbed in examination of the flaccid body of an elderly female.

Sheehan turned again to Campbell who had just lifted a small pair of tweezers from the tray beside him and, taking the corpse's right hand in his, he extracted a small strand of elastic rubber, perhaps a tenth of an inch in length, from under one of the fingernails. He held it up for the detectives to see.

"What is it?" Sheehan asked, staring at it.

"It's a tiny piece of white elastic."

"So, what do you make of it?"

"I've just told you. I don't know."

"There was a load of sex paraphernalia in that room. Anything spring to mind that might have stuff like this in it?"

The doctor burst out laughing. "What kind of life do you think I live, Jim? How would I have a clue about something like that?" He grinned at Stewart. "Sex toys, indeed."

"Could it have come from the killer, do you think?"

"I have to imagine that it did. He's got fairly long nails, this guy, well manicured. I suppose if there was any kind of struggle or activity, this could have caught on one of those nails. I'm sure it wasn't there while he was alive. He would definitely have noticed it and removed it." He stroked his chin and stared directly at the detective. "Or, the hand may have come into contact with an ambulance attendant or something while they were packing the corpse for removal and this snagged on the fingernail, wherever it came from."

"I'll have somebody's guts for garters if that proves to be the case," Sheehan growled. "Bag it for me, will you, Dick? Maybe forensics can find out what it is. Or maybe even harvest a speck of DNA from it."

Campbell's mouth went down. "Mmmm!"

"Mmmm what?"

He shrugged. "They might, but it won't be easy." He walked over to a shelf and placed the elastic in a small plastic evidence bag. "Here you go, Jim. Let me know what you find out about it. I'd be curious to know what it is."

"Thanks, Dick," Sheehan said, handing the bag to Stewart. He looked back down at the corpse. "So, what else can you tell us?"

"Well, one thing is different, I mean, apart from the fact that the killer carelessly overlooked that tiny item."

"Let me guess," Sheehan interjected. "Unlike the other two, this victim was drugged before he was killed, right?"

Campbell's head went back, and he stared quizzically at his friend. "Okay! I'll bite. How did you know?"

"Simple deduction," Sheehan replied.

Campbell's eyes narrowed suspiciously as his gaze moved from Sheehan to Stewart. "He's playing with me, right?"

Stewart said, straight-faced, "I really couldn't say, Doctor."

"Look, Dick," Sheehan explained casually. "Our killer's profile is telling us that he is a small, probably slight man, maybe even a woman. Our victim here is stocky, strong. If he was in the heat of a sexual encounter that night when he was murdered, our killer would never have been capable of physically overpowering him. The only way the perp could have carried out the killing the way he did was by drugging the victim at some point beforehand. So, there you go. Q.E.D."

Campbell looked far from convinced but he tossed his head and changed the subject. "I found some fibres on the judge's corpse."

Sheehan was immediately attentive. "Fibres?"

"Yep! Looks like they might have come from a camel-hair overcoat."

"Oh, very clever, Dick. You had me going there."

Campbell shrugged. "I did find fibres."

"Yes, and you saw the coat during your examination of the body at the murder scene."

"Yes. Actually, I meant to ask. What was the overcoat doing there?"

"The person who discovered the body, Edgar Doran, felt that he couldn't leave it lying exposed the way it was, and threw his overcoat on top of it. I gave him a bit of a rollicking for doing that. Think he cost us anything?"

"Not sure," he replied. Then he pointed again to an area of the victim's abdomen. "Okay, I was messin' with you about the fibres, but I did find a tiny hair on the judge's corpse. The judge's hair is white; this one is dark. So it isn't the judge's. It might have come from the killer, or it equally might have come from Edgar Doran when he was throwing the coat over the body."

Sheehan frowned thoughtfully. "Our killer wears some kind of protective clothing. He's leaving us nothing, so it's probably Doran's. Bag it anyway, and we'll get forensics to have a look at it." He looked at his watch. "Anything else?"

Campbell spread his hands. "Not sure of its relevance, but two of your victims, the judge and Stevens, were sexually very active, in all sorts of deviant ways, I would guess. The teacher, not so much."

Sheehan grimaced. "The teacher is kind of the odd man out in this trio. We've been trying to find ways to connect him to the other two. You've just made him even more of a disconnect."

Campbell grunted. "Oh, dear! That was careless of me. It has to be annoying when pesky facts get in the way of your famed deductive skills."

Sheehan tried to give him a hard stare but the twinkle in his eyes rendered the effort futile. "We'll let ourselves out, Dick. Let us know if anything else strikes you."

The pathologist bowed theatrically. "Good day to you, Jim, and good day to you, too, Sergeant Stewart."

TWENTY-FOUR
Monday, 20th August. Evening

Stewart was cooking dinner. A simple dish of brown beef stew was simmering in a pot on the hob. It was something Tom liked to eat with mashed potatoes, carrots, and HP sauce. From the tension revealed by her body language, and the way she was throwing cutlery on to the table, it was obvious that there was more than brown stew simmering in that kitchen. She looked up sharply when she heard Allen's key in the door, and her lips tightened.

Allen shouted from the front door, "I'm home." Then he appeared at the kitchen door and said with a smile, "Hi!"

She glared at him, refusing to respond to his greeting.

Allen's smile faded. "What?" he said, uncertainly.

"What?" she snapped. "What do you mean, what?"

"What's buggin' you?"

"I'll tell you what's buggin' me. You trying to disgrace me in front of the team today, that's what's buggin' me."

"Disgrace you?"

"Yes. And you think the chief didn't notice? He had to butt in and cut you off, for God's sake. The embarrassment of it!"

Allen was still a few steps behind. With a puzzled frown, he said, "Where does the embarrassment come in?"

"You started telling me off for doing my job. The chief was very pleased with what I'd done and what I'd found. But you? 'Big risk', you shouted." She threw a couple of napkins on the table as if somehow they had mortally offended her. "I'm a fully trained detective sergeant. I can do my job without somebody trying to make it look that I'm a silly little woman running myself into trouble."

Allen looked contrite. "Sorry. I wasn't thinking about it like that. I was just concerned."

"Do you get concerned when the chief or any of the others on the team go out and do their jobs?"

"I said I'm sorry. I was worried about you."

"Worry? What about respect? Do you think I'm not capable of doing my job? Do you think I'm too stupid to find my way around the Dark Web without getting caught? Do you think you have to dive to my rescue at the slightest wee thing?"

"Okay," Allen said, his tone reasonable, not allowing her anger to affect him. "Let me ask you a question. Do you think if I was in trouble that Geoff wouldn't be diving straight in to help me? Or if Geoff was in trouble, d'you think I wouldn't rush to help him? It's called having your partner's back."

"That's different. You don't belittle each other doing that."

"I wasn't trying to belittle you."

"You made it very clear that you thought I was too fragile or something. You were almost telling me not to take risks like that again. Is it the fact that I'm a woman, or do you just think I can't handle the job?"

Allen eyed her for a minute. "No, I don't think that," he said. "I think you are the most intelligent, most creative, most intuitive, most tech savvy, most well-trained, most courageous ... uh ... most beautiful cop in the PSNI. I don't doubt your skills even for a minute."

Stewart stared at him, suddenly off-guard.

Allen's face was expressionless. "And if your life is in danger any time in the future, I'll just go into a wee nearby shop, buy a packet of fags, and smoke in the car until you've got yourself sorted out."

She turned to serve some stew into a dish on the table. "Not funny," she said, but she was hiding a smile.

He stepped up behind her, put his arms around her and snuggled the back of her neck. "I'm sorry. I didn't mean it the way you think I did. I heard what everybody was saying about the Dark Web and I was just suddenly terrified that somebody awful would latch on to you from its depths and I wouldn't be able to help."

She resisted for a few minutes. Then she turned and put her arms around him, but her expression remained serious. "I'm a fully-fledged member of the team, Tom. I do what you do. Don't say things in front of the guys that make me look inferior."

"I really am sorry," he repeated. "It won't happen again. I promise." He kissed her on the nose. "Are we good?"

She grinned, despite herself, and punched Allen hard on the arm. "If my life ever is in danger, you better not be smoking in a parked car somewhere."

TWENTY-FIVE
Monday, 20th August. Evening

Another round of interviews with the judge's group had produced little information except to show that a number of them had passable alibis for the evening of Stevens' murder, although these still had to be checked out. Five of them had not—Judge Adams, Professor Gallagher, Oliver Kane, Jaclyn Kennedy, and Robert Bryant. Each had claimed to be at home that evening. Adams expressed considerable resentment that he should even have been an object of suspicion and could barely bring himself to say that he was at home. When asked if he could prove he was at home, Kane, in his cold, calculating way had answered flatly, 'Can you prove I wasn't?'

"Are you enjoying the movie, Jim?" Margaret asked, her expression innocent.

Sheehan started slightly, glancing at his wife in the armchair opposite him. "Uh, yeah, it's okay."

"So what do you think happened to Julie's boyfriend?"

"Julie?"

Margaret smiled. "You've no idea what this is about, have you?"

Jim grinned sheepishly. "My mind must have wandered."

Margaret switched off the television. "All right. What is it? Your brow has been so furrowed this past half hour, I think those wrinkles are going to become permanent."

Jim smiled again. "Ah, the usual. Some stuff came in today and it has set the old brain running. Stewart discovered that the killer is writing blogs on the Dark Web about the murders, very detailed stuff that only the killer could know."

"The Dark Web?"

"Aye! Dangerous place. It's like Google, but it's the haunt of all sorts of depraved and shady types doing criminal and other deals that can't be detected in the normal way." He smiled at her. "No place for an innocent like you."

"Humph! So what was Stewart doing there?"

"Something she heard made her think she might find some stuff there about our suspects. Instead, she found our murderer."

"Good grief!"

"Well, she found our murderer, blowing and bumming about his exploits, but he's anonymous because of the encrypted nature of the Dark Web and, according to Stewart, he's going to stay anonymous."

"Did he leave any clues?"

"Sort of. We had a conference call from Professor Greenwald during our debrief today. Our killer is a narcissistic psychopath."

"Of course he is. I'll bet Sergeant McCullough appreciated that little gem," Margaret said, grinning."

"He did, yeah! We had already worked out that our killer is short, extremely well educated and probably very clever. Four of our key suspects fit that profile. He's also quite mad. He writes about the killings in the style a nineteenth-century novelist, philosophising about justice and vengeance and stuff like that. He wants to boast about what he does, but he also wants to convince his readers that he is not guilty of anything. Crazy stuff. Nigel says he craves adulation, and he's acting out a scenario in his mind that somehow replays something that happened to someone he had feelings for."

"Didn't know psychopaths had feelings."

"New research says they can, under certain circumstances. So, that's about where the team is in its thinking."

"But not you?"

"Ah, no, I'm no further on than the rest of them. It's just that when I read the first blog, it immediately triggered a memory. Well, not a memory, because I don't know what it was, but it was some kind of connection, a sentence or a phrase, maybe even a word. Something in that blog just jumped out at my subconscious." He blew a frustrated breath through tight lips. "But I just can't reach it."

"A memory from where?"

"That's the point. I don't know. I have a strong feeling that the connection was to one of the interviews I conducted, or maybe even to something one of the team said."

"Like what?"

"Dunno. I've tried to go back over all the interviews in my mind, but nothing jumps out at me." He grimaced. "But I know there's a connection between one of them and the first blog, and it's killing me that I just can't get it."

"Don't think about it and maybe it'll suddenly come to you."

"Aye, right. It's the same with that schoolteacher's face. I know I saw it somewhere. But where? I mean, I know I've never spoken to or met the guy. I have absolutely no recollection of his voice. But his face ... it's driving me nuts." He bent forward and rubbed his hands through his hair. "But what's most annoying, this has all triggered off something else that I heard at one of my interviews, and I know, totally know, it's important. But I can't get that either. It's all smoke. I sorta sense it, but the minute I try to touch it, it floats away."

Margaret smiled. "How many times have I heard this? Your inner brain makes connections that nobody else's ever makes, but even your own surface brain is initially left lagging behind." She smiled again. "But it'll catch up; it always does."

"Aye, right. But right now, my brain's all over the place, second guessing itself." He reached for the TV remote control. "To tell the truth," he added, before switching the television back on, "the team is bulling to see what's in that locked safe. They think they'll find all the answers there. Me, I'm not so sure. I'm beginning to get the uneasy feeling that we might be looking at this from the wrong perspective." He gave her a defeated grin. "But what other perspective is there?" He switched the television on. "What's that you were saying about Julie?"

TWENTY-SIX
Tuesday, 21st August. Morning

Parking his car some distance from the crowd of gawkers jostling around an opening in a high dilapidated fence, Detective Robert Williams of Belfast's Policing 'A' District, pushed his way through the craning heads, and flashed his warrant card at the two officers protecting the gate. The gateway was sealed off with yellow police tape, but the officers allowed the inspector to pass while they calmly and proficiently kept the crowd at bay. Their eyes, however, searched restlessly for any unusual facial clues, atypical body tics, or simply signs of something other than mere curiosity that someone in the crowd before them might be exhibiting. Williams nodded approval. It was known that on occasion, the killer in such instances could well be part of the crowd, his ego driving him there to observe the impact of his handiwork. He noted, too, that there were already some members of the press, holding their press passes high and seeking privileged access to the crime scene. *Not a chance*, he thought. Press and members of the public were deliberately kept in as much ignorance as possible, not only to preserve the scene but to prevent any leakage of details about the crime. Too often in the past, information from a crime scene hampered the investigation and had led to hoax calls and false confessions.

Once inside, Williams paused to survey the area, a piece of wasteland, partially cleared by some building machinery, but currently left devoid of protection or attention. SOCOs in pale blue protective Tyvek suits, armed with cameras, lights, or sticks, walked or crawled the scene, searching for clues, large, small or infinitesimal, marking out footprints, tyre tracks or other scuff marks that might have been left by the perpetrator.

Two teenagers, segregated from the crowd, were held to one side by an officer who was interrogating them and taking notes. Away from the gate, some yards along the inside of the fence, a makeshift tent had been erected, and close to it, pieces of transparent waterproof sheeting had been draped over what he could make out to be a battered suitcase and some clothes. There were waterproof sheets spread over some patches of ground as well, which experience told him almost certainly contained footprints, scuff marks, and maybe tyre tracks or blood spatter.

It was a scene Williams had seen many times, but one that never failed to clutch at his stomach as he wondered who the unfortunate victim might be this time. As he made his way towards the tent, he watched the photographers painstakingly snap pictures of areas and items, alongside each of which were small cards with numbers on them. While they were carefully placed to portray height, distance and radius for the photographs, Williams knew that the numbered markers would also be used to cross reference any evidence against future reports that might be made or, indeed, they could often find themselves as numbered exhibits in subsequent court proceedings.

As he stood there, he couldn't help wondering. *Could this be the one?* Williams was nearing the end of his career yet, despite limited talent and an almost pathological inability to make any decision that contravened 'the rules', he continued to harbour hope that he would one day make Chief Inspector. But to do that he would need to bring a major case to a successful conclusion, and that was something he had not yet done. He did have his chance a while back with the murder of that social worker, but it turned out that her death was linked to a series of other deaths in Jim Sheehan's patch. He had fought at the time to hold on to the case, but the Assistant Chief Constable had insisted that he hand it over to Sheehan. He heaved a sigh. Jim was a friend and a great fellow, but he had made Chief Inspector at a young age and all the breaks seemed to fall his way.

Williams was too decent a human being to wallow in jealousy, but he did experience a twinge of envy. A wry grin curved his lips. He wasn't just envious of Sheehan's promotion. He had to admit that he was envious, too, of his friend's talents. Jim was a brilliant detective who had the respect both of his fellow officers and the authorities. That, together with a penchant for operating outside of 'the book' if it would yield results, made it inevitable that he would solve practically every crime that landed on his doorstep. *Success equals promotion. And, no doubt there's more to come.*

He nodded to the officer guarding the tent which was being kept closed until the pathologist arrived and, steeling himself for the gruesome scene he knew awaited him, he gestured to the SOCO to lead him in. The body on the floor was that of a huge muscular man, naked, and covered in tattoos. Part of a heavy cylindrical object protruded from his rectum and his head had been beaten to a bloodied mush. Accustomed as he was to murder scenes, Williams felt bile rise towards his throat and only with difficulty was he able to swallow it. Taking a few seconds to compose himself, he muttered, "My God. Who on earth could do something like this to a fellow human being?"

The SOCO who had accompanied him inside said with some cynicism, "This is Northern Ireland, Inspector."

Williams' lips tightened. "What's that sticking out of him?"

"Far as I can gather, it's a police truncheon, sir."

Williams stared at it, puzzled. It didn't fit at all what he was thinking, but he asked the question anyway. "This down to any paramilitary feud you might know about?"

"No idea, sir, but it sure as hell is vicious. No question about that. Sorta thing they'd do."

"Who found the body?"

"Two lads larking about, sir. Officer Grimes is talking to them now."

"Was he the first officer on the scene?"

"Yes, sir."

Glad of the opportunity to leave the grisly spectacle, Williams said, "I'll have a word with him." He paused, pointing at the naked body. "Cover that until the medical officers get here, would you, please?" A sensitive and gentle man, Williams seldom gave orders that didn't also contain an element of request.

Face grim, he made his way to the officer and two youths he had noticed on the way in. He nodded to the officer who had already recognised him and gave the two teenage boys a hard stare. Around sixteen years of age, skinny, wearing anoraks with the hoods up, both returned the detective's stare with insolent expressions. Williams turned again to Grimes. "So, what's the story?"

Grimes said, "These two young citizens were walking past this fence, erected a few weeks ago by Keenan and McDonald's Builders." He gestured to the youth on his left. "Francis Kelly here bumped into the gate by accident and—" He referred to his notebook. "—it sorta, kinda fell open." His voice adopted a sarcastic tone as he continued to read. "Concerned that there might be materials in the yard that people could easily steal, and, doing their civic duty, they went in to check before contacting the police. It was then that they noticed the body."

"Gave us a terrible shock, sir," Kelly volunteered.

"Never seen a dead body before, sir," the other youth added.

"Kevin Morgan here is the proud owner of a mobile phone, sir," Grimes said. "He phoned 999 and—"

"Did you touch the body?" Williams asked, interrupting Grimes' ponderous saga.

Both youths shook their heads furiously. "No way," Kelly said. "It scared the life out of us."

"We just went back out of the gate and waited for the cops," Morgan added.

"We were here within a few minutes," Grimes said, "and immediately cordoned off the area. The yellow tape must have attracted those nosey parkers milling around outside."

"And you saw no one else?" Williams asked the youths.

Grimes assumed a peeved expression. "I have been through this with them, sir. The gate was closed when they arrived, and the yard was empty. I noticed some car tracks beside the body. Got those covered right away. But whatever actually happened here, happened some time before these kids discovered the body. During the night would be my guess. Rigor mortis is well established."

"Okay," Williams said. "You've got their names and addresses?"

Grimes gave the inspector an oblique look, and then, eyebrows down, thumbed through his notes. "Let me see." After fiddling with the book for a few seconds, he held it out in front of him with both hands as if he was having trouble reading it. "Oh, yes. Here they are." He put the notebook back in his pockets. "Both addresses, sir," he added without expression.

Deserved that, Williams thought. *Stupid question.* Aloud he said, "Thank you for your prompt action, boys. You can go home now. If we need anything more from you, we'll get in touch."

"Is there a reward?" Morgan asked.

Williams glanced at him briefly before saying, "I haven't heard. If there is, we'll let you know. Run along now." He turned to Grimes as the boys trudged to the gate. "Any theories?"

"Not really, sir," Grimes responded, pleased that he had been consulted. "All those tattoos. Could be some sort of paramilitary beating that went too far."

"Hmmm! That was my own first thought."

As he was speaking, two figures, enveloped from head to foot in pale blue coveralls, came through the gate carrying medical briefcases. Williams recognised Doctors Campbell and Jones, and saying, "Excuse me, Officer Grimes, and thanks," he hurried over to the two pathologists.

"Hello, Dick. Hello, Doctor Jones. The body is in the tent. It's pretty grim."

"Hello, Bob," Campbell said, not pausing. "Give us a few minutes to have a look and then we'll chat."

Williams nodded and turned towards the gate when he heard an ambulance arrive. He watched as the vehicle lumbered slowly up to the tent and stopped. A couple of paramedics emerged and headed to the back of the vehicle for a stretcher and some covering. Williams joined them. "Good morning, gentlemen. The medical examiner has just arrived. He'll be a few minutes."

The paramedics shrugged. One pulled out a packet of cigarettes, offered one to his companion and held the pack towards Williams. The inspector shook his head in polite refusal.

"What do we have, d'ye know?" the man asked, putting his cigarettes away and accepting a light from his companion.

"Sorry. I've no information at this point." He left them and flagged down a passing SOCO, a slight man, who gazed at him enquiringly with a reserved manner. Taking him to one side, Williams said quietly, "Excuse me, Officer." Then he paused, studying the man. "Do I know you?"

"No, sir. I'm new," the man said. "George Rice."

"Good to meet you, George," Williams said perfunctorily. "Did you find out anything about the victim from those clothes or the suitcase?" He waved a thumb in the direction of the covered objects.

"Very little in the case, sir," Rice said quietly. "A couple of pairs of jeans, a few tee shirts, some underwear. That's it. A few pounds in his pocket." He held up a finger, his face showing a flicker of animation for the first time. "However, there's a couple of interesting things. We dusted the suitcase and found several of what were obviously the victim's prints. But we also found fresh thumb, middle and forefinger prints that definitely do not belong to the victim."

"Excellent. What was the other thing?"

"There was a letter in the jeans he was wearing from the Probation Office. It's bagged as evidence, but basically, it's an instruction to the victim to meet with his probation officer, Gerald Gribbon, in a couple of days. Our victim's name is Thomas McStravick, and reading between the lines, it appears that he's not long released from prison."

Williams was conscious that the man's speech patterns lacked the normal short-cuts and abbreviations normally used by his men, but he mentally shrugged the observation away. His lips went down at the edges and he looked perplexed. "Odd."

Rice nodded agreement. "Singularly grotesque, sir, with that prison guard's truncheon lodged in his rectum."

"Is that what it is?"

"Sorry, sir. I just assumed that's what it was. I don't really know."

"You think some prison guard came after him to exact some sort of revenge?"

"I wouldn't have a clue, sir. But he's big, sir. Gives the impression of having been rather uncouth. I would imagine that he might have been the type of prisoner to have given the guards a hard time."

Williams nodded solemn agreement and dismissed the SOCO with a cursory, "Okay, George. Thanks." He surveyed the crime scene once more and expelled a heavy breath, head shaking slowly from side to side. Sheehan had more than once said to him, "It's the small things, Bob. Keep your eye out for the small things." *Small things? Where the heck do you even start?* His lips twisted in a wry grin. That was the difference between Sheehan and every other detective on the force. He saw small things where no one else would see anything. He had extraordinary insight and a great memory for detail. Solutions just seemed to fall into place in his ever-churning brain.

He looked up as Campbell and Jones emerged from the tent. Jones was wrapping the strap around a camera that he had used to take photographs of the victim. Then he bent to pick up the two medical briefcases and headed towards the gate.

Campbell called to the waiting paramedics. "Get the body to the mortuary now, boys. I'll be right behind you."

Williams wandered over. "Well?"

"Hi again, Bob," Campbell said. "You might want to phone Jim Sheehan about this."

Williams closed his eyes for a second, depressed. *Shit. Not again.* "What do you mean, phone Sheehan, Dick? This is my patch."

Campbell shrugged. "Yes, but this is the fourth body I've seen in the past couple of weeks with a police truncheon sticking out of it. The other three were on Sheehan's patch. Looks like the same MO." He hesitated. "Well, pretty much."

Williams picked up on the slight doubt. "Is there something different about this one?"

"Well, all the other victims were dispatched with a single blow to the head. This victim's head has suffered a sustained and frenzied hammering. It's a mess."

"Copycat, do you think?" Williams asked, still clinging to a small hope that this might still be his case.

Campbell shrugged. "Hard to say. Jim'll know."

"You say policeman's truncheon?" William's pressed. "Could it be a prison guard's truncheon, do you think?"

Campbell made a face. "Is there a difference? That's what our perp has been using, wherever he's getting them. I think modern prison guards now use an expandable straight baton, same as the police. This truncheon is different. Old-style." He stepped aside as the two paramedics exited the tent with a covered corpse on the stretcher. He watched them load the body into the ambulance and then glanced around. "Jones gone already? I'm off, Bob," he said, heading towards the gate. Turning and walking backwards for a few steps, he added, "Give Jim a ring, will you, please? Tell him to come to the mortuary as soon as he can." A quick wave and he was gone.

Williams reached for his mobile phone, already despondent. There was only one way this was going to go. He dialled and waited.

"Sheehan."

"Hi, Jim. It's Bob Williams."

"Bob? Good to hear from you. How're things?"

"Grand, Jim. Grand. We've found a body over here in a disused building site. Dick Campbell has taken it away to the mortuary. He wants you there as soon as possible. Thinks it might be one for you."

"Oh, dear God. Not another one. Have you identified the victim?"

"Yes, an ex-jailbird called McStravick."

Sheehan was silent for a second. Then he said, "Ah! So that's where he went to."

Williams was puzzled. "Come again, Jim?"

"A couple of my guys have been trying to interview McStravick about a case we're working on. They haven't been able to find him." He paused seeking a delicate way to frame his next question. "Was there, uh, a police truncheon—?"

"There was," Williams interjected. "Ugly sight. So, there've been others?"

"Aye! This guy's the fourth."

Williams made a hissing sound through his teeth. "Nasty. Anything I can do to help?"

"Yes, please, Bob. Can you arrange for every single forensics item, including clothes and anything else found at the scene, to be sent to Bill Larkin for examination? Be very thorough, please, Bob, because to date we have virtually nothing."

"Will do."

"I don't suppose your SOCOs found anything of interest?"

Williams gave the matter a second's thought. "Maybe. There's an old suitcase here. McStravick must have been heading somewhere. One of the SOCOs, a new guy, uh, George Rice—"

"Oh, yes. I've met him," Sheehan said. "Very serious?"

"That's him. He tells me he's found loads of McStravick's prints on the case, obviously, but he's also found a couple of others, fresh, not the victim's."

"Geez, Bob. Protect those prints with your life," Sheehan said excitedly. "This might be our perp's first mistake."

"I'll see they're kept safe, Jim."

"Thanks, Bob. We'll chat soon."

Williams disconsolately put his phone back in his pocket and went in search of the Crime Scene Supervisor.

TWENTY-SEVEN
Tuesday, 21st August. Morning

Despite Allen's misgivings, Stewart continued to surf the Dark Web looking for further posts from Nemein. Since the entries usually followed a killing, she was not expecting to find any further posts on this morning. However, a new blog had, in fact, been posted sometime during the night, and she read it now with increasing tension. The killer had struck again and yet they had no reports of any new killing. She finished reading the blog quickly, almost turning away in disgust as she neared the end. The chief had been talking on the phone with someone while she had been searching, but she became aware that there was now silence in his office. She quickly printed out a copy of the blog and brought it to him.

"Oh, dear," he said, reaching out to take the copy from her. "A blog about McStravick, right?"

Stewart was surprised. "How did you know, Chief?"

"I've just had Bob Williams on the phone. They found McStravick's body on his turf, but Dick has put him wise about whose case it is. Dick wants us over to the mortuary right away." He looked at his watch. "Go and get the car, and I'll meet you at the gate in about ten minutes." He held up the printed sheets. "I'll just have a quick run through this now."

ΝΕΜΕΙΝ'Σ ΒΛΟΓ

Ηατε

Hello again, and welcome to my increasing legion of new fans. Several thousand hits! That is gratifying and confirms that my loyal followers understand and approve my theories about the separation between act and intention. I do hope my post-mortem scribblings afford you food for thought, as well as some arresting images to flash upon your inward eye which, as Wordsworth tells us, 'is the bliss of solitude'. Thank you also for your many encouraging comments. Sadly, with the limited time available to me, I cannot acknowledge all of them individually, but I do appreciate the interest you are taking in my quest, and the support that you offer.

Latterly, I have been pondering the idea of HATE. Isolated from context, it seems to be a concept that veers towards the ignoble when compared with the more lofty abstractions analysed in my earlier blogs. But what if we examine it in terms of its origin, in terms of its purpose, in terms of its emotional content or, perhaps more importantly, in terms of its lack of emotional content. Might we possibly discover in its depths, something dignified, something honourable, something noble?

Seeking justice, seeking revenge, seeking satisfaction, these can be noble. BUT, improperly focussed, buried too deeply in emotion, they can draw on the energy of HATE. That in itself is not necessarily an evil. But a HATE that drives a person to act with blind, unthinking passion, to act without purpose or control, to act without cool logic underpinning the process, is a HATE that has already conquered both the will and the spirit of the doer, a hate that has reduced him or her to irrational savagery.

The Christian Church offers an interesting aphorism: Hate the sin, not the sinner. Now there is a noble aspiration. And how has it worked out for the Church? Christians from time immemorial have been fed the belief that they were the true believers, the people with the answers, the chosen. Inevitably, they looked on other churches, other people of no church, initially with concern, and ultimately with suspicion. They are so wrong, goes the thinking. They don't understand. They cannot possibly know the truth of how life should be lived. And so, Christians became imbued with the philosophy that they were superior to all others, God's chosen, with a mission to redeem the world, a mission that led to those great acts of godly love through the ages as Christians sought to convert the pagan ... the Crusades, the Spanish Inquisition, the murderous witch trials, the 'just' wars, the holy wars, the slaughtering of heretics. Great acts of Christian love? These global tragedies, my friends, were prompted by a philosophy of contempt for others who were deemed ignorant, and in their ignorance, inevitably sinful, worthy of hate. 'Hate only the sin' was never within the normal curve of human psychology. Christians have been, and continue to be, because of their supreme sense of their own righteousness, slowly indoctrinated with an insidious creed of HATE.

Hate is all around us. In Northern Ireland, fixers of the past attempt to glorify the violence of the 'troubles' as a fight for freedom, as an era of courage and self-sacrifice by the 'volunteers'. Tell that to the innocent victims, the thousands of innocent victims, casually blown to pieces by cowards who sought easy targets to make their murderous points. Here were evil men ostensibly at war with the forces of an occupying government, but who were, in fact, motivated by hatred and bigotry, and who killed and maimed indiscriminately in the pursuit of their spurious ideology.

And yet, was there justification? Protestant Unionism held sway in Northern Ireland at that time and, to Nationalist and Catholic eyes, the principal objective of Unionists, apart from loyalty to the British Crown, was to ensure that the nationalists were effectively forced to remain second-class citizens. They were to be denied access to high-profile jobs; they were to be given little or no say in government. The working-class nationalists knew heavy unemployment and little social mobility. Their housing was grubby, crowded and impoverished. Here was a powder keg waiting to explode. Hate was the match that lit the flame.

Hate is all around us. Many of us are infected by its power and its force without realising it. I, myself, have had to stop and consider the possibility that the events in my life have cast a pall over my own soul, have tested my objectivity, have impinged upon the purity of my intentions. But in the very act of doubt, I pause. I plumb the depths of my consciousness and am thus enabled to restore my impartiality.

Hate is all around us. But, despite provocation or just cause, the noble soul can rise above it. That I can work detached from emotion was evident to me during my most recent encounter. This perpetrator was, in life, vicious, cruel, vile, without honour, without scruple. A creature born to be hated; a creature who has given me personal and prodigious cause to wallow in hatred for him.

This one was under the impression that his appalling act had escaped undetected. But such is the honour among thieves that a little monetary persuasion, judiciously applied, can loosen the tightest of lips. The trail was simple to follow. A short series of inducements provided a snippet here, a fragment there, until the entire picture materialised. And yet, although my suspicions were validated and confirmed, such was the shock and the horror of the revealed truth, that I was filled with rage, with loathing, with unalloyed hatred. I railed at the heavens. I screamed into the darkness. I cursed my very existence. But eventually, through the haze of emotional torment, discipline made itself felt and self-mastery became once again my goal.

Luigi Guissani speaks of a state of 'emotional imperturbability', a frozen wasteland of the heart where one no longer has to engage with outer stimuli of any kind, where the heart is cut off from feelings, and cold aloofness reigns. I focussed my energies inwards and sought that mastery of will that would allow my heart, my very soul, to remain implacably untouched by the tragic revelation my enquiries had uncovered. Oh yes, I did have monumental reason to hate, but when I embarked on this phase of my mission, I was again in control. In a strange way, part of me was outside my body, calmly and dispassionately directing my behaviours.

The beast—and that is how I must define this loathsome animal, a brute in mind and in body, a troglodyte with no redeeming features—was ultimately easier quarry than I might have presupposed. As with all the other transgressors who have been prey to my hunt, I monitored his movements for several days until I knew his habits as intimately as my own.

As might be expected from one whose brain functions only on the most basic level, his evening haunt, every evening without fail, was a sleazy, down-at-heel drinking den, a squalid tavern that offended my own fastidious sensibilities to their very limit. And yet, despite my extreme distaste, I found myself drinking alone, sometime after dark had descended, in a corner of those shoddy surrounds, a corner which I already knew was the chosen station of my boorish target.

It was not long before he arrived carrying a battered suitcase, and, as I had surmised, he thundered to my location with black anger suffusing his face. "What the hell are you doing in my seat, you poncy fuck?" was his less-than-gracious greeting.

I arose immediately, of course, and apologised most profusely. "I am so sorry," I said. "I was unaware that I was intruding on someone's space. Please, allow me to buy you a drink by way of apology."

I rather imagine my vocabulary and manner of speech tested his puny intellect, but he did understand the part of my dialogue that involved a drink without cost. He stared at me with his bulbous eyes while his tiny brain wrestled for a response. What he eventually decided upon was a lacklustre, "All right."

I pointed to a nearby empty chair and said, "Would you mind if I sat with you for a few moments while I finish my drink?"

Puzzlement was the predominant aspect of his countenance. I should imagine that the customary response of persons of my ilk, when confronted with a brute of such savage mien, would be hurried flight with, perhaps, one fearful backward glance. My calm reaction, therefore, probably surprised him. His small brain, I have little doubt, was still engaged with the concept of a free libation and therefore left him incapable of additional cerebration. Thus, he grunted a second time, "All right."

I pulled the chair forward and gestured for him to sit. Once he had done so, I followed suit and, pointing to the suitcase, I said innocently, "Travelling?"

This clearly touched a nerve since the brute's face was suffused with a sudden scowl and a black glare. The arrival of the bartender at that juncture tempered the burgeoning anger. One long, thirsty swallow all but drained the glass.

"Allow me to get you another," I said, and before waiting for his permission which, doubtless, would have been readily accorded, I followed the bartender to the bar rather than call him back. This allowed me to purchase a further drink at the bar and place it on a small, round tray. By dint of some careful prestidigitation, I was able to drop the contents of a small phial into the black liquid. "Here you are, my friend," I said heartily on my return, setting the second drink on the table.

My heartiness earned me another suspicious glance. There is little doubt that the strangeness of the encounter limited his ability to think, and ultimately his ability to act. Thus, he continued to re-act, and I continued to control the conversation. I pointed to the travelling bag. "Are you waiting for a bus, or going to a hotel?"

Again that angry scowl. "My stupid brother has thrown me out of his house."

I understood immediately, and rendered the moment less fractious by remarking sympathetically, "Family. Who can understand them?"

He stared at me, again unsure, but he did decide to reply, "Bloody right."

I gave him an earnest look. "Am I to assume that you find yourself without lodgings for this evening?"

I could almost hear the wheels of his little brain slowly turning as he strove to establish the import of my comment. Eventually he said, "Aye! Not sure what I'm gonna do."

I spread my hands as if what I was about to say was the most natural thing in the world. "Why don't I offer you a room at my dwelling until you find yourself more permanent lodging?"

Everything I said seemed to baffle him but, nevertheless, his suspicions were once again aroused, "Why would you do that?"

"My dear friend," I said easily, "I can see you are troubled. I can see you are in need. Only the hardest of hearts could deny you the support you require."

He looked around the bar to see if anyone else was listening to this most weird of conversations, almost as if to confirm that it was indeed taking place. No one, however, was showing any interest. In turning, his knee caught the side of his suitcase causing it to fall flat on the floor. I quickly reached forwards and obligingly replaced the bag in its upright position. Clearly disconcerted by my mannerly act and grappling with inner questions, the answers to which were quite beyond him, he turned to me and said, "Are you some sort of Salvation Army type?"

"I suppose you might say that," I replied. Anything to bring this tedious conversation to an end and to allow me to rid myself of this fellow's most odious presence. Pointing to his second drink, I added, "Why don't you finish that, and I'll take you to my place right now and get you settled."

Mistrust again clouded his countenance, but at the same time a spark of sly cunning flashed in his suddenly hooded eyes. "Okay," he said, and with one long, gulping swallow, emptied the glass. He wiped his lips with the back of his hand, belched loudly, and said, "Right, let's go."

I was forced to walk quickly ahead of him to conceal the disgust that must surely have impressed itself upon my countenance. The brute was singularly lacking in even the most basic elements of etiquette. I continued to engage him in some form of inane conversation as we walked to my car which I had parked around a street corner several yards away to ensure some modicum of security from prying eyes.

As we talked, his speech became more slurred and he began to stagger. He stopped and supported himself against the wall of a house with one hand, still holding his suitcase in the other, and shook his head, saying, "Must've tossed that bloody pint down too fast."

I took his elbow. "Come. It's only a few steps more."

We barely made it to the car where he collapsed into the rear seat, unable to move. He remained to a degree lucid, however, and now even his minimal intelligence had detected that something was amiss. "Wha's matter wi' me?"

I told him in no uncertain terms what the matter with him was. I told him in no uncertain terms what he had done in the past to destroy my life. And I told him in no uncertain terms, and with a great deal of embellishment, exactly what was about to happen to him. Struggling to move but failing, he pleaded for mercy, even started to blubber. How utterly distasteful! I could not even look at him.

I drove to a place I had reconnoitred some days earlier, some miles away on the other side of the city. A high, dilapidated fence surrounded a patch of bare ground that was waiting for a building crew to begin work on it. As with a number of such sites in the city, time seemed to be of little import and thus the area had lain untouched for several months. There was a corrugated gate with a feeble lock which I had earlier picked. It was the work of but a few moments to open the gate, drive my car inside and close the gate again. I knew that I would remain undisturbed for the rest of the evening, but I raised my head and listened very carefully for some minutes to ensure that this night was to be no different from any other night.

I correct myself. This night was going to be very different from other nights, for this patch of ground, and for my now almost comatose companion. And that said, those of my faithful followers who have been reading these accounts, will know what next transpired. I dressed quickly in my protective suit, and with some difficulty, given the evil-doer's considerable bulk, I dragged him from the car. I stripped him of his clothes, tossed his suitcase to one side and sat him on the ground. You will appreciate how much more awkward it would have been for me to crush his skull had I lain him flat.

Despite the strong sedative he had taken, Hypnovel, if you must know, he was still vaguely conscious, and in his stupor fought to remain sitting rather than allow himself to fall. I quickly procured my Instrument of Justice from my car and, allowing myself no time to gloat, swung the truncheon with all the force I could muster against the back of the reprobate's head.

Had this vile creature not carried out the dreadful deed that robbed me of my life's purpose, it is likely that none of the other transgressors would have had to pay any penalty, and thus the retribution I have been forced to seek might never have had to plague my life. Each of the others, unwittingly perhaps, but inevitably and uncaringly, led my life's soul mate to this uncouth creature. All shared, therefore, in the guilt. Nothing that this monster did, however, was unwitting. His actions were spawned from unbridled lechery and unadulterated malevolence. It is upon him, therefore, that the direct responsibility for the fatal tragic act must fall.

The sudden intensity of this awareness, the realisation that the vile predator whom I had for so long sought was now at my feet, at my mercy, brought on me, my dear followers, a sudden ecstasy of rage. I am obliged to confess that for some moments, therefore, I could no longer retain my emotional imperturbability and, in unrestrained fury, I swung again at the murderous brute ... and again ... and again ... until his head was a bloody mass of gristle and pulp.

Aware eventually of my loss of control, and breathing heavily, I pushed the odious creature on to his side and eventually on to his very ample stomach. Taking no time to savour the moment, I squashed the truncheon with as much vigour as I could muster far into the villain's rectum and, having divested myself of the protective suit and replaced it in its carrier bag, I hurriedly departed the scene.

As I rushed away, I was aware that there remained yet one more guilty party who has to pay for his role in this harrowing drama. But this one is not to die. This one is to suffer the torments of the damned. And suffer he will, my dear followers, suffer he will, and for the rest of his life. The exquisite tribulation I have planned for him would terrify even Machiavelli.

Wait in patience, dear friends, for the final chapter of this desperate saga.

Your friend and mentor,

Nemein.

TWENTY-EIGHT
Tuesday, 21st August. Late morning

Sheehan, with Stewart just a step behind, entered the mortuary. Jones was weighing some organs at a nearby steel table, while Campbell was busy taking photographs of McStravick's internal organs. He looked up in time to see Sheehan's expression of distaste.

"You should be used to this by now, Jim," the doctor said, before bowing gallantly to Stewart. "And how are you this fine morning, Sergeant?"

Stewart smiled a greeting to both doctors and said, "I'm very well, Doctor, but—" She nodded towards the gaping, Y-shaped incision Campbell had been photographing. "—I would have been happy enough not to have seen that."

"You're still relatively new to this, Denise, but just for your information, there's a great deal of detail on the human body, detail that can be easily overlooked by even the most competent of professionals." He paused and looked at her over the top of his spectacles. "Well, maybe not me." He beamed at Jim and went on, "These details must be photographed because they can prove essential in determining cause of death. And, of course, the photographs will be used later in court to offer members of the jury full details of any injuries to the organs without exposing them to too much gore."

Stewart's wrinkling nose betrayed the fact that she wasn't enamoured by the word 'gore'.

"For this reason," Campbell went on, "medical examiners need the highest possible quality photographs of every inch of skin. In fact, we start photographing and X-raying even before we touch the body."

"You seem to be taking excessive care with this one, Dick," Sheehan said. "Any reason for that?"

"Excuse me, Chief Inspector." Campbell gave Sheehan a faux-glare. "I take great care with all my work." He looked back at the corpse. "However, yes, I suppose I am giving this one a little extra attention."

"And you're doing that because?"

"There's been a change in the MO."

"This victim's head has been beaten to a pulp instead of the single blunt force trauma that killed the others?" Sheehan said.

Campbell stepped back and waved a hand at the body. "Please," he said caustically, "tell us more."

Sheehan pretended to study the body. "Mmmm! Do I detect indicators that the victim was sedated before death?"

Campbell stepped forward quickly, surprised, and studied the body. "Where do you see that?"

"Experience, Dick. What were you saying about the extra attention?"

Campbell gave him a sideways look and a frown before continuing, "Well, if the MO has changed, we can't afford to make assumptions. Yes, the brutality of the head trauma would have been more than enough to cause death, but we have to double check. I just want to ensure that nothing other than the vicious blows to the head have contributed to the cause of death."

"What exactly are you looking for?"

"I'm trying to make sure there was no poison involved, for example. We're looking for needle marks or other minor trauma that might lead us in a different direction."

"Okay. So you haven't found anything other than the Hypnovel?"

Campbell's head shot up again, really puzzled this time. "For heaven's sake, Jim. Have you gone all clairvoyant or what?" He noticed Stewart stifling a grin. "All right. What's going on here?"

Stewart glanced at Sheehan, smiling. "You should tell him, Chief."

Campbell glared at his friend. "Well?"

Sheehan grinned and said, "Our killer is writing blogs about his murders on the Dark Web. Stewart here discovered them. We've actually seen a detailed description of how this particular murder was carried out even though we didn't know where the body was. Stewart downloaded the blog just before we left the station. The others haven't seen it yet."

"Good heavens," Campbell exclaimed. "That's really weird." He glanced up with a grin. "I think Bob Williams will be disappointed. He was hoping there'd be enough subtle differences in the MO to make this a copycat killing. I think he really wanted this one."

"I'll chat with him later. I'm afraid the blog makes it clear that this was just the next one on our killer's list."

Campbell nodded. "You're right. Same perp, I'd say. Nothing new. Drugged and battered. That's it, as far as I can see."

"No tiny forensics of any kind?"

"Nothing. Your killer obviously wears some kind of protective gear."

Sheehan nodded. "Yeah! He said that in the blog." He looked at his watch. "Nothing new on any of the others?"

"No. Forensics haven't got back to me with a DNA report on the hair or the piece of elastic. I'll let you know as soon as I hear."

"Okay, Dick. Thanks. We'll go on. Talk again soon."

TWENTY-NINE
Tuesday, 21st August. Afternoon.

S heehan tapped his pencil on his desk to hush the chattering team. "Okay. We'll get started. Sergeant Larkin has asked me to call you all together because he has significant news to impart. I can only hope it's something to do with the safe." He nodded to the bespectacled sergeant. "The floor's yours, Bill."

Larkin got to his feet. "Thanks, Chief. And you're right. We got the safe opened."

Some whistles and hoots greeted this announcement. "Way to go, Bill." This from Allen.

"So, what was in it?" Sheehan said, sounding a lot more casual than he felt.

"I don't have any of the actual contents with me," Larkin said. "They've been lodged in evidence, but I took some notes. You're not going to believe what I have here."

"It's going to be hard to believe it if we don't know what it is," Sheehan said dryly.

Larkin said, "Sorry, Chief. Well, to start with there was nearly a quarter of a million in cash." Larkin looked up from his notes and added, "Not big into paying his taxes, obviously."

Nobody was amused. Larkin's tendency to lead up to a point from some distance back was almost intolerable at this juncture.

"Big money, Sergeant," Miller said, "but scarcely cause for disbelief."

"Well, try this," Larkin answered. "Our Brexiteers are not Brexiteers at all. They're all members of a top-secret and hugely expensive Sex Club that caters for the most depraved and perverted sexual tastes. No desire, no matter how warped or degenerate, cannot be catered for. I've seen the menu, excuse me, the *Liste des Activités*, and the prices. Geez. I thought I'd seen it all and that I was too long in the tooth to be shocked." He shook his head, almost in bewilderment. "But this stuff is sickening."

"What can you tell us about it, Bill?" Allen asked, almost slack-jawed.

"Well, it seems that the judge originally had a small side-line. People in certain circles would learn on a secret grapevine that Judge Neeson had the connections to put them in touch with people of similar tastes for gratification of all sorts of kinky needs. Apparently, the word drifted around certain discreet circles, and demand for his services grew to such an extent that he could no longer cope with it. This led to the creation of a new club called *Fulfilment for the Enlightened*. Membership costs the earth, but scores of high-fliers, and not only from Northern Ireland, have been lining up to join. That party at the judge's that night was a brief induction before introducing these new members to The Club's delights."

"Any names?" Connors asked.

"Shit loads. Uh, sorry, Chief. I mean, you have doctors, lawyers, judges, royalty, government officials, millionaire businessmen ... there's just no end to the list."

McCullough spoke, sounding uncertain, "A hardcore secret society for very rich people with exotic sexual tastes. Is this something that the police need concern themselves with?"

"Too right, Mac," Larkin replied. "This isn't just some jaded elite playing perverted party games. Maybe some of the things they do could just be on the side of legal, like fetish balls, maybe, but when it comes to paedophiles' abuse of very young children kidnapped from their own homes, youths and young girls and women kidnapped and imprisoned in dungeons below the place, to engage in horrid activities...." Larkin stopped to stare around the room, his eyes distressed. "Honest to God, it's unbelievable. Lots of what goes on isn't about sex at all. Sado-maschochism of the most extreme sort, torture, cruel games that sometimes go way over the limit and actually end in death, even creating their own snuff movies."

"You're not serious?" Connors' shock removed all menace from his usual growl.

"Yeah, I'm telling you. Way, way, waay outside the law. Judge Neeson has meticulously noted these, what he calls, 'unfortunate incidents'. He relates how he had to cover up the deaths and get rid of the corpses. He notes the names of the participants, dates, full descriptions of the events. It's bloody disgusting and sick-making and ... and...." He paused again, disgusted. "It's a blackmailer's motherlode."

"Maybe that's what the guy who was blackmailing the judge had on him," McBride suggested.

"If The Club is all that t-t-top secret and exclusive, then the b-b-blackmailer had to be a member," McNeill stated. "He couldn't have known about it if he wasn't m-m-moving in those circles."

"You're probably right," Larkin said. "There's a load of stuff the judge wrote about a young lad he and Adams had the hots for. The kid went off with somebody else and Neeson blamed Adams for that."

"Yes," Sheehan said. "Detective Connors got a whiff of that a while back when he was looking into their backgrounds."

Both Connors and Miller were nodding agreement as he spoke.

"Yeah, but there was a bit more to it," Larkin said. "Apparently Neeson offered the young fella a load of money for one night's work in The Club. You might say, he made him an offer he couldn't refuse. No details, but whoever the client was and whatever he tried to do—and looking at that menu, I'm sure it was bloody awful—somehow the young lad ended up killing him. Manslaughter, the judge's notes say." He waved his own notes. "These are only jottings and I'm a bit iffy on the details. It seems that the judge tried to cover the whole thing up by restaging the killing in the victim's own house. The judge made sure that there were loads of prints, DNA and other forensic evidence that led straight to the young fellow." He pointed to his notes again, looking disgusted. "But here's the thing. He persuaded the young chap to take the fall and confess to the deed on the understanding that he would give him the most minimal sentence he could in court. But when it came time to deliver the sentence, the vindictive bastard threw the book at the kid. Gave him six or seven years, I think. Adams was fit to be tied. Accused Neeson was getting payback because the lad had rejected him earlier and threatened to expose him. But Neeson apparently had other stuff on Adams, and so they just hated each other from a distance and did nothing."

"So what are we waiting for?" Connors asked truculently. "There's your killer. Why aren't we arresting the bastard?"

Sheehan said, "We've been through this before. Adams obviously has plenty of reason to hate Neeson, but there still remains the question over his motive for killing the others."

"Doesn't mean there isn't one," Connors said. "We just need to find it."

"Yes, and if it's there, we'll find it. But it's going to be tough. This whole business about The Club is going to lead to a huge investigation, arrests, trials. There's a huge scandal brewing. There'll be a media frenzy when the word gets out, reputations thrashed, questions in Stormont." He was shaking his head, his expression serious as he visualised the furore that was just a couple of days away.

"Geez, Chief," Miller said, sounding stunned. "Where do we even start?"

"Bill told me before the meeting that copies of the judge's notes were sent to the Assistant Chief Constable the minute they were found. He's been on the phone to me. The ACC's putting a special Task Force together even as we speak. We will have some involvement, especially as far as identifying our serial killer is concerned. So, while the Task Force will be rounding up the big fish in The Club, we'll still have to deal with our own original suspects."

"Maybe that's the connection with the teacher," McCullough said. "He must have been a member of this Club as well."

"From the sound of what Bill has just told us," Allen said, "I'd say our suspect pool has expanded outa sight."

"I agree with Tom," McNeill said. "P-p-people like that would have no problem committing m-m-murder to stop anyone revealing those things they were d-d-doing."

"There must be dozens there with motive to murder the judge," Connors said, "and, indeed, to murder anyone else who might be a threat to them."

Sheehan was frowning, not fully agreeing. "Makes sense, I suppose, but the latest killing calls that whole line of thinking into question."

"Latest killing?" Miller's surprise raised the tone of his voice a few notches.

"Yes. Sergeant Stewart found another blog this morning. You'll have copies in a few minutes. We've already been to see the body."

"Which of them is it this t-t-time?" McNeill asked.

Sheehan said, "Well, it explains why Miller and Connor were unable to carry out their interrogations of released jailbird, Thomas McStravick. He's the latest victim, and he was not someone who got in the way. He was deliberately targeted and is definitely a piece of our killer's jigsaw."

"Hell, where does he fit in with all those millionaires?" McCullough asked, clearly confused.

"My thinking exactly," Sheehan replied. "Are we looking at this from the correct perspective?"

"What do you mean, Chief?" Larkin asked.

"Well, although Mac thinks the teacher might be a member of The Club, we have no evidence of that yet. What if he isn't? That would mean two out of the four dead are anomalies. That has me wondering."

Stewart rose from her desk and handed copies of the latest blog to the team. There was silence while they studied the pages.

Miller was the first to speak. "My God, he's really got it in for the final victim, whoever he, or she, is."

"We're going to have to stop the killer before he gets to him," Allen said firmly. "Where do we start, Chief?"

Sheehan shrugged. "Until we find a different turning, I suppose we'll have to continue following the path we're on. I suggest we start by calling in our four primary suspects. They're facing arrest anyway, so we can hold them for a couple of days. Maybe we'll get lucky and one of them will crack."

Connors was shaking his head. "Bloody hell, this is going to be a serious mess. If our killer isn't one of those four, we're going to be blown seriously off track. We'll be back looking for needles in haystacks." He blew out an exasperated breath. "What's wrong with these bloody peoples' heads, anyway?"

"What exactly is the ACC doing?" Stewart said to Larkin.

"Everything's being kept very hush-hush until the members of The Club have been identified. Some of them have private planes and stuff, and many are from England and even parts of Europe. It's seriously huge. British cops. Interpol. There's going to be a massive big sweep today or tomorrow and, whatever about the continent, all the Northern Ireland and English members will be pulled into stations all over the country. There'll be all sorts of legal crap with extradition requests for the members from Europe. They've the money to buy top lawyers, pay out massive bribes. God knows what'll happen there."

"Holy shit!" Miller moaned. "If one of them's our killer, we're done."

"I think our killer's definitely nearer to home," Sheehan said. "We'll get these interrogations done and see where they lead."

Miller sensed something unspoken in Sheehan's tone. "You know something, Chief, don't you?" he said. "Come on, give us a clue."

Sheehan grinned. "You all have the same clues I do, and I have to be honest, I find some of them very confusing."

"What do you mean, Chief?" McBride asked.

"Well, if we consider the basic investigative requirements—means, motive, opportunity—our key suspects from The Club are all serious runners. But in view of the McStravick angle and the possibility that we might have to step even a little bit outside of this group to consider other options, you hit a brick wall when you start looking for motive."

"You're hiding something, Chief," Allen pressed.

Sheehan, still grinning, shook his head. "Not really, but I always try to look at other options where possible. This case makes that tough." He shrugged. "We'll plod along, building up evidence, and see where that takes us." He paused, while gathering up his folders then said, "Tom and Geoff, will you take on the interrogation of that professor, Edith Gallagher? And don't go easy on her because she's a woman." He nodded to Miller. "Simon, you and Declan see what you can squeeze out of Jaclyn Kennedy. She's a dark horse, that one. Stewart and I will question Adams and Kane."

He looked down at McCullough, his expression thoughtful. "Mac, could you and your young partner organise a line-up with that big fellow Robinson in it? Bring in Doran to have a look at it. Get them all to read aloud from a piece of paper, something like, *'Where's the bloody second safe, you wee bastard'*. Robinson matches the description of the big guy who kidnapped Doran. If Doran can identify his voice, maybe we can get that nasty piece of work off the streets right away. That'd be a start."

THIRTY
Wednesday, 22nd August. Afternoon

"You see," McCullough was explaining to Doran, as they waited, "what we do is get six big guys, roughly the same height and build as your abductor and we—" He looked up as McBride uttered a polite but obviously fake cough. "What is it, son?"

"Uh, Mr Doran is well qualified in legal matters, Sergeant. He probably knows all about identity parades."

They stood in a small ante-room in front of a large window that looked into a bare room, at the far side of which was a white wall with height markings on it. Also present in the ante-room was a thin, balding man dressed in a navy, pin-stripe suit. He stared at the others through gold-rimmed glasses, his lips compressed, his bearing vigilant, but he did not speak. He was a solicitor representing Mr Robinson, although neither of the policemen addressed him directly, nor had Doran been introduced to him at that point.

Doran smiled at McBride. "Obviously I am aware of identity parades and their purpose, Detective, but to be honest, I have never actually been present at one."

"Well," McCullough said, throwing the solicitor a sideways glance, "there's not much we're allowed to say to you. The process has to be scrupulously fair." He waved a hand at the solicitor. "This gentleman, Mr Cosgrove, is here to ensure that no rules are broken."

Doran glanced at Cosgrove. "The suspect's solicitor, I presume?"

Cosgrove gave no sign he heard him.

"We're going to bring in six people and line them up at that far wall." McCullough pointed through the window, "And don't worry. None of them can see us. This window's a one-way mirror. You, of course, will be able to see them clearly. But, as I was saying earlier, to be fair to the suspect, all six will be of equal size and similar proportions, and all will be wearing balaclavas."

"Good gracious!" Doran exclaimed. "I don't think I'd be much help in identifying the man who abducted me if they all look the same."

"We understand that," McCullough said, "but you did hear him speak, right?"

"I did. Quite a lot, in fact."

"That's what we're going to focus on," McBride interjected. "We'll ask each person in the line-up to read a sentence using words that were said to you during the time you were being beaten in that garage. There might be a chance you'll recognise the voice of your abductor." He hesitated when Mr Cosgrove straightened and moved slightly forward before adding hastily, "However, we have to be scrupulously fair, so neither the sergeant nor I will be allowed to say or do anything that might help you to identify the suspect. Not that we could," he added, again glancing again at Cosgrove. "We're not allowed to know which one he is."

"Just listen to the voices," McCullough said. "If you're sure that one of the voices you hear is your abductor's, then tell us. If you can't positively identify any of the men in the line-up, that's okay." He shrugged. "We'll have to live with that." He sounded, however, as if living with it was the last thing he wanted.

"The thing is," McBride added, "we'll need you to be absolutely sure if you identify anyone. Anything less than total certainty won't stand up in court."

Doran nodded, looking slightly uncomfortable. "I'll do my best, Detective."

Again, Mr Cosgrove signalled silent disapproval of the tone of the conversation.

McCullough, watching the solicitor for any reaction, added, "And as Detective McBride said, neither of us knows which of the six is the suspect. So don't be trying to read any imaginary clues from our body language. There won't be any."

Doran nodded, seeming to steel himself for an ordeal.

"Okay," McCullough said. Pressing a button, he spoke into a small microphone that was attached to the wall just below the mirror, "Send them in, Officer, please."

Six large men paraded into the room in single file, the one in the lead walking to the extreme end of the wall, the others following. All were dressed in grey, tailored suits, and all stood with their backs to the wall, arms hanging by their sides, each holding a slip of paper in his right hand. The wall markings showed that all of them were well over six feet in height.

McBride stepped back from the mirror while McCullough issued instructions at the microphone. Both detectives now exhibited traces of tension. Normally it would have taken some days to set up such a line-up, but since the detectives were already sure they had their suspect, the other five members of the line-up were actually serving police-officers, drafted in at short notice. The identity parade would be used simply as confirmation that their suspect was, in fact, the person who had abducted and assaulted Doran. Any arrest, however, depended upon their witness being able to make a positive identification. The slightest hesitation or doubt on Doran's part and Cosgrove would have Robinson whisked out of there in a matter of minutes.

"Number One," McCullough barked into the mike. "Read your sentence."

Number One was clearly never destined to experience a career change from law-enforcement to the theatre. In a voice that lacked any variety or emotion, he intoned, "Where is the bloody second safe, you wee bastard?"

Doran was now close to the mirror, his head to one side in a listening attitude. He glanced at McCullough and gave him the slightest of head shakes.

"Number Two," McCullough repeated. "Read your sentence."

Number Two spoke his line with slightly more vigour, but with a voice as dry as dust. "Where is the bloody second safe, you wee bastard?"

Again Doran listened carefully for a few seconds before shaking his head once more.

"Number Three," McCullough called.

Number Three may or may not have been harbouring secret thespian aspirations but he did sound as if he had given the line considerable practice. He proclaimed the words harshly and with some heat, "Where's the bloody second safe, you wee bastard?"

Doran again listened carefully, but this time a slight smile creased his lips. "No," he mouthed inaudibly, "not him."

"Number Four," McCullough again shouted into the microphone.

Number Four apparently shared Number One's utter lack of histrionic endeavour. Dry, monotonous, devoid of all inflection, he said, "Where is the bloody second safe, you wee bastard?"

Doran closed his eyes, and listened with great attention, still seeming to hear the voice several seconds after the speaker had finished. He signalled to McCullough to turn off the microphone. "Are you permitted to instruct that man to read the line again?" he whispered.

"To be fair to the process," McCullough answered, "you'll have to hear the other two first. But yes, when all six have read the line, you can request to hear any of them read again."

"Okay," Doran said. "Please continue."

Numbers Five and Six read their lines in flat, uninvolved tones, but Doran appeared to have lost interest at this point. "Now can I hear Number Four again," he asked, seeming to fight impatience.

"Number Four," McCullough spoke into the microphone once more. "Read your line again."

Number Four cleared his throat before saying the words. He read without any flow, enunciating each word separately from the others.

Doran listened carefully, his eyes closed. Eventually he said, with some excitement. "He's trying to disguise his voice, but I am one hundred percent certain that Number Four is the person who abducted and assaulted me."

McCullough said carefully, staring pointedly at Cosgrove. "You have no doubt that this is the man who abducted you?"

"Absolutely none," Doran said with a hint of anger rising in his voice.

McCullough switched on the microphone again. "Take off your balaclavas, gentlemen."

All six men pulled the balaclavas from their heads. Five of them looked unconcerned. Number Four, Patrick Robinson, looked grim and angry.

McCullough spoke again into the microphone. "Everyone leave except Number Four, please."

As the others were filing out, Doran's rising anger was replaced by puzzlement. "There was a Patrick Robinson on the list of invitees to the judge's soirée," he whispered to McCullough, nodding towards the suspect. "Is that the same Robinson?"

"The Chief Inspector will explain," McCullough whispered back. Bending forward once again, he spoke to the suspect, intoning familiar lines with something of the same dryness as the officers in the parade. "Mr Robinson, a witness has identified you as the perpetrator of a kidnapping and an assault. An officer will now take you to one of the interrogation rooms where you will be charged and held in custody until a court hearing can be arranged for your arraignment. You may lodge a request for bail at that time."

Even as McCullough was speaking, Cosgrove marched out of the room without a word to any of them.

Doran was still staring intently at the suspect. "Will I be expected to confirm this identification in court?"

"Hopefully," McBride said, "but all we have so far is your uncorroborated statement. We're going to need a bit more. I don't suppose you've thought of anything else in the meantime that might be helpful to us?"

Doran hesitated.

McBride said quickly, "Anything at all. Doesn't matter how irrelevant it might seem."

"Well, shortly after I returned to my apartment from hospital, I was cleaning up and found a small button. My guess is that it might have come from the sleeve of a man's jacket. I noticed it because it doesn't match anything I wear. I thought perhaps it might belong to the Chief Inspector and intended to ask him about it. But…." He stared from one detective to the other. "Could it have come from Robinson's jacket when he grabbed me, do you think?"

McCullough showed some excitement. "Do you still have it?"

"Yes, it's on my desk in a small glass dish that I keep paper clips in. I didn't want to throw it out."

"Great. We'll pick it up later and get a warrant to search Robinson's house. There's other stuff going on, so there'll be no trouble with the warrant."

Doran nodded and said quietly, "You'll understand if I say that I hope your search is successful and that you will find enough evidence to lock that ... that...." His lips tightened as he fought to control his anger. "I just hope he goes to jail for a very long time."

"We understand, Mr Doran. If the evidence is there, we'll find it," McBride assured him as he led him out of the room. "Thank you very much for your help today. We really appreciate it."

THIRTY-ONE
Wednesday, 22nd August. Late afternoon

Interrogation Room 2 in Strandtown Police Station is bare and functional. It contains no furnishings other than a single table with two chairs on either side of it. On the table is a recording device, beside which are some blank sheets of headed paper and a couple of ballpoint pens.

Late in the afternoon, a short time after the identity parade, Sergeant McCullough and Detective McBride sat at one side of the table facing Patrick Robinson and his solicitor. McCullough reached out to the recording device and switched it on. Looking at his watch, he said tonelessly, "Interview with Mr Patrick Robinson conducted on Wednesday, twenty-second of August, two thousand and eighteen. Present in the room are Detective Sergeant McCullough, Detective McBride, Mr Patrick Robinson, and his solicitor, Mr Kieran Cosgrove. The time is three forty-four p.m."

He sat back, arms folded across his ample girth, and offered Robinson a silent glare.

Cosgrove, with a glare of his own, waited only a beat before saying, "Is this to be an interrogation following stipulated guidelines, Sergeant, or an exercise in intimidation?"

McCullough might not have been the brightest spark in Sheehan's team but he had years of experience and was thoroughly versed in all matters of police procedures. Cosgrove's intervention did not faze him in the slightest.

Staring at the solicitor, he growled, "Just trying to collect my thoughts. And you butting in before I even get time to open my mouth is not helping. So, could you hold your horses, please, until you actually have something to shout about?"

Cosgrove's prim lips tightened in distaste. Intellectual cut and thrust were his stock in trade. McCullough's coarseness rendered him temporarily speechless.

McCullough turned his attention to Robinson once more. "Where were you on the evening of Tuesday the fourteenth of August between ten o'clock and midnight?"

Robinson, sitting back on his chair with his own arms folded and a faint sneer on his face, said coolly, "That was a couple of weeks ago. I wouldn't have a clue."

It was obvious that McCullough was less than happy with the suspect's answer, or with his attitude, but he held himself in check. "It was just over one week ago. You got Alzheimer's or something?"

"Sergeant..." Cosgrove started.

McCullough waved a dismissive hand at the solicitor and continued. "What do you usually do on a Tuesday night?"

Robinson shrugged. "Depends. Sometimes I stay in and watch TV. Sometimes I go out with friends."

McCullough pushed a blank sheet of paper towards the suspect and picked up one of the pens. "Would you please write down the names, addresses and phone numbers of the two friends you were out with on the night of Tuesday, the fourteenth."

"What are you talking about?" Robinson said.

"Sergeant McCullough," Cosgrove snapped. "We have not established that Mr Robinson was out with friends on the night of the fourteenth. Would you confine your questioning to the facts, please?"

"Oh, but we have," McCullough replied. "We have the evidence of a key witness confirming that your client, together with two thugs, kidnapped and assaulted Mr Edgar Doran on that Tuesday night."

Robinson reacted furiously, but Cosgrove put a restraining hand on his arm. "Sergeant, what you have is a person who heard six people muttering through heavy balaclava masks and identified one of them as a voice he heard for a few minutes over a week ago. Good luck trying to make that stand up in court."

"It will," McCullough said, nonchalantly examining his fingernails, "especially when we support it with very incriminating physical evidence."

McBride stiffened and glanced sideways at his superior. The lie had rolled very easily off the sergeant's tongue. The warrant to search Robinson's house had not yet even been applied for.

"What evidence?" Cosgrove asked coldly.

"You will be informed in due course," McCullough said, smug now. He could see that the two men at the other side of the table were suddenly rattled. "So, Mr Robinson," he went on, waving the pen at the suspect. "My best advice to you is to confess to the abduction right now. It'll go much easier for you at sentencing."

Robinson looked concerned but Cosgrove said, "Don't be ridiculous. My client has no intention of confessing to a crime he didn't commit."

McCullough tossed the pen on to the table as if in disgust. "Okay. So what did you want with that safe, anyway?"

Cosgrove reached across and grasped his client's forearm to stop his response. "We deny all knowledge of this issue, and my client particularly denies knowledge of whatever safe you refer to."

McCullough stared intently into Robinson's eyes. "Let's talk about that Club, then."

Robinson may or may not have had hobbies. If he did, poker wasn't one of them. The shock that covered his face was a clear admission of guilt. His lips moved but he seemed lost for a response.

McBride hid his eyes behind a hand that he was using to rub his brow. His superior was discussing this topic before the Assistant Chief Constable was ready to launch his offensive. He leaned sideways to speak to his sergeant, but McCullough turned towards him with a confident expression. "It's okay, Detective. I know what I'm doing."

Cosgrove watched this interplay closely, but if he had any idea what was going on between the two policemen, his lowered eyebrows indicated otherwise. "What Club?" he asked, glancing his puzzlement at his client. The solicitor appeared suddenly to be unsure of himself.

"Well," McCullough almost drawled, "it's actually a confidential thing right now. I can't tell you about it because my superiors are getting ready to deal with it. But your client knows all about it, don't you, Mr Robinson?"

"No comment," was the best Robinson could muster.

McCullough uttered what seemed to be a mixture of snort and laugh. "Oh, you'll comment, Mr Robinson. You'll comment. You see, we found that safe you were so anxious to get your hands on, and we've seen what's inside of it. My Gawd, you and your pals are in it up to your necks."

Robinson paled, again shocked to his core. "It was just a swingers club," he spluttered. "We were doing nothing illegal."

"Hah!" McCullough barked, his voice suddenly filled with anger. "Paedophilia, murder, human trafficking, kidnapping and imprisonment, underage sex and all sorts of physical abuse. I could go on. So, Mr Robinson, what do you mean by nothing illegal?"

As he listened, Robinson was suddenly hyperventilating. "I don't know anything about any of that".

"You're a signed-up member of The Club, Mr Robinson." McCullough spat out the name contemptuously. "You'd have seen what was available. Your so-called ignorance means nothing. You're guilty by association and, believe me, you'll spend a long time behind bars."

Cosgrove had been severely rattled by what the sergeant was saying, but he gathered himself to challenge McCullough's guilt by association gambit. "Excuse me, Detective," he said, coldly, "there's no law for guilty by association. In fact, it's known as a fallacy, the *ad hominem* fallacy. People are charged as *parties* to a crime, not because they are somehow connected to one by being in the wrong place at the wrong time."

"There's still accessory after the fact," McBride cut in. "Your client was fully *au fait* with what The Club was offering before he applied for membership. I doubt if his argument that he didn't know about it will hold water in court."

McCullough sat back in his chair, arms folded, mouth tight, nodding full agreement with his young partner. There was no indication in his demeanour that he was struggling with the legal niceties.

"Excuse me, Detective. You know very well that mere presence at the scene of a crime is not enough for a charge to be brought. Accessory liability requires proof of a conduct element accompanied by the necessary mental element. There needs to be some kind of active encouragement of the crime."

McBride nodded. "That's true. I'm quite familiar with R. v Jogee, so you might also have added that if the crime required a particular intent, the accessory had to intend to assist or encourage the principal to act with such intent."

Cosgrove eyed him warily. "Precisely," he said. "So you agree?"

McBride shook his head. "No, I don't. As you know, it's all about interpretation. If the court hears that your client joined this club fully cognizant of its depraved and decadent offerings, a judge or jury will have no trouble arriving at a reasonable inference of intent, and an affirmation of encouragement of any crimes past and future committed by The Club."

Cosgrove glanced sideways at his client, clearly perplexed. "There are issues here to which I have not been made party. I request that you put a temporary halt to this interrogation. I need some moments to confer with my client."

McCullough looked at his watch. "My partner and I don't have all day. We'll give you ten minutes." He reached for the recorder and, before switching it off, intoned, "Interview temporarily suspended at four minutes past four." He rose from the table, McBride rising with him. "Remember, ten minutes," he said, heading for the door with McBride on his heels.

Once outside, as they stood waiting in the hallway, McCullough said, "Great stuff in there, partner. I didn't know what you were going on about, but Cosgrove did, and you clearly had him on the run."

"Thanks, Sarge," McBride said, "but I was lucky. I had an assignment to do on that very issue a couple of weeks ago."

Despite his glee, McCullough became aware that the young detective's expression was sombre. "So what's with the long face?" he asked.

"It's just … I mean, d'you think we were wise telling them about that safe now. The chief—"

"Ah, don't be worrying about that, son," McCullough cut in. "At some point Robinson will have to tell Cosgrove about The Club and the safe. Then it'll be into client confidentiality and all that stuff. So it won't leave this room."

McBride still looked uneasy. "It'll be on the recording."

"Not a problem. Look, you're new to this. When we've finished the interrogation, we'll have to seal that master copy of the recording in the suspect's presence. There'll be a second recording which will later be used as a working copy." He patted his young colleague on the shoulder. "We can simply make sure that neither of them leaves our possession until the word about The Club is out. And, believe me, something that big? The ACC will be on the ball about it in no time, if he isn't already."

McBride relaxed. "Robinson has a point about only being a new member who knows nothing about the murders and trafficking."

"He can't make that argument if he saw the menu Bill was talking about. And he must have. You don't join a club with sky-high entrance fees without finding out what you can about it. I don't know much about law, but I'm pretty sure, uh, whaddya call it, prior knowledge or something, will go strongly against him. You're the law student. You saw the stuff from the safe. And what you were saying about..." He made some small circles in the air with his right hand.

"Accessory after the fact."

"Yeah, that. I'm telling you, he knew what was on offer before he joined The Club. He's on very sticky ground and he knows it."

McBride nodded. "Probably why Cosgrove wanted a recess."

"Aye! But I've something else up my sleeve. I've been down this path loads of times before. That stuff about murder and trafficking is scary, and very heavy duty compared to just giving somebody a hiding. If my guess is right, Cosgrove is right now giving his client the advice that's gonna get us the confession we need to charge the big bastard with kidnapping, assault and battery." He looked at his watch. "We'll give them another couple of minutes."

"You sure scared the hell out of them, Sarge."

McCullough grinned. "That was the idea, son."

"You scared the hell outa me, too. I've only just made detective and I could see my career going up in smoke."

McCullough gave him a sympathetic grin and a slap on the side of his upper arm. "When you been around the Chief as long as I have, you'll learn that results mean everything to him. He'll not give a rat's ass if we detour slightly off track to get them. All we're going to get is a clap on the back...." His expression changed, his normal truculence replaced by something akin to regret. "Not that I've ever had many of those."

"Well, as far as I'm concerned, Sarge, you did a really first-class job in there."

McCullough was still thinking about claps on the back. "Didn't really deserve them in the past, son," he said, "but that whole business with them Satanists. Makes you think."

It was McBride's turn to slap his superior on the arm. "And thinking's what you're doing, Sarge. Let's go back in and see what effect your thinking has had on our client."

They went back into the room. Cosgrove was still huddled in whispered consultation with his client, but they separated and sat back on their chairs, silently watching the two detectives as they took their seats.

Cosgrove cleared his throat. "Sergeant, before you turn the recorder back on, my client requests that we be permitted to discuss a hypothetical situation with you."

McCullough glanced at his partner, reluctant to admit that he didn't know what Cosgrove was talking about. McBride gave him a slight affirmative nod. The bulky sergeant then shrugged and said neutrally, "Okay. Let's hear what you have to say."

"Just assuming my client might know something about Mr Doran's abduction...." He held up a hand. "We're not admitting anything, you understand, just raising a hypothetical assumption which would lead to a hypothetical question."

McCullough still retained his severe expression, but he was not following the solicitor. However, he simply said, "And that would be...?"

"It's this." He raised an admonitory finger. "Hypothetically, remember. Would there be any possibility, should my client choose to admit to some involvement in the abduction of Mr Doran, that you could ignore all and any charges relating to his membership in The Club?"

McCullough glanced again at his colleague. He had no idea whether or not he was in any position to make such an offer. McBride's blank expression indicated that he wasn't sure either. *Wing it, McCullough*, he advised himself. *Throw in a couple of white lies if you have to.* He tightened his lips, nodded almost imperceptibly as he eyed the two men at the other side of the table, offering the impression that he was giving the matter serious thought. Then he said, "Not so fast."

Cosgrove looked puzzled. "Not so fast?"

"There's still the little matter of Judge Neeson's murder. Did your client have anything to do with that?"

"What?" Robinson almost jumped out of his seat.

McCullough shrugged. "Somebody in your group was blackmailing him," he said, his tone matter-of-fact, positive. "The judge's notes show he was holding a lot of damning information on all of you. It had to be you, or one of your pals who murdered him."

"I had absolutely nothing to do with that," Robinson spluttered.

"You're a violent man, Mr Robinson," McCullough said. "Your abuse of Mr Doran is more than enough evidence of that. Killing somebody would not be difficult for you."

"I didn't do it." Robinson was becoming increasingly agitated.

"I'm not convinced, but we'll leave that for a moment. Do you know which member of your group was blackmailing the judge?"

Robinson was almost gasping. "No, I don't. I had absolutely no idea anyone was blackmailing him."

Cosgrove laid a placating hand on his client's shoulder. "Just be silent, Patrick. Let me deal with this." He turned to McCullough, angry at this response. "Do you have any evidence to support these outlandish accusations?"

"We have a great deal of evidence that points either to your client or to one of the group he's a part of," McCullough lied. "If he wants to talk about this, uh, hy-hy ... this deal, he'll need to tell us what he knows." He pointed to the recorder. "This isn't being recorded, so he won't be incriminating himself if he wants to help us out here."

"But I don't know anything," Robinson protested.

"A judge who was part of your Club group was murdered, and none of you even discussed it?" McBride finally contributed, his voice dripping with scepticism.

Robinson stopped protesting, appearing rattled. For once, Cosgrove simply waited. "Well, we did talk about it one evening at The Club. In fact, my business partner, Jaclyn Kennedy, asked the group point blank if any of them had done it."

"And?" McCullough said.

"Everybody suddenly went stone-faced. Judge Adams told her not to be silly and to stick to the issue we were discussing."

"So, who did it?"

Robinson looked blank. "I've no idea."

"But you must have your suspicions. If it wasn't you, that is," McCullough said.

His little addendum got him the result he needed. "I have no evidence, but if I had to guess, I'd go for Judge Adams. Word is he absolutely hated Neeson. If Neeson had anything on him, he could easily have killed him to keep him quiet."

"Any of the others?"

"Kane hated the judge as well, something in their past. I don't know what it was. But he's the devil's own job to read. Face like a blank wall. You never know what he's thinking. But either of them could have done it. They're seriously cold."

"Hmmph! What about one of the wimmen, Kennedy, for example?"

"Jaclyn? No way. She's a thinker, not a doer. If she did involve herself in anything, she would have to give it a great deal of serious thought. She'd figure out all the options and moves. She's very intense, very clever. She would take ages...." He faltered as if his train of thought was suddenly puzzling him. "She would have to do some concentrated planning before she'd commit herself to an action like that." He turned to look at Cosgrove, his expression confused.

McCullough thought about that for a minute. Then he said, "So she could have done it?"

"Can't see it," Robinson replied, but there was no longer the same conviction in his denial.

"What about the law professor? Could she have done it, do you think?"

"I don't really know much about her. I couldn't say."

McCullough glanced at McBride, offering him a chance to speak. McBride shook his head. McCullough lifted one of the pens again and said, "Okay. Let's get back to this deal thing." He pushed one of the blank pages at Robinson and handed him the pen. "Let's pretend that your offer was real. Write down the details of the abduction and assault of Doran, your own involvement in it, and the names and addresses of the two thugs you hired to help you, and I'll drop any charges relating to The Club." He ignored the nervous glance his partner gave him.

Robinson glanced at Cosgrove who nodded, grim-faced.

THIRTY-TWO
Wednesday, 22nd August. Evening

Sheehan replaced his phone on its receiver and went to the door of his office. "They're raiding The Club," he called over to Stewart who was working at her desk. "I'm taking a run over there now. Serious and degrading stuff, I'm told." He hesitated and looked at his watch. "You don't need to come. You can go on home if you want to."

Stewart bridled. "Sir, it's enough I have to fight about stuff like this with Tom without you starting."

"I only meant—"

"You only meant that I'm a woman, sir, somebody who needs to be protected from the darker side of police work." She got up from her desk and faced him. "I said it to Tom, and I'm saying it to you. I'm a fully trained detective sergeant, sir. I take what the job throws at me, just as Tom does, just as you do, good or bad, pretty or ugly, safe or dangerous. It's my duty. The fact that I'm female is utterly irrelevant."

Sheehan held up his hands in a gesture of surrender. "Sorry, sorry. I didn't mean—"

"You did, sir," Stewart snapped, still irked. "You're the one who's always talking about unconscious bias—"

Sheehan cut in. "Okay! Okay! You're right. You've made your point. My mistake. It won't happen again. Now let's go." He stalked out of the room, but stopped just outside the door and said, with one finger in the air, "BUT, if you had let me finish what I tried several times to say, you'd have discovered that my concern was about making you work unpaid overtime by accompanying me. It's day's end. That's why I suggested that you could go home if you wanted to." He ignored her open-mouthed reaction and added, "Okay, go and get the car. I've one call to make. I'll meet you at the gate."

She nodded and edged past him, clearly mortified.

Sheehan watched her as she went down the corridor. Shaking his head, he muttered, "Women." Then, aware of the irony, he grimaced. *Oh, crap. Good job she didn't hear that.* He headed back into his office, shaking his head and fighting a sheepish grin.

Pulling his phone to his ear, he dialled the Station Desk Sergeant. When the sergeant replied, Sheehan spoke fast and urgently. "Harry, DCI Sheehan here. There'll be all sorts of fancy arrests coming in shortly. You might recognise some of them. Listen to nobody. Y' hear me? Tell anybody with funny ideas that your instructions come from me."

"Okay, Chief. What do you want me to do?"

"Whatever about the other suspects, and there will probably be several of them, make sure that Judge Adams, Permanent Secretary Oliver Kane, Professor Edith Gallagher, and Industrialist Jaclyn Kennedy, are all kept separate and fully isolated from each other. Got that? They are not allowed to communicate in any way, and that goes for their lawyers, too."

* * *

"Well, that explains it," Sheehan muttered, as Stewart coasted slowly along a country road searching for the private road that would lead to The Club.

"Explains what, Chief?"

"Why there have been no complaints about large cars coming and going at all hours of the day and night."

"Middle of nowhere, Chief. These people pay for privacy as much as anything else, and they've got it here in spades."

Sheehan pointed. "There y'are. There's your entrance."

"I googled the map of this place earlier, Chief. There's still nearly a mile to the house."

"Huh! They sure weren't going to be disturbed."

They drove on in silence until they emerged on a large expanse of ground covered in red pebbles in front of a magnificent three-storey Tudor house, built sometime in the 1930s. Dark wooden beams relieved the white walls, which were adorned with large bay windows, and topped by turrets and a red slate roof that featured a large number of heights and ridges. There was no indication that an extension had ever been added to the house, but Sheehan noted that it was exceptionally long and, while he could not see the back part, he could easily imagine that the house contained many rooms of different sizes and shapes.

Peace may have been the owner's quest and aim, but there was no peace now. A number of police vehicles were parked on the pebbled area, armed officers with pistols and submachine guns were patrolling the grounds, white-suited SOCOs were wandering in and out of the large front door, some officers were leading people in handcuffs to the cars, many of them protesting loudly and angrily. Some, both male and female, dressed in white shirts and black trousers succumbed quietly to their arrests.

Probably staff, Sheehan mused.

As he and Stewart climbed from the car, he noticed Superintendent Joseph Owens talking to a knot of officers. He strolled over and said to the superintendent's back, "Interesting place, sir."

Owens turned and smiled when he recognised the owner of the voice. "Hello, Jim," he said, giving Stewart a brief nod as well. "Sergeant."

"Afternoon, sir," Stewart said.

Owens spoke to Sheehan again. "Some can of worms you've opened here, Jim." His head was shaking from side to side, his expression close to bewildered. "We picked tough men for the Task Force, but some of them have been coming out of there vomiting."

"Yes, we have some notion of the depravity that went on in there."

"Do you, Jim? Do you really?" Owens was hyper, deeply affected by what he had seen and learned about the house. He began pacing towards the entrance, calling over his right shoulder, "Come on. Let me show you."

Even as they entered the great hall, Stewart nudged Sheehan and pointed with a sideways tilt of her head. Four young children, three girls and a boy, maybe four or five years of age, were sitting beside each other on a sofa in a nearby drawing room. Their faces were solemn, their eyes round and unblinking as they stared at a young policeman who was on one knee in front of them, trying to get them to speak.

Owens followed their gaze. "Traumatised," he explained. "We're waiting for Social Services."

"The young cop looks as traumatised as they are," Sheehan said dryly.

Owens nodded. "Probably."

As they moved towards the end of the hall, they saw a number of other rooms, SOCOs and officers walking in and out of them. Many were expensively decorated, some in garish reds and purples. One looked like a small cinematographic studio, loaded with equipment, a screen and projection cameras.

"They make all sorts of porno movies here, even worse, snuff movies. And people pay thousands for the privilege of acting in them. And, of course, one of our forensic accountants has discovered that Judge Neeson was selling these movies all over the world and making a fortune from them." As they continued walking, Owens added, grimly, "There are loads of rooms like these all over the house. Some are done up like blue or pink nurseries, full of toys, children's clothes...." He ground to a halt, lips tight, head shaking again. Then he went on, "There are bordellos, small cinemas, rooms with several beds, large halls with weird decor, from World War II Germanic style to rooms filled with occult paraphernalia. It's bloody madness. From what we've been able to piece together so far, members were allowed to engage in excessive drinking and unlimited sexual activity within The Club's rooms and grounds. Many MPs, top professionals, lawyers, doctors, government officials, civil servants, priests, monks, members of royal and near royal families, millionaires, movie stars...." He shook his head, still appalled at what he had learned. "You wouldn't believe the list. Some reputations are going to be ground into the dust before all of this is finished."

They had reached a door at the end of the hall. Just as Owens made to open it, it swung inwards, and a young man, probably early twenties, and naked but for a blood-spattered pair of cut-off jeans, staggered into view, his right hand holding on to the arm of a policeman as if it was a stair-rail. His back and legs were lacerated with old and fresh whip lashes and purple bruises. He was gaunt, emaciated, and clearly exhausted. Sheehan guessed that the policeman had lent him his arm in that odd way to avoid touching him and rendering the pain worse.

The policeman waved at someone behind Sheehan. Two paramedics had just come in and when they saw the youth, one stalled momentarily but, apart from a meaningful glance at his partner, said nothing. They quickly went to the stumbling youth and led him out to their ambulance.

The door was at the top of a flight of stairs. "Down here," Owens said.

He led them into a stone cellar, or what could more properly be described as a dungeon, with two prison cells made from rough stone walls and iron gates. The cells had iron restraining rings on the walls, stone floors, and tables covered with mediaeval instruments of torture such as thumb screws, a flagrum with several thongs weighted with lead pellets, a heretic's fork, head crushers, knee splitters, as well as a rack, a Chinese Iron Maiden, a Judas Chair and other instruments, small and large, that would eventually be identified by the Task Force's researchers.

Sheehan stared at them, disturbed. "Like the Spanish Inquisition," he muttered.

"Look at the floor," Owens said.

Sheehan and Stewart looked down. The stone floor seemed to be painted red and brown, but both detectives quickly realised that it was not painted but covered in what were clearly old and new blood stains.

"What in God's name was going on down here?" Stewart breathed, shocked.

"Whatever it was, it wasn't in God's name," Sheehan growled. He turned to Owens. "I've seen enough, Joe. Get us out of here."

"You haven't seen the quarter of it," Owens said, leading them back up the stairs. "Wait 'till you see what we found in the office." As they emerged from the door again, Owens shouted to a SOCO just about to enter one of the rooms in the hall. "George, bring us a copy of that menu, will you?"

"Bill Larkin mentioned a menu," Sheehan said.

"Yes," Owens said, "but a menu like no other menu you've ever seen."

While they were waiting for George to come back, Owens explained that this raid was one of a number, coordinated with other forces in Ireland, England, and with Interpol on the Continent. "We didn't get that many arrests here," he explained. "I think activity fell off a bit after the judge was murdered. But there'll be many arrests today all over Ireland, the British Isles, and abroad. The investigations, charges, and trials will probably take years. However, the judge's safe contains loads of incriminating evidence. It'll take time to get through it all, but...." His grim expression said what he couldn't find words for.

"What about Judge Adams, Oliver Kane and the others we were investigating who led us to this Club? Any sign of them?"

"Officers have been sent to arrest them even as we speak. The ACC instructed us to send them to Strandtown Station."

"Good," Sheehan said curtly.

Owens glanced at him. "You think one of them is your killer?"

"Hopefully we'll find out within the next day or so after we've interrogated them."

George arrived back, and Sheehan suddenly realised it was the SOCO he had met at a couple of the other crime scenes. His eyebrows went up. *Gets around a bit, doesn't he?* But he gave the man a friendly nod and said nothing as Rice handed Owens what looked like the kind of large leather menus found in expensive restaurants. This one was red leather, with hand-stitched edges, and gold embossed writing at the front. Owens handed it to Sheehan who stared at the gold writing:

LISTE

des

ACTIVITÉS

[pour votre délectation et votre plaisir]

He glanced at Stewart who said, disgust evident in her tone, "List of activities for your delight and pleasure, Chief."

Sheehan raised an eyebrow. "What's with the French?"

"Maybe they thought English was too uncouth, sir. Maybe they wanted to be like expensive restaurants, you know, using French to create an aura of elegance and privilege."

"Elegance and privilege," Sheehan muttered. "Aye, right."

Sheehan held the menu up so that Stewart could see it as well. Owens pointed to a Latin phrase at the top of the page. "That's The Club's motto, apparently. One of the SOCOs translated it on his smart phone: *Do what you will shall be the whole of the Law.*"

Sheehan and Stewart studied the menu, their faces wrinkling with revulsion the more they read:

FULFILMENT FOR THE ENLIGHTENED
Quid faciendum sit summa legis

MENU OF AVAILABLE ACTIVITIES

[Special requests will be considered but may take time to provide.]

1. Any kind of sex: hetero, lesbian, homo. Beautiful partners. £1000

2. Wild sex parties: luxurious food and drink, fancy dress. Eighteenth century, Nazi, futuristic, minimalistic. Patrons' choice always. £2000

3. Convivial 'Hellfire Club' dinners, and sex with "the sisterhood" (local girls or prostitutes who dress as nuns). £2000

4. Young boys, pre-teens. £5000

5. Children (3 to 6 years), male or female, available for paedophile tastes. £10,000

6. Coven activity, black masses with wild orgies. Guest Satanists to advise and provide an authentic experience. £10,000

7. Black Mass orgies with human sacrifice. £50,000

SPECIALS

8. Pornographic Movies: Make (and star in) your own pornographic movie. Beautiful actresses supplied. Top of the range equipment. Advice and technical support every step of the way. £25,000

9. Snuff Movies: Make and star in your own snuff movie. Top of the range equipment. Advice and technical support if required. Training in advance on use of equipment if desired. Disposition of bodies by The Club. Full discretion guaranteed. £100,000

10. Torture Dungeon. Mediaeval torture instruments of every sort available for use. Young men provided for sadistic torture and murder. Privacy and circumspection guaranteed. Bodies disposed of with utmost discretion by The Club. £130.000

THIRTY-THREE
Thursday, 23rd August. Mid-morning

"Gee, God! Perversion doesn't even come close to describing that stuff. That's absolutely bloody horrible." Connors was speaking for himself, but he was echoing the thoughts of the other team members who were again gathered together in the Serious Crimes Room. Sheehan, with Stewart pitching in occasionally, had given the team a summary of what they had found and learned from their visit to The Club the evening before.

"When Stewart and I saw that depraved menu," Sheehan said, "it was about as much as we could take. We got outa there and let the Task Force get on with it."

"If they need any help rounding up those bastards," Miller said, "count me in. No overtime required. Arrogant perverts! Think money allows them to do anything they like."

"Don't worry. Superintendent Owens was very shaken by what they found at The Club," Sheehan said, "but he will make darn sure that every one of those degenerates is caught and put away for a very long time."

"Were many arrests made?" McBride asked.

"Only a few of the staff, and a couple of members who had dropped by," Sheehan told him. "It seems that activities were sporadic after the judge's death. But there won't be a problem. Notebooks full of names and addresses were found in the judge's office safe. Looks like he was setting himself up for some lucrative blackmail in the future. Thanks to his greed, few if any of The Club's members will escape the full weight of the law."

"Where are they all?" McCullough asked.

"All over the place ... England, France, Belgium, Germany. One guy from South Africa flies in on his own plane from time to time. He's one evil, depraved son of a bitch. Records indicate that at least three young men had been whipped and beaten to death in the dungeons, and the South African guy is the chief suspect. Interpol is trying to track him down."

Most of the team were shaking their heads in disgust.

"What are we going to d-d-do about it?" McNeill asked. "Or does it all g-g-go over to the T-T-Task Force now?"

"No need to worry," Sheehan replied. "The Task Force has it well in hand and they have loads of help from law enforcement agencies in the other countries."

"What about our suspects?" Allen asked. "Does the Task Force get them?"

"No. They are in the process of arresting the group that were at the judge's that night, all right, but since they are still officially regarded as suspects for the Dark Web murders, our team gets initial access to them. We'll be interviewing them separately here in Strandtown to see what we can squeeze out of them." He paused to give them a meaningful look before adding, "And there'll be no kid gloves this time."

"They'll be looking for bail," McCullough said.

"No bail until all have been interrogated and charged with whatever charges might apply."

"The money they have," Allen said, "they could easily abscond if they get bail."

"True. But if the judge has any wit, it's unlikely bail will be granted in circumstances like these."

Solemn faces stared back at the chief but, apart from one or two grim nods, no one spoke.

"In the meantime," Stewart said, "there's been another development, or the threat of one."

Eyes stared at her.

Rising from her desk, she distributed some pages to the members of the team. "There's been another blog," she explained as she walked around. "I took another trawl through the Dark Web while I was waiting for you all to arrive and I found this. It's quite disturbing. Study it now and we'll discuss it in a few minutes."

Eyes turned to the sheets they had been handed, faces concentrated as they read.

ΝΕΜΕΙΝ'Σ ΒΛΟΓ
Σατισφαξτιον

A final 'Hello' to my faithful followers. This, I suspect, may be my last blog, for a time, at least. Hopefully you will find it will stimulate your interest, as you tell me the others have done. You have been faithful, supportive and encouraging. You have my sincere thanks and my best wishes for your individual futures. You will seek answers after you have read through this post, perhaps with a twinge of disappointment. Do not worry, however. Keep your eyes on the local press in the days that follow, and the answers you seek will be found. Thank you again, my friends, and please bear with me now as I consider one final element in the psychology of retribution.

Coming to the end of a long and stressful crusade, I have had occasion to consider the concept of Satisfaction. I have sought Justice. I have questioned the extent to which Vengeance might legitimately be deemed an element of Justice. I have pondered the degree to which my actions may have been Justified, given their genesis and their purpose. I have even contemplated the possibility that the purity of my intentions might somehow have been contaminated by Hate. By dint of logical argument, however, I believe I have legitimised the inherent nature of my actions.

From the many positive responses I have had from you, my dear followers, I can see that it is unnecessary for me to pursue further this line of self-justification, since all of you have given me your unmitigated support and constant encouragement. For that I thank you most sincerely from the depths of my being. The path I was duty-bound to follow was lonely, friendless, and filled with the possibility of calamitous pitfalls. With your invaluable endorsement, with the awareness that so many of you were accompanying my every move in spirit, I was able to proceed with the conviction I needed to retain my firmness of purpose.

But I digress. I near the end of my journey and have recently had occasion to consider the extent to which my undertakings have offered me Satisfaction. And that is when I realised that to know whether or not Satisfaction is available to me is a question not easily answered. To do that, I first must need define what it is.

And therein lies a difficulty. Satisfaction is one of those words people readily understand. They nod, they signal agreement when it is mentioned. But dig a little deeper and the word reveals itself to have many layers of meaning and, indeed, might well pertain to a state that can be as much illusory as real.

First let me say that satisfaction has many synonyms, but each in its own way is nuanced, and thus none of the synonyms truly define the concept. A quick search produces such words as: achievement, gratification, happiness, contentedness, security. pleasure, pride, relief, vindication, gladness…. I could go on, but my point is that an examination of each of these words makes it clear that they are not fully synonymous with each other, nor indeed, with the essence of what Satisfaction truly is.

There are those who seek Satisfaction in a relatively modern form of meditation called 'mindfulness'. This ideal is very strongly correlated with Eastern mysticism. Lin-Chi once suggested that instead of looking outside, we should turn our inner light upon ourselves. But I ask: Look into ourselves and see what? If Satisfaction is not already present within us, then it will not be seen. Something much darker, however, might reside in our inner being. And then what? Once when Hamlet was castigating his mother, forcing her to look deep into her own psyche, she was forced to cry aloud:

O Hamlet, speak no more!
Thou turn'st mine eyes into my very soul,
And there I see such black and grainèd spots
As will not leave their tinct.

No! I do not believe that entering into the realm of mental oblivion, or deep inner awareness, is useful or purposeful, or that it will somehow lead to Satisfaction.

Is Satisfaction, then, to be found in the achievement of goals? I would doubt that. Attaining desired outcomes may provide fleeting moments of gratification, the kind of Satisfaction I would term 'illusory'. But there remains the deep part of one's psyche that seeks for, yearns for, something more than the ephemeral.

Does Satisfaction come from having everything one wants from life? Again, I think not. It is too easy to create scenarios where people have all that they believe life can offer and still continue to harbour an inner restlessness that confirms true Satisfaction is missing.

Missing? Unfulfilled? These words lead me to the concept of 'fulfilment'. Can Satisfaction be the existence of some deeply felt inner serenity that we may not even be capable of apprehending, but a state that allows us the consciousness of a well-being that pervades our emotions, that impacts positively upon our sense of ourselves and our view of the world? If so, how is such a felicitous mode of being to be acquired?

Here, I am sure, is where the answer is found. I do not believe that Satisfaction can be deliberately sought. I rather imagine that it is a kind of by-product of our manner of living, a consequence of discovering one's purpose in life. In the diligent and earnest pursuit of that purpose, one precipitates life's eventualities to coalesce in a way that is both beneficial and benign, impacting propitiously on that broiling inner unrest which is the customary lot of the human spirit. And there, unsought but present, lies true Satisfaction.

And so, again I muse, have I achieved Satisfaction? And my answer, I write with regret, is a hollow 'No.' Until the one final act of retribution that still remains has been accomplished, my spirit, my psyche, will continue to churn, to seethe, to smoulder, until this one, the originator of the entire chain of events that has led to this point, has been made to pay.

The final perpetrator will not die. It will be his lot to suffer the torments of the damned for the rest of his life. Oh, do I have the most exquisite dilemma for him with which to climax my crusade for justice? His body will remain unscathed, but his spirit will be lacerated beyond imagination. I will present him with a choice, a choice no one should ever have to make, a single fatality to obviate a double fatality. Will he choose? Can he choose? Can he NOT choose? Oh, my entire psyche squirms, crawls, convulses at even the intimation of a moment of such delicious angst.

I now know that the detectives working these cases, while floundering in ever-increasing ignorance and frustration, have discovered my blogs.

Well, bully for them! That they should have taken so long to do so is unlikely to inspire the populace with any confidence in their abilities. However, as I have just asserted, there remains one more malefactor. Can the forces of law even speculate on what I have planned for him, or, indeed, can they interpret information which I append below to determine the identity of my final target?

How much help do they need? I dare say I almost feel sorry for them, crawling around in a dark space like tiny ants not knowing which way to turn. Thus, to adjust the odds in a game they have played so poorly, I offer a final, monumental clue. For those who have eyes to see, here is a pointer (and a promise) to the individual who is the final link in the chain of miscreants whose callous disinterest led to the brutal extinction of a noble soul.

Justice Served
Justice demands that redress must be paid,
Impossible the choice that needs must be made.
Madness shall follow the path that you take,
Suff'ring and torture will hunt in its wake.
Horror will ravage the span of your time,
Every mem'ry will wallow in slime.
Extreme be the torment to gnaw at your soul,
Heartbreak and mis'ry beyond your control.
Anguish and grief, there'll be no release,
Never again shall your spirit know peace.

Decipher it those who can.

To my friends and followers, a final thank you, and a reluctant adieu. May we meet again.

> *Nemein*

*   *   *

"Don't get it. He that has eyes to see? What the hell is there to see?" Connors' tone betrayed his frustration.

"Obviously he's planning some serious torture for whoever it is," Miller said.

"Yeah, emotional or mental torture. But what?" Allen sounded as frustrated as Connors.

"Whoever he's targeting has to make a choice between one fatality or two fatalities. What's that about?" Stewart asked.

"That's right," McBride said. "Does this mean the final victim has to allow somebody to be killed in order to save two others from being killed?"

More blank stares.

"What about those apostrophes? They look a bit funny. Anything cryptic there?" Connors suggested.

"Or maybe there's something about the l-l-letters that are m-m-missing," McNeill mused. "Any clues there?"

Sheehan stared at the lines. "An 'e' from *suffering*, an 'o' from *memory*, and an 'e' from 'every. E, O, E?" He shook his head. "Says nothing to me."

Blank eyes stared at their sheets.

"Nope. Says zip to me, too," McCullough volunteered. He was happy to admit ignorance when the issue was complex.

"Maybe it's just fancy, old-fashioned poetry," Miller mused. "We had a bit of that sort of stuff at school. Y'know, Wordsworth, or somebody like that. Commas for letters all over the place."

"Apostrophes," Stewart corrected. "And I think you're right. I believe the omissions simply reduce the number of syllables in those words to help with the metre, which looks a bit like iambic pentameter, except that this one has only four double beats instead of five. I really don't think the apostrophes are cryptic. They're just like poetry from a century or two ago."

Questioning eyes turned to look at her.

She shrugged. "Advanced level Literature, okay?"

"It's like Geoff said a while back," Allen said. "All of our killer's writing is a bit old-fashioned, blogs and all, like out of an old book. This is no different."

Sheehan gave him a speculative look but said nothing.

Miller said, "Fair enough. But how does that help us?"

Allen shrugged. "Just an observation, but sort of agreeing with Denise. The apostrophes don't mean anything."

"He said the clue is monumental and there for anybody who has eyes to see," Miller said. "We're missing something very obvious."

"Aye, right," Sheehan said. "So tell us what it is. All I can see there is the usual self-serving, pseudo-intellectual bollox, and then some seriously threatening stuff." He read from his sheet. *"His body will remain unscathed, but his spirit will be lacerated beyond imagination.* I mean, this guy's seriously clever. This threat, whatever it is, will have all that evil imagination and malevolence behind it. I dread to think what he's planning."

"And against whom," Stewart added, tight-lipped. "Where do we even start to look for the next victim?"

"Next victim, or l-l-last victim? He's talking about c-c-coming to an end of his quest. Could be only one m-m-more killing. We really need to s-s-save this last one."

"He's not going to kill him," Allen corrected his partner. "He's setting him up for some kind of terrible torture. We need to find him. But how?"

Connors blew a heavy expulsion of breath through his lips. "He says the answer to that is in the poem."

There was a moment's bewildered silence. It was broken by McBride who said, hesitantly, "The clue might be in the title."

"Justice Served?" Miller asked, questioningly. "Don't see it."

"The two words begin with J and S. J for Jim, S for Sheehan?"

Sheehan raised an eyebrow. "Thank you very much, Detective."

"C'mon." Allen said. "That's really pushing it. The guy said a *monumental* clue. That's just a graspin'-at-straws kinda clue. Coincidence, nothing more."

"And if the title's the clue," Sheehan argued, "why go the bother of writing this complex poem? Are we to assume that after he put all this effort into writing the thing, it's only persiflage to direct our attention away from the two initials in the title?"

"Well, if you put it like that, sir. But I was thinking that Jim Sheehan was the clue and the rest of the stuff is letting you know what he's going to do to you, sir." He shrugged. "It was just a thought."

"Not wishful thinking, I hope," Sheehan said, grinning. Then, more seriously, he added, "Actually, it was a rather clever thought but, hopefully, a misdirected one. I mean, why would I be in his sights?"

"I can't imagine, sir, unless he's peeved at you chasing around trying to catch him."

Sheehan studied his sheet again, musing, "We may not have found the connection yet but there is something linking all of these killings. Each of the victims has clearly been part of an event of some kind that set our blogger off on his murderous spree." He pointed at the sheet he was holding. "There it is, in the line just above the poem." He read it aloud, "…chain of miscreants whose callous disinterest led to the brutal extinction of a noble soul. Looks like the victims have somehow been involved, as a group, in the killing of someone important to our blogger." He shuddered. "The unfortunate person whose spirit is to be lacerated beyond imagination is a final part of that chain. God help him."

"Makes sense, sir," McBride conceded. "Put like that, well, he's been going on about justice being served all through the other blogs. I suppose it's only natural he would use this as a title for his final major threat." He grinned, a bit shamefaced. "And you can be absolutely sure, Chief, this is one time when I'm very happy to be wrong."

"Chief's right, Malachy," Miller said. "It's obvious from the tone of the poem that whoever the target is, has been the object of this guy's hate for a long time, not just since we started this investigation."

"Give him his due, he really has us ch-ch-chasing our tails now," McNeill said.

"You gonna be writing some fan mail to his blog?" Connors growled.

"Just sayin'. We're all over the p-p-place and diving on every l-l-little thing for a clue, even way-out mad things." He glanced at McBride. "No offence."

McBride grinned. "None taken."

Sheehan was staring at his sheet, his expression baffled. "We need a cryptographer."

"A what?" McCullough asked.

Sheehan glanced at him. "Somebody who can decipher clues hidden in writing like this."

McCullough sat back, his face screwed up. Clearly something was puzzling him. "That crypt ... crypto ... thing you were talking about, Chief. I knew I heard that word before. It reminded me of something. Back during 'the troubles', there was a guy worked out of our station with Special Branch for a while, uh, must be twenty-five years ago. He was great at codes. Helped the Branch to crack all sorts of IRA secret messages."

"He still about?" Connors asked.

McCullough spread his hands. "Don't know. He's a good deal older than me. Probably retired now."

"Any chance you remember his name?" Allen said.

McCullough's face was contorted as he put his brain through some unwonted activity. "Uh, something to do with a ... a ... shed."

"Shed? For God's sake, Sergeant." Connors' patience was shredded.

"Well, that's what's in my head. Gimmie a minute. It's ... it's ... oh, aye! Gardener. Sam Gardener."

Several pairs of eyes shot ceilingwards.

Sheehan glanced at Stewart. "Google him, Sergeant, will you, please? Find out if he has an address, or if he's even still alive."

Stewart nodded and immediately started typing.

"Maybe we should get back to the interrogation rooms and beat the answers out of those bloody Club members," Connors snarled. "All this feckin' talking isn't getting us anywhere."

"We put Robinson through the wringer," McBride said. "I'm prepared to bet my job that he genuinely has no idea who the killer is."

"One of them's bound to bloody know," Connors snapped. "Where else are we going to start looking? They're all involved."

Stewart looked up from her laptop. "Sir, I have quite a history on Samuel Gardener here. Also an address and a phone number."

There was silence for a second. Sheehan was sitting stock still at his desk, an expression of shock on his face, clearly oblivious to what Stewart had just said. His voice, sounding as if he had been hit by a brick, filled the room. "Oh ... my ... God! What did you say, Declan?"

Connors, sounding uncertain, said uneasily," I said, uh, where else are we going to start looking? They're all involved. I meant with The Club, sir."

Sheehan put his head in his hands, "Oh, my God, where else? Where else? How could I have been so bloody stupid?"

All eyes were fixed on him now.

"Sir?" Stewart said.

"I broke all my own rules," Sheehan said, almost moaning. "I let myself be sucked into that whole Club business, just like the rest of you. I assumed that we'd find all the answers there. I mean, I did have some thoughts, small things that kept pointing ... but they didn't make any sense. I mean, where was the motive, the connections? I couldn't see. Bloody hell! How stupid can you get?"

"Chief, you're not making any sense," Miller said.

"Because Judge Neeson and Stevens had an obvious connection through The Club, we assumed that the other two victims were connected to The Club as well, and thus connected with each other." He looked at the team, almost despairing. "But we haven't been able to find any evidence to connect the teacher with The Club, and I've been driving myself nuts wondering what on earth kind of connection the other victims could have with a brute like McStravick."

"We're still looking in to that, Chief," Connors said defensively. "We haven't had a lot of time."

"Yes, but don't you see?" Sheehan cut in, his voice near to desperation. "We've been looking at this all wrong. The whole Club association has thrown us all out of whack. We let that be the basis of our thinking. I broke one of my own most stringent rules—don't make assumptions until all the evidence is in." He leaned back in his chair, his hands across his face, muttering almost under his breath, "You stupid idiot. You stupid bloody idiot."

"Sir," Allen said. "What other connection could there be?"

"One a child could make," Sheehan almost snapped, "if his brain wasn't distracted by that bloody Club. Okay. You tell me. Where would you find a connection between a judge, a barrister, a criminal, and a layman?"

Miller was on to it right away. "Holy shit. A jury trial."

"Exactly," Sheehan said, almost groaning, "and we have completely missed that all this time. There's been a trial somewhere, and I bet that's where I saw Redmond's face. He must have been on the jury." He shook his head. "I've been to court so many times … so many people. I still can't remember a thing about him other than his face."

"What about McStravick? What's his connection?" McCullough asked. "Was he the one on trial?"

Sheehan was leaning forward, his face in his hands again. "Don't know. Don't know. Don't know." Then he looked up. "Dammit! I need more facts. That trial's the key. We need to find which one."

"Redmond was probably the foreman of the jury, Chief," McBride said. "That would explain why the killer singled him out."

Sheehan was on his feet like a jack-in-the-box. Raising his arm, he kept pointing vigorously at the young detective with each word he uttered. "Yes! Yes! Yes! Good man. Good man." He turned to Stewart. "Sergeant, we're off."

And with that he moved hurriedly, gathering up his files and folders, and dashed into his own office where he dumped them on his desk. Despite his haste, he allowed himself time to phone the front desk. "Harry, DCI Sheehan. Find the number of the Courts Records Office, will you. Tell them to expect me in a few minutes and to start looking for any court trials with a Seamus Redmond as the jury foreman."

"Seamus Redmond?"

"Yes. He was a school headmaster."

"Will do, Chief."

As he rushed back into the main room again, Stewart, confused, said, "Off, sir?"

"Yes. I have a feeling Redmond might have been the jury foreman at a trial I was a witness at. Court records will have Redmond's name, Stewart, and which jury he served on. If we can find out which one." He headed quickly for the door. "Come on, Stewart, we're going to the Court Buildings. We need to get access to those records right away." He stopped and turned back to the team, still sounding pumped up when he said, "The rest of you keep working on that poem. Try to figure out that clue."

"Sir, I found Gardener's name and address," Stewart repeated.

"You did? Brilliant! Okay. Allen, get that address from Stewart's laptop. Drag the guy in here right away and see if he can decipher that poem and work out who the final victim is. Soon as you know who it is, warn him

right away and send a team to protect him. Contact us when you find out."
He charged towards the door. "Let's go, Stewart."

THIRTY-FOUR

Thursday, 23rd August. Early afternoon

A s they sped along the Newtownards Road on the way to the Royal Courts of Justice, Sheehan's inner agitation was plain. He stared silently through the windscreen, his expression intent, his eyes unseeing. Stewart, who was driving, glanced at him a couple of times. If she was harbouring any notion of questioning her superior about what was troubling him, the tautness of his demeanour made it clear that now was not a good time to interrupt his train of thought.

Sheehan's mobile sounded in his pocket. His expression didn't change, nor apparently did his train of thought, as he reached absently for the phone and brought it to his mouth. "Sheehan," he muttered, still fixated on the ideas that were charging through his head.

"Jim?" Margaret's voice was high-pitched and sounded stressed.

Sheehan became instantly alert. In the millisecond he had heard that single, quavering syllable, he became instantly aware that his wife was in trouble, serious trouble.

"Margaret?" His own voice mirrored the anxiety in his wife's. "What is it?"

"Jim." Margaret was tearful. "There's a man wearing a balaclava here, holding a gun to my head. You are to tell me exactly where you are or he will shoot me."

"Jesus!" The violence of Sheehan's exclamation caused Stewart to swerve, almost colliding with the car alongside her. "We're on the Newtownards Road heading for the Court Buildings."

Another voice came on to the line, obviously disguised. "Very good, Chief Inspector. Now listen carefully. Keep your phone open, instruct your sergeant to park the car, and phone your home landline. If she has not made the call within fifteen seconds, I will shoot your wife without compunction, and leave."

Sheehan's voice was almost a hysterical croak as he barked a command, "Stop driving, Stewart. Park here."

Not knowing what was happening, Stewart hesitated. "Sir...?"

"Now, for fuck's sake, Stewart. Stop!! You have ... eight seconds to phone my home number or Margaret dies."

Despite having no idea what was happening, Stewart could see that her boss was terrified. With commendable composure, she obeyed his instructions. Taking barely a second to park and knock the car out of gear, she hurriedly searched her jacket pockets for her mobile.

As Sheehan shouted the numbers to her, the disguised voice sounded in his ear, emotionless, implacable. "Four seconds."

"Wait! Wait!" Sheehan cried. "She's dialling. She's dialling."

His breath stuck in his throat as he waited for what seemed interminable minutes before he heard, distant but clear on his own mobile, the sound of his home phone ringing. This was followed immediately by, "Excellent, Chief Inspector, you made it with a second to spare. Please excuse me, the other phone is ringing. I must answer it. But do not attempt for one second to hang up on this call." The menace in the voice was unmistakable.

He watched, his stomach muscles rigid with anxiety, as Stewart listened to inaudible instructions on her phone. Suddenly her lips tightened and, lowering the window beside her, she threw her phone out into the speeding traffic.

Sheehan was shocked. "What the hell, Stewart...?"

The voice came back to him. "We can't have your sergeant using her phone to contact anyone, Chief Inspector, nor indeed, can we have anyone using the GPS on her phone to track your whereabouts." There was a brief pause, during which Sheehan struggled to regain some control. Panic was not going to contribute anything useful. Then came the rasping voice again. "Now, Chief Inspector, do you know who I am?"

"Nemein," Sheehan gritted.

"Excellent deduction, Chief Inspector. Now, before your own phone goes the way of your sergeant's, I am going to give you a few instructions. These must be followed to the letter. If I detect anything even slightly untoward, your lovely wife will be no more. I am Nemein. You know that I will not hesitate to do what is needed."

"Leave my wife alone," Sheehan said. "I'll do whatever you say."

"A sensible choice. You are currently parked on the Newtownards Road. First, I want you to place the blue police light on the roof of your car and flag down one of the cars passing right now. Offer the driver your car in exchange for his and tell him he can pick his own car up at Strandtown Station in three hours. Brook no denial. Exercise your full inspectorial authority if he demurs. Go now, and keep your phone open so that I can listen."

"We both have to get out of the car," Sheehan said to Stewart as he went around to the front and flagged down a passing motorist who was driving a black Audi. The mystified driver stopped, wound down his window, and said uncertainly, "I haven't been speeding, sir."

"I know," Sheehan said curtly. "Please get out of the car."

"But...?"

"Sir, please don't make me ask you again."

The driver, a young man in his late twenties, got out of the car and stood beside it. "What did I do? I'm entitled to know," he blustered.

"Nothing," Sheehan said. "I need your car. Get into mine and drive away. Go to Strandtown Station in about three hours and you can get your own car back."

The young man was mystified. "But...?"

"Get in, now, and drive away. Go!" Sheehan ordered forcefully. "I have no time to argue with you."

The young man, frustrated but with no option, got into the police car and drove off.

"Good," said the voice on the phone when Sheehan put it to his ear again. "Who knows what fancy technology your car might have that would allow some nosy policeman to pinpoint its whereabouts. Okay, just a second, please." After a brief pause, Nemein spoke again. "Now, I am checking the map on your wife's laptop as we speak. The route from there to your home at Connsbrook Avenue is clearly marked and is timed as twenty-one minutes for a pedestrian, and nine minutes by car. I understand that you will have heavy city traffic to contend with, as well as traffic lights, and no siren regrettably, but you will be here in your own house, with your sergeant, inside of seven minutes. The penalty for failure will be the death of your wife. Now, leave your phone turned on and throw it out on to the road. The sounds of the traffic will let me know that you have done as I command. The time starts now."

Sheehan threw his mobile out into the passing traffic and instructed Stewart urgently as they both climbed into the Audi. "We have seven minutes to get from here to my house. Start driving."

Stewart wasted no time with pointless argument. Throwing the car into gear, she shot out into the traffic, driving at almost reckless speed. She passed one vehicle on the inside, shot across its nose to pass another, as she sought the lane she needed. She was subjected to some angry horn-blowing by shocked drivers in the other cars but ignored them. Sheehan was swerving in his seat, arms almost raised, shouting and pointing, "Watch that guy on your left, Stewart. There. There's a space, two cars ahead."

Stewart, eyes never leaving the road, said coolly to her superior, "Sir, we have a better chance of getting there alive if you wouldn't keep distracting me. I know what I'm doing."

Traffic was heavy as they charged towards the Sydenham Road. There were several lanes filled bumper to bumper with impatient drivers as they sought access either to the M3 and the Sydenham Bypass to the George Best City Airport, or the M4 and M5 to the Ulster University and other points northeast.

Stewart skilfully, if more than a touch insanely, wove her way in and out of the packed cars along Sydenham Road, dodging erratically across lanes, squeezing into minimal spaces. Her aggressive driving earned her a cacophony of horn-blowing and numerous angry hand gestures from drivers' windows. Coming to a roundabout, she screeched left into Mersey Street and floored the accelerator. Thankfully the traffic was lighter here and, touching almost eighty miles per hour, she raced along for a few hundred yards until she saw the turning for Connsbrook Avenue. Braking heavily, tyres screaming protest, car almost on two wheels, she negotiated the turn and tore up to the end of the cul-de-sac where the Sheehan's lived. Sheehan was out of the car and charging to his front door even before Stewart had brought the car to a halt.

As he raced into the hall, Sheehan was confronted by a slight, short figure, holding a gun in his right hand and staring at a watch on his left wrist. He was wearing a woollen balaclava mask that covered his head and face, leaving only his eyes showing. Incongruously, he was also wearing a dark, tailored suit.

He stepped back as Stewart arrived, panting, behind her boss. "Again, seconds to spare, Chief Inspector," the rasping voice said. "Welcome to your humble abode." Despite the wordplay, the voice was cold, humourless. He gestured with the gun, stepping back yet again to allow them to pass. "Please come into the dining room."

The sight that greeted Sheehan made his blood run cold. The dining table had been pushed back to a wall and three chairs now sat in the middle of the room. One of them was a dining armchair, arranged so that it faced two side chairs, both placed side by side a couple of feet in front of it. Margaret was tied to one of the side chairs, strong nylon cable ties around her ankles, her hands fastened behind the back of the chair. A strip of heavy duct tape was stuck across her lips.

Sheehan made to rush forward but the voice behind the mask barked sharply, "Desist, Chief Inspector. You know better than that. Please sit on the armchair and do not move in any way until you are instructed otherwise."

Sheehan did as he was told, staring into his wife's terrified eyes as he sat in front of her. "Don't worry, Margaret," he said, striving to sound calm. "We'll sort this out."

"Touching, Chief Inspector," the masked intruder mocked. "However, the only one who will be sorting anything out here will be me." He turned to Stewart who was standing uncertainly just inside the door. Waving his gun, he motioned her further into the room. "You see a number of cable ties on the table there, Sergeant," he said. "I want you to tie your superior's ankles tightly to the legs of his chair. Do it now, and do it properly. Remember I am watching your every move. Please do not do anything silly."

Stewart grabbed a couple of ties and, giving her boss a despairing look, she knelt at his feet and tied his ankles tightly to the chair.

"Excellent, Sergeant," Nemein said. "Now, tie his left wrist to the arm of the chair." He paused and added menacingly, "Tightly, Sergeant. You will be aware that I do not tolerate sloppy work."

He watched closely while Stewart carried out his instructions. She stared sullenly at him when she had finished.

"Very good." The rasping voice sounded almost pleased. "Now this last tie is a little more complicated but I'm sure that you are capable of dealing with it." He spoke to Sheehan. "Chief Inspector. Could I ask you, please, to place your right arm and the edge of your hand on the chair arm?" He watched as Sheehan did so, ignoring the detective's angry stare. "Thank you. Now, keeping the edge of your hand on the chair arm, would you please hold your hand firmly open with your thumb pointing upwards."

Sheehan held his hand as instructed, still staring daggers at the killer.

"Excellent," Nemein said. "Now, Sergeant, I need your help again. Taking care not to disturb the Chief's hand, please tie his wrist to the chair as tightly as you can. Remember, I will check your handiwork when you are finished. Don't risk unpleasant consequences."

When Stewart was finished, Nemein closely examined her handiwork. The glittering eyes buried in the mask turned to Sheehan. "Can you move your hand, Chief Inspector?"

Sheehan wriggled his hand a bit and said dourly, "Just about."

The eyes stared at him, attempting to force the detective into submission. Eventually they turned back to Stewart. "Now, Sergeant. Would you please sit in that empty chair beside Mrs Sheehan?"

Margaret stared wildly at Stewart and turned to her husband, her eyes wide with questions and fear.

"It's okay, Margaret. It's okay," Sheehan said helplessly.

"Indeed, your husband does have it in his power to make it okay for you, Mrs, Sheehan," Nemein's tone was implacable, indifferent. "Please be patient and let us see how events transpire." He went to the table, picked up some more cable ties and handed one to Stewart, "Sergeant, please tie your right ankle as tightly as you can to the leg of the chair you are sitting on." When Stewart did so, Nemein instructed her to fasten her other ankle as well. When he instructed her to put her arms around the back of the chair, Stewart signalled resistance, but Nemein waved the gun again and warned, "One wrong move could result in three very bloody deaths, Sergeant. Now join your hands together and don't move."

It was the work of seconds for Nemein to render Stewart as helpless as the other two. He checked the bonds for firmness and then cut a strip from a roll of duct tape that was sitting on a nearby dresser. He covered Stewart's mouth with it, indifferent to her initial difficulty in breathing. "Comfortable?" he asked callously.

Stewart stared daggers at him as he stepped back a couple of paces. He studied the tableau for a few seconds, and even behind the mask, it was possible for the others to sense that he was strangely moved. "Exactly as I had envisaged it," he said. "I can barely believe that this momentous conclusion is finally being realised." Seeing Sheehan's eyes fixed on him, he put a theatrical hand to his heart and said, "Be still, my palpitating heart!"

THIRTY-FIVE
Thursday, 23rd August, Afternoon

McCullough's phone rang, and he put it to his ear. He listened for a few seconds and put the phone back in his pocket. "That's reception," he told the others. "Sam Gardener's just arrived. I'll go down and get him."

The team was still in the Serious Crimes Room, studying the cryptic poem Nemein had written. In the interim, McBride had used his computer skills to project the poem, via a PowerPoint presentation, on to one of the white evidence screens. The team was now studying the screen, reading and re-reading the poem as they sought for clues that might help them identify the next victim. At this point, however, they were no further forward than they had been when Sheehan dashed out.

They heard the elevator doors in the corridor opening and seconds later McCullough led their visitor into the room. He was elderly, white-haired, a bit stooped, but as he glanced around the room, there was a sharp, intelligent twinkle in his eye that belied the dry nature of the work he had done during his employment years.

"This is Sam Gardener," McCullough said to the team. "He has kindly offered to help us break this code."

Gardener raised an arm in greeting, smiling in acknowledgement of the nods he was receiving. But it was clear that he was keen to see what was causing the problem and turned quickly to the screen. He seemed unable to take his eyes from the poem, and he fiddled a hand behind him, seeking to locate the empty chair that had been left for him a few paces in front of the screen. He was already searching for hidden clues even before he had settled awkwardly on the seat.

"So this is the famous poem Sergeant McCullough has been telling me about," he said heartily. He stared intently at it for a few moments more and said off-handedly to McCullough, "So what do you think we have here, Sergeant? Code or cipher?"

McCullough looked blank, his eyes searching for help from his colleagues. None was forthcoming. "Your guess is as good as mine, Sam," he finally hazarded.

Miller laughed. "I'd say Sam's guess might have the edge, Sarge."

"What's the difference, sir?" McBride asked.

"Well, when you substitute one word or sentence with another word, or even mix them up in certain ways, you're using a code. When you mix up the letters, or replace them with alternative letters, you are using a cipher."

Blank eyes stared at other blank eyes, but no one pushed Gardener for further explanation.

The elderly cryptographer sat in his chair, hunched forwards, elbows on his knees, reading slowly through the text. His expression was a mixture of concern and puzzlement. "Good gracious. Your villain certainly has it in for his next victim. This is horrendous."

"See anything that might lead us to the monumental clue he says is there?" Connors asked.

"Not yet, I'm afraid. If this is a code, the surface text is remarkably complete and uncluttered." He studied the screen again, muttering to himself. He turned to McCullough. "Could I have something to write on, please?"

McCullough lifted a couple of blank pages from his desk and handed them to him.

Gardener took a pen from his pocket and wrote a couple of lines on one of the pages. Then he crossed them out with some violence. Again, after another close examination of the poem, he wrote some further lines of notes, almost immediately scratching his pen through them as well, looking irritated. "It's not a transposition cipher either," he muttered, sounding cross. "So what the heck is it?" He sat back on the chair and folded his arms, still staring intently at the screen. "If this is code and there was an algorithm used to encipher it, I can't for the life of me spot any trace of it. And even if I did, we'd need the key used with the algorithm to decipher the message."

He leaned forward more urgently, eyebrows down as he studied the screen more intently. It was obvious he was determined to break the code, or whatever it was. Further minutes elicited only a mumbled, "No excessive use of single letters, or of the most common ones." He blew air through frustrated lips. "Thought maybe the letters after the apostrophes might have been significant." He shook his head. "No. The apostrophes are definitely metrical breaks, nothing else." Shaking his head vigorously, he leaned forward again. "Gotta be something here I'm not seeing."

The detectives continued to watch him closely, not moving, afraid to speak lest they interrupted the cryptographer's concentration.

Several minutes passed until Gardener sat back, looking disgusted. "Are you sure there is a monumental clue in here? If this is a code or a cipher, there would be little tells, tiny off-key letters or words. But there's nothing here that I can see—" He stopped suddenly, staring once more at the screen, his eyes crinkling, a smile starting to break on his lips. Then he uttered a huge guffaw. "You cheeky chap," he chortled.

"What is it?" Miller asked, frowning.

Gardener sat back in his chair, arms wide. "It's a simple acrostic," he almost bellowed, still chortling. "Don't know how I missed it. Must have been distracted by those heavy-duty threats in the poem." He waved his hand at the screen. "They're not so common now," he explained, "but my dad used to play around with them when we were kids. Used to amuse us."

Connors, ever bullish, snapped, "Play the bloody hell around with what?"

"Acrostics. They were actually very common in medieval literature. Poets would use them to highlight the name of their patrons, or maybe make a prayer to a saint. Common in German, too, and but rare in other languages."

"What the hell are you talking about?" Allen interrupted, his patience as thin as Connors'. "How does this help us? Have you deciphered the clue?"

Gardener laughed again, clearly pleased that this particular test had not defeated him. "No deciphering needed." He seemed unaware, or maybe unfazed, by the growing restlessness in the room. He continued to lecture like an eccentric university professor. "Often the ease with which you become aware that you are looking at an acrostic can depend on the intention of its creator. In some cases an author wants the acrostic to be perceived by an observant reader, so he'll embellish the key capitals with ornate decoration, or something like that. However, the author might seek to conceal the message rather than make it obvious. He can do this by formatting the key letters to make them identical with the surrounding text. That way they won't stand out." He pointed again at the poem. "That's what your fiendish blogger has done. He has made the text so graphic and so horrible, and with its own built-in enigmas, that it was bound to distract the eye from the perfectly plain clue that he has left. I mean, I am very familiar with these things, but this one almost eluded even me."

"You by any chance related to our pathologist, Doctor Richard Campbell?" Miller asked peevishly.

Gardener looked puzzled. "Nooo ... why?"

"In the middle of all that persiflage—" Miller's patience, like that of his colleagues, was gone. "—is there a point you can make that might help us? What plain bloody clue are you talking about?"

"Oh, sorry." Gardener looked surprised. "I thought you understood once I identified the poem as an acrostic. It's a simple trick the poet uses. Look at it." He pointed to the first three lines.

Justice demands that redress must be paid,
Impossible the choice that needs must be made.
Madness shall follow the path that you take,

"The first letter of every line," he explained, "put together in order, spell out a word or a phrase. In this case ... em ... we start with Justice. That gives us a J. Then we get an I from Impossible. And then an M from Madness. He spelt out the letters ... J –I –M." He paused. "Is that a name? Do you know anyone called Jim?"

Miller was way ahead of him. Pointing at the screen, he began calling out the first letters of each succeeding line.

Suff'ring and torture will hunt in its wake.
Horror will ravage the span of your time,

Every mem'ry will wallow in slime.
Extreme be the torment to gnaw at your soul,
Heartbreak and mis'ry beyond your control.
Anguish and grief, there'll be no release,
Never again shall your spirit know peace.

"S- H –E- E- H- A- N." He was shouting the letters. "It's the chief. Holy shit! He's the final victim." He looked round wildly. "Where did he say he was going?"

"He and Stewart have gone to the Court Buildings to check on some trial records," McBride reminded him.

Miller grabbed his mobile phone. "We need to contact him right away and let him know he's in serious danger." He dialled quickly and listened for a second or two. He ended the call, hands opening and closing fretfully. "Engaged," he spat out.

"I'll phone Denise," Allen said, his voice thick with sudden anxiety. He too listened for a few seconds. "It's dead," he said, his face ashen. "Something's happened. We need to find them." His voice rose in pitch as panic began to set in.

McNeill put a soothing hand on his shoulder. "Don't go jumping to c-c-conclusions, Tom. There could be any n-n-number of explanations for this." The others, however, looked as anxious as Allen, apart from Gardener, who remained in his seat, a fascinated observer.

"I'll phone the Courts Records Office," Allen said, madly googling the number on his phone app. Finding it, he called the numbers out to McNeill. "Okay. Call them back to me," he said, preparing to dial. A few seconds later a voice sounded in his ear, "Courts Records Office. How can I help you?"

"Detective Sergeant Allen here, Strandtown Station," he said hurriedly. "We're trying to trace Chief Inspector Sheehan. He was heading for your office a while ago. Is he there yet?" Allen couldn't keep the tremor out of his voice.

There was a brief pause while the speaker conferred with a colleague. "Yes, we did get a message to say he was on his way to check some trial records, but he doesn't seem to have arrived yet."

"You're sure?"

"Well, he didn't check in with us, as would be normal. Sorry, I don't think he's here."

"Okay, thanks," Allen said, hanging up. He looked desperately at his colleagues. "Now what?"

Anxious eyes stared back at him.

Connors was already phoning the desk sergeant. "Harry, Declan Connors. We're concerned about DCI Sheehan. He's in some sort of trouble and we can't locate him. Find out which car Sergeant Stewart took out of the pool and track down their GPS, will you? ASAP, Harry, okay?" About to hang up, he brought the phone back to his ear and shouted, "Harry, you still there? Aye! Would you get somebody to drive Mr Gardener home, please? He'll be down in a couple of minutes." He glanced meaningfully at McCullough who ushered Gardener out the room with a mixture of thanks and apologies.

At that point, Miller turned and rushed towards Sheehan's private office. "T'hell with the chief's privacy," he shouted as he ran. "There might be something in his files."

Allen was right behind him, and the two began pulling pages out of the folders on the desk, desperately searching for something that might point them in a direction, any direction.

Miller stopped dead as he stared at a single A4 sheet in his hand. "Holy shit!" he exclaimed and, leaving a mystified Allen standing there, he rushed back into the squad room waving the page. "Everybody," he shouted, almost beside himself. "You're not going to believe this."

THIRTY-SIX
Thursday, 23rd August. Late afternoon

"**Y**ou could breathe a lot better if you'd remove that heavy balaclava," Sheehan said caustically. "And you're going to rip your throat to shreds if you keep rasping like that."

Nemein glared at him, his eyes glittering with anger. "Are you hoping to make me reveal myself?"

"Reveal yourself?" Sheehan offered him a scathing glance. "Huh! I've known for days who you are. Take that silly mask off, Edgar. You aren't fooling anyone."

Again the killer gave the detective a long, piercing look and, still glaring at him, he removed the balaclava, instinctively patting his hair down with the other hand. "How did you know?"

It was indeed Edgar Doran, but his demeanour was far from the mild, irresolute persona he had presented in their previous encounters. Here was a man forceful, decisive, very much in control of his surroundings. The exposure of his true identity must have been a shock to him, but he appeared much less dismayed than Sheehan might have expected.

Sheehan shrugged. "As I so often say to my sergeant, it's the small things, Edgar. Small things offer pointers until a pattern eventually emerges."

"Your reputation is well deserved, Chief Inspector," Doran said, trying to regain his aplomb. "Would you care to elucidate?"

Glad of the opportunity to keep their captor talking, Sheehan said, "Of course. But there are some gaps, obviously, and I'll need some input from you to put the whole picture together."

Doran offered no response.

"Well, believe it or not, your vocabulary was the first small thing that caught my attention. Your first blog used the word 'punctilious'. It's probably ten years since I came across that word, maybe more. Actually missed that for a while. Knew there was something in the blog, however, that I should be seeing. Then a few days later, I remembered what was bugging me. That word. I had heard it recently. You used it during my first interview with you. You were talking about how punctilious the judge was in keeping his appointments. Not that it made you the killer, of course, or even a suspect, but it set my mind along certain tracks. Little things. It's amazing how the little things add up. Word like that cropping up a couple of times in a couple of days? Gotta be a bit more than a coincidence. I probably wouldn't come across it again for several more years ... or not! Because, what do you know, there it was again in the second blog. The teacher was *punctilious in his habits.* You need to get yourself a broader vocabulary, Edgar."

Doran listened with great intensity, eyes blazing, but refused to respond to the jibe.

"Same with 'must need' or 'must needs'. You used that expression when I was talking to you, and it's all over the place in your blogs. I don't think I've heard anyone else use that phrase in conversation ... ever. But when I saw it on the blog it jumped out at me because, like punctilious, I knew I had heard it only a couple of days before. Was that coincidence?" He shook his head. "I don't believe in coincidences."

"Clutching at straws, Chief Inspector," Doran sneered

"No, Edgar. Small things. Initially, of course, I just noted them for what they were, random connections. I had absolutely no reason to suspect you. But it did throw your name up."

Doran continued to stare at him.

"In the first blog you also described your killer blow," Sheehan went on, "an elegant sweep upwards, you said. Upwards? The killer had to be short. You'll forgive me, Edgar, if I point out that you are somewhat deficient in the height department. Vertically challenged, I believe, is the politically correct usage."

Doran didn't reply, but his eyes were spots of fire.

"My old brain wrestled with that, too, wondering, just wondering," Sheehan continued. "I mean, the investigation was hardly started and stuff is already pointing at you."

"Very thin, Chief Inspector. Very thin."

"I would be the first to agree, Edgar. Very thin. I didn't know what to make of it." He paused to stare meaningfully at his captor. "Small things, Edgar. Like when that business about the blackmailer came up that first time I interviewed you, you were taking about having to meet him. You had already pointed out that you had not yet met with the judge that evening, so I asked you where you got the money to bring to the blackmailer. That clearly threw you. For a second you didn't know what I was talking about. 'Money?' you said, clearly at a loss. Remember?" It was obvious to Sheehan from Doran's expression that he did remember. "I'll be honest," Sheehan went on, "it didn't register with me at the time, and you did indeed come up with a fast and clever response to get yourself back on track again. Only later, added to other little things, did I begin to wonder about that, too."

Doran's expression was scathing. "Would you seriously expect to convince anyone with that litany of irrelevances?"

"I very much doubt it. But I emphasise, Edgar, they weren't clues. Just small things that set my mind off in a certain direction." He tried to make himself more comfortable in his chair before continuing. "Then my mind started gnawing at a couple of sentences you used in your first and second blogs. I know them almost by heart. In your first blog you said something like: *I have experienced the application of Justice. I have seen the dispassionate and uncaring face of so-called retributive Justice. I have seen the ramifications of Justice as its ripples spread beyond the ken of the principal actors. I have seen great harm result from the cold-hearted dictates of shallow judges who remain impervious to the evil they cause.* Who sees stuff like that except the law profession?"

"Humph! Weak, Sheehan. Very weak. This could easily have been written by a victim of the system."

"I know, Edgar, I know. On its own, it could have meant anything, led anywhere. But it didn't, Edgar. Your name buzzed into my head. You fit,

Edgar. Of course, I was still only at the stage of asking myself, 'Why?' But there were too many 'Whys', Edgar, and too many of them pushing me towards you."

He squirmed in his seat again. His sciatica was beginning to bother him, but he tried to ignore it. "Like that other little slip you made in your second blog."

"Slip? I don't make slips, Sheehan," Doran said haughtily.

"Well, that's debatable, isn't it? You said: '*I am fortunate in that I have some access to the dark underbelly of society, and thus privy to skeletons lurking in many cupboards.*' Who would be privy to secret information of that kind? Maybe a priest in confession?" He offered Doran a sceptical glance. "Hardly fits. Oh, yes. I spent a lot of time wrestling with that one, especially because of the comment that followed a couple of lines later: '*...records to which I have convenient access.*' Who would have that kind of access?" He raised his eyebrows. "Some sort of criminal blackmailer? Possible. We already had one as part of our whole crime scenario. A psychiatrist? A counsellor? They have access to loads of secrets. But something about it led me to the legal profession. Solicitor/client privilege." He stared at his captor. "You might not have been a solicitor or a barrister, but by your own admission you had intimate access to all the judge's papers."

"Oh, dear, Chief Inspector. Are you seriously suggesting—"

"At this point," Sheehan cut in, "or rather, at that point, I wasn't seriously suggesting anything. I was just seeing these things, but some pesky little guy at the back of my brain kept pointing me to you." He shrugged his shoulders. "And once I started to look at you, other little things began to bother me, like the coat you threw over the body. You're way too forensically savvy to have made a clumsy error like that. I'm guessing now you were thinking that if, in spite of your care, you might have left a minimal forensic clue leading to you, you could always argue that it happened when you were covering the body with the coat." He gave Doran a direct look. "And we did find a dark hair ... but I'll come back to that. The point is, these small things set my subconscious along a specific track which was now ready for further clues coming in—"

"Subconscious?" Doran sneered. "Sounds to me as if you were fully aware."

"The awareness only came later, Edgar. You're getting a hindsight view right now. But at the time I didn't quite know what was going on in my subconscious, but there was stuff definitely churning about in there. Naturally, I got Stewart here to run a normal check on you. She talked about your job and the criteria that had been listed in the advertisement for a Judge's Judicial Assistant." His brow furrowed. "Among them was something like 'high-level computer skills'. These were skills our blogger had in spades."

"Hardly unusual in this technological era," Doran sneered.

"And then there were all those books in your apartment when we called to see you after your abduction. Looked like shelves of legal tomes, but I noticed one shelf was filled with leather-bound British classics: Austen, Wells, the Brontës, Thackeray, Dickens, Stevenson, Scott, Trollope, Hardy, and several others. The blogger's language could have come straight out of eighteenth and nineteenth century literature, and not too many of the people we came across in the case could have boasted a collection like yours. You'd have been steeped in it, like our killer." Doran moved to speak, but Sheehan cut in quickly, "Yes. Yes. All circumstantial and far out. But the small things kept piling up."

"You know you could never have convinced the Public Prosecutor's Office to go to court with conjecture as vague as that," Doran scoffed. "I wouldn't even dignify it with the adjective 'circumstantial'."

"No, but it left me prepared for when you started to make the real mistakes."

"Real mistakes?" Doran's expression was suddenly thunderous, his ego unable to accept the idea. "Now I know you're lying. I was very careful not to make any mistakes."

"No? You don't know that you left your fingerprints on McStravick's suitcase?"

Doran uttered a disparaging bark. "This ridiculous ruse is beneath you, Chief Inspector. You won't bluff me that easily. There can't be any fingerprints. I was wearing rubber gloves the whole time."

"Were you wearing them in the pub when you bent down to pick up the suitcase after McStravick had knocked it down? That is clearly described in your blog."

Doran blanched, staring at the Chief Inspector as if he wanted to attack him. He calmed himself and, breathing heavily through his nose, said, "That won't matter. My prints are not on the police files, so all your forensics team has is a set of unidentifiable prints. They won't lead back to me."

"False comfort, Edgar. You see, I had already figured out who you were before I came here. I have left several mentions of you as a key suspect in my personal files. People will see those, and they'll come looking for samples of your prints." He adopted a neutral tone, imitating a tired policeman trying to convince a witness. "Just to exclude you from further hassle, sir…" Then giving Doran a hard look, he added, "…not! And there's more physical evidence, evidence that will lead to your arrest."

"Hah!" Doran mocked, but the sound had a hollow ring.

"Well, let me tell you. A tiny piece of white elastic got snagged in Steven's fingernail on the evening of his murder. It baffled me for a while. I couldn't figure out what it might be or where it might have come from. I asked around, but the others didn't know either. Then I had an image of you that night at your apartment, and it struck me that it might have come from a support bandage of some kind. Oh, yes, once I got that idea, I looked it up on the Internet. It came from what's known as an 'ace wrap'. That has small strips of elastic in it to keep the support tight. But of course you know that. You were wearing one on your arm that time Stewart and I visited you. The murder of Stevens took place shortly after that. No doubt you still needed the support."

Doran's lips were tightly compressed, as if he couldn't trust himself to speak. The detective's words were playing havoc with his god-complex.

"Oh, on that, by the way," Sheehan went on. "A couple of days before Stevens' murder, you were pretty beat-up. How did you manage to, what was it you said, *'play the coquette'* or whatever? You must still have been hurting. And those facial bruises...?"

"No problem, Chief Inspector. All carefully considered in advance. I always kept in soft lighting, judicious use of make up to cover the bruises and, of course, my iron control that enabled me to eliminate any telltale winces when pain struck."

"Admirable," Sheehan said, continuing to play for time. "Have to say, when I read the blog and remembered the state you were in a day or two before, I was thrown off track for a while."

"So why didn't you look elsewhere?"

"Actually, we were looking at others, and seriously. But the small things, Edgar, the small things. You have no idea how they prick."

"Continue to enlighten me, Chief Inspector."

"Well, there's the hair I mentioned earlier, the one that you dropped on Neeson's body when you were throwing the coat over it. I presume you had already divested yourself of your protective clothing by then. The hair, of course, wasn't significant in itself, but it gave us your DNA which, I have no doubt, will match the DNA found on the piece of elastic. Hard evidence, Edgar. Hard evidence that will send you to jail for life."

"Not going to happen, Chief Inspector," Doran jeered. "As soon as we have finished our business here, I'm off to new climes. Fresh fields and pastures new, as the poet said. My plane out of Northern Ireland leaves in a few hours to a faraway country where your colleagues will never find me." He shrugged unconcernedly. "And even if they do, which frankly won't happen, I am going to a country that has no extradition treaty with Britain."

Sheehan strove to conceal his shock by remaining silent.

"What's the matter, Chief Inspector?" Doran said caustically. "Cat got your tongue?"

"They'll come looking for you."

"And where will they look? Did they solve my little puzzle?"

"Yes, they know I'm your next victim."

Doran frowned. The mockery had left his voice. "I have to admit I'm surprised. Who worked it out?"

"McBride did. It was in the title. Justice Served. The first letters of each word are J and S. Jim Sheehan.

For a moment Doran looked initially perplexed, then amused, before bursting into a high-pitched laugh. "Well, how utterly ironic."

"Ironic?"

"Yes, it has to do with first letters." He uttered that mirthless laugh again. "But not those letters. It had not even occurred to me that those initials could be interpreted in that way." He shook his head slowly from side to side, still bemused. "I spoke in my blogs a few times about justice being served and thus it seemed a singularly apt title for your poem." He laughed again. "What a complete coincidence! This is most amusing."

He continued to look distracted for a few moments. Then his expression became serious. "But you know, of course, that I don't believe you. I offered them a monumental clue." He emphasised the word *'monumental'*. "That feeble effort of McBride's is anything but monumental. I have no doubt your team dismissed it as a ... a stretch, you would call it. They'll have to solve the acrostic before they truly know you are the final chapter of my vendetta."

"Acrostic?" Sheehan had never come across the term.

"Yes. An old-fashioned type of poem with slightly cryptic, uh, edges." He grinned at his own wit. "McBride should have looked at the actual lines of the poem if he wanted to look at first letters. The first letter of every line, taken in order, spell your name."

Sheehan had studied the poem enough times to have it committed to memory. He closed his eyes and visualised the lines and their first letters. Grudging admiration was his first reaction. "Clever, Edgar. Very clever."

"I don't need your praise, Detective," Doran said loftily. "I am fully aware of my own brilliance." He gave Sheehan an oblique look. "So, is our conversation over?"

"Maybe you'd explain why the old-fashioned truncheons."

Doran uttered a dismissive grunt. "No hidden purpose, Detective. I purchased a number from the Dark Web. Old-style or modern. Irrelevant. They were good enough for my purpose."

"Which was?"

"Enough chatter, Chief Inspector," Doran said, looking at his watch. "I really am quite anxious to progress to the next phase of the proceedings."

THIRTY-SEVEN
Thursday, 23rd August. Late afternoon

Miller stopped waving the page about and placed it on the nearest desk for all to see. The team crowded round, anxious to learn what was so exercising their colleague. In the middle of the page was a wide ellipse with the name DORAN written inside it, followed by two question marks. Pointing towards the ellipse, all around its circumference, were several arrows. A small phrase was scribbled along the length of each arrow.

"Can you read any of what's written there?" McCullough asked.

McBride, who was closer, said, "They're little comments indicating why he thinks Doran is a suspect. One says that he's small like the killer. Another says he has a collection of classical fiction, which the killer has obviously studied."

"There's a couple of useful ones further round," Miller said. "Look! Finger prints on McStravick's case. And there! That little bit of elastic has come from a bandage of some kind." He looked up. "Wasn't Doran wearing some sort of medical support thing on his arm?"

"This is coming way out of left field," Connors said dubiously. "Doran? Seriously? Didn't he get the livin' crap kicked out of him? I think the chief is reaching a bit here, desperate for a suspect."

"You're right about left f-f-field," McNeill agreed. "Complete sh-sh-shock to me. But this is the chief. He s-s-sees things we never see."

"He's got me convinced," Miller said, reading a few more of the comments.

"Okay! Okay! The bastard's the killer," Allen interrupted, clearly still wound up. "We're wasting valuable time arguing about it. The real question is, where do we even start to look for him?"

Anxious eyes continued to stare at the page as if seeking inspiration.

"Okay," McBride said. "Let's apply a little logic to the situation. What sort of space would he need if he has two kidnapped detectives with him?"

"Not his office, that's for sure," McCullough said. "Anybody could walk in."

"And if he wants peace and time to do whatever it is he's planning, it won't be outside either," Connors said. "Even a small wood or a field, anybody could come walkin' along."

"He'll need somewhere quiet where he's unlikely to be disturbed," McBride offered. "And he's going to need a while. According to that poem he wrote, he's working on some scenario that'll take a bit of time."

"The judge's h-h-house," McNeill shouted. "That's still t-t-taped off, but he has his own key. He won't be d-d-disturbed there."

"I think that's it, Geoff," Allen said excitedly, already moving. "Right! Let's go."

"Hold on, Tom," Miller said. "There are other options."

"Like what?" Allen was almost truculent.

"Well, Doran will be assuming that no one suspects him. He could be at his own apartment. Nobody's likely to go there either. He'd have all the time he needs."

"Oh!" Allen was torn. He could see that Miller's suggestion made sense. "We're going to have to split up," he said.

"There might be one other place," McBride said, a touch hesitantly. "Maybe I'm barking way up a wrong tree, but didn't the blog imply that the victim was going to have to choose between two people. Maybe Mrs Sheehan is also involved. What if Doran had already gone to the chief's house and kidnapped her? If he phoned the chief and said he has his wife, I mean, he'd drop everything and run. He wouldn't stop for a second."

Miller clicked his fingers, saying at the same time. "A pound to a penny that's why he hasn't contacted us. Doran's threatened Mrs Sheehan in some way, forcing the chief to keep schtum."

"Don't forget he's got Denise with him," Allen cut in. "She's in danger, too."

"Don't worry, Tom," McNeill said. "She can l-l-look after herself."

"Aye, like the judge, and Stevens, and even that brute McStravick, looked after themselves," Allen snapped back. "This mad man is fiendishly clever. If he's got them...." He didn't finish the sentence.

At that point Connors' desk phone rang. He rushed to pick it up. "Harry?" He listened for a few minutes, his expression a mixture of puzzlement and concern. "Thanks, Harry. Talk soon," he said, hanging up. "The chief's car is already back in the compound. Some guy drove it in a couple of minutes ago. Apparently, the chief flagged him down, grabbed the guy's keys and gave him the keys to the police car."

"Bastard," Miller said. "Nemein knew we could track its GPS. He must be holding something serious over the chief to make him do something like that."

"What was the guy driving?" Allen asked impatiently.

"A black Audi Sport. Number plate DLA 3497. Harry already has the word out to watch for it."

"Okay," Miller said decisively. "Tom, you and Geoff go to the judge's house. McBride and the sarge will go to Doran's apartment. Declan and I will go to the boss's place."

Allen was already heading for the door, shouting over his shoulder. "And the first one to learn anything, phone the rest of us immediately. Come, Geoff. Let's go."

THIRTY-EIGHT

Thursday, 23rd August. Early evening

"**O**ur conversation is hardly over, Edgar," Sheehan said, still hoping to keep Doran talking. "I've been completely open with you about my deductions, but I still have a lot of questions. What was your motive for the killings, for example? I mean, you know that we had ourselves tied up in knots searching for a Club connection that didn't exist, but I have only just realised that the victims are connected by some sort of jury trial. Neeson would have been the presiding judge. Stevens, I would guess, was the prosecuting barrister. And Redmond would have been the jury foreman. But I can't see what connection McStravick might have had with the others, and no clear motive springs out at me."

Doran eyed him contemptuously. "If you're stalling for time, I can assure you, Chief Inspector, help is not on its way. And regarding your feeble attempts to identify my motivation, it is of no consequence to me whether or not your puny intellect is satisfied. I now have other matters to attend to—" He paused, offering Sheehan a sardonic stare. "—matters that will require your involvement and your complete attention."

"But what about the blackmailer?" Sheehan urged, almost desperately. "There's a mystery there." He sought to appeal to the psychopath's ego. "Surely it would please you to rub my nose in the stupid way I allowed you to pull the wool over my eyes with that clever ploy? I mean, there was no sign of him on the parking garage CCTV footage. Indeed, you claimed that you were there but there was no sign of you on the footage either. I have to say, I found that very odd. And then the so-called blackmailer seemed to disappear off the scene altogether after the first murder. Was there a blackmailer at all, or was he a figment of your fiendish imagination?"

Doran's expression didn't change but his stillness made it clear that his vanity was vying with his desire to proceed with business. "Oh, there was a blackmailer all right," he said eventually. "It's just that the blackmailer was me. When you started asking questions, I simply gave you the same story I gave the judge. Of course I wasn't on the CCTV footage. I didn't actually act out the scenario I gave the judge. It was a small ruse, but it had you chasing your tail. That was satisfying."

"I'm sure. But why were you blackmailing the judge?"

"The first obvious reason is that I needed a lot of money to pay for the investigation I had to conduct in order to identify all the actors in my revenge saga. That was a costly process, and not just investigative costs. I had to offer several bribes to unsavoury characters before I was finally led to the truth." He offered the detective a mirthless grin. "So, you see, the judge's regular contributions to my cash flow were extremely useful." He reached out and checked the tightness of the ties on Sheehan's wrists, scarcely aware that he was doing so. He stepped back and continued to speak, "But I also wanted the judge running scared so that I would have easy access to his house late at night when the time came to consummate his demise. That would give me time to execute him and clean up afterwards. Obviously, his holding that party at his house was a bonus I couldn't ignore. I chose that night to ensure that suspicion fell on everyone but me."

"You played your part very well," Sheehan said. "Self-effacing, timid, helpful."

"Easy when you have considerable intellect and are in full control of your emotions."

"It also helps if you're a psychopath," Sheehan said dryly.

Doran eyes glittered as he stared at the detective. "I can always change my mind and kill you, too."

"You knew about the second safe, didn't you?"

"Of course. Who do you think fixed it for your blundering forensics officer to trip over?"

"Richardson was convinced you couldn't have taken that beating without revealing what you knew. He's convinced you knew nothing."

"Control, Inspector. Control. His blows were ultimately futile. The mind is a powerful weapon in all sorts of circumstances. That oaf was no match for me."

"And yet, you decided to give up the safe?"

"You think I was going to ignore what Richardson and his two thugs did to me? I wanted to make sure that he would pay, him and that vile Club."

"You could have made a fortune blackmailing the judge if you'd let him live. You threw rather a lot of money away, did you not?"

"You demonstrate little understanding of the nature of retribution, Chief Inspector," Doran jeered. "Money would never compensate me for allowing that evil wretch to live." Then he added with a smirk, "But that is not to say that I didn't profit from knowing about the second safe, and its combination code. The judge was unaware that I knew about either."

"Profit?"

"Of course. The judge was charging phenomenal prices to millionaires for the services he offered at The Club, so his safe was a valuable source of funds for me. Obviously, I had to leave a couple of hundred thousand in it to convince your plodding colleagues that it had not been tampered with. A paltry sum, however, given the judge's prices. He could make that much in less than a week." Doran uttered a mirthless laugh. "I told you I am heading for new climes, but I am not departing unprepared. My new life will be funded by some five million pounds worth of diamonds, and nearly a further million in Sovereign Bonds, that the judge had amassed in his private safe. Those I had obviously apportioned to myself before making the safe available to the authorities." He looked at his watch and said briskly, "Now, Chief Inspector, I have indulged your curiosity long enough. It's time."

Taking a small pistol from his pocket, he walked over to Sheehan and placed it in his hand. "Do you find that you can hold that comfortably?"

Sheehan glowered at him.

"Move your hand, please. Can you point the gun right and left?"

Sheehan continued his sullen scowl, hand totally still.

Doran breathed a theatrical sigh. He raised his own gun and pointed it at Margaret. "Very well, if you insist on forcing my hand."

Sheehan immediately began to move the pistol right and left, a couple of inches in either direction, and shouted, "Stop! Stop! I'm moving it. Don't do anything rash."

Doran glared at him. "You really shouldn't continue to try my patience, Chief Inspector. This is a moment of great import." He pointed again. "Can you move the pistol in any other direction?"

Sheehan tried. "No."

"Good. Wouldn't want you turning it on yourself." He raised one eyebrow but his expression remained grim. "Or, indeed, on me. In fact," he added, "just to be on the safe side, I'll observe events from over your right shoulder." He went behind Sheehan and stood slightly to the right of him, his back to the dining-room door. When he spoke again, his voice was filled with sudden menace. "Now, Chief Inspector, you have a choice to make."

"Choice?" Sheehan's heart was pounding. He knew exactly what was coming next.

"Yes. Two very important people in your life are sitting in front of you, your lovely wife, and your loyal partner. I want you to kill one of them with that pistol."

"That's madness," Sheehan cried, frantically seeking some argument to dissuade Doran.

"Not madness," Doran said coldly. "Justice."

"But why would I...?"

"Because," Doran interrupted, "if you don't shoot one of them, I will kill them both. At least, if you make a choice, one will survive."

Sheehan's clenched left fist was white with tension, his chin tucked down into his chest, his face tight with desperation. He was shaking his head from side to side, saying in a tortured voice, "No. No. I can't do this ... I can't ... This is inhumane."

"This is justice," came the cold, dispassionate voice from behind him, "and I have waited a long time for it. Choose, Sheehan. My patience is wearing thin."

Veins were bulging out on the sides of Sheehan's forehead, sweat dripping into his eyes as he raised his head to stare at the two women. His tortured eyes pleaded for forgiveness as he looked first at one and then the other. Margaret's eyes were half closed, but she nodded calmly at him. He could hear her voice in his head, '*I've had a good life, Jim. Denise is only starting out. Choose me.*'

Stewart's eyes were wide, moving desperately in their sockets, her head shaking violently from side to side as she tried to get him to understand her thoughts. He didn't need to understand them. They rang clearly in his head, words that she had uttered to him only yesterday, '*I said it to Tom, and I'm saying it to you. I'm a fully trained detective sergeant, sir. I take what the job throws at me, just as Tom does, just as you do, good or bad, pretty or ugly, safe or dangerous. It's my duty. The fact that I'm female is utterly irrelevant.*' She could never have known that it would come to this, yet the words were followed by a loud echo in his head, '*Choose me!*'

Sheehan closed his eyes, heart pounding. "Oh, God, I can't. I can't. Please, God, I beg you. Stop this," he groaned, unaware that he had been speaking aloud.

"Your God has no place here, Sheehan," came the remorseless voice behind him. "Choose."

He looked again at his wife. She had her eyes closed, praying. Sensing his gaze, she opened them again and gave him a soulful look that he couldn't interpret. Forgiveness? Love? Resignation?

Wretchedness flooded through his entire body. Help was probably on its way, but it was going to be too late. He knew that now. He had only seconds left. He tried to turn his head to Doran, tormented beyond bearing. "Shoot me, Doran. Shoot me," he begged, seeking even at this eleventh hour to appeal to some vestige of humanity in the psychopath's soul. "I'm the one who offended you. I'm the one who should pay."

"And pay you will," came the implacable response. "You'll pay in reams of unalloyed spiritual and emotional torture." The tone became peremptory. "Now, one last time, Sheehan. Choose!"

Sheehan heard the rustle of clothing as Doran lifted an arm to look at his watch. "You have ten seconds."

Sheehan's face was an agonised grimace of despair as his finger curled on the trigger, although the gun was still pointed at a space somewhere between the two women. His breathing had become erratic and ragged, his body was starting to shake, as he came to the stomach-churning realisation that time had run out, that he now had to make the unthinkable choice. His gaze rested on the two women, filled with desperation, imploring forgiveness, craving understanding. He heard a harsh intake of breath behind him as his finger tightened on the trigger, heard the hammer's startlingly loud, inexorable click as it started back with infinite slowness...

...and he heard the sound of sudden scuffle behind him, sensing rather than seeing a dark shadow race across him. Instinctively he relaxed his grip on the trigger, confused and disoriented, but he became aware that Miller was already holding his wrist, trying to pry the pistol from his grasp. "It's okay, Chief," Miller was shouting as he pulled the pistol from Sheehan's hand. "It's okay. You're safe."

Drawn to the sounds behind him, still almost in a daze, Sheehan uttered a silent, "Thank you, God," and turned his head to see Doran's diminutive frame almost lost against Connor's massive bulk, struggling futilely to free himself from Connor's huge arm which was locked tightly around his neck and pulling him up from the floor. Connors' right hand darted erratically after the gun that Doran was waving about. He managed to grasp the killer's wrist and force it upwards, causing Doran to fire two futile shots into the ceiling.

Doran, virtually immobilised and hoisted well off the ground, continued to rage and kick, snarling in his throat like a cornered animal. The big detective half-hurled him against the wall without releasing him, and banged the psychopath's hand so violently against it, that the gun was knocked flying from his grasp. McBride, who had just entered the room with McCullough, immediately picked it up and moved off to one side.

Connors then released his stranglehold on Doran's neck and pulled him round to face him. Seizing Doran's left shoulder in a vice-like clasp, and holding him at arm's length, he drew back his huge right fist and powered it into the side of Doran's head with all the violence of his pent-up anger. "That's for that poor wee dog, you worthless piece of scum," he spat out as he stared down at the instantly unconscious figure.

At that point, Sheehan turned back to Miller and, struggling to hide his emotions, growled, "Get these bloody things off me."

Miller, never without tools about his person, whipped out a penknife and cut the ties.

Sheehan bent immediately to Margaret, stretching his hand towards Miller. "Gimme that," he said, and grabbing the knife, he freed Margaret from her ties. She fell instantly into his arms, weeping with relief.

"It's okay," he said, holding her tightly and smoothing her hair. "It's okay." He sat her gently back on her chair. "Just a second," he said, turning to Stewart and cutting her free, too

She stood up from the chair, rubbing her wrists. Nothing in her demeanour revealed the heart-pounding relief she must have been feeling. But when her eyes suddenly caught sight of Allen dashing into the room, the corners of her mouth trembled and her face started to pucker. Allen reached her in time to catch her as she collapsed, enveloping her in his arms and asking repeatedly, "Are you all right? Are you all right?" She didn't answer but clung to him, shaking like a leaf.

Miller noted her trembles and said, "It's the shock." And even as he was speaking, he headed for the kitchen, adding, "Hot tea. That's the answer. I'll go and make some."

As Sheehan reached again for Margaret, he began to feel his own legs trembling and stumbled backwards.

Connors caught him and sat him back down in his chair. "Take it easy there, Chief," he said. "You've just been through a very traumatic experience."

McNeill, who was standing close by, added, "The shock isn't g-g-going to go away easily. It could go on f-f-for weeks. The two of you will h-h-have to talk to somebody."

"Aye, right," Sheehan muttered. Turning to Connors he said, "How did you find us?"

Connors told him about the solving of the acrostic clue and the decision to split into three teams. Miller had just arrived back with a tray bearing three mugs of steaming tea, and said as he handed out the mugs, "We drove here like bats outa hell and when we saw the Audi and another strange car in the drive, we knew immediately that we had found you. We weren't exactly sure how to proceed but when we got to the front door, we noticed that it was slightly open—"

"We guessed you did that on purpose," Connors cut in, "so we sneaked into the hall and heard voices. We heard the threat about the gun and were still dithering about the risk of barging in. But when we heard yer man giving you ten seconds—"

"We knew it was all or nothing." It was Miller's turn to cut in. "We just dived in there. Geez, it was scary, Chief. Connors grabbed the bastard while

I rushed to try and get the gun from you before it went off. My heart was in my bloody mouth the whole time until that pistol was safely in my hand."

Sheehan stared at the members of his team. They were all there. His throat was constricted, and he wasn't sure if he could even speak. *Your emotions are all over the place, Sheehan. Get a grip.* But he managed to say, "Thanks, Declan. You handled our kidnapper very well."

"That skinny wee runt?" Connors scoffed. "He's lucky I didn't break him in two."

Sheehan grinned and turned to Miller. "Thanks, Simon." His gaze took in the whole team. "Thanks, all of you. We can never repay you for what you've done here today."

"Aw, will you quit, Chief," Connors said, grinning awkwardly. "You'd have done the same for any of us."

"In a heartbeat," Miller added.

"Well, one good thing comes out of all this, anyway," McCullough said.

"You mean apart from a couple of lives being saved?" Miller said.

"Oh, em, of course. Certainly. That was the whole point of the rescue." McCullough was suddenly flustered. "I only meant—"

"It's okay, Mac," Sheehan said, intrigued. "Enlighten us."

"It's just that we don't have to interrogate those obnoxious Club members any more, or listen to their lies, or put up with their bloody arrogance. To be honest, I'm glad to be shot of them."

"True," Sheehan nodded. "I agree with you totally, Mac. That is something to be thankful for. The ACC's Task Force is going to have to deal with them, and all the other guttersnipes their investigation uncovers. And good luck to them. We're well out of it."

There was a groan from the floor as Doran began to regain consciousness.

Sheehan couldn't look at him. "Get that thing outa my sight, Connors, will you? I'll see you later at the station."

Connors grabbed the confused Doran by the scruff of the neck and dragged him along the floor and out of the room. Miller followed, shrugging at Sheehan with a wry grin as they left the room. The others, except Allen, trooped out after them

Sheehan glanced over at Stewart who had by now achieved some modicum of control and was chatting quietly with Margaret. Allen was standing quietly to one side, allowing them to talk.

"Tom," Sheehan said, "would you take Denise on home, please? No need to report back to work until you both feel like it. In the meantime, I'm going to stay here a while with Margaret."

Allen nodded and Stewart stopped to face Sheehan as she prepared to leave. Holding her boss's eyes, she said, "Sir, we're never going to refer to this again, or talk about it ... ever."

Sheehan studied her earnest face. Then he said, deadpan, "Refer to what, Sergeant?"

It was her turn to study him. She waited a couple of seconds before offering him the tiniest of nods. "Aye, right!" she said.

THIRTY-NINE
Thursday, 23rd August. Evening

Interrogation Room 3 is the same bare, functional space as the other Interrogation Rooms, but with one addition. Serious Crimes suspects tend to be interrogated there, so the table has, in addition to a recorder, pens and paper, a heavy metal ring built into the suspect's side. Edgar Doran sat alone at this table, his wrists in handcuffs. The cuffs were attached to each other by a thick chain about twelve inches long, which was looped through the ring in front of him. He could therefore move his hands and arms to either side about a foot or so, but that was the extent of his movement.

When Sheehan, accompanied by Stewart who had refused Allen's pleas to stay at home, entered the room, Doran leaped from his chair. He was stopped short by the chained cuffs and was forced to remain bent over as he hurled insults and swear words at the two detectives. "You should be dead, you bitch," he snarled at Stewart. "And you should be in mental agony, you bastard," he roared at Sheehan. "Get out of here. Get out of here. You destroyed my plans. You ruined my life." He was spitting and almost foaming at the mouth, so intense was his rage. "Go!" he screamed. "Go! I refuse to speak to either of you."

"Sit down," Sheehan snapped. "You will be interrogated like every other prisoner."

Doran continued to spit and swear. "I will not be interrogated by you, you piece of shit." He began pulling and rattling violently at the chains, abrading his wrists and starting to draw blood. He seemed impervious to the pain, tearing and struggling with the chain as if determined to rip the ring from its niche on the table.

"Get out! Get out! I won't listen." Doran kept pulling on the chain and starting to sing loudly out of tune. "La, la, la, la. I can't ... hear ... you."

"Sing all you want," Sheehan shouted back at him. "Forensics have confirmed that it is your fingerprints that were found on McStravick's suitcase and that it is your DNA both on the hair and the piece of elastic. You're going down, Doran, and you're going down for a long, long time."

"You ... don't ... have ... mo ... tive." Doran continued to sing the words in some sort of bizarre rhythm, still tearing the skin off his wrists with the handcuffs. "Stupid Sheehan ... Stupid Sheehan ... Going to court ... without a mo ...tive. Ha, ha, ha! La, la, la!" Then changing mood suddenly, he began screaming invective again. "Get out, you bastard. Get out to fuck! Out! Out!" He was pulling madly at the chain again, tearing skin off his wrists which were now covered in blood.

Stewart pulled at Sheehan's sleeve. "Sir, maybe we should go back out and talk about this. He's going to do himself some serious damage."

"Out! Out! Out!" Doran continued to shout, his voice becoming hoarse and ragged.

His face like thunder, Sheehan turned on his heel and stalked out, the prisoner's invective still ringing in his ears. "The bastard's not going to get away with that," he snapped at Stewart once they were outside and the door was closed behind them. "He's going to have to talk to us at some point."

"Maybe, Chief," Stewart agreed. "But not right this minute."

Sheehan was still breathing heavily as he fought his anger. He looked straight through Stewart for some seconds until his expression cleared and he reached into his pocket for his mobile phone. He dialled and waited. When he got an answer, he said, "McBride, you still at the station?" He listened to the response and continued speaking, "Okay. Get yourself down here to Interrogation Room 3."

"Sir?" Stewart said with raised eyebrows.

"Doran thinks he's so bloody smart. Well, we'll fight smart with smarter. I've put my money on McBride before, and I'm going to do it again."

"I'm not with you, Chief."

"Doran likes good-looking young men, right?"

Stewart nodded uncertainly.

"And McBride has proved himself to be intelligent, creative, and resourceful, right?"

Stewart nodded again.

"And you heard McCullough at one of the debriefs saying that McBride has a great career as an actor if he quits police work, right?"

Stewart nodded for the third time, really puzzled now.

"Okay. McBride goes in there and plays the part of a naive, inexperienced young guard, just there to ensure that Doran doesn't do himself harm. He's smart enough to find a way to take advantage of that." He looked up. "Here he comes now."

McBride, almost running, joined them, looking enquiringly at Sheehan. Sheehan explained what he wanted and said, "Stewart and I will be watching through the one-way mirror in the ante-room."

*   *   *

Doran was still glowering when McBride entered the interrogation room. He looked up at the young policeman and snarled, "Are you here to waste my time, too?"

McBride held up two defensive hands, one of which was holding a kindle reader. "Nothing like that, Mr Doran. It's just that the senior detectives are going to be very busy for some time and I've been instructed to remain with you. Apparently, you tried to harm yourself earlier...." His eye caught the bloodied wrists, and putting an effeminate hand to his mouth, he said, wide-eyed, "Oh my goodness, what have you done to yourself?"

"It's these bloody handcuffs," Doran grunted.

"Dear God, I can't leave you like that. Excuse me." He rushed out of the room again and returned with a first-aid box, a cloth and a dish of water.

"So what are you doing here?" Doran asked, as McBride gently cleaned the blood from the badly scraped wrists and spread some salve on them. He reached into the box and took out a roll of gauze and a pair of scissors.

Keeping himself and the scissors at a safe distance from Doran, he cut off a couple of lengths and made a makeshift bandage around each wrist. While he was doing that, he said, "I'm supposed to keep an eye on you for a while."

"How long is a while?" Doran snapped.

"Don't know, I'm afraid," McBride said calmly. "I presume you're aware that there's been a number of significant arrests today, so all the senior detectives are conducting interrogations. Obviously, I don't have the experience or the skills to help with that..." He rolled his eyes and made a face. "...so I get to sit with you." He held up his kindle. "I would like to pass the time reading, if you wouldn't mind." Then appearing to realise that he had forgotten his manners, he said solicitously, "Oh, sorry, can I get you something? Coffee? A soft drink? Water?"

"No. I'm fine for now," Doran replied, eyeing the young policeman with some suspicion.

McBride just smiled. He opened his kindle and appeared almost immediately to be engrossed in what he was reading.

After watching him for some minutes, Doran asked, "What are you reading?"

McBride gave him a sheepish grin. "You'll probably think I'm odd, but I'm reading Vanity Fair by William Makepeace Thackeray."

"What! A policeman who reads classical literature? That's a first."

"I studied English Literature for my Advanced Level GCSEs," McBride said, "and got to love the nineteenth-century novelists: Brontë, Austen, Dickens, Hardy, Wells, Trollope, and all the others. There's something about that era that really appeals to me and...." He paused, seemingly embarrassed to go on.

Doran was intrigued in spite of his circumstances. "You were going to say?"

McBride uttered a self-deprecating chuckle and said, "Well, I'm studying Law at Queen's University in the evenings, and I find it a calming contrast to walk away from the dry, legalistic tomes I have to wrestle with, and lose myself from time to time in a world of lovely old patterns of etiquette, customs, manners, and dignity, that are completely lost to our generation."

"That's surprising," Doran said admiringly. "Most unusual." He seemed suddenly taken with this handsome young man who had been sent to guard him. "And I agree with you wholeheartedly. Would you believe that I have a whole library at home with all those authors in it, and indeed, I have been through that same educational route myself."

McBride affected surprise. "You have?" Adding as an afterthought, "Ah, that explains it."

"Explains what?"

"I've already deduced from reading your blogs that you were more than familiar with the classics. Your own writing style seems very much influenced by them. Which makes me wonder...?" He hesitated and then waved a dismissive hand. "Sorry, none of my business."

"It's okay," Doran assured him. "What were you about to say?"

"Well, you are obviously educated and well read. Forgive me, but I just can't see you as a murderer."

Doran's lips tightened and his bearing became diffused with a sudden anger. "I'm not. I was forced to kill, but not of my own volition. And it wasn't murder. It was justice."

"Yes, you make that point many times in your blogs. Uh, may I say they were very well written."

Doran was pleased. His anger passed. "Thank you," he said, smirking. "It seemed to me, given the nature of the arguments I was to engage in, and their intricacy, that the classical style was eminently suited to them."

McBride appeared to think about that. "You know," he said, "that makes perfect sense." He laid his kindle reader on the table and leaned forward earnestly, seemingly very interested now in this discussion. "If I may be so bold, however, there is one glaring omission in your blogs."

"Glaring omission?" Doran was immediately on the defensive.

"Oh, your arguments are very well rehearsed, complex, of course, but concise. However, readers with a rational mind would fail to be convinced about the level of aggravation you claim to have suffered."

"Level of aggravation? Claimed? Let me tell you, young man, I was driven almost to the edge of madness."

McBride held up his hands and sat back. "Sorry, Mr Doran. None of my business. Just got a bit carried away with the logic of the argument. My apologies, sir." McBride reached for his kindle again, hoping that the mark of respect and his retreat from the conversation would further persuade Doran to disclose his motives.

"It's okay," Doran replied, mollified. "What logic?"

McBride put the kindle back on the table and said, almost reluctantly, "It's just that you are an exceptionally clever man, sir, and I would surmise that you are sufficiently well versed in the basics of logic to understand that broad claims without supporting evidence are seldom convincing."

Doran studied him. He was obviously quite taken with the polite young policeman who read literature and could argue logic with him. However, he cast a glance at the mirror on the wall and raised his eyebrows.

McBride followed his gaze and rolled his eyes again. "I doubt if anyone would be interested in watching me sitting here reading my kindle, sir. Heck, I'm practically invisible. They don't even see me when I'm in the squad room."

"What? A bright young chap like you?"

"Kind of you to say so, sir. But no, I'm far too young and inexperienced at this point to be given any notice or, indeed…" He allowed a note of dissatisfaction to enter his voice. "…any responsibility." His frowned as if irritated and picked up his kindle again.

Doran studied him for a while. Then, as if making up his mind about something, he said, "Are the details of our conversation likely to reach the ears of Chief Inspector Sheehan?"

"Hah!" McBride's tone was derisory. "Like the Chief Inspector is likely to talk to somebody like me, even for a second. That's quite amusing, sir."

"True, I suppose. The chief inspector is, indeed, insufferably arrogant." Again that speculative pause before he continued, "I would like to tell you a story. I once knew a young man, decent, respectable, who decided to admit to his parents when he turned eighteen that he was gay. They were staunch Presbyterians and immediately threw him out on to the street without qualm. I came across him a few days later, thin, hungry, begging for pennies to buy a bite to eat. There was something in him that struck me as worthwhile, so I took him home, gave him access to my bath and facilities, lent him some fresh clothes, and offered him my spare room for the night."

"That was very charitable of you, sir," McBride said.

Doran shrugged. "How often do the good characters in the literature you read perform such acts of charity?" He smiled to show that he was one of the good ones. "As it turned out, we found an affinity for each other and he continued to live with me. In fact, that was a period of singular experiences for me. I had an intellectual awareness from my reading of such concepts as companionship, friendship, even love and self-sacrifice. But I had no emotional connection with them. Something changed in me as my relationship with the young man developed, and suddenly I knew, knew in my being as opposed to my mind, what it meant to be lonely, to have feelings for someone, and later—" He pursed his lips. "—to understand the devastating nature of raw, uncontrollable grief." He breathed heavily for some seconds, clearly needing to regain control of his emotions.

"Anyway, my new friend and I had a happy and fulfilling existence. He had some O-levels, so I helped him find a job to ensure that he would have access to some financial independence and, I suppose, to a sense of self-worth. It might have been Karma, or it might have been pure coincidence, but it happened that the job he found was as a clerical assistant in Judge Neeson's office. I knew nothing about the judge at the time...."

He studied the bandages on his wrists, remembering. He remained like that for some minutes, brow furrowed. When he looked up at McBride again, he said, "That's when things started to go wrong. Judge Neeson, and from time to time, Judge Adams, would see the quiet, good-looking youth in the office and try to engage him in conversation." He waved a cuffed hand, slightly startled by the rattle he made. "Both of them were notoriously infamous for their predilections for young men, you understand. My young friend, however, whose name, by the way, was Kevin Lane, chose to reject their overtures, until one afternoon Judge Neeson offered Kevin a thousand pounds for one night's work." He shook his head in disgust. "Kevin, of course, had no idea what was in store for him. The judge simply told him he needed a personable young man to help him entertain some important guests."

McBride affected wide-eyed interest. "Don't tell me it was something to do with that awful Club all the talk is about today?"

Doran nodded. "I'm afraid so. The job was to offer private entertainment to a sadistic brute whose idea of fun was to whip, bite, beat with sticks and chains, and engage in all sorts of sexual depravity. Kevin could never have coped with any of that, and when the pervert began to abuse him, he put out his two arms to push him away. The vile creature caught his feet in a blanket that had slipped off the bed during the struggle and smashed his head against a marble fireplace. He died almost instantly. Cerebral haemorrhage."

"Oh dear," McBride said, with a sympathetic shake of his head. "I dread to hear what's coming."

"You can guess, I'm sure," Doran said. "I'll be brief. Neeson got his 'clean-up team', as he called it, to take the victim back to his own house, and restage the whole incident there. He threatened Kevin with a life sentence for murder unless he maintained a total silence about the entire incident. He also told him that should the matter ever come to light, he should confess to the killing and accept a manslaughter charge. Kevin was to admit that he had innocently accepted an invitation for a meal at this man's home, that he had been attacked, that he had defended himself, and that the man fell and smashed his head on his own fireplace. He was to keep repeating that story and never mention The Club. Neeson assured Kevin that if he kept his head and did as he was told, he could arrange things so that he, Neeson, would be the presiding judge at his trial and that any sentence Kevin received would be minimal." Doran sat back, seemingly disquieted by these memories. "I wouldn't mind a drink of coffee now, if that would be all right. My throat is becoming quite dry."

McBride jumped up obediently. "Certainly, sir. Not a problem. Back in a few minutes."

*   *   *

In the anteroom, Sheehan and Stewart were listening to every word. Sheehan, still watching intently through the one-way mirror, said quietly, "Told you McBride was the key. He fed Doran's pathological ego with that innocent act and clever little asides. Vanity like that, Doran had no chance. He's supposed to be the master criminal but McBride's playing him like a fish. He's got Doran singing his head off in a way I never could. Definitely going places, that young fella."

"Any of this ringing bells with you, Chief?"

"I think so. That trial's starting to come back to me. I can see Redmond clearly now. The victim was a young man, Stevens was the barrister. There was something...." He paused, searching his memory. "Oh, yes, Stevens was going after him in court with everything he had. Way over the top. I remember being disturbed by that. He must have been in collusion with

Neeson. I remember speaking up for the youth. I said something to the effect that I was now unsure of the charges, and that I believed the incident was self-defence rather than manslaughter. Of course, the judge ignored me completely." He paused again before muttering, "Now, why would I have done that?"

Stewart said, "Maybe you felt sorry for him, sir. Judging from Doran's story, the kid was obviously an innocent abroad."

"Oh, yes. I remember now. I was the investigating officer in that case, four or five years ago. There was plenty of DNA and fingerprints at the scene but, to me, there was something not right about it. Doc Campbell and I had a wee talk about the way the body was lying, and the nature of the wound in relation to the area where the head was supposed to have struck. Both of us were convinced the position of the body had somehow been interfered with." He frowned at the memory. "The young lad had been caught shop-lifting not long before, and his fingerprints and DNA were on record, so we found him almost immediately. The one thing that had me puzzled, however, was the amount of evidence that forensics found— fingerprints, DNA evidence, other minor forensic details—all loaded against the boy. It almost looked like a frame-up, but I put it down to the kid's inexperience and lack of awareness."

"Judging from what Doran has been saying, I'd say the judge made sure that you would find all that evidence," Stewart said, lips tight, obviously disgusted at what had happened to the youngster.

"No doubt," Sheehan agreed. "When we pulled him in, he looked young, innocent, and very scared. I remember being concerned for him and tried to get him to open up, maybe plead self-defence or something. That would certainly have made sense. Yet at the time, it was the staged look of the scene that made me dubious about any possibility of self-defence." He shook his head. "The more I questioned him and the more he kept dishing out exactly the same story, the more I began to wonder. He was scared to deviate even from one word. The same story over and over. But there was nothing I could do. The crime scene didn't jibe with what he was saying. We had him dead to rights. And there was the persistent confession. I couldn't ignore that. All I could do was pass the result of my investigation on to Prosecutions and let them decide what to do about it."

"So what sent Doran off at the deep end?"

"Well, despite all his promises, Neeson tore the young lad's character to shreds in his summing up and threw the book at him. Gave him six or seven years, if I remember correctly."

"That was definitely nasty," Stewart said. "Probably peeved because the kid rejected his advances. But do you think it was reason enough to send Doran off on his rampage?"

"No. There had to be something else," Sheehan agreed. "Oh, McBride's back. Maybe we'll get the rest of the story."

As they turned again to the window, Stewart said, straight-faced, "I'm not altogether sure Doran was right about you being insufferably arrogant, sir."

Sheehan ignored her.

*   *   *

"I wasn't sure how you liked your coffee, sir," McBride said, placing a cup on the table with a small jug. "I've brought black, but here's some milk in case you want it."

"Black's fine," Doran said grandly, as if he was being served at a restaurant. He sipped the coffee. "Ah, very hot. Just the way I like it. Thank you, Detective."

"You're welcome, sir," McBride replied respectfully. He sat back toying with his kindle reader. "Uh, I don't mean to pressure you, sir, but you left off your story at a very climactic point. Any chance you could tell me the rest of it? I would love to hear it—" He held up a diffident hand. "—but only if you want to."

"Of course, Detective. I was just about to continue. Yes, your nosey Inspector Sheehan, as he was at the time, was handed the case and he soon uncovered Kevin's involvement. I have no doubt Neeson littered the crime scene with evidence that led directly to Kevin. And, of course, there was a trial, a most horrendous farce. Stevens, the barrister, went after Kevin as if he was Jack the Ripper, no doubt prompted by Neeson, who also made Kevin out to be almost a deranged killer in his summing up. And, inevitable as I now see, he sentenced Kevin to the maximum tariff available. So much for his vile promises."

"That's terrible, sir," McBride sympathised, holding his head slightly to one side. "Why do you think he was so cruel?"

"Humph! Jealousy. Bruised ego. The judge always had to get his own way. He would have hated any form of rejection, especially from a callow youth like Kevin. It took very little to bring out the worst in him."

"But...?" McBride said, before hesitating and stopping altogether.

Doran raised his eyebrows, encouraging him to continue.

"It's just ... well, you see, sir, I heard about your quest for justice. This hardly seems—"

"Of course it doesn't, Detective," Doran said sharply. "I had infinitely more reason than that to pursue my quest. The day after Kevin had been incarcerated, I went to visit him at Magilligan Prison. I was forced to wait at Reception while guards went in and out, some giving me strange looks and exhibiting a general air of unease. That had me worried from the outset. But it was nothing to the pain and desolation I suffered, my entire being screaming denial, when a guard eventually came to inform me that Prisoner ... they gave me some number that I can't remember, had suffered sudden death by misadventure." Doran's face was suffused with anger. "I was devastated. I pleaded and begged for more information but all I got was the same answer, over and over, death by misadventure. Eventually I was forced to leave and, no, I could not have access to the body. It was being held at the prison mortuary for a post-mortem examination."

Doran stopped speaking, clearly suffering distress as the memories crowded in on him. Eventually he continued, "I won't bore you with the emotional trauma I experienced at the time, and for many weeks afterwards. I was a mess. But there came a morning when my former self reasserted itself. I found myself once again in an emotional wasteland, still conscious of my loss, but able to view it with a cold and implacable eye. I was removed from all feeling except a dark and deep desire to exact retribution from all those who were directly responsible for Kevin's death."

"Did you know who they were?"

"Of course not, but in its detached state, my mind was able to devise a course of action that would ensure every iota of information that I needed to discover and punish the guilty would eventually be mine. At that moment, I determined to acquire paralegal qualifications, graduate *summa cum laude*, secure myself a post in Judge Neeson's offices, work morning, noon and night to win his approval and trust. It was the span of a few moments to formulate the plan; it took four years to bring it to fruition."

"Four years of study?"

"No. I completed my studies in two years by taking extra semesters and modules in the summer months. But getting work in the Judge's offices and making myself indispensable to him took a further two years." He waved a dismissive hand. "The point is that I finally had access to all of the judge's private papers and personal information. I even learned about that depraved Club he founded. He didn't know I was aware of that, but it allowed me to blackmail him and so fund my search for information. Neeson, Stevens, Redmond, and that nosy detective, Sheehan, I already knew about."

"I don't wish to sound argumentative, sir," McBride interrupted, "but do you not think Sheehan was just doing his job?"

Doran snorted. "Doing his job? If he had been half competent, he would have figured out the truth and realised that Kevin had acted in self-defence. Utterly reprehensible! No charges should have been made. Instead that callous bungler simply threw my friend to the wolves. He was the worst of them."

McBride made a face and said placatingly, "I see where you're coming from."

Doran nodded, completely convinced that he now had the young detective's endorsement. "Uncovering precisely what happened at the prison was the difficult part. But with the money I took from the judge, I was able to find out what prisoners were incarcerated in Magilligan at the time. It took time, but I contacted quite a number of them and by dropping a number of judicious bribes, I gained enough pieces of information to allow me to finally discover the truth. McStravick and a moronic companion had tried to rape Kevin in the prison showers on his first evening there, but in their brutal and uncontrolled passion, they pushed him violently against the shower wall and smashed the back of his head." Again, he lapsed into silence, seeming to study the bandages on his wrists. Eventually he raised his head. "Do you know what makes a secret a secret, Detective?"

McBride, nonplussed, hazarded, "Something that nobody knows."

Doran grinned mirthlessly. "Someone would have to know it, Detective. It's a secret when only one person knows it. When it is shared, even with a single other, it is no longer a secret. McStravick thought his secret was safe, but his faithless partner in crime was happy to divulge all he knew for a few measly pounds." He scowled and added harshly, "McStravick's companion, a chap called Moan, and the Prison Governor who so cold-bloodedly insisted that the prison doctor record the death as accidental, still remain targets for my wrath and they will one day earn their just dues." He pondered that for a while, seemingly oblivious to the fact that he was about to spend many years in prison. After some moments, he raised his hands a little causing the chain to rattle. "Anyway, I now had the last piece in the puzzle. I was ready to initiate my vendetta. And each of those involved in Kevin's death would die as he died, with the back of their skulls crushed, and their rectums impaled as a symbol of McStravick's evil intentions."

*   *   *

Sheehan turned away from the window, his expression troubled.

"Something wrong, Chief?" Stewart asked.

He sighed heavily. "I didn't know about the young fellow."

"You didn't know what? That he was dead?"

"Uh huh!" He shook his head. "I suppose if it was signed off as an accident in the prison, there wouldn't have been any fuss about it. And I never met the parents. So, the information just never got to me."

"Sad ending."

"Yep! Poor kid. What a life! A whole series of misfortunes, and not a single one of them his fault." He shrugged and shook his head again, visibly upset. He turned back to the window and glanced once more into the interrogation room. After staring at the handcuffed Doran for some minutes, he said, "Well, now we know. Means, opportunity, physical evidence ... and now, motive." His gaze moved to McBride. "Add an intelligent and very credible witness in young McBride, and Doran's goose, as they say in common or garden parlance, is well and truly cooked."

As they walked out of the anteroom, Stewart said, "Are you not going in there, Chief?"

"For what? To gloat?" He shook his head. "To want to do that, I would need to care about what Doran thinks. He's done and dusted now, Stewart. What he thinks or what he feels no longer mean a thing to me. He'll find out soon enough how young McBride played him. That'll torture him as much as his imprisonment."

EPILOGUE
Friday, 24th August, 2018

T he following article appeared on the front page of The Belfast Telegraph on Friday, 24th August 2018. While Shaun Black earned acknowledgement for the photographs, it was clear that neither he nor the writer of the article, Amanda Whitby, were permitted access to The Club's premises. Black's photographs were simply a few external shots of the building, taken from different perspectives.

COUNTRY MANSION FAÇADE FOR DEN OF INIQUITY
Story by Amanda Whitby
Photographs by Shaun Black

Yesterday evening, Thursday 23rd August, police swooped down on a large isolated mansion situated in the heart of the County Down countryside. In minutes the house's expansive grounds were swarming with armed police, some with rifles and wearing bullet-proof vests. Also involved in the raid were SOCOs in white scene-of-crime suits, a couple of ambulances with teams of paramedics, and a senior detective to direct operations. The armed policemen threw flash bombs into the house through the front door and through windows, to stun those holed up inside, before racing in and leading them out under restraint.

This reporter spoke to Detective Superintendent Joseph Owens who led the operation. He informed us that the arresting officers took away some members of staff and four loudly protesting club members. "What was going on in that place would absolutely turn the stomach of any right-minded person," he said. "It is disgusting stuff."

The Superintendent also added that while The Club's degenerate activities involved incredible extremes of corruption and decadence, his Task Force was particularly concerned with trying to help a number of young children who had been sexually abused. The extent of this particular form of depravity was such that some of his own officers have been traumatised by what they have seen and learned. One horrendous discovery was the shocking number of abused children found in The Club's secret records, information made all the more horrific by the revelation that once The Club had used them to satisfy the perverted lusts of members, these innocent children were passed on to other perverts in other clubs.

Owens said they hoped to trace any young victims—girls and boys, some of whom appeared to be only about three or four years old—and offer them support and counselling. He added, however, that "...with the number involved it will be a very difficult task, but it is one that we will not give up on until the kidnapped children are returned to their parents, and all of these perverted criminals have been identified and arrested."

Scores of high-profile citizens from Northern Ireland, and further afield, have joined this top-secret sex club, grandiosely named *Fulfilment for the Enlightened*, an exclusive members-only den of iniquity, based in this sedate country mansion just outside Belfast. Sources close to this newspaper have also revealed that many other members come from the British Isles, Europe, and one from as far away as South Africa.

Since the house is at the end of a long drive in a secluded country area, no one in the surrounding neighbourhood had any inkling of the dissolute activities that were taking place there. Eamon Gallogly, who lives about half a mile from the house, said, "I've occasionally seen some very upmarket cars coming and going, but I just thought it was the rich visiting the rich."

Medical consultants, judges, senior civil servants, industrialists, minor royalty figures, and even some high-profile members of the clergy, are among the members of this hardcore secret society. Names are not permitted for publication at this stage since the crimes and the details of The Club's activities are currently *sub judice*, but members with influence are already petitioning for interdictions to bar any media from ever publishing their names and other details.

Membership to this elite Club tends to be by invitation only, but information about the unnatural activities it offers have been leaked on to the Dark Web, and other members have been recruited from there. However, despite the renowned security of the Deep Web, Superintendent Owens declared that, "People who engage in these kinds of warped practices have felt relatively secure up until now in the knowledge that the Deep Web is virtually unpoliced. This coordinated action around the world has demonstrated that this is no longer the case."

This reporter understands that the activities of The Club were so vile that the phrases 'wild sex parties' and 'fetish balls' would be considered normal, even banal, in comparison to some of the services The Club is said to have provided to wealthy perverts, paedophiles, and yes, sadists, for whom cost is no barrier.

Police officials from the home countries of members, including members of Interpol Headquarters in France, had teleconferenced very hurriedly when information about The Club was supplied by Detective Chief Inspector Jim Sheehan. The DCI came across the house and its lurid secrets while investigating a series of murders connected with The Club. With the information DCI Sheehan was able to provide, coordinated plans for raids across the continent were prepared in record time. Charges have not yet been filed and will differ from country to country according to their different judicial systems.

British police helped coordinate the raids in Britain, Europe, and even South Africa, on the homes of prominent citizens—government officials, members of the legal profession, doctors, politicians, millionaires, even high-level clergy. Interpol headquarters in France said that when British authorities had sought their assistance, it became clear that the arrests of members in the different European countries would have to be very precisely coordinated. Despite the limited time available, however, the entire international operation was successful.

A number of arrests have been made in yesterday evening's police raids across the British Isles and Europe. In cooperation with other police forces and Interpol, the PSNI reports that twenty-two people were arrested in Northern Ireland, twenty-nine addresses were raided in England, seventeen in Germany, twelve in Italy, ten in Norway, and one or two in Belgium, France, Sweden and Spain. Unfortunately, it is anticipated that several of the trials will take years to make it to court, since hugely wealthy Club members will employ top legal teams to win bail and delay trial dates almost indefinitely.

But regarding the arrests already made in Northern Ireland, particularly in the Belfast area, a source has informed this paper that charges are imminent, charges that will range from the serious offense of sexual abuse of children and a variety of other degenerate and illicit practices, to involvement in the suspicious circumstances surrounding the disappearance of some of the children, teenage foreign girls, young men, all of whom had once apparently been imprisoned in The Club's 'dungeon'.

Probably the saddest element of this sorry saga is the fact that the majority of The Club's members are pillars of society. They are supposed to represent what is best in us—medicine, law, education, commerce, politics, even church. What is to become of us if such depravity becomes the norm? Or, more disturbingly, has it already become the norm, skulking in dark places unfamiliar to those of us who live 'ordinary' lives? Frighteningly, given the many revelations that continue to appear in our press and other forms of media, it would seem that such corruption is ever-rising and becoming unstoppable. It becomes increasingly obvious that those who seek and gain authority in today's amoral climate seem incapable of resisting its lure. Power corrupts, and those who gain access to the controls of society's different strata seem to lose touch with the ancient virtues that gave our culture its value and its worth.

This is disturbing. Do we still need, even yet, to learn the lessons from history, how the increasing licentiousness of those who ran empires led to their destruction and downfall: The Roman Empire, the Ottoman Empire, the Yuan and other great world powers? We can no longer afford to be complacent. The awful revelations of yesterday's events have shown how perversion can lurk at the very heart of our country's authority. We still have a democracy. We still have a vote. It is more important now than ever to use that vote to bring into authority worthy people who will work tirelessly to root out all forms of corruption and perversion from whatever dark corners of our society it tries to secrete itself in.

And yet we must not forget that there remain people of integrity who continue to perform their duties and work tirelessly for our society's good. We salute in particular, those men and women of the PSNI, under the leadership of such worthy men as Superintendent Owens and Detective Chief Inspector Sheehan. Their integrity and remorseless commitment to duty are instrumental in keeping our country safe.

Thank you for choosing this book. If you enjoyed The Dark Web Murders, *please consider telling your friends or leaving a review on Amazon, Goodreads or the site where you bought it. Word of mouth is an author's best friend and much appreciated.*

If you would like a free e-book of the first book in this series The Doom Murders, *please email me at* brianohare26@hotmail.co.uk *and I will send you a copy. Be assured that your name and email address will be secure and that this information will never be sold or disclosed by me to any other party.*

ABOUT THE AUTHOR

Because of a childhood disease that required a liver transplant, Doctor Brian O'Hare took early retirement in 1998 from his post as Assistant Director of the Southern Regional College in Newry in Northern Ireland. He now enjoys full health, plays golf several times a week, and travels occasionally. He is author of several academic works as well as two memoirs, and three award winning fiction novels, including the Crimson Cloak's Inspector Sheehan Mystery Series.

Look for the first three award-winning books in the Sheehan series, *The Doom Murders*, *The 11.05 Murders*, and *The Coven Murders*, available from a variety of distributors such as Amazon, Smashwords, Barnes and Noble, Ingram, and the Crimson Cloak Publishing shop at: http://www.crimsoncloakpublishing.com/. There are also three Crimson Short Stories featuring Inspector Sheehan: *Murder at Loftus House*, *Murder at the Roadside Cafe*, and *Murder at the Woodlands Care Home*.

Also by Brian O'Hare:
The Miracle Ship– award winning religious non-fiction.
Fallen Men – award winning contemporary fiction.
A Spiritual Odyssey– a spiritual/medical memoir.

Social Media Links
Web: http://brianohareauthor.blogspot.co.uk.
FB: https://www.facebook.com/inspectorsheehan
FB: https://www.facebook.com/brian.ohare.96
Twitter: @Brian O'Hare26

ALSO BY BRIAN O'HARE

THE DOOM MURDERS

[Vol. 1 of the Inspector Sheehan Mysteries Series]

Prominent figures in Belfast are being murdered. The bodies are left naked and posed in grotesquely distorted shapes. No clues are left at the forensically immaculate crime scenes except odd theatrical props and some concealed random numbers and letters left by the killer. How are the victims linked? What is the connection between these killings and a famous mediaeval painting of The Last Judgement? Chief Inspector Jim Sheehan is baffled. Faced with one of the most complex cases of his career, he turns to an eminent professor at Queen's University and a senior cleric who is a biblical expert. With their help, Sheehan begins to piece together some understanding of the killer's psychopathy but can he learn enough to identify the killer and put an end to the murders?

The Doom Murders has been the recipient of three literary awards - The IDB Award in 2014; The New Apple Award, 2014, for Excellence in Independent Publishing; and the 2015 Readers' Favourite International Book Awards (Bronze Medal Winner).

"The Chief Inspector, Jim Sheehan, is drawn so deftly and with such genuineness, you can feel him breathing." (Eugene Fournier, novelist and screenwriter, film and TV)

"The most subtle of clues are intricately interwoven into the storyline, and even the most astute mystery buff is apt to miss them." (Donna Cummins, Author of the Blacklick Valley Mystery Series)

"Incredibly addictive page turner." (Meghan, Amazon Top 1000 Reviewer)

"O'Hare leans toward the human side of his characters, imbuing them with a real-world presence that is in turn witty and passionate." (Roy T. James, for Readers' Favourite)

THE 11:05 MURDERS

[Vol. 2 of the Inspector Sheehan Mysteries Series]

Three people are murdered on separate Tuesday evenings at precisely 11.05. Random clues point to random suspects, but too many questions remain unanswered. Why 11.05pm for each killing? Is there any connection between these deaths and a rape that occurred at Queen's university twelve years before? What is the connection between the killings and Sergeant Stewart's mystery informant? Who is the violent stalker who twice nearly kills Detective Allen? What is his connection, if any, to the murders? This is a murderer who comes and goes as he pleases. Even when the police know the target, the date and the time of his next murder, he still kills his victim, kidnaps a key member of the team, and escapes without being apprehended. Who can hope to catch a killer who is so ruthlessly clever and efficient? Inspector Sheehan has literally only minutes to make sense of these questions if he is to save his colleague's life.

The 11.05 Murders has won Top Medal Honours for its category in the The New Apple Award, 2015, for Excellence in Independent Publishing

The first thing I thought after reading this book is: why isn't Brian O'Hare better known in the crime writing world? This man is extremely talented, and his book a wonderful 'whodunnit' that left me guessing until the end. [Joseph Sousa, Crime-writer]

Head and shoulders above most mystery authors who are published today, Brian O'Hare deserves far wider recognition. You won't regret purchasing his books. [CBT, Amazon Reviewer]

Brian O'Hare is an intelligent and compassionate storyteller who takes his chosen genre a decent literary distance beyond your average 'whodunnit'. [Robin Chambers, author]

An explosive mystery that keeps you guessing until the very end, riddled with unseen surprises and breathless suspense! [Wesley Thomas, writer and blogger]

THE COVEN MURDERS

[Vol. 3 of the Inspector Sheehan Mysteries Series]

Published 2018

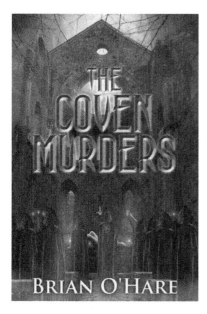

The Coven Murders opens with a horrifying account of a ritual Black Mass and a human sacrifice in an abandoned church. Twenty- one years later, near an old ruined church in an area of outstanding natural beauty, Chief Inspector Sheehan and his team discover the skeleton of a young woman. But what seems initially to be a straightforward case, brings the team into conflict with a powerful Satanist who has plans to offer up to Satan another human sacrifice on the evening of the great Illuminati feast of Lughnasa. Several murders occur, baffling the Inspector until he makes a connection between the modern murders and the twenty-one-year-old skeleton. The team's pursuit of the murderer and their determination to protect a young woman who is targeted by the coven, lead to a horrific climax in a hellish underground crypt where Sheehan and his team, supported by an exorcist and a bishop, attempt to do battle with the coven and a powerful demon, Baphomet, jeopardising not only their lives, but risking the wrath of Satan upon their immortal souls.

A whirlwind of a ride, frightening, disturbing, and so intent do we become in rescuing the sacrificial victim in time that we almost forget that the murderer has not yet been named. Hang on, because the final scene is a shocker! [C. Todd, Amazon Review]

It's impossible to get into without some serious spoilers, so I'll leave you with this: It will make the hairs on your arms and neck stand up straight. [Kendra Morgan, Amazon Customer]

The end took me completely by surprise. I'm willing to bet there are few out there who will guess this one. Denna Holm, Para-normal and Sci-fi novelist.

Head and shoulders above most mystery authors who are published today, Brian O'Hare deserves far wider recognition. [A.C. Amazon reviewer]

Printed in Great Britain
by Amazon